Zeke Borshellac

※

James Damis

Sagging Meniscus

© 2024 by James Damis

All Rights Reserved.

Set in Mrs Eaves with LaTeX.

ISBN: 978-1-963846-04-1 (paperback)
ISBN: 978-1-963846-05-8 (ebook)
Library of Congress Control Number: 2024938678

Sagging Meniscus Press
Montclair, New Jersey
saggingmeniscus.com

Contents

One · *1*

Two · *22*

Three · *43*

Four · *62*

Five · *86*

Six · *107*

Seven · *129*

Eight · *149*

Nine · *167*

Ten · *190*

Eleven · *214*

Twelve · *236*

Thirteen · *256*

Fourteen · *278*

Fifteen · *291*

Sixteen · *310*

Seventeen · *327*

Eighteen · *348*

Nineteen · *367*

Twenty · *386*

Twenty-One · *407*

Twenty-Two · *429*

The Songs of Zeke Borshellac · *449*

For my wife Beth and daughter Audrey
and my parents
who've always been in my corner

ZEKE BORSHELAC

ONE

ZEKE BORSHELLAC raced through the black wet woods, threading his frantic stride between the dense murky multitude of trees while suspecting the furious fishermen who'd been giving him chase had quit and turned back. He had been fingered by none other than Ma Moody, the strumpet hag of the wharves, as the thief who stole their trawl of fish, but their fear of becoming gravely lost, Borshellac thought, ended their thirst for vengeance. A fleeting vindication flitted across his mind before he crashed smack into a large oak and dropped to the moist thawed earth like a pulverized puppet. Nearly unconscious, the smell he'd delighted in since boyhood, that of woodland earth thawing in early spring, left him in a wistful, melancholy reverie. His faithful sheepdog Balthazar, at his side throughout the flight and now all atwitter with solicitude, sought to revive his master with sharp pokes of his snout while licking his face in a frenzy. As the cobwebs lifted and Zeke slowly rose again, his mind returned to the fishermen and how gratified they would have been to see him slam into that tree and injure himself and now he felt they were responsible insofar as their accusation was baseless. So he blamed them as he began weaving again amidst the timber, sluggishly now, wobbly even, like a beaten boxer desperately wading into his opponent, but then he smiled with not a little glee recalling that he actually had glommed a passel of porgies and had them wrapped in brown paper in his frock. Now he wished he had stolen the entire trawl, but it was the sodden hooligans of the wharves who lifted much of the net's contents and fled, losing a fair amount along the way. The blunder he rued was pocketing the spillage fish fetched for him by Balthazar and being seen by Ma Moody as she was taking a break seated on a capstan, whittling and smoking a cigarillo. She was a spiteful sea hag, sadistic even, Borshellac thought in indignant stupefaction. On the wharves she was feared by all and cognizant of everything, considered virulent, perhaps eccentric, even unhinged, but paradoxically, "one of our own." He cursed Ma Moody and recognized now she was going to have her jaboneys work him over had he not fled when he did in the wee hours, but she still managed to sic the fishermen on him. *I will cook their fish and savor it tonight!* he swore out loud, though not sure he would even find his way out of the darkness and trees. He thought he heard rustling and footfalls somewhere and he began running again thinking it them still coming and he turned to scour the darkness and vegetation without stopping, only to once more smack head-on into a fine strong tree and be clobbered and sent sprawling on his back. The intervention again of his sheepdog roused him from a brief slumber. Groggy, now he recalled the violent cry of one of the fisherman, the burly, cross-eyed one with a fancy frescoed rubber cummerbund, known as "Devilcake": "I will gut you like a hammerhead with my shank, you gutless gonoph!" Then he heard the echoes of a man's demented guffaws carry throughout the woods, not the same man, not Devilcake, Borshellac was sure inasmuch as the laughter was choppy, shrill, interposed with gravelly gurgling spasms of side-splitting, that of a foreigner, he pegged it, or more precisely, a Burmese. It was pitch black in the woods and the rain filtered through the trees dousing the earth and Borshellac pushed onward, teetering and stumbling, as if his life depended on his ability to continue. And he was walloped by other trees just the same and kept getting up from the muddy ground, musing at times on why he invariably seemed to end up running, when all he wanted was to live righteously and do some good helping people, live a life of the mind and find himself, and enjoy a good meal now and again, such as roasted pork chops. He also pondered his desolation and whether he was so used to it that he unconsciously perpetuated it and when people turned on him he secretly sided with them, his punishment the familiar disaffected loneliness and melancholy. Maybe it

ONE

was simply an adverse stretch, the string of promising new beginnings that degenerated into abject fiascos in the last several places he lived, the most recent in the little harbor burg of Bluddenville. Borshellac had no maritime background and zero capability as a fisherman, but after being blown overboard from the steamer he was sailing on to a potential position as a scullion in Bayonne, New Jersey, the fishing vessel rescuing him delivered him to their native Bluddenville and there Zeke had an epiphany to finally put some roots down. In the seaport the only paths one could pursue were apprenticing on a fishing boat or catching on with one of the many criminal enterprises long plaguing the streets of the faded old town. Naturally, Zeke chose fishing and did so with more ardor and passion than probably anyone who ever donned the black rubber floppy hat and long slicker and buckled boots to report for duty as a trainee on a trawler.

He now finally slowed to a halt as the rain came down furiously through the trees, and he took what shelter he could from an arbor of sorts under a crowded cluster of great branches. Here Zeke rested, sitting on a large rock and locating the pint of rum tucked away in his frock. He took a swig and lifted his head towards the leafy, leaky roof and began a reflection on what happened to him in Bluddenville and the vocations he practiced there all in the name of helping others. It had been some time since he had been honest with himself and truly taken inventory of a life that increasingly seemed lost in the itinerant eddies of forgotten backwaters, amidst the lurking snares and shadowy webs of far-flung ruination. Here the hope of work and friends and a hometown had turned ugly, like sun-ripened tomatoes rotting in a storm cellar, transmogrifying into disappointment and disgust and eventuating in folks condemning and execrating his character and running him out of their town. But his first days in Bluddenville, following up with the captain of the weathered tub that saved him, all seemed quite sanguine in that grizzled Bunt Ketchum, the notorious crotchety old salt who once bludgeoned a shirking seaman into unconsciousness with a live trout and strung his limp form high on a spar as an example, improbably took a shine to the earnest strange fellow his men pulled out of the sea with his lungs taking water. In the beginning Ketchum found the raw newcomer's unbridled zest for his every duty, regardless of how menial or servile, quite refreshing from his usual crew of hardened veterans who had been through it all and bitterly knew the toll the rough nature of their work eventually took. But slowly his impression of Zeke's potential as a fisherman began to darken and grow suspicious. The new recruit's enthusiasm never waned or wavered, instead it only intensified to levels that presented disturbing images to Ketchum and the men. Stationed down in the galley as the cook's assistant, Zeke worked hard in preparing food but his chronic seasickness proved an insurmountable obstacle insofar as it induced a steady stream of vomiting, which led to the crew objecting to such an individual handling their victuals. Ketchum had little choice but to yank him from the galley and install him on deck as a general assistant and porter. While the ravages of his seasickness did not abate, Zeke was able to better control the upchucking by dashing towards the sides and sending the foul effluences overboard, although the suddenness of some eruptions prevented him from doing so cleanly. More than a few times an unsuspecting fisherman found himself on the receiving end of an errant discharge, and Borshellac's sincere apologies were hardly sufficient for these hardy maritime men. While novices assigned grunt duties were subject to hazing on fishing boats as a rule, Borshellac's failures in the kitchen and now on deck by sliming one after the other with his puke left him wide open to their epic fishermen hi-jinks. He soon became a regular victim of their bastinadoes and cat-o'-nine-tails and frequent launchings into the drink via their massive catapult. But through it all the tyro swabby never capitulated, refused to complain, and simply kept picking himself up from the deck or swimming back on board to grab hold of his mop and make sure the boat glistened. While Borshellac's tremendous will and tolerance for punishment impressed some seamen enough to lay off with the bastinado and whip, others were indifferent to his efforts and a small band of liquored-up mates perceived Zeke's limitless durability as a personal affront and a challenge to take him down. Bunt Ketchum knew

ONE

about these roughnecks' goal but turned a blind eye, and many of the crew who'd come to respect Zeke's gameness suspected a vicious prank of some kind was about to befall their polarizing crewmate. Such began Zeke's descent into grim misery trapped aboard a boat in the sunless void of remote ocean.

One night they spirited him straight from sleep in his bunk, Devilcake and another called Ticky Gwashler and others, and took him down in the bowels of the ship and strapped him to a bench so he had to watch their crude, violent, though at times poignant "Fish Story Free-for-All" during which the crocked fishermen manipulated fish chosen from a great pile of them down there and acted out lurid tales of revenge and star-crossed lovers and unspeakably tragic fates for the fish characters. The ploy was to initially beguile the immobilized viewer into finding the characters amusing, the story intriguing, as they did here with a sizable carp named Larry Skompis who injured his main fin while playing ninepins and later when resting in Honolulu is deceived by a monkfish to invest his savings in hair tonic, which he sips and to which finds himself addicted until a female barracuda he falls in love with nurses him to health before selling Larry to a Chinatown merchant and is soon destined for a trencherman's table, an outrage for which he'd wreak destruction in the form of hepatitis B. The Fish Story Free-for-Alls were designed to "hook" the viewer early through engaging piscatorial portraits and suspenseful drama so that when the fishermen puppeteers veered sharply into more maddeningly dadaist territory there was exasperation coupled with consternation and finally, utter dread and panic. The Free-for-Alls flourished in the 19th Century mainly around the unadulterated New England fishing ports of Gloucester and New Haven and a young William Dean Howells, Zeke would later learn, was believed to have been subjected to a particularly brutal and cathartic one while at sea that left him supine and caterwauling like a rutting cat for days on end until his shipmates dropped him off on a schooner sailing for Cuba.

Zeke fell hard and fast for the misadventures of the big carp Skompis and was especially moved by the Chinatown scenes of plotting vengeance, brilliantly captured, he thought, by Ticky Gwashler, who he thought was channeling his own disgruntled rage towards Bunt Ketchum. When Devilcake came barging in holding five mackerels aloft and singing a grating chantey in Portugese, Zeke reacted with the desired annoyance on cue. "Why this is an outrage!" he cried. "You gypped the audience out of Larry's fate!"

"Audience?!" Devilcake roared with derision. "You mean *you*, don't you, Shellacko?" The deliberate mispronunciation of his surname rankled Zeke more and he called for his leather straps to be untied so he could vacate the theater area. Now Devilcake, a towering cross-eyed lummox with a strangely swollen scarred face may have been frightening, but did not seem a shrewd, cerebral sort in the least, and this very paradox was his greatest strength.

Zeke's indignation and request to leave played exactly into Devilcake's hand, his savvy as a Free-for-All scrapper nonpareil. Suddenly freed and adjacent his fish puppeteers Borshellac could hardly contain his disappointment and groused to Ticky Gwashler: "You, sir, are a gifted actor wasting your abilities in the pedestrian pursuit of fish."

Gwashler, the alcoholic harpoonist known as "The Nihilist Fisherman" in a series of monologues he had performed in seaport dives near Narraganset years earlier, knew their mark would take the bait. "And *you, sir*," he declaimed in his resounding old "stage" voice, "are a stodgy ninny who is about to implode from deserved revulsion." He now held up Larry Skompis, still in his costume of sport coat and turtleneck and very much alive.

"Larry! It's Larry!" exclaimed Zeke, noting Ticky Gwashler had a half of a lemon in his hand and laughed sadistically as he sprinkled the sour juice on Larry and in a lightning flash took a large bite out of the poor carp's twitchy dorsal flesh. Devilcake jumped in with Carol Fragge, the Barracuda femme fatale, and he likewise squeezed lemon over her top and sunk his long yellow teeth into her glistening side. More fishermen charged in with other fish characters and began eating them alive and Zeke, saddened, nauseated, and scared of all the deranged biting, broke for the stairs desperate to reach the deck and fresh air and sanity, but the fishermen quickly tackled him and hoisted him over their heads and violently passed him around in some strange sport which they were now engaged, a wild crashing game of teams fighting over "the bait buster," i.e., Zeke. They were all ripped, stinko drunk with several jugs of rum going around and a hashish hookah to boot, beating the hell out of one another in their peculiar sport with rules cryptic and the bait buster taking the brunt of the battering as he got thrown around. Now old Bunt Ketchum countenanced the time-honored traditions and recognized their value in building character and guts in worthy fishermen, but he had his limits and when the irascible captain caught wind of what bedlam had broken out below in the galley, he appeared on the steps above screaming incoherent threats promising mutineer charges and summary executions for anyone not on deck working in seconds. Naturally, all obeyed the command with the exception of Zeke, groggy and badly hurt in the melee, which was an unacceptable excuse as far as Ketchum was concerned.

"You are a contemptible, pathetic lump of a human being, Borshellac, and the lowest of worms ever to envision a career in fishing," he railed. "Well, we'll either make a fisherman out of you or your dead carcass will end up feeding the flesh-eaters in the bottom of the sea!" Strewn on his side in a bloody sprawl, Zeke could not rise and defend his dignity with the vigor he felt it deserved, though did manage to query about a "third option, such as my imminent exile to landlubbering forever?" Ketchum only snarled some incomprehensible seadog cuss words as he grabbed the back of his frock and dragged him up the stairs and tossed his limp form across the deck where it remained supine. The raging captain hollered for the men to gather round and pronounced they were going to forge a fisherman out of that half-conscious "benighted galoot." The men knew what that meant and Devilcake and two others picked him up by the extremities and Zeke began grumbling and groaning until he realized they were going to send him overboard and he started yelling: "Sweet Jesus the bastards are dumping me in a watery grave!"

Bunt Ketchum bade them pause a moment for him to lean over and declare to his troubled work-in-progress in a distinctly paternal, wise counsel way: "What you fail to grasp, Shellacker, my boy, is that the best fishermen instinctually know that to succeed they must learn to *think like fish*. Coco Plastermann, maybe the greatest fisher there ever was, wore a four-inch Mecklenburg fish hook in his tongue for four years, a year per inch, easily breaking the smelts catch mark before succumbing to tetanus poisoning. Plastermann *wanted* it, and now we're going to see how much the hell you want it, Borshellac!" He nodded and all watched as they hurled Zeke over the side, only to eventually fish him out with their great trawler netting, and they repeated this over and over until Zeke seemed delirious and crazy and flopped and wriggled like a giant salmon every time in the tangled netting as they hauled him aboard. Then came the burying of the spunky greenhorn under increasingly massive piles of freshly caught fish, each time presenting a greater challenge for him to somehow grope and find a way back to daylight. Three grueling times he made it too, each victory only assuring him a place on the bottom of greater mountains of fish, shad and cod and chub and char among many, until the fourth and last one Zeke felt like a goner under several tons of squirming sea life, bream and haddock and sole and halibut to name just a few, and he began to understand the abject futility of struggling to emerge once more. At length, Zeke gave up the ghost, surrendering to the seeming grisly interment beneath the vast gallimaufry of newly caught fish. Now he ruminated on his too short life and the promise he would never live up to, and he thought of his family and the occasional road trips they used to take, such as the one to Coney Island for the freak show. He recalled his fascination with the fat boy who was born with a turtle shell and how this exotic blubbery chap disappeared into his shell and when he got too close to inquire if it was hot in there a stubby hand shot out to tweak his nose. Zeke thought it strange the memories that come back in spades at the end, and he felt an itch on his nose but his arms were pinned down beneath the fish pile. And some fish heads were nibbling his ears, his fingers, his neck, their oleaginous scaly flesh pressing

ONE

against his face, stiff fins jabbed him everywhere like fiberglass saws, and the gills throbbed in increasing alarm without water. The foul confluence of fish effluvia assaulted Zeke with dreadful stench, though now too he could smell the great quantities of fish they were frying up there in massive skillets and they were boisterously ebullient, knocking back rum as usual he figured, and belting out old seadog numbers. He mainly felt forlorn and forgotten under the immense pile and renounced his fisherman folly and remembered tenderly his dog Grainy Lackawana, a spirited irrepressible Irish Wolfhound who ran away from the Borshellac flat when Zeke was only eleven and a family friend, Deacon Malk, a street juggler, spotted the canine a couple years later being walked by a wealthy margarine heiress in Norwalk, Connecticut, tidings which left the heartbroken boy even more disconsolate. "Old Grainy looked content, cheerful, and well-fed," Malk remarked callously, "splitting in retrospect looks like the smart move." Borshellac's breath now grew labored in his smothering grave of fish and he let out a sob as Malk's words echoed in his mind. *Even Grainy jumped ship on me . . . Grainy Lackawana, the one true friend I thought I had . . . come back, Grainy . . .* Maybe he didn't mean to move on, he mused, but it just worked out that way? Maybe Lackawana sold his young master short? That young master deserved better, he told himself. *It wasn't meant to be like this, always degenerating into wreckage after such sanguinity . . .* The terrible weight and grotesquery and implacability of the fish on top of him seemed peremptory, but Zeke recollected that his entire existence until now had been a relentless struggle to release this irreducible inviolable *nitty gritty*, this *something,* that was in him and had to come out. He wasn't too sure what the hell it exactly was but knew it was extraordinary and profound and valuable to others and uniquely him, Zeke Borshellac. Well, there had to be more inside than all the puke he'd been upchucking, he reasoned. So he couldn't let it die down there beneath the avalanche of fish. Zeke had suffered much in his twenty-seven years up until then but had a premonition of the unknown mysterious *goodness* to come and resolved to fight on until then. All the guilt he had to live with was like that sick amassment of fish over him now, he thought, and wanted to give the boy he was who lost his dog another chance and now he grew angry and began shifting and stirring and shaking and then flailing and slithering and clambering his way out from the fish—who seemed annoyed by his jostling and their captive felt their baleful constellation of fish eyes bore into his soul—and he summoned deep reckonings within himself—and instinctually hollowed out a Pompano head with his hands and forcefully slid his own head into it before bolting up the stairs like a lurid mythical sea creature, his long lanky frame strikingly macabre, a gilled monster from beyond seeking vengeance, soaking in fish entrails and slimes and while the fishermen were carrying on guzzling and gorging he furtively insinuated his way amongst them and brandished the bastinado and began fulminating in an eerie, muffled tone that he was going to "fulfill a destiny born in my bones, a good life in which I am proficient at some worthy craft. I will find my calling, despite it hiding in darkness!" Devilcake and some others lunged for the lunatic ranting fishhead, but Zeke pivoted in time and caught one of the assailants in the back with a wild swing of the bastinado. Someone sliced him across the chest with an angler's chiv and he screamed that he would never go fishing again and Ticky Gwashler huzzaed snidely. Blood covered Zeke's torso in grand guignol fashion and his ululating anguish left most of the crew apprehensive of him, cowered by the aberrant form they now thought could be a marine poltergeist. He looked inside himself further and found a boost of moxie. *I am not one of you brutish bastards, not of your foul fishing kind, and I will find out just who Zeke Borshellac is! This much is incontrovertible—he is a good man with something inside him that must come out!* And with that he began puking the longest, most powerful sluice of green vomit anyone on that ship ever witnessed. And after smacking a few fisherman with the bastinado and dodging their attempts to capture him he managed to launch himself from the great catapult, his trail of fresh puke describing a brilliant, almost phosphorescent rainbow that froze for a moment in stark relief against the crepuscular briny night air hanging over the ocean.

ONE

Zeke exulted in his magnificent escape from his tormentors and even appreciated his seasickness striking him for once when it could be used advantageously, but flopping with serious splashes into the ocean soon brought his celebratory self-satisfaction to a jarring realization that he had propelled himself a good distance into the sea with nary a buoy or flotation device anywhere to be seen. Zeke treaded water for a while as the notion of his foolhardy impetuous mistake only burgeoned into a full-blown crisis, his choice in the end being *drown* or *try to swim back to the fishing boat and grovel with apologies*. Naturally, Zeke chose the latter and began his desperate way across the water. He could make out the distant outline of the trawler on the gray horizon and frantically swam towards it, the final vestiges of twilight fast fading and the boat intermittently dissolving into the ocean mists. Zeke powered through the water with his long wiry limbs, fear of fatigue preempting even the slightest slowing of his rhythmic strokes. Never much of a swimmer, facing his own mortality head on proved the mightiest of motivators for the fisherman manqué. But the flesh ineluctably succumbed at some nameless juncture and for Zeke time tilted down as the night fell hard and darkness enveloped his swim, and the wind grew gusty, the water rougher, and the trawler vanished altogether from his view. He lost stamina and petered out until he attempted to conserve his strength by floating, but after a while he could hardly sustain his breathing above water. Zeke made his peace with submerging for good when he bumped blindly into a clump of driftwood and vulcanized rubber toys somehow entangled together. He latched on and thanked the vast black firmament the clump was enough to keep him afloat. One of the toys was a large rubber fish with penetrating eyes that spooked Zeke and left him anxious the pile of fish he'd escaped had somehow sent this one to finish off his mind. Zeke held onto the driftwood and avoided the rubber fish eyes and waited for fate to rescue him, though knew as the long harrowing minutes somehow passed his chances did not look promising. His benumbed extremities were turning more and more violet in spidery intersecting veins and his consciousness had begun to ebb when he became aware that he and his clump of wood and rubber were caught in a current, which soon seemed more of a potent riptide. The air was very still now, so the force behind the steady flow puzzled the depleted Zeke, until he made out a line of cordage or hawser far off to one side, and while the dark overcast haze precluded much more visibility he did notice more and more fish swimming alongside him. Very quickly Zeke felt the flow zooming with a choppy force and saw the density of accompanying fish multiply tenfold, and then he picked up the telltale sign of another hawser rope, this one with sturdy meshwork attached trailing underneath and no doubt connecting elsewhere. Zeke understood that he had been caught in a great sweeping trawler and immediately his trepidations suspected the very boat he catapulted from had now captured him, the worn tub of old Bunt Ketchum and his mad gang of drunken seadogs. Of course, he first and foremost greeted this development with the requisite dose of gratefulness, for at least he would be spared a cruel fate at the bottom of the ocean, but for how long once they had their traitor back on board? Now he was surrounded by thousands of frenetic fish who sensed their bad turn and he thought of the pompano head and disguising himself once again as the massive nets were being hauled in. An unutterable panic suddenly came over him like a metal head clamp boring into his unsuspecting skull, and a queasy dread that nearly immobilized him like a dead jellyfish left him susceptible to drowning before ever being caught. He cursed the vast multitude of fish traveling with him in the net, believing they were in some sort of cahoots with Ketchum's crew, herding him into their grasp once more, though he felt the poor fish probably thought *he was responsible for rounding them up*. He noticed a speckled halibut moving quite slowly and appearing worse for wear, when the will to act seized him: *yes, this halibut would save him* . . . he would co-opt the old halibut's head and make it his own to thwart any recognition. He dug a clam shucker out of his pants' pocket and deliriously lunged for the halibut and it was flopping and splashing in the netting like a baby sparrow in a birdbath, deftly avoiding Zeke's charge, only to be worn down by the whilom fisherman's relentless pursuit. Finally, Zeke simply jumped the enormous fish and after a desperate struggle that would become timeless lore to the people of the wharves, Borshellac carved off the halibut's head, his upper half really, furiously hollowed it out and stuck his own dome inside. It disguised and confused his shipmates enough to escape the ship, now it would work the same way in enabling his undetected return, he reasoned. In the netting scramble Zeke positioned himself in the midst of the heap of fish, his torso and limbs hidden and only the halibut head peeping through. Once Ketchum ordered the catch thrown through the deck hole into the galley, Zeke planned to hide down there. But the trawler haul was not sent below, instead he found himself crashing on the foredeck near portside, a thousand panicky fish falling mostly on him, and Zeke was badly shaken. Slowly he shook off the convulsive fish and in an unsteady daze got to his feet, felt the halibut head securely in place, and now eyed the fishing crew encircling him and his piscatorial captives. He knew not one of them. There was no Bunt Ketchum or Devilcake or Ticky Gwashler, just strange men gazing at him in stark silence. More than thirty fishermen stood stock-still around him, foreign men he figured by their olive-skinned features and silky colorful garb, baggy genie pants with flashy sashes. They just remained motionless like that, staring in a kind of stupefaction. Then one of them began playing a long instrument like the bassoon, a curious woodwind for sure, and another accompanied him on the ukulele and Zeke sought to break the ice by dancing to their song. Movement certainly helped palliate the unbearable tension and presentiment the strange ship cast over him. The men seemed to like this so he continued moving to the music in an improvised series of twirls and spins and reeling leaping frolicking and they chuckled to one another and spoke in guttural voices oddly tonal, an unidentifiable foreign tongue Zeke concluded.

    Once he grew tired and ceased hoofing it two of their ranks came towards him to take him to a small cabin below deck near starboard, where a bespectacled bearded old fellow reclined smoking a corncob pipe, attired in a squid patterned rubber tunic and traditional fisherman's hat, albeit several bright pompoms of a coagulated sallow putty dangled from its crown. Zeke inquired when the boat would be returning to harbor. The old man stared back at him without a word, stroking his beard meditatively and finally grunting something indecipherable and threatening. Zeke asked: "What?" The old man repeated in a shriller voice what he had first said and seemed irked. Zeke regretted asking him "What?" insofar as the man apparently had no real grasp of English.

"You . . . fishhead!" the old man bellowed suddenly.

"Yes, I am a fish creature. But I want to go ashore! I want to return to the land. I am a seasick fish fellow, you might say, and I am hoping your fine ship will sail me back to solid earth."

The old man examined the halibut head with his hands and scrutinized the line at which fish turned into young man, kneading with authority Zeke's neck and upper torso area. *"You fake fishhead!"* he now pronounced. The floor heaved and they were jostled, a storm or squall apparently coming in all of a sudden. Consternation flared in Zeke as thoughts of his predilection for the puke came now concomitant with a woozy swoon.

"They throw you back if discovered to be fake."

That was not Zeke's first choice, perishing in the ocean. The old man drew on his corncob and Zeke thought his clouds of smoke smelled like bad fish, realizing too it could have actually been the fumes of his own fishhead. "You cannot take off fishhead. They think you magic fish fellow from deep sea . . . will bring them good luck and keep this vessel safe."

Zeke thought the old man had a screw loose yet was immensely relieved he spoke at least a broken English. "If you can see right through my disguise, what makes you think the crew up there won't?"

The old man chortled with a grunt and stood up and conked his head on a steel pipe and yelled in that foreign language a visceral murderous series of sentences. He then threw some carbuncled shad in a pan and turned on a burner flame of a hidden stove behind him. "We eat fish together, you, me." He slapped his chest and motioned with his chopping hand towards Zeke. "You must be magic fish fellow or you die with fish overboard. They will not question you're the real McConkey from the deep sea because *I* vouch for your authenticity."

Zeke did not know how to receive this news. It was kind of the old man to want to protect him, but Zeke was too cynical not to expect the other shoe to fall. "Why would you do that? Why care about me? By the way, it's real *McCoy*."

The old man drank from a flying fish engraved verdigris tankard now and poured some abalone infused hot rum into a similar tankard for his guest. He snorted a laugh and they clanked vessels and drank. Zeke's esophagus throbbed in overpowered shock and he doubled over to collect himself. Now the old man replied: "I need helper on ship. I work too much making all spirits friendly to fishermen on ocean. Now you will do a lot of the . . . how do you say . . . *showmanship* necessary."

"That's some mighty potent rum, pal," Zeke began. "So, you want me to put on some kind of shows? What are you talking about? I just want to go ashore!"

The old man grinned knowingly at his puzzled recruit and turned to check on the sizzling flying fish, flipping them with a deft thrust of the pan, presently serving their meal. Zeke was hungry and scarfed down the succulent fish with gusto. "The toasty carbuncles add crunchy zip!" the old man commented. He was watching him with favorable regard and relit his corncob and swigged more rum, settled back, and commenced unbosoming his own story as means of enlightenment to the circumstances of their sea exigencies. Over three years had elapsed since the retired cooper and scrimshaw artisan and grandfather of three went for a fateful dip in the remote lagoon off Frunderbach Point and found himself snatched up by the foreign fishing vessel of unknown origin. The 72-year-old insisted he was simply practicing his butterfly stroke, but the captain claimed credit for saving him from certain drowning. The fishermen found the old-timer charming and a steady, calming presence, which quickly became a shamanlike role bestowing propitious conditions and spiritual advice to the reverential crew. He became known to them (at least phonetically) as Parabola Pumas and he constantly had to develop and broaden the character mystically so they wouldn't turn on him and throw him overboard. He picked up enough of their language to communicate with the men, though their country of origin remained an enigma to him. It even occurred to Pumas, he related in an aside, that some of the fisherman themselves have no memory of their homeland years. "When at sea a long time I understand now how this *fog of ocean* envelops one. You merge with the water, the spray, the waves, the vessel, the daily regimen of fishing, and most of all, the *fish*." After he said this to Zeke he threw back a gulp of hot rum and said, looking away: "It's happening to me, my fishhead friend. I feel myself more and more identifying with Parabola Pumas, recognizing the vital role he plays with these fishermen—I even think in their tongue now—while at the same time there is the gnawing notion that my family neglected me in my sunset years, the paucity of visits, the like . . . but this thinking is . . . insidious . . . the sea does that . . . I really must get back home. It's been almost four years . . ."

The two men bonded in their calamitous maritime misadventures and forged a rum-soaked pact to aid one another's struggle to escape the shanghaied sea life aboard their aberrant ship. They worked on Zeke's fishhead figure as a mysterious creature caught in the ship's trawler for an unknown cosmic purpose, and over a couple of hours of hot rum and pan-fried flying fish they arrived at four irreducible elements to the fishhead persona. First, the fishhead would remain squarely, securely, and immovably on Zeke's head, inasmuch as exposure of fakery would mean both being sent overboard. Second, routines of abstract one-act plays rich in blank verse and fishermen songs would be performed by the fishhead fellow at precise intervals four times a day. Third, the fishhead fellow would speak his own language, a throaty mélange of Teutonic and guttural sounds that no one else followed. And fourth, the fishhead fellow would ululate in the manner of an eerie hybrid fish man and engage in good-natured didoes with the crew, such as lifting one's flask of rum ration and dashing away after secretly fastening the victim's fancy sash to the forecastle binnacle.

ONE

Zeke wakened to find his achy hung-over form strewn in the pantry closet with a heap of onions and rutabagas among other root vegetables and squinted at the pale morning light seeping through. The events of the previous day barraged him, his arrival via trawler, the odd foreign fishing boat hauling him in, and his long drunken meeting with Parabola Pumas and their four-point plan of escape to land, which now in the harshly sobered dawn seemed utterly bootless as a vehicle to effect their deliverance. He placed his fingers on his face as he caught sight of his fishhead lying among a group of turnips and parsnips, and loath as he was to wear it again, he recalled the admonition of Pumas and jammed his skull back into the congealing goo and rank flesh of the hollowed halibut. Zeke climbed on deck and located Pumas near the bow with his arms raised high and eyes shut, some metaphysical pose no doubt, Zeke figured. He stated his objections to the four-point plan and a quarrel between the men broke out. A few fishermen caught the spectacle and Zeke knew he had to simmer down, so he consolidated his chagrin into one question: "And what if I simply refuse to carry out my part of the plan?"

Pumas showed that amused smile again and pulled out his corncob and fired it up. "You *will* uphold your end of it, or I notify the captain at once that you are fake and you *will* go overboard. So you better start performing what we talked about soon!"

Zeke bristled at such a threat. "I thought if they uncover my being a fake we both go overboard?"

Pumas guffawed with scorn. "If *they* expose you, yes, but if *I* alert them of your fraudulence . . . then I am above suspicion and you go over alone."

The fishermen began stirring on deck, preparing the great nets and windlasses and capstans, climbing the mizzenmast and readying the topsails, greeting their strange new shipmate with incomprehensible salutations, and Zeke pondered his predicament and saw his sentence in that moment, trapped among them as the ocean creature they caught, mystical and providential, a fishhead freak of a talisman tasked with the tall order of amusing, edifying, and inspiring them through the four-point plan he no longer embraced. But old Pumas meant business, knowing his new partner meant less of a shaman load for him, and he had him over a barrel.

Zeke began later that morning staging his first play in which he portrayed a kind but naïve flounder who discovers fishing as a hobby and catches his father and devours him sautéed with lemon and chives before realizing his crime. *Floundering with Belly Full of Poor Papa* was the showstopper he slapped together, which smoothly segued into the free verse uncompromising poem, *Fishsticks in the Crawlspace, Half-Cooked,* and the lugubrious ballad *Apace Molders a Moon Pie.* He worked up some peppy nautical numbers too, Sousa inspired pure baroque celebratory sounds sung with reckless abandon and the ship's bassoonist and ukulele strummer providing instrumental interludes when the transported fishhead fellow marched about in his signature high-stepping spasmodic improvisation. The fishermen, unable to comprehend the content of Zeke's performances, were nonetheless transfixed by the raw spectacle of the fishhead fellow hearkening some screwball compulsion to plumb deeply within and find expression for an unholy, unhinged mélange of mindless conceit and self-debasement. Zeke established a routine of three shows a day; one shortly after daybreak (*matins,* he called the opener), early afternoon (*sunnyside skidoo*), and one in the evening (*vespers*), a gratifying but punishing load of work made all the more grueling by his halibut head emitting an increasingly foul odor from the rotting fish interior. The fishermen were usually working while he was performing, which integrated Zeke into their arduous mission to catch more fish and the strange finned figure preternaturally drew their interest and attention and cooperation. The fish character was developing exponentially through these early live shows and Zeke truly lost himself in concocting clever new ideas, the fishhead fellow he created sustaining his very will to endure. He fretted that he, like Pumas, might become slowly usurped and taken over by the panicky hybrid sea creature he'd come to grudgingly respect while growing more and more uneasy inhabiting.

ONE

After several weeks the freshness of his act began to wane and the fishermen hardly paused to take note of their resident performer anymore, though the few times Zeke stopped in the middle of a show the men very quickly went into a violent uproar and in a flash their fishhead fellow was resuming his act. He grew melancholy realizing he'd been relegated to ambient noise, like the periodic ringing of church bells so part of a town's landscape only their silence would elicit a reaction. But Zeke Borshellac had a survivor's perseverance in him and thrived in his three shows daily, churning out plays almost effortlessly, such as *Catfish Confidential*, *Mud Flaps Mojo*, and *Monkfish Lasso Pasquinade*, all searing examinations of the quiet lives of fish and their ongoing systematic slaughter, and veering into big soaring operatic songs of lives torn apart by long fishing expeditions and the disasters befalling the men aboard who perish and leave wives and children behind. "*The sea gives us life and swallows others in death, like Captain Schlugelpan, who tumbled into a roiling high tide, drunk and happy.*" The fisherman seemed to latch onto the mention of Schlugelpan in this song, and Zeke was amused by their pronunciation of his name: Kappa Shushupah. He could never forget the image of these odd hard-nosed fisherman scampering higgledy-piggledy with impish grins, their billowing silky genie pants reflecting the sun rays on the ocean horizon, a few rowdier ones slinging fresh caught sole with their flashy sashes at one another's heads, all shrieking "Kappa Shushupah!" and laughing, later on roistering over rum with an equally baffling joie de vivre. Zeke bore them no ill will, he rather enjoyed their uncommunicative company, the camaraderie among them to which he was ineluctably alien. He found their arcane culture impenetrable and fascinating and struck up an acquaintance with the captain, a rotund, large-eared chap with a croaking incessant chuckle and a penchant for pounding the fishhead fellow, or as they called him "Sfrugzer Flogesh," on the back as hard as he could. There too was a détente with Pumas and they on occasion played pinochle in the galley while downing rum, the optimism shared only weeks earlier now gone in their grim resignation to the long voyage against their wills. Zeke knew he should have hated Pumas for coercing his participation in their ill-conceived drunken scheme, but he decided to eschew those obvious sentiments. It could have been worse than stuck on that ship, he knew. But lying in his hard too-small bunk at night Zeke thought of his life aboard that ship hiding in a foul fishhead (changed blessedly by filching a halibut now and then from a fresh haul) and honing performances for mysterious fishermen not particularly invested in his form of live art, and he could never imagine his younger self, the ten-year old Zeke Borshellac dreaming of adventure and making his mark one day as an explorer or visionary or simply a bold, unconquerable man of the world, that boy born to a pretty tavern wench and a lushhound liveryman, who ran wild in the stark countryside with his pack of loose lads doing as they pleased, *he* would take his chances jumping overboard rather than sticking such a grim grind out. Pumas would expatiate on the salutary need of adjusting one's expectations, the contentedness of yielding to resignation, of finding a new, useful existence within the inevitable confinements of life's vagaries. The old man would affect the intellectual as he delivered such deadening words, stroking his beard, relighting his corncob, twitching his noggin to twirl the putty pom poms dangling from his fisherman's hat. Zeke swore he would never succumb to such constraints, would never surrender the faint flickers of exultant illimitable yearning that yet survived in his dormant soul, that nebulous notion to emerge as a substantial man of parts with skills and knowledge and yes, the capability of great transcendent love with the right woman, he held onto that much lying in the darkness of his cold cramped bunk at night as the ship rocked against waves, his fetid fishhead on a shelf beside him. But this vestige of fortitude was waning every day as he went ever deeper into his fishhead fellow performances and his body ached with overworked exhaustion and pustules and cankers sprouted on his face and neck from the halibut entrails and his terrible puking resumed like a broken spigot twisting amuck.

    And then, one morning at daybreak Zeke awakened in his bunk to hear the extraordinary sounds of people and horse hooves on cobblestone and a kind of bustle that betokened something other than their vessel and the ocean, and he put on his fishhead and scampered on deck and beheld the wondrous sights of a busy harbor where his dark ship had apparently docked. And just like that, in a straightforward manner he never imagined, his long ungodly ordeal had come to a sudden end. He let out a glorious laugh as his chest heaved with heartfelt gratefulness and he peered across the bow at the brisk commotion of commerce pulsing along the wharves and the cobblestone streets and old brick buildings and felt all the exhilaration of knowing he had been granted a new life, land once more would be under his feet. He searched for Pumas and found him in the forecastle orating before a group of squatting fisherman in their guttural tongue, oscillating a length of hawser line with a bream and moonfish dangling, incense smoke emanating from his tunic, now swinging the hawser line over the men's heads as Zeke interrupted with a shout: "Pumas! We have docked in a harbor! Come with me, let's hurry and disembark from this godforsaken tub while we have the chance!"

Pumas completed his pagan maritime ritual and slowly turned to his comrade. "They will not let you, Borshellac. They will tie you up and torture you and throw you overboard tonight. Don't be a fool. It is over. There is no way out for us." The fishermen were conversing confusedly and watching Zeke closely, moving towards him.

"You are a scared old man who gave up your freedom for this madness!" He pulled off his fishhead and threw it at Pumas and the fishermen and yelled: "Good-bye and go to hell you bastards!" And he ran across the deck as fishermen now saw he was a fake all that time and they gave him chase screaming in their infernal tongue and very nearly caught him before Zeke leaped from the bow onto an old weather-beaten stretch of pier that trembled under his weight as he bolted over it and into the chaos of the crowd, losing his pursuers forever.

Two

ZEKE KEPT RUNNING for what seemed to him most of that splendid early spring morning, across the town square with an imposing fountain sculpture of a wild-eyed fisherman astride a giant seahorse aiming his harpoon at a defiant merman creature mirthful and holding a bottle of wine as he sends gushing jets from his mouth, dashing through the fish market with its familiar stench and the condemned fish ebbing in their last dying twitches and the many already deceased—was that Larry Skompis? his split-second mind registered a large carp, instantly knowing it wasn't of course—and he proceeded down narrow sloping cobblestone alleys, tore through a dry goods marketplace and raced towards the wooded lowlands near a stream, where he slowed enough to breathe deeply and take stock of himself now at liberty once more to decide his life path and treasure the sunshine of a fine cool new day and the pungent March earth under his tread. He then ran until he ached with fatigue and grew winded, walking now while intermittently looking back over his shoulder for signs of pursuers, and he ran and walked in intervals for a good while more along a dirt thoroughfare en route to the next burg. As the shank of evening came along with a gustier wind of chilly air Zeke's joy of escape had already faded into anxiety over where he might find work since he was nearly broke, and more immediately, where he might sleep and cadge something to eat that night. He stumbled onto a rotting shed from another era and crawled inside for a few hours of fitful slumber, before identifying wild blackberry plants and stocking up for the resumed journey. It was only the beginning for Zeke of discovering the true depths of hard times that had befallen the land, as he rambled

TWO

for several days through villages and small cities and saw the sobering reality of desperate people all looking for food and work. There were hoboes around campfires singing in bitter, unyielding voices songs of the struggle and the wonder of sneaky pete, more highwaymen laying for travelers who were increasingly broke until highwaymen began mugging one another, and once chancing upon a workers' shape-up outside a foundry factory front gate and joining the massive throng but his beaten-down, tired self was not even considered.

One night Zeke teamed up with a group of hoboes who were woefully lost searching for train tracks and seemed to accept the young, tattered wayfarer's company, enough so to share a bunch of *mickies*, or potatoes they roasted over flames at their night camp. They were passing around a magnum of muscatel and chomping their fire-cooked steaming hot potatoes and sharing tales of the unforgiving economic struggle they were up against. Zeke's turn came and he hesitantly began telling them about his first brutal experience on a fishing trawler, which had ironically rescued him from drowning. He knocked back substantial pulls of muscatel and his eyes seemed nutty as he tried to diminish any notion of himself as a professional fisherman, yet anyone could see he still wanted to be taken somewhat seriously. The hoboes listened attentively and there were some grunts and garbled snarls of empathy as Zeke recounted his plight aboard Bunt Ketchum's tub, though one lean rugged hobo with a broken nose and scarred cheek, the evident honcho of this crew who until now had said nothing, now piped up: "Seems to me, *brother*, from where I'm sitting, this Ketchum wasn't so bad. Hell, the man pulled your drowning ass from the sea and gave you a shot working on his ship. If you washed out, *brother*, it would be best you owned up to it and knock off your goddamned bellyaching." The hobo paused to address his cronies now. "This hoople had an opportunity, a golden one in a job on that boat, and he spit the bit. He don't deserve our simpatico! Hell, he's probably still got some of that fishin' pay in his pocket!" Now the group looked at Zeke with narrowed censorious eyes and before he could begin to scram the half-crocked hoboes had jumped him and turned him upside down emptying his pockets, lifting the last few coins he had to his name. Thusly fleeced, they kicked his sprawled form sufficiently to spend their anger at the "loser who had no claim to calling himself a hobo," as the hard-nosed leader they called Scud put it and left him there in the dim glow of the ebbing embers of their fire.

Zeke soon stirred, sore and aching but relieved they were gone and equally consoled by their neglecting to take with them their magnum of muscatel, still lying beside him in shadows. He crawled towards the bottle and quenched at least some of his pain with an extended swig. It felt like he kept arriving at new low points, lowering the bar of a new nadir, but at least this time he had his nepenthe in the muscatel. He drank some more, incapable of pondering upon a step forward. But then he heard muffled voices coming from the old rail yard, the unmistakable sound of Scud and his hoboes returning, no doubt for their forgotten wine, and Zeke hightailed it in the opposite direction as fast as his beaten-up form would allow. Behind him were Scud's cries of ire, ordering his crew to fan out and "nab that grape glomming rat bastard!" But Zeke had an excellent jump on them and, as he had done before, maintained his skedaddle at a good clip—the magnum under his arm like a football—for what seemed to him most of the evening, or simply as long as his legs and wind would hold up, halting for necessary respites during which he'd down the blessed muscatel. For the arduousness of his flight was more than matched by the psychological existential struggle he fought within himself, a desperate self-examination of his very worth and usefulness as a working man, an unforgiving interrogation of his character and courage, insofar as the damning words of Scud's indictment of his fishing folly reverberated viciously and indelibly in his thoughts. The nepenthe muscatel would help blunt the irreconcilable trauma of Scud's words as Zeke moved through dark desolate trails beyond hilly woodland, athwart lonely country towns and along the cobblestoned lanes of burgeoning cities, down their alleys and across their shaky footbridges, foraging for sustenance where broke travelers look, back doors of inns beseeching kindly cooks, the earth's bounties in berries wild and farm crops unwatched, and Zeke wrestled with the choices he had made and the man he aspired to become as he belted muscatel and replaced the magnum with new bottles he pilfered from shops out of necessity. Over and over Zeke told himself that he had persevered through will and endurance and guts to emerge from Bunt Ketchum's boat, and he had shown even greater survival instincts and strength to escape the second, foreign ship, but it was no matter, nothing could stave off the insidious spread of self-doubt vitiating his core identity, his young man's soul. Zeke Borshellac always carried in him the zephyrs, the woolgathering, of great dreams and singular achievements, unique to him and his sensibility and destiny, the wherewithal of potential that was in him and had to come out . . . and now doubt, furtive and debilitating, shared that inner sanctum. Zeke swilled muscatel in ever increasing amounts and covered more ground every day in his drunken journey, penetrating back country and regions remote and lost, abysmally astray and stumbling ever onward into the dark chasm of mocking purlieus. His worsening condition was too wrung-out and bone-weary to continue much longer, the incessant lapping up of muscatel had deadened him altogether, albeit paradoxically vivifying his spirit in wild thrusts here and there. He performed an old soft shoe number for a few rats gathered by a sewer drain, and he sporadically burst into "Greensleeves" when his reflection would appear in a window or large puddle.

It was weeks of sleeping outside under trees or in old sheds of desuetude, scaring up wild berries or raiding hardscrabble farmers' crops, generally going hungry and fading in viable cognition, and then came the dark old city with the hard inky rain, the howling black squalls, the soot begrimed brick buildings and the dubious forsaken souls creeping about with larceny or battery or fear driving them, and he came upon the archaic creaky harbor and the fishing vessels and the threat of dark watery williwaws ever over the streets and the harbor's rough tides and Borshellac recognized through his wine-soused eyeballs that he indeed had wended his way back to Bluddenville. Anguish stabbed at him now as he recalled the start he had here not so long ago when he procured a berth on Ketchum's trawler and the eager exuberance with which he brought to the opportunity of apprentice fisherman. Zeke now hit the sneaky pete hard and tottered down by the piers, breaking out some soft shoe while sticking out his tongue for some sooty rain, and tumbling more than once as he made his way towards the darker, dim section most avoided. A light shone faintly from a window of a lopsided shack built beside the piers, a soot-coated wooden shanty with irregular unsightly additions that whistled splitting the black squalls, and Zeke instinctually reeled and lurched his way towards it, its soft glow refracting and wiggling in wet reflections before him. The whipping rain pelted him as he waded across the sudden puddle-pond gushing around his movement, and he paused to pull out his muscatel for a chug and survey the elements with a goofy appreciation before plodding and splashing ahead. And then he fell down in a sloshed heap, the waterline cresting inches from his nose, and he lay there soaking and alone and nearly unconscious. Not a soul was about as Zeke slept strewn on the flooded cobblestones. Until a figure emerged from the shanty and proceeded towards the fallen rambler, a personage familiar to all who frequented the crude, disreputable world of the Bluddenville wharves and the iniquities laced therein. She had glimpsed Zeke's collapse from her window and now moved with deliberate strides across the watery stones as if she'd done it many times before. Her old-time black-rubber rain boots with buckles and long raggedy slatted skirt, not unlike the dreary curtains that have hung forever in the hourly fleabag hotels she haunted, were well-known to locals, along with the speckled black and gray beehive coiffure she wore like a modified Prussian helmet, all part of the jib one Ma Moody cut in the underworld of the wharves and greater harbor. Now she bent over the sodden form and grasped his torn frock, yanking his torso upright and assessing his scraped somnolent mug, slapping his cheeks with increasing vigor to little avail, a few groans and grunts, before dragging him over the cobblestones towards her shanty. With firm grips under his arms from behind she backpedaled the good two-hundred feet to the shelter of a backroom bunk, a feat she managed quite summarily. Of meager frame and well past her scrappiest prime, she still exhibited a raw-boned fortitude that made her an indomitable force in her own right.

Zeke remained semiconscious and quite incoherent as he lay supine in his newfound comfort, unaware of Ma Moody's hovering ministrations bedside as she jovially prepared a cup of tea with sugar for him. "So you come to see me, eh? Can't say I've seen you before. Well, welly, you almost made it, boy, but you fell short . . ." She let out a horselaugh. "And I mean *bellyflopper*, boy! Went down hard, you did. Well, welly, you were splicing the main brace too much . . ." She now adjusted his head on the pillows and brought the steaming cup to Zeke's mouth, inducing him to sip some. She laughed again and said: "You boys tank up till pie-eyed, sure, sure, probably down at Gilhooley's or The Red Harpoon, and then you want your poontang . . ." More laughs. "Well, welly, Ma will finish you off, don't you worry 'bout that, boy, cause there ain't nothing Ma can't do when it comes to getting them ashes hauled . . . oh, it'll cost you extra, boy, but none of my fellas ever complained afterwards, that's a bona fide fact." Now Ma Moody certainly perceived in her whipsawed stinko customer a challenge of serious proportions, though when she began her dexterous manipulations of his limp body there was more than her professional pride at stake, she wanted his money and her own ethics would not allow her to collect it unless she brought him around. She was all business and went to work on his anesthetized flesh with a surgical precision, using her hands and tongue and small but willfully effectual breasts to recharge the half-dead man and extract a rise from him, incrementally, through fierce labors and techniques acquired over years of becoming the queen strumpet of the wharves. Like a master mechanic attending to a broken-down jalopy, Ma Moody entered a whirlwind of tactile procedures and maneuvers like nothing Zeke had ever felt, revving up and re-animating his private parts into a significant concupiscence. And then, when she had his engine purring with pent-up power she mounted him and rode her looped boy hard and long, knowing just when to give it the gun and when to slow down into a sweet and delightful cruise. Ma Moody loved her trade because she was so good at it, the unqualified best many harbor habitués felt, notwithstanding her scant pulchritude. And despite being dead drunk and barely conscious, Zeke was roused enough to experience the very best sex of his life, long, durable coitus that would be only remembered in the morning in a bleary haze, like a wet dream that hardly could have been real. Only Ma Moody could have done it, devoured and drawn from his flaccid ruins the kind of volcanic Dionysian balling that seemed far, far beyond the boundaries of carnal pleasure, straining all credulity by even the recipient come morn, only the succubus haunting the wharves at night as the squalls bluster through could have done it.

Zeke opened his eyes in the same bunk, squinting in the pale light of dawn streaking towards him, the faint cries of gulls gliding over the harbor the only sounds. His head hurt and limbs were all sore and he hardly recalled how he got there in that bunk when he smelled a strong pungent steam and then there was Ma Moody with a snaggletooth grin and a great metal bowl under one arm, stirring the hot contents with a wooden spoon. "So, you have risen, eh boy? Well, welly, I have your breakfast ready, the finest furmity there ever was." She propped him up with an authoritative tug and ladled him a wooden bowlful and Zeke shoveled a spoonful in his mouth and the spicy wheat and milk and cornmeal and fatback beans filled him with warmth and surprise it was so good, which he attributed to his ravenous hunger.

His cognizance of Ma Moody was opaque, faint, filtered through the boozy layers of a hard wham-bam night, but he did know she did him a good turn, pulled his wasted form across the cobblestone square and into her shanty. She put him in that bed and afforded him the chance to recover and rest from the merciless torrents of the night, and Zeke was grateful now. "You rescued me last night," he said, "and I will ever be beholden to you."

She smiled crookedly and stroked his hair with her hand. "I seen you out there lurching about on your way to see ol' Ma, and when you hit the deck I thought I can't let a fine young man with such good taste drown in that floodin'."

TWO

Zeke became quizzical at her remark. "I got quite a bag on last night," he began, "so I don't recall where I was going before you came out of nowhere to lug me to your place. You think I was coming to see you, but I don't believe I even knew you before last night."

She let rip a guffaw and replied: "Looky boy, you don't have to *know* Ma Moody as much as *heard* about her to understand why you were coming across the street in this here direction."

"I was probably just searching for a place to get out of the rain."

"Pshaw!" she cried with a cackle. "Any port in a storm, eh? That's what the fellas like to say . . ." She grabbed a bottle of applejack and dumped some in her cup of unknown contents before taking a gulp with her eyes closed. When opened her eyes now had a demented glint in them and she wiped her mouth with her elbow and uttered in a cocky murmur: "But when it comes right down to it, boy, there is only one real port in these parts. They come down to see ol' Ma Moody."

Zeke's head had throbbing pain in it but only dim recollections of his long night so his savior's remarks were puzzling and more than a little egomaniacal for him, as he couldn't imagine why all these fellows were coming to see her. Certainly not for sexual commerce. But he certainly appreciated her hospitality and tactfully said: "I'm sure glad you saw me out there."

She poured more applejack into her cup and chugged some before jabbing Zeke's side playfully, replying: "Business is business, boy! Now you get some rest and gather your strength." She fed him a hot spoonful of furmity and chuckled as he swallowed it. "Well, welly, when you're all together and ready you just slap together some frogskins to the tune of two sawbucks—check that, two sawskis and a fin— and shell 'em out for ol' Ma, y'hear?"

She plied him with some fine steaming hickory java and several more spoonfuls of her furmity and it occurred to Zeke that she was hitting her ward up for remuneration, which made him think much less of his savior. And being broke, her request for payment caused him considerable unease and disquiet, disremembering, of course, the crazed carnal congress of the drunken unconscious night. Finally, finishing his breakfast and slowly finding his feet in a woozy upright stance, he made a clean breast of his poverty. "I'm sorry to have to divulge the true status of my finances, ma'm, but I am dead busted. I acknowledge my great debt to the shelter you provided me. Can I pay you your fee once I scrape a sum together?"

Ma Moody no longer punctuated her words with her singular laughter and grins, but now faced a dilemma she was quite unaccustomed to in her tenure as queen strumpet of the wharves. She had to ponder what this troubled slim stranger had declared in an earnest manner, that he could not pay. She could have called in the goons to have them teach the loopy crum-bum a bruising lesson never to be forgotten, or she could cash in her chips in other ways, such as enlisting the lad in some sticky errands she needed performed. "Here's what we are going to do, poor fellow. I have a piece of work for you, and upon its completion we will be even." Zeke rather liked the arrangement, right away wondering if it could lead to regular work. He said it just so happens he was looking for work on land, as his experiences fishing had been horrendous.

Her eyes narrowed and she smiled faintly. "Don't you worry, boy, your dogs are hoofin' on solid ground with Ma Moody. First I want you to go see an associate of mine, Cal Crimcastle. Tell Cal I sent you to lend them a hand whipping that dump into shape." When Zeke asked the kind of dump he'd be rehabilitating she replied: "Oh, a house nobody lived in for years that I'm claiming. It's going to be all the rage around these parts, and ol' Ma'll be cashin' in."

A couple of hours later Zeke's ride, a horse-drawn tin-knocker's rattle-trap flagged down by Ma Moody, clip-clopped down a narrow sinuous byway and came to a halt. "That's the joint, mister," the old tin-knocker announced with a sigh. "Ma Moody ought to be satisfied I got you here. Make sure she knows." The house was set back from the road and seemed half-swallowed by the encroaching overgrowth and too far gone to Zeke for restoration, but then he heard hammering and sawing sounds reverberating from within and thought of Ma Moody's will to build her own gambling den and told himself he wouldn't bet against her. He watched the tin-knocker recede down the lane, shaking and jostling in the most clamorous way, until he stood there alone in the stark still rustic recesses of the city. He began towards the crumbling front steps and the peeling-paint front door. He heard them working in there so after his knocking went unanswered he simply entered and was stunned to see the wreckage and decrepitude which greeted him. A dim dusty gloom hung over everything, the motley mounds of accumulated debris, the worn broken furniture, and the sawing of a staircase by a pudgy man of fifty or so with a long black beard and wearing a striped uniform of gray and brown that seemed like a sailor of a far-flung navy. It was Cal Crimcastle and Zeke tried to catch his attention by yelling over but he was so focused on his sawing it seemed nothing could break his concentration. There was occasional hammering coming from upstairs and now Zeke sought another set of stairs to climb up there but settled for clambering atop the front porch and crossing the roof to enter through a second story window.

As he moved from room to room in search of the individual hammering it became much more difficult when the hammering stopped altogether. "Hello? Ma Moody sent me to help you out!" he now exclaimed. He crept about from one junk-strewn room to another calling out again for the hammerer to show himself. And as he turned a corner into the last room an arm suddenly came from behind to put him into a headlock, and Zeke struggled to extricate himself only to be thrown hard against the wall and collapse. When he collected himself enough to look up at his adversary, he saw a rugged red-haired fellow in a green turtleneck glaring back, brandishing a prodigious hammer with a foot-long head.

"Spit it out, kid! What's your business coming here?"

Zeke stammered his being sent by Ma Moody. Now Cal Crimcastle joined them and said disgustedly: "This must be the help she's been promising us. We need three or four tradesmen with proven skills and she sends us this stiff." They both cursed a bit and asked Zeke about his experience and his honest answers left them more irate.

"I have a debt to work off here," Zeke said, "and while I'm a novice in the construction trades I can assure you I am a hard worker."

The two men murmured to each other before the red-haired fellow, O'Connell, spoke with a finality: "We'll see what you got, kid. Crim and I will give you a try-out. If you crap-out . . . well, you'll find out." The men walked their apprentice down the functioning staircase to the kitchen table where Crimcastle opened a blueprint of the house and taped it to the wall. He held a long measuring stick with which he hit the room design he was addressing, breaking into long disquisitions on the juxtaposition of erecting structures and their subsequent demolition. He now padded around the seated Zeke, the stick held behind his back as he seemed to ruminate on his next words. "I don't know if we can deliver the kind of gambling palace Ma Moody wants." He paused and poured himself a shot of rum from a bottle sitting on the counter by the sink. "She pushes hard for the impossible . . . then assigns blame. It could end bad."

O'Connell rose from his chair, grabbed the rum and took a big swig from the bottle and wiped his mouth with the back of his hand. He paced around, appropriating the measuring stick as his own prop in expounding on the herculean task ahead of them. "Ma Moody ain't the sort anyone ought to trifle with, and I for one have nothing but immense respect for the 'ol hag. She's asking a lot here, much of the specs describe completely new rooms, kitchens, bathrooms, main floor, bar . . . that's where Crim and I come in. We're builders, erectors . . . this place needs demolitionists first. That's where you come in, pal. That's why I figure Ma Moody sent you down here."

Zeke thought about O'Connell's statement and was puzzled. "She never really inquired about my experience as a demolitionist. I told you, I am paying off a debt."

"Times are tough, chief. This is an opportunity you can make the most outta, if you're smart," Crimcastle counseled.

Zeke's heart leapt now as his hunch seemed to have some validity. A job on land was his biggest goal. O'Connell fixed him a good glass of rum and bade him knock it back. He slapped his back with a hearty laugh. "She must've seen something in you, kid. Maybe the spark of a true demolitionist she gleaned in ya. They say all of us are either erectors or demolitionists. You're the latter, or at least Ma Moody has you so pegged . . . now Crim and I will try you out and see if you cut the mustard."

Zeke stood up straight and smiled at his new colleagues, meeting their eyes when he declared: "Well, you fellas will not be disappointed. I'm going to smash this joint to smithereens. I'm your demolitionist and nothing will remain upright after I'm done with it."

They nodded towards him with tenuous confidence and began showing him the walls that still had to come down and the furniture that had to go and where the floors had to be cut open for the new staircases and the attic's dismantling and the removal of the sun room, not to mention the ripping out of all the windows except a single bay variety in the parlor (which itself had to be utterly razed). Naturally, Zeke asked for a point of clarification about the bay window remaining intact when the parlor itself would have to be totally leveled. O'Connell snapped in exasperation: "Ma Moody wants that bay window, pal. Don't overthink it or get cute with us. She wants to place a fantail Chesterfield in that window where she could sit and keep watch over the goings-on. If you don't preserve the bay, you will have failed for sure." Zeke gazed at the window in the parlor on the blueprint and saw her seated bolt upright in her fancy chair looking daggers at him. "Yeah, don't flub the goddamned bay window, chief," Crimcastle piped up. "You ever meet her son Gunther?" asked O'Connell. "He's a monster of a vicious thug who will work over and even murder anyone who gives his mother a hard time. He revels in his menace and drinks more beer than anyone alive. A case a day to Gunther is nothin' and he makes it look easy." Crimcastle speculated: "Gunther goes six-five, two-sixty, the son-of-a-bitch is an animal. Usually knocks back two cases a day, like water to the big bastard. If he turns on you . . . he'll usually kill you."

Zeke felt a chill of misgivings. "How does he feel about the house here?" he asked.

The men looked puzzled by the question. "It doesn't matter," Crimcastle replied, "as long as Ma Moody is happy, Gunther is happy." Zeke became introspective, receding towards the wreckage of the adjoining dining room. "Hey, don't worry about him, chief. Gunther will probably like you. You're both demolitionists," O'Connell called to him.

And the daily pattern of work on the project was thereafter settled. Shortly after this conversation Crimcastle and O'Connell told Zeke they had meetings to attend about the "natural esthetic" of the eventual new structure and they were responsible for creating that "vision." Builders need to ruminate and reflect. Zeke was the demolitionist and he had his mission to commence at once. They parted and went straight to the Jolly Roger Tavern across town where they settled in for some fine dark rum and shepherd's pie and many belly laughs with an associate of theirs whose waterfront gang never warmed to the notion of Ma Moody rehabilitating the old house into a gambling palace. They gleefully told this man, a dour dandy named Stu Leapers in a piebald ascot and a khaki jungle suit, that manna from heaven came knocking on their door in the form of a malleable clodhopper called Zeke Borshellac.

After his travails at sea and the hard economic times buffeting him on land, Zeke could not pass up a chance at steady employment, and the more he cogitated on the nature of his assignment the more he thought he understood about the natural facility for demolition Crimcastle and O'Connell saw in him. He began to conjure up a case for his fulfillment of a formidable destiny in destruction. It all began to make perfect sense insofar as the drunken debauchery and utter chaos surrounding his early years being raised in a tavern by a rambunctious wench, who loved him in her way and did her best by him, but nonetheless it left a loathing and disgust in him that only intensified over time. His coming of age led to a fruitless struggle to find a better life. He recognized the quagmire of despair that ineluctably led him to Ma Moody and her netherworld, an uncanny sea hag who can identify him for who he truly is and what kind of existence he can truly thrive in. His life was in shambles, he thought, he had proven indisputably to be a master of self-destruction, so why not embrace the scorched earth policy towards everything? There was ultimately freedom in absolute demolition, he reasoned, because wrecking something, totaling it, tearing it apart and pulverizing it, eliminates an inevitable source of anxiety and compels one to believe in starting over. Demolition therefore means creation. Annihilation is renewal. Ruination equals rebirth. He would bust the place up and find liberation. He had several massive sledgehammers, all varieties of hacksaws, and tremendous will and stamina as he began in an artful, almost ritualistic manner to knock the abandoned house down. He chose the largest sledgehammer, the one with a four-foot mahogany handle and a two-foot, forty-pound steel head, and warmed up with it performing swinging revolutions in many angles before hoisting it high over his head and circumscribing oblong orbits in vigorous rhythmic intensity. In this manner, swinging the sledgehammer until arms ached with strain and breaking only for swigs of rum, Zeke moved past all vestiges of apprehension and found a serene zone within with which to launch his assault on the house. He summoned all of the rage buried deep in his darkest recesses, all of the cumulative anger stored in there which chronicled the shaft life had shown him so far and let rip a great cry of the aggrieved beast who had enough and wanted payback. Zeke tore into the interior wall of the kitchen first, slamming it with strong blows until it began to crumble and plaster dust filled the air and wood buckled in splintered shafts. He gained confidence like an animal drawing first blood, became even more animated now as he swung the sledgehammer with crocked abandon. Zeke transformed himself into a human cyclone, relentless, random in his targets, a rum-soaked mind awash in notions of providentially making his mark as a force of nature, a pure demolitionist. His movements increasingly maintained a crazy syncopation, as if he were performing on stage for an audience and he was the antagonist caught up in his Sturm and Drang tragedy in which little but doom awaited him, unless he tore the house down in time.

The first day Zeke worked well into the night, hardly taking a break, and the next morning Crimcastle and O'Connell found him passed out on the ground floor amidst collapsed beams and insulation and sawed pieces of stairs. An empty bottle of rum lay beside him on a shattered bookcase. "Well, it looks like our boy is making some progress," Crimcastle chuckled.

O'Connell was less pleased. "It will take the kid forever at this rate." He cracked open the fresh half-gallon of rum he brought and took a hit and gazed at O'Connell. "Maybe we ought to pitch in ourselves, Crim. The sooner we destroy this place the faster we collect our envelopes from Leapers."

Crimcastle now went for the rum and seemed uneasy after his gulp. He shook his head. "It's got to be all the kid's doing. Ma can't connect us to it."

O'Connell grimaced in confusion. "Tell me again why the Moravian wants the place razed? I understand he's threatened by Ma growing her gambling interests, but she's going to build her palace regardless."

Crimcastle peered out the window at a cardinal landing on a nearby tree. He turned towards Zeke, snoring again now, and spoke with exasperation. "What the hell do I know, except what Leapers was talking about that once the dump is completely down they think that pettifogger shyster of theirs could tie them up legally . . . no more squatter's rights or whatever. Now let's get this galoot up."

"All right then, the kid's gonna have to work harder. I could use the spondulics sooner instead of later," O'Connell acquiesced, before delivering an ample kick to Zeke's side which elicited a groan. The men watched their demolitionist slowly rise and nearly stumble over nearby detritus as he stretched and rubbed his eyes from rays of sunlight penetrating the new holes in the house.

"I don't like being kicked," Zeke grumbled.

"Well, who does, pal? But you're on the clock and you have work to do," Crimcastle explained. They left him the bottle of rum and bid him adieu to attend another meeting to "finalize the design," and in-

TWO

side the hour they were on their stools at the Jolly Roger sipping fine dark rum. In a battered old cupboard lying on the floor, he found a rusty tin containing some hard biscuits, and while stale and bitter he gobbled them up straightaway and washed them down with rum. His warm-up preparation now became more involved, as he began swinging the great sledgehammer in a variety of loops as he had the day before, but this morning when he was circling it high over his head he started to sing old songs at the top of his lungs while running in place, forgotten old songs such as "Tailor, Shorten My Trousers, Please," "In a Canoe With Mrs. Ledoux," "Pixie Dust and Spoetzle," and the pirate chantey "Skeleton Charlie at Dead Man's Jamboree." He so enjoyed the deeper engagement of his new prep routine he kept singing and swinging his sledgehammer for over an hour, adding intervals of very regimented choreography as well, and during his rum break he was sweaty and fatigued but felt alive and very gratified with his assignment and prospects, and as he chugged more rum he noticed he was not alone. A small puppy, a shaggy sheepdog pup it appeared, had been perched on a broken wobbly chair taking in his show. Now generally, puppies and demolitionists do not make the best of bedfellows, but Zeke had an abiding admiration for canines and, of course, a hole in his heart ever since his beloved dog Grainy Lackawana ran away when he was a boy and was remarkably discovered a few years later happily living with another family. The loss of Grainy was a grievous memory, albeit his being found in such a way was hard for him. Zeke petted his furry visitor now and fed him a hard biscuit. He held him in his arms and talked to him, told him about old Grainy. He sang one of the old forty-niner songs to his new puppy friend, "Klondike Cappy Gets Shot by His Patootie." Finally, Zeke carried the scraggly sheepdog puppy outside and set him on some tall grass. "So long, buddy, I have to go to work. Stay out of there cause I'm knocking it down and you could get yourself hurt." He petted him once more and locked eyes with the strange canine for the longest time and thought they bonded on a mysterious, profound level. "Come around here a little later, ya hear? I'll have a biscuit for you and we'll talk some more." Zeke had a new spring in his step turning to his task, as he carried a new sense of someone, even if only a canine, being on his side. He swung wild and hard and did so with an abundance of determination and ferocity, amalgamating on a subconscious level his unorthodox herky-jerky dance patterns and his belting out the old songs into a daylong opera of some arcane kind, and the wood broke and split and crashed down and the plaster powder was like glittery mist and Zeke hammered like a young man desperate to bust out of his penurious constraints, his imprisonment as an unskilled nobody, and he knew he had an audience watching him from somewhere outside, a kindred spirit also up against the lonely hard knocks of an indifferent world, his new sheepdog puppy pal was firmly in his corner he knew.

At a furious pace powered by his singular performance he demolished more wall and floor and bashed through ceilings too, and as the crepuscular shanks of evening fell much of the house had already fallen, but he was far from finished when he finally gave out and lay strewn amidst the wreckage, sloshed and spent beyond all limits, and when his colleagues found him the next morning his young canine friend was curled up snoozing right beside him. Crimcastle and O'Connell noted the progress but had concerns the job could drag on for a week. Leapers had applied new pressure to accelerate matters in a lit tirade at the Jolly Roger. "He could pull back the overture on us unless we get it done fast," O'Connell said, wary of Zeke's efficacy as the demolitionist snored steadily beneath him.

"The bastard is getting antsy, no doubt. We ain't gonna blow it though," Crimcastle affirmed. He drew two very large stogies from his jacket, handed one to O'Connell and struck a wooden match to light them both up. They smoked in silence for a minute enjoying the pungent tobacco, lost in puffing ruminations. Crimcastle now grinned after a big whiff and sending a cloud of smoke wafting above them. He fired up a match and held it while meeting O'Connell's eyes, which quickly showed he grasped his intent.

"And who do you propose as the torch?" O'Connell played along.

TWO

Crimcastle blew out the match and looked down at Zeke snoring vociferously and tossed the still smoking match onto him. O'Connell's mien was skeptical, but Crimcastle was bullish on the notion and he poked him with a long piece of wood to waken him. Zeke stirred and collected himself in coming to consciousness while the pup jumped up barking at the two men. "Shut up you dumb mutt!" Crimcastle bellowed.

"Hey, don't say that! He's a good dog," Zeke snapped, now getting up quickly.

Crimcastle laughed. "Oh, so our demolitionist made a little friend." He grew serious then: "Listen, kid, you need to wrap up this job then you could play with your damn dog all you want." Zeke quieted the angry puppy down to listen to them.

O'Connell poured him some rum and gave him a stogie and Crimcastle lit him up, holding out the match to observe it continue to burn. "Tonight's your last night to get it down," he said, "and there are other more sure*fire* ways of meeting that deadline." He chucked the pack of matches at him and Zeke snatched them at the last second and eyed them apprehensively.

"I'm no arsonist. The sledgehammer will do. I'll finish tonight. Besides, what about the bay window for Ma Moody? Fire will wipe everything out."

O'Connell let out a guffaw. "Kid, you can't preserve the bay window when the wall itself has to come down. Ma Moody will understand that."

Zeke puffed his cigar and moved towards the bay window for a better look. "I'll save the woman her bay window. I owe her that."

The men chuckled and Crimcastle slapped him on the back. The puppy barked and growled, but Zeke told him it was okay. "That's the can-do attitude I like to see, kid. You got that spunk in ya. But the spunk might need a few sparks. Remember that."

O'Connell grabbed him playfully by the back of his neck. "Knock yourself out, kid. Do it your way, but get it done by tomorrow. You don't know who you're dealing with." And with that the men were off to The

Jolly Roger to down fine dark rum with Stu Leapers, who was eager to hear of their latest timetable and would report everything to The Moravian that evening.

Zeke and the sheepdog pup ate their breakfast of stale bitter biscuits outside, washed down with rum and water respectively. "I'm going to have to call you something," Zeke said, and thought for a while before coming up with Balthazar, which sounded like a Shakespearean character that seemed to have a noble bearing to it. When asked if that would do, Zeke saw approval in his bright-eyed countenance and his drooping tongue. Soon it was time to begin his work and he petted and hugged Balthazar, lectured him not to come inside while he was engaged in demolition and told him they would meet up once again after the building was razed. "We will stay friends, Balthazar," he called back to him just before he went back inside. "You and me . . . I guess we need each other. I'll take good care of you. You've already done a lot for me." The little pup barked twice and wagged his tail, gazing at his Zeke as he disappeared into the house he had to demolish. He began the same warm-up movements, swinging the largest sledgehammer in every conceivable circle before hoisting it overhead in a horizontal path of whorl and breaking into the old songs while revving up the idiosyncratic but methodical choreography of the performance. Zeke invoked a dark fierce province from the deepest reaches of his soul and it took more warming up in a sustained feverish harum-scarum doubling-down of destructive vehemence, and his swings were blindingly fast and encompassed all manner of geometrical circumscriptions, even done one-handed, and his footwork too picked up speed and improvisation in free-form capricious excursions, and when he on this morning first put hammer to house it was with a new explosive ruinous violence that seemed beyond him the day before. He was wholly taken over by a maniacal, dementedly rhythmic implacable force to demolish once and for all the structure that defied his violent efforts, the walls and roof and ceilings that hemmed him in like a rejected mutton-headed stiff that never got his shot and Zeke tapped that fury as he swung his sledgehammer like a hell-bent marauder of the Middle Ages. His rum breaks were more infrequent but downed more rum to fuel his mad assault, and a second half-gallon was opened. There was a rage buried deep in the core of Zeke Borshellac and he had it now dug up and mined and called forth in powering his sledgehammer like it had grown onto his arms and was part of him and his newfound deliveryman of cumulative wrath. He moved in sudden mad intricate flights that defied all terpsichorean plausibility, yet always maintained control over the integration of a long-view marathon opera. He sang the old songs like never before, louder and with more fervor and urgency; "Pancakes on a Promontory in Toledo," "Fritz in the Pumphouse," "I Love Mr. Marshmallow But Not Today," "Marbles in My Head Make Me Who I Am," "The Rolling Pin Imp Came to the Party," "Hootenanny Hellcats in Polka Dot," and the famous miners' number "Fourteen Clams For Forty-eight Fellers." Zeke sang them all with all he had in him, and his mighty performance was indeed informed and enhanced by knowing that his little pal Balthazar was out there somewhere listening. More rum went down as the afternoon waned and he required more strength to knock down more house, as too much still stood, and the edges of twilight brought new exigencies to reckon with as the incipience of doubt manifested in his fight against time. The arrival of night occasioned a panicky madness that brought him a final surge of potent fortitude that seemed to turn as a major part of the roof collapsed and the sunroom seemed to teeter, but the shift of mass detritus only presented further impediments of access to key areas. Zeke tore into the stubborn structures with a last desperate push, but he was enveloped in mass wreckage which boxed him out and clearing the refuse out was a job of days not hours. He was snozzled and exhausted and could hardly remain upright much longer, let alone continue his mission, and the evening stretched now towards midnight. He knew consciousness had its own clock in his condition. He took a long pull of rum and eyed the book of wooden matches Crimcastle and O'Connell left him. He saw with some pride the still intact bay window he intended to carve out and present to Ma Moody. His drunken rationale somehow figured he could set fire to the intractable zones of the project and he'd avoid the bay window with these spot fires. At first he had several small scattered blazes going and thought it could work, but the drunken demolitionist was far out of his field when he resorted to flames. The independent fires burned bigger and bigger and had an inexorable combustion to join forces and become one great conflagration and Zeke could do nothing now but scamper outside and bear witness to the ever-swelling mad inferno and he watched it accomplish with consuming efficiency what he fell short of, and then he saw it begin to devour the venerated bay window and there on a board he saw his pal Balthazar trapped in the encroaching flames and Zeke ran in without hesitation dodging roaring fire all around to reach him and climbed up to take him in his arms and dive out and roll in the muddy grass to dampen where he'd caught fire. He held his puppy tight and moved away from the burning house and saw Balthazar was okay as he headed for the woods.

Three

Moving swiftly amid the density of trees in darkness Zeke was felled by several branches and trunks, recovering each time with somewhat diminished resilience and fortitude though Balthazar's licks of concern were ample exhortation to push onward. The new team drew strength from one another in their flight and Zeke only thought about leaving the dreadful world of demolition and conflagration behind. He scrambled breakneck through the woodland for as long as he could short of dropping before coming upon a moonlit clearing of fluttering high grass and patches of brush near a gurgling stream. They drank the cool fresh water and jumped in and Zeke felt renewed with a sanguine residue intact as the honey red glint of moonbeams spread over the landscape. Patches of blackberry plants were in abundance close by upon which they gorged themselves before lying on the grassy banks and watching the pale light shimmer in the flowing stream. Zeke gazed upon his new puppy and felt grateful the plucky canine came into his lonely life, the notion of another solo skedaddle from another inflamed gang of maniacs seemed unthinkable now. Balthazar soon rose to all fours and shook his wet shaggy coat with the intense vibration dogs use to dry themselves. "You have natural moves like that when you need them," Zeke said, "ways of acting built into you to accomplish tasks." The puppy scratched his ear with his paw and then fixed Zeke with a curious look. "Your purpose in life is born in your blood and there is a lot to be said for that, Balt. Now take me. I have no notion of where I ought to make my mark, the right path to my true destiny. Except I do know that I am decidedly no fisherman and indubitably someone who will never again consider a career in demolition." He tossed a rock into the stream and saw it skim the surface three times before disappearing. "But I will say this, my good pup, I ain't about to give up on what I have inside me . . . cause whatever it is will make or break me but I'm determined to let it out." Balthazar snuggled beside him, stretching himself dramatically as Zeke petted him. "We'll keep it moving, Balt, you and me. And let's be sure to appreciate this fine night out here away from all the people who are pursuing us, and I'll ponder a vocation more suitable to my capabilities." He chuckled and shook his head. "All I keep coming back to is dedicating myself to improving folks' lives, even in some small way, so I guess I'm a sort of cornball in that regard." And with such noble thoughts prominent in his ruminations Zeke drifted into the gentle arms of Morpheus, where Balthazar had already succumbed, and there they slept on the grass of a singular woodland evening by the burble of a stream, a soft wind on their moonlit unconscious faces, united in their journey to a better life.

A thin yellowish gray heralded daybreak and their verdant bivouac suddenly was over. Zeke was determined to continue deep into the forest and put as many miles between them and Bluddenville as possible before making camp again for a night's rest. Through the wooded density they marched, following meager trails overgrown with brush and scrub, Balthazar at his master's heel with every stride. Zeke regretted his willingness to trust Crimcastle and Connelly and the eagerness with which he tackled his duties in the demolition of the Ma Moody house. He felt chastened by the debacle and swore to examine the nature of any future opportunities more fully before throwing himself whole hog into the work. As they climbed many hills and forded across several hard-charging streams, penetrating into a remote wilderness devoid of anyone before them, Zeke turned inward, musing on the ultimate questions of the grand scheme of the universe, whether random and meaningless or the product of an incomprehensible design. Trekking in the far reaches of forests will induce eschatological reflections, Zeke knew, and his raw glimpse into the oblique mysteries in such natural surroundings made him lean towards ascribing to there being a master plan. But he knew his mind could shift on this in another setting, albeit he felt heartened enough by his tentative incomplete conclusions. It was late when they made camp, again by a stream though in a dale dotted with wildflowers, and Zeke lit a fire and cooked a bunch of roots and dandelions and a few small sea creatures that roasted remarkably well which he and his pup enjoyed immensely.

They were hampered the next morning by an intermittent drizzle, which grew into a steady shower by midday and poured for a period until they made an early camp under a bower that Zeke fortified with all manner of branch and loose bush. He lit a campfire and cooked up a concoction of wild berries and mushrooms and they sat close for warmth against the windy wet night. Zeke thought of the hardships of his boyhood and occasionally bunking in the livery stable to watch over his drunken father, who often fulminated in long-winded dirges on the disintegration of civil society, always ending up decrying "the good eggs who inevitably surrender to the bad apples and enable the rat bastards to ruin the rudiments of everything that makes life worth living." Now on this raw wet evening with Balthazar curled up beside him Zeke found himself murmuring his father's soused words of so many years earlier, words he knew by heart ever since, and he said them a few times in escalating volume and varying cadence and sentence accents. He began to address his puppy with these utterances, gazing upon the canine as if almost expecting a response, and then divining an insight communicated as they locked eyes: *I don't care what your father said to you while intoxicated, I'm tired after the long day and I don't know what you are talking about anyway.* Zeke chuckled and told his pup how much he valued his forthrightness, plain-spokenness, his reluctance to mince words. "You are indeed a dog of dogs who speaks the truth. That's what I'm after myself. In the end, that's about all we have."

Noises came out of the rainy black woods somewhere, fast amplifying sounds of movement through the thick wet overgrowth and Zeke rose to look around. The rustle of brush and snap of twig and steady advance of heavy tread struck Zeke as horses in the fleeting moments before the two men on horseback suddenly appeared in the flickers of light twinkling from the ebbing fire. They seemed like two imposing statues, men with shadowy faces and long raincoats and wide-brimmed hats on massive beasts, figures of menace there now out of nowhere towering over Zeke. One rider guided his horse a little closer and a shaky dim light revealed his hard squinty stare and large smeller as he commanded with stentorian authority: "Get up all your dough and hand it over. Go on!"

Zeke replied with fear and earnestness, half wondering if these highwaymen were not phantasms or sprung from a nightmare he was having. Indeed, he was broke and wanted them to understand that and simply stated that fact.

"That is a bald-faced lie and you know it. Don't insult us. Let's address this postulate you cite like intelligent men, shall we? A wayfarer traversing these woods at night must have dough on him!"

Zeke nodded in agreement before a dose of doubt came over him. "And why is that exactly?" he asked. "It doesn't seem that expensive to me out here."

The highwayman's eyes glowered like a jack-o'-lantern's as the tense silence dragged on until his angered voice posed a question: "Are you some kind of wise guy, mister? Cause you really ought to quit the goofy act and pay heed to my demand."

The other highwayman on horseback was riding around Zeke and his pup, wearing a freakish grin and brandishing an enormous pistol, twirling it in his fingers once and remarking that Balthazar was "a handsome puppy who we could take with us, Lester." He cocked the hammer with a click and pulled up his horse with a flourish in front of Zeke, training the pistol on his head. "I'm going to make it real simple for you since you strike me as the simpleton sort. It may be a hackneyed phrase in our profession, but no one can gainsay its effectiveness. *Your money or your life, pal!*"

Now this highwayman was a hot sketch with a certain mercurial irascibility to him who struck Zeke as a fellow who was not completely comfortable with his robbery occupation. "I have no money whatsoever, sir," he tried to explain. "I would surrender it for sure if I had any, but I am flat broke."

The highwayman trotted his horse even closer with his pistol aimed at Zeke's head, and there was a long tense silence until Lester called to his partner: "Plug the rat son of a bitch, Rollo." But Rollo instead holstered his pistol and guffawed like an unhinged preacher of fire and brimstone. "I tell you what I'm going to do with you, simpleton, I'm going to show you the dark elements of these woods. I'm going to frighten you out of your dim wits by showboating in an ass-backwards manner."

Perplexity now left Zeke speechless, though relieved he no longer stared down the business end of the large pistol. "I am quite happy to watch your show, mister, but I must warn you it will not enable your stick-up to be successful insofar as I will remain destitute," he said.

But the unorthodox highwayman had already positioned himself standing upright *backwards* on his horse and was galloping about in crazy eight figures, or so he declaimed in a thunderous rodomontade from the wooded blackness. Zeke could only make him out as he came charging out of the still darkness and raced by him and his exasperated cohort Lester. "It is astonishing he can ride through the dark forest and not crash into a tree! I can't run through it at night without continually clocking myself," Zeke remarked to Lester.

"He's a talented horseman, but *an ineffectual highwayman!*" Lester replied, fulminating the last part so his partner may hear him. Soon Rollo came tearing back in from the woods and he rebutted Lester with a mordant attack of his own: "You are jealous Lester because you cannot hold a candle to my horsemanship or my propensity and mastery of the bloodless boost! You have become irrelevant and useless next to my wizardry, and so you backbite." In tense awkward silence Lester and Zeke (Balthazar had dozed off by now) waited for his next appearance after his cycle in the woods, at which time Lester was ready and laced into him: "You belong in a circus, Rollo, doing damn equestrian stunts with the clowns. *Not on the highway pawning off your poltroon-*

ery as some sort of avant-garde technique of thievery!" The next time Rollo came roaring through they traded insults again, but the horseman now brandished a switch he must have snapped off in passing, and he swung it at Lester who snatched hold of it and pulled his partner off the speeding equine.

Moments later Lester was kneeling over his fallen pal with trepidation over the extent of his injuries, albeit once it was determined Rollo was banged up but otherwise unhurt the men began their quarrel where they had left off. Zeke had been ready to seize the chance to bolt and as he was awakening his pup for the getaway his robbers simultaneously picked up on his making a move. "Don't even think about it, pal! Rollo and I might lock horns on occasion but make no mistake our rolling you is the priority," Lester bellowed.

Rollo switched gears too and slowly rose to approach Zeke and snarl: "You gotta give up the scratch," he ordered with his cannon of a gun conspicuous now.

"Go on, Rollo," Lester urged petulantly, "Search the man! Turn the bastard upside down and shake the loot loose from his hidden pockets!"

Rollo, baby-faced and roly-poly beside the lean Lester, bristled at the order and replied that upside down searches were not among his many fortes, and "why don't you handle that chore yourself since you're so adept at it?"

Lester frowned at his partner. "Because when you have conquered a maneuver, zest deserts it, atrophy rots it. This dictum applies to all movements of sophistication, but none more than the upside down shake-out for me."

Rollo chortled. "And yet the man persists in fabricating utter twaddle such as we just heard. Have you no shame, Lester? I am starting to believe what they have been saying, that you don't have a shake-out maneuver because no one has actually seen it."

The quarrel, Zeke sensed, would escalate into the worst kind of shouting match in which the participants fail to actually shout as they incrementally become convinced of each other being right. So he attempted to move their otiose robbery of him along by standing on his head. "What's this here? I thought I told you no funny business, nimrod?" Lester snapped, puzzled.

But Rollo grinned appreciatively at their victim's act of obeisance. "Don't you get it? Rather than being shaken out by us, this gee is doing it to himself. That's initiative you don't see enough of anymore!" The highwaymen now each took hold of one of Zeke's legs, just below the knee (or above, actually, in the upside down perspective) and lifted him a couple of feet from the earth and shook, shivered, and swung him every which way until they plumb tuckered themselves out. They put his head back down and looked at one another stewing in ire. While Zeke's pockets shed a congeries of bric-a-brac, including an expired seahorse, a skein of pipe cleaner, a bottle cap with an eyeball painted on it, and smashed shards of scrimshaw, there indeed was not a red cent to drop. "Maybe this stiff is devoid of mazoola," Rollo mused in frustration.

"Nah, I think he's just clever at caching it." Lester grabbed Zeke's leg hard and exhorted his partner to "heave him up again, we're close to cracking the rat son-of-a-bitch." They yanked him higher now and shook him more violently and Zeke said he would prove his destitution if only they would let him go. "Stop jiving us, you wealthy dolt! I can smell the simoleons on a jaboney like you," Lester declared. They shook him harder and a second seahorse spilled out of Zeke's pocket, this one larger and exotic with black glass eyeballs that became odd points of fascination for the two highwaymen as they shook their mark ever more viciously. And Balthazar, still half dozing, wakened suddenly and saw his pal in trouble and instantly began barking and gnawing at his tormenters' trouser bottoms. Rollo yelled, "You mangy cur, I'll kill you!" And Lester kicked the puppy, only grazing him, as they now let go of Zeke and he came crashing down on his head, nearly knocking himself unconscious until he heard his puppy whimpering over his master's injuries. In his grogginess Zeke imagined the highwaymen were going to dognap Balthazar, and he flew into a crazed rage and lunged for the frightened pup and scooped him into his arm. Lester's horse, an impressive appaloosa who had been quietly stationed closer to the woodland, now had become spooked and was bucking and kicking as Lester struggled to calm him. Zeke seized the opening to charge Lester and clip him with a Sunday punch on the button, staggering him, affording Borshellac the chance to snatch his pistol. But now Rollo squared towards Zeke with his pistol trained on him. "Don't get cute, mister, or I'm going to let you have it," he warned.

Zeke considered the situation for a moment. "You took the words right out of my mouth, Rollo," he countered. They remained in a stand-off taking measure of one another for the longest time. "You'll crack, chief, and then I'll pump you. You are the quivery sort of dodo who will drift into sleep eventually . . ."

Zeke smirked at him and said: "It's one gun apiece, Rollo. You could be the one to dig himself a nod and I'll be there to shoot you if I still feel like it."

They settled in for a duel of endurance, the loaded weapons a deterrence to either party's action, and Rollo and Lester only escalating their bickering over whose fault it was the robbery went awry. Lester kept harping on the postulate that had Rollo turned Zeke upside down in the first place as he told him to do, they wouldn't be in their current predicament. Rollo's rebuttal centered on their processes and methodology having long been in need of an overhaul and upside down shakeouts were only a symptom of much larger malfunction, albeit upon sharper pique did not hesitate to add that it was indeed his partner's inattentiveness that enabled Zeke to disarm him.

As the night wore on, they made adjustments to accommodate the increasing physical discomfort of the gun barrel impasse. By degrees their mutual interest in such relaxation resulted in the three men seated on rocks around a fire, Balthazar reclined before the glowing warmth and the horses leashed to nearby trees. While Zeke understood the stakes could not be higher in the contest to remain awake the longest, and he had to outlast both his adversaries, as the night endured with its black curtain unrelenting, he no longer could imagine either highwayman murdering him. And he felt they recognized in him the same aversion to plugging them. So when Rollo began to hint at breaking out a bottle of fine gin he had packed with his horse, Zeke cottoned to the idea of the three passing it around once it became clear he would be welcome to partake. And so the skids of palaver slowly grew greased and as bibulous fellows are wont to do, they told stories from their pasts.

Lester remembered the time as a lad when his father and his Uncle Rutherford took a ride on a hot air balloon and they emergency landed on an island near Roanoke and the locals thought his uncle was some dark prophet of doom, since he cussed and barked at folks and at six-foot ten was an imposing figure, but when he played banjo at their Snowflake Ball by a fluke they embraced him and built him a cabin near a stream where the three of them spent that winter trapping and salmon fishing. It was a heartfelt remembrance and the hardened outlaw nearly teared up but caught himself in time and coughed a lot instead.

Rollo recalled running away from his home in the mountains as a stripling and after two days bumming around the streets of Wheeling he came upon a group of hospital patients on a retreat engaged in a fierce game of tetherball. There were about fifteen of them attired in loose-fitting pale-yellow pajama-like suits, a motley collection of men mostly bearded and bespectacled and infused with a mad desire to win the tetherball contest. Rollo watched them and caught the attention of their handlers, beefy old men in lab coats and rubber boots who invited the youngster to take part in the picnic they were also providing the patients. He ate fishcakes and some tapioca pudding. Soon Rollo found himself not only playing for a team but showing a unique ability to spike the ball with startling power and to dominate the struggles in the tetherball scrums. Afterwards, he knew he had found his sport, but arriving home two days later not a soul in the mountains had ever heard of tetherball and some thought him soft in the head for talking it up.

Zeke listened to the highwaymen with interest and thought about the wayward paths people find themselves in their lives and whether there is intrinsic meaning in these episodes or is it up to us to decipher the seemingly haphazard occurrences that concatenate existence. Zeke reflected on being accosted by the highwaymen and the chance of it turning out as it had, the three of them flapping their jaws over a bottle of juniper juice while ostensibly still holding pistols on one another. And their horses elicited his woolgathering more than anything, reminding him of his troubled boyhood at the rough tavern with his prostitute mother and the frequent bloody brawls propelled by his boozehound father who worked and lived at the livery stable a mile away. Caleb Borshellac was a well-known equestrian skilled in every facet of horsemanship whose accomplishments in stables caring for and training horses were nonpareil, although his self-destructive alcoholic binges and accompanying violent episodes made him a persona non grata in many circles of the region. Zeke's mother would say that Caleb's overweening devotion to his horses was what broke up their marriage, somehow disregarding his failure to show up for their shotgun wedding owing to his passing out in the Snedde sisters' outhouse from too much corn whiskey. Whenever Zeke saw his father the man was wobbly and surly from toping and he usually had to skedaddle real fast as annoyed constables always seemed to be chasing him. It was during these brief interludes that Zeke would experience his most memorable moments with his tragic father. Zeke told his new bottle pals one such recollection of his father charging upon a bronco into the darkened hayloft building where Zeke slept adjacent the tavern. He was wakened suddenly with an unspeakable fear over the mad horseman appearing like a wraith with a burning phosphorescent coil encircling his chapeau. A stranger from the dark yelled that the growing flames would soon engulf the hayloft structure entirely and Zeke inquired the name of the stranger. "Who goes there?" he demanded.

"You cannot know me," came the cryptic reply.

Now young Zeke saw that the horseman, on his huge equine as it kicked high on its hind legs, bellowing like a delirious ghoul, was his father. "Daddy! Why does your odd cap burn? Is it on purpose? The fire is as beautiful as it is baleful," the awe-struck son cried.

THREE

A nameless roar of sick laughter came from the horseman's throat and he led his magnificent wild steed through a complicated series of caracoles and canters and piaffers, punctuated by incandescent sparkles shooting from his chapeau, and Zeke never would feel as frightened and exhilarated at the same time again.

The boy quickly swooned into a private abyss of stupefaction and the voice of the stranger from the dark corner came again: "You cannot see me nor stop me. Despair like mine can never be known, truly known. It engulfs one in darkness and conflagration ravages all. You ask why. Why does one fellow crave mutton for supper and the next one made sick at its sight? There are no answers, only notions of the unknowable."

Zeke took his sip of gin and felt the cold insufferable ache of a fear, a fear he knew well since that day, and concomitantly felt again the warmth and fondness that had welled up in him over seeing his father on horseback, the dreadful figure of his old man, simply because his father had taken the time that evening to ride over for a visit. Sitting on a rock swilling gin he wrestled with the stark fear and the abiding hope of connecting with his father and he remembered how he walked towards the paternal horseman and met his eyes for a second before bottle rockets seemed to launch off his chapeau's glowing coil, and he only could ask the father he only knew from afar: "Daddy, why does your odd cap burn and shoot off bottle rockets to boot?" His father smiled with a crazy glint in his eye which said: *how can a man answer such a question?* And he turned towards the dark corner where the strange voice had emanated and the horseman and boy waited for a figure, a creature, to emerge, but only a tiny little fat man in a pastel paisley suit and a trilby came out to lecture them in a strange guttural tongue.

Zeke now downed more gin and withdrew into a deep introspection, as he marveled at his detailed memory of this episode, except the distinction between dreaming the encounter and it really happening all those years ago had utterly blurred and he felt a doleful resignation in never knowing the truth of that day in the hayloft. He had asked his father soon afterwards whether he had any memory of the surprise visit and he did not, though the man had difficulty recalling many recent experiences owing to his chronic drunkenness. "The anxiety and ambiguousness of living too close to the shadows . . . the edges of murky perceptions . . . has bedeviled my existence since days such as the one I just related," Zeke divulged to his swigging interlocutors. They sat in a protracted silence now that their stories had been told, the pre-dawn crepuscular still distant as the darkness swelled with a chorus of crickets and the hooting of owls. "I don't understand why you fellows rob people. I mean *how* can you do it? It just ain't right," Zeke finally piped up. "You guys ought to be in the jailhouse for trying to roll me. If I had half a mind for vengeance, I'd haul your butts down to the sheriff and you'd be locked up for a while." He was studying their expressions and saw them meet eyes with uneasiness and he chuckled. "Well, I guess you can consider yourselves lucky cause I don't see myself doing any of that."

Lester said with a twisted grin: "It seems you forgot that we are holding one of the roscoes too. I wouldn't be planning no victory parties just yet, even the fantasy kind."

Zeke shook his head in exasperation. "Look, we know we're not going to shoot each other. You fellows don't seem the sort now that I know you more, and I certainly am not. But sticking up innocent, indigent folks like myself seems the work of malevolent misanthropes and I want to know what is the impetus of such actions?"

Lester and Rollo looked at one another and Lester was the one to reply: "Desperate times, desperate acts, there is no work and we need to eat. Existence requires moolah last time I checked."

Zeke grunted. "No way being broke justifies trying to rob some poor bastard," he said.

Lester cleared his throat with a great harrumph and squinted his eyes before he spoke: "We don't target the indigent. That would be asinine and futile. Rollo and I need a modest take from our loot, but let me be clear, mister, this is way bigger than us. You don't think we keep all the scratch we boost, do you? After we skim our small hauls off the

THREE

top the rest all goes to the Rambling Hoboes of America Fund, headquartered in Passaic, New Jersey."

Zeke had to process this information for a while before responding: "So you're part of a group of bandits who fancy themselves some sort of Robin Hoods?"

Rollo interjected with a shrill dismissal of such a categorization, asking about "these hoods" and betraying his utter unfamiliarity with the hero of Sherwood Forest. Lester quickly evinced a deep understanding of the Robin Hood legend but rejected any such comparison with their work, deprecating the classic tales as pandering literature which oversimplifies the perennial struggle between the landed aristocracy and the working class, which disregards the complicated and subjective troubles inherent in any society where the vast hordes must work for the few lords of property and commerce who control the economies.

Zeke thought for a moment but rejoined with a tinge of pertinacity: "Ok, but he still robbed from the rich and gave to the poor. Which is your m.o., am I wrong?"

Lester grimaced and snarled: "It's a superficial and invidious comparison. There was actually a legendary figure from Thuringia in Germany who came after Hood in forced forest noblesse oblige via mugging who was a much closer model for what we are trying to accomplish. His name was Dieter Schrampenkrieg and he deployed nothing but brass knuckles and a cool con of blandishments."

Zeke waited for him to go on and explain how they were more like Schrampenkrieg, but only silence came so he asked Lester himself. Lester only chortled with an underlying pensiveness. "The Bashful Sandblaster, as he was known, was a social champion for the ages," Lester offered wistfully without answering the question. "A light-heavyweight who punched like a mule and could take you out with either hand," Rollo added to his partner's irked look of daggers.

"So he was a boxer?" Zeke asked, puzzled now.

"Well, yeah . . . in his younger days he had some bouts," Lester explained, "but he soon turned to the noble vocation of highwayman who mostly used his gift for soft-soap and jawboning to lift the cash out of most swells' pockets, while the others were treated to blows with the brass knuckles."

Zeke wanted to know if the name came from his days in the ring and Rollo immediately answered a resounding yes while Lester twisted his face disgustedly, declaring, "No, his boxing career was cut short quickly by a calamitous trip to the Yukon where he certainly would have perished on the tundra if not for a quick-thinking Eskimo who pulled him to safety." Lester now really tried to remember the Eskimo's name and kept thinking he had it but only grew more frustrated, while Rollo thought it may have been Thurman, which only enraged Lester. Schrampenkreig, they told Zeke in closing, soon returned to pulling stick-ups in places like Leipzig and Rottershausen and he became so skilled at his craft that folks often sent him more cash long after the initial robbery."

"A lot of the swells, or really the folks who fancied themselves swells but really weren't, wanted to get rolled by Dieter Schrampenkrieg for the cachet of it cause Schramps was becoming so notorious," Rollo noted. Lester chuckled. "That's where Schrampen Campin' came from," Lester said, "the well-heeled set up picnic camps roadside in the bush hoping to catch a glimpse of Schrampenkrieg and let him clean them out in the bargain. They'd have some high-toned jamborees at Schramp Camps. Brahms supposedly played at one outside of Frankenwald."

The three men went on like this knocking back gin and regaling one another with byzantine tales that invariably returned to the profession of highwayman and how they came to it and the so-called Rambling Hoboes of America Fund (RHAF) that seemed to justify the wild outlaw lifestyle the quarreling partners were holding forth about. Guilt curdled inside Zeke as he couldn't shake the idea of adventure and wild kicks riding as a highwayman stirred in him. He looked at the two men across from him. "You guys ever shoot anyone with your firearms?"

THREE

They both shook their heads. "They're just props to get folks to buy into the act," Lester assured.

Zeke could tell they sensed his intrigue in their trade and seemed to want him to join them. "So much of it is in the presentation the heist really takes care of itself."

Zeke was imagining himself a desperado of a group of outlaw riders who scare up big dough for the Rambling Hoboes, a mad, destructive notion on one hand but also one of daring adrenaline nights and driven by altruism and humanity and benevolence towards fellow citizens who've been felled by hard times. Zeke felt it, that consensus emanating from his gut that demanded to be heard and would have to come out. He knew he'd found his next vocation, a capricious pull on his imagination but ineluctable, one crazy path indeed. He gazed at Balthazar, who had wakened just then and was sitting up with a searching expression on his face. Such was Zeke's intuitive understanding of his puppy that he recognized in his eyes an entreaty not to abandon him now that he was riding off with a band of highwaymen. He saw concern in his canine eyes that even if he brought him on their nighttime sorties he would be neglected and become a burden for Zeke. "Don't worry, Balty, you're always riding with me. I wouldn't let you down like that. We're going to have fun and do some good for the hoboes to boot," he assured the pup, who barked excitedly and darted over to his master and licked his face before settling down beside him.

"Schrampenkrieg had a dog, you know," Rollo began, "a magnificent Malamute he acquired during his convalescence in Alaska with the Eskimos."

Zeke swigged the gin bottle and petted his pup. "Is that so? Did the dog join him on his night rides?"

"Oh sure," Lester piped up, "he pretty much let Hooklestupf do as he pleased. The Bashful Sandblaster loved that Malamute like nobody's business." Rollo grinned and nodded knowingly.

"Was that his name, Hooklestump?" Zeke asked.

The two men broke into laughter, enough so Balthazar barked. "Hooklestupf!" Lester corrected in the German pronunciation. "There are legends about the Sandblaster's dog, that he drank four liters of beer a day and would ride on the back of an uncanny mountain goat trained by an Eskimo shaman called Yule Crayfish."

There was a silence as the wind blew up some dirt and the trees soughed. "Yeah, I wish I could have met that Hooklestupf," Rollo pined, "there was a dog for the ages. And Yule Crayfish was an artist too. Painted that goat in over one hundred portraits. Nobody knows that. They had them at the Folk Art Festival in Halifax."

Lester frowned and let out a grumble. "Crayfish was a bitter sanctimonious crackpot! I read his book and he disparaged the Sandblaster as an opportunist and the Malamute as a lazy lush who ruined his precious goat. Poor Lute was traumatized, he claimed. Who the hell names a goat Lute?"

"Was he the Eskimo who pulled Schrampenkrieg to safety on the tundra?" Zeke thought to inquire. The men burst into laughter. "Crayfish?! He couldn't rescue a pocket watch from a tattered old vest. No, the Eskimo who saved the Sandblaster up there . . . his name is on the tip of my tongue—"

Rollo chimed in: "I still think it might have been Thurman . . ."

And once again, as Lester strained his memory for the name he blew his top over his partner's suggestion. "It ain't goddamn Thurman, okay?! That much I know!"

The men continued to imbibe gin and palaver in such a manner that one would think they had forgotten about their pistols and the standoff in which they were engaged. But no one truly forgets that someone has a firearm he is ready to use on one. The gin kept the tension at more of a low hum undercurrent, which in some ways seemed to infuse their talk with a crackling kind of exigency. Zeke indicated he would throw in with their cause because he admired the importance of putting themselves personally on the line to fight economic oppression. But he had ideas he wanted to brainstorm with them, concepts and imagery with which to stamp their iconoclasm in the newspapers, and so over a fresh bottle of gin that Rollo found on his horse they began to exchange thoughts over the soft glow of the stoked fire and the swaying trees surrounding them. It took them through the night in their lambent woodland lacuna, until the first pale mists of daybreak came calling, but they hammered home a rough blueprint for the kind of highwaymen they wanted to be and be known as far and wide to all travelers of the night, which they swore to hereafter rule as quicksilver desperadoes of the darkness. The legacy and tenets of Dieter Schrampenkrieg would be central to their theme and purpose in roadside robbery, principally in his schematic designs and "tactics of antipodes" which combined creating shadowy monstrous ballyhoo of fear and lightning strikes overwhelming targets and then pulling "the Phantasmagoric Switcheroo" to utterly foul them up and leave them malleable to your message. "Like pieces of putty in the hand which one molds his art," Lester quoted Schrampenkrieg as saying, noting he later amended the statement to the singular "piece" of putty, conceding that it would be hard to mold multiple putty pieces simultaneously.

Zeke well-nigh exulted in the animated colloquy on such intellectual and esthetic components of this new way of advancing the highwayman aura and potential. He couldn't remember the last time he felt so alive. He just could hardly wait to saddle up and lurk under cover of brush for a night coach to come rolling by so he could "scare the ever-livin' bejesus out of the high-hattin' fat cat bastards" (said to impress his new associates) right before they stupefied them with the Switcheroo. He used the term raison d'etre several times in straining to encompass a larger point, namely, that one's personal raison d'etre ought to in some irreducible seminal way line up with the raison d'etre of one's working group and with that of society itself, but he had trouble pronouncing it and it sounded like "raisin debt" and a quarrel ensued as a piqued Rollo yammered that he didn't even like raisins so why would he take Zeke's?

But the disagreements in their freewheeling wee-hours discourse were minor and for the most part swiftly circumnavigated, for once Lester and Rollo were able to make the leap into a broader form of conceptual banditry and fully embrace the performance and message that so excited Zeke then the incipient brand of the new way fell into place. They admitted they were really more conventional highwaymen, and not very successful ones, who aspired to adopt the techniques of The Bashful Sandblaster but never really had the kind of committed confidence and streak of madness that required. "All along we were riding hard, pulling jobs . . . botching 'em here and there . . . and we always venerated the Sandblaster and all he accomplished, but never made the adjustment," Lester lamented.

But now the three partners were ready for wholesale change and it came together organically, sprung from their dormant recesses and forged into a singular force of fear and showmanship. "Will our band be known primarily as criminals or artists? Inextricably we are bound to both to ride as planned, but I believe it is imperative we choose our fundamental identity," Zeke challenged them amidst debate over procedural niceties. There was, of course, never any doubt what the answer would be. There would be the roscoes, the brute force and ferocity of halting the coaches and subduing every iota of resistance, the general swagger and thuggishness inherent in such rapid and utter seizure. But the heart of the presentation, the desideratum of rendering the experience at once frightening as death and as a transformational and unforgettably illuminating and stirring encounter was unquestionably the element of performance artistry the highwaymen would present. They would call for a "suggested donation" for the RHAF, though this would be a euphemism, sardonically deployed as part of the show, but there would be no doubt everyone was expected to cough up every last dime on them.

"They have to know we mean business," Zeke emphasized, "but by the same token we can't go around shooting anyone. Towards that end we'll have to show 'em our dexterity with the roscoes, dazzle 'em the way gunslingers twirl their pieces 'round with their fingers." He pulled out his own piece and tried to demonstrate this to no avail, the gun dropping to the ground several times. The men had themselves a chuckle as Zeke vowed to practice up on the move, but they were only marginally better when their turns came. "Well, I guess we all need to work on it," Zeke said with a grin of his own. "We ought to be like the James Gang with these things when we're through."

Their long gin-soaked chinfest conceived the major components of the group: 1) they would call themselves The Wild Man Riders of the Reckoning, 2) they would wear buckskin outfits with cerulean fringes from the sleeves and lime green cowboy handkerchiefs embroidered with mad dancing skeletons sporting top hats would cover their necks and mouths as dust protectors, and classic old top hats would jauntily sit atop their own domes, 3) their slogan would be "Through Fear Comes Loot and Laughter, Occasionally Catharsis," 4) they would create and perform an unlimited number of original shows for their affluent victims with which to utterly overwhelm them with perplexity and thrilling wonder and everlasting epiphanies. A theme underscoring much of the droll and outlandish elements, such as the screwy, arcane performances they would foist upon their prey, was the long-term goal of creating and magnifying through the newspapers their own singular legend and ensuring it endured and was bruited far and wide, deepening their mythic sweeping fame. Not only would their legacy as the greatest band of highwaymen be secured but their power to effect significant change for common folks who wanted to be able to dream big once again would be fortified. Of course, it would be difficult to gainsay that their swilling copious amounts of gin all night contributed to some degree to the lofty ambitions and the downright loopy irrationality woven through their manifesto of a new perspective predicated on the Schrampenkrieg philosophies. Nonetheless, as aforementioned, the crocked cohorts stayed the course beating their gums until the silvery ashen mists of dawn snuck up on them, but they were so rapt in their plan it wasn't until the morning was well under way before they finally realized, with a frightened jolt, the day had indeed arrived.

Four

It was Zeke who first identified a source of shortfall which threatened to undermine their entire grand plan to create an indelible team of outlaw madcap riders: they only had two horses among the three of them and this would not do. It hit Zeke hard that he needed a horse badly and rued his entire horseless existence until then. He pronounced in a low determined voice that he would find a suitable horse right away, and Lester and Rollo pledged their help before they poured themselves another nightcap and slipped back into snoring slumbers amidst the morning light illuminating the forest clearing. They finally wakened to a gray windy day with pockets of sun streaks poking through, and as the developments of the evening gradually returned to Zeke he initially felt it was all a crazy castle in the air and it wouldn't have taken very much for him to scotch the whole deal out of doubt. Such as one of his new cronies evincing a case of cold feet, or embarrassment over the sort of irreverent performance agenda they had outlined. But no such prod came from Lester and Rollo, instead they intensified their zeal for getting to work on the great project that, they noted, Dieter Schrampenkrieg himself would have valued and approved. And so the men found themselves once more confronted by their first significant setback, Zeke had no horse and would need one to become the highwayman he envisioned, riding athwart forest evenings and laying off road for opportunities to ambush wayfarers. In short order they arrived at the inescapable conclusion that since they were broke there was but one route to procuring a horse for Zeke: they would have to steal one. The punishment for horse thievery was seven years in the hoosegow and a hefty tariff attached indefinitely to one's interstate movement of sundries, poultry, as well as livestock in the breadbasket states. Now seven years in the can was a formidable chunk of time, nothing to thumb one's nose at and Zeke duly took measure of the risk, while flouting the glaring otiosity of the tariff as "the kind of moronic diddly-squat that makes the low lives feel superior to the legislature who concocted the asinine penalty in the first place." Rollo buttressed his seething contempt for the tariff by launching into a mawkish account of an old-timer, Hi Lentils, who was a convicted horse thief and rather than leave his beloved pet pelican named Artie behind in Macon, Georgia, to "visit his grandchildren up north, he stuck it out down there looking out for that damn pelican."

After Rollo no one spoke for a while, as if he said it all with his pelican story, but Zeke really had no idea what he was talking about and a sudden cold apprehension cut through him as he pondered upon often feeling that way about other people going on and on about arcane esoterica he could not fathom or even care to grasp. He looked at his puppy, who was wide awake for some time and savoring the portions of pemmican Zeke cadged from his partners for him, and told him "it was high time we swiped a fine equine for our new enterprise, eh Baltsy?" The pup barked twice and Zeke chuckled at his affirmation, though Lester remarked he only wanted more of their pemmican, adding: "Now about this horse situation, or lack of one, well I think I have a notion—"

Rollo interjected with a pleased smile: "I know where you're heading with this . . ." They met eyes for a couple of seconds and said at almost the same time, "Old Man Grackler."

He was an old onion farmer whose house and hardscrabble acreage was about ten miles away where he lived with his younger brother, Osmund, an obese French horn player out of work for years, and their unstable, loner cousin Simon who had been residing in a makeshift treehouse for months since the old man banished him from the premises after catching him smashing onions for sport, or possibly spite. This is what they told Zeke about the farm folk they were propounding from which to steal a horse. "The horse barn is a good two-hundred feet from the farmhouse, and Simon's treehouse is clear across one of the fields," Lester explained, "so we can slip in tonight while they're all sleeping and clip ourselves the best nag the old bastard has in there."

Some caws and chirps emanated from a nearby tree but the birds could not be seen, and then another hidden creature let out a shrill cry that seemed to be telling everyone to shut up. "Simon is the one we'll have watch out for," Rollo said, "he's known to roam on the soil at night. He's not right in the head, you know."

"You fellows seem to know an awful lot about this farm family. How so?"

Lester smiled at the memory. "They used to sell an onion stew at a little farm stand in front of the place. We occasionally would stop there and boy, oh boy that was some fine stew." Rollo seconded the encomium of the Grackler stew: "The finest stew anywhere, they made it fresh every day with many varieties of the onions they grew. It was almost miraculous how they produced such a tasty stew on a daily basis, a mystery to real devotees as to what made it so good."

Zeke started to feel a tad peckish after the gastronomical talk. "What was in this fabled stew?" he asked with a hint of skepticism.

"Onions," Lester snapped, "all kinds."

"And a killer sauce with singular spicy meat chunks," added Rollo.

The thought of such a hearty stew further awakened Zeke's appetite and he lamented: "It's too bad we couldn't grab ourselves some of their stew since we're going to be there anyway. But horse thievery and stew eating just don't align right, fellows, a fact we just have to recognize."

The men agreed as they broke camp and began the tough ride over hilly, severe terrain towards the Grackler farm, Zeke alternating his time on board his new cronies' horses and Balthazar rolled snugly into a coarse Indian blanket Rollo had tucked into his saddle. They made it to a thick forest rise that opened to a great valley of swaying tall grass, beyond which they could see the farmhouse and barn in the distance.

FOUR

It was twilight and they decided to settle in and make a fire to roast some wild dandelions, mushrooms, and berries they'd picked along the way. They first passed around a fresh bottle of gin and had a free-form bull session in which their ideas and anxieties were expressed with respect to their vision and hopes for the new career of a gang of highwaymen riding for a righteous cause. They spoke of their simpatico with the hoboes and how they too may have turned towards the hobo life if not for a break here or there, but long gaps of silence accrued, and it was Zeke who realized they had to eat the damn wild pickings already since they were famished. But this only sent the bottle around more so with more agonizing vacillation, this time over whether they should ignore their qualms about toxicity within the wild plant and fungi life to satiate their ravenous hungers. Zeke and Lester, in the end, opted out, while Rollo then went to town scarfing down the entire medley of their natural pickings and gloating smugly in his relishing his feast without being stricken dead. In such a manner, the partners engaged in raillery and ridicule as a means to stay loose before tending to the business of lifting a horse in the dead of night. Most memorably, they would later agree, was Rollo's sudden gasping and staggering and clutching his chest and falling as if dead, only to jump up and laugh madly at eliciting their concern. He managed to pull off this fake seizure and succumbing to poisoning routine a total of three times before the fourth attempt of flailing and choking completely failed to fool his partners.

Zeke found himself swigging the gin harder as the evening advanced towards the wee hours when they would break into the barn. He understood why the juniper juice became to him like water to a dizzy nomad lost in the Gobi. It was in fact palpable to him since the moment he and his partners realized they would have to glom him a horse if he were to join them as a highwayman. An old fear, long dormant since he last rode as a stripling, began to manifest deep in his inner being, incipiently and insidiously, this terrible fear of horses Zeke felt since his boyhood when his drunken delirious father rode his magnificent lightning steed with the fireball eyes all over the countryside with reckless howling abandon. And he would seek the boy out, as Zeke related to his partners earlier in his recounting of the dreamlike horseback hayloft intrusion, and sweep his son up onto the furious beast and charge maniacally until ineluctably they would be thrown by the violent bucks of the mad bronco Scunj. Zeke was terrified of Scunj and he was certain his father's beloved bronco would one day trample him out of some benighted jealousy. His father brought him his own bronco pony, Jockamo Chop Chop, and they'd ride through the night on black treacherous roads, daring their horses to throw them off and kill them and one night Zeke soared from the back of crazy Jockamo Chop Chop and landed in an irrigation tank where his father left him to fend for himself. He spent three days in the tank struggling not to drown and wondering where his sick old man went. He yelled for him and Jockamo to no avail. Zeke was finally rescued by a lost census taker who was looking for Okies, yet Oklahoma was more than six-hundred and fifty miles away, and the poor fellow would continue to ask Zeke strange census questions throughout saving him and another week past that. "The son of a bitch was no census taker," he hollered now in remembrance. "He was trying to roll me with his razzle-dazzle interrogatory subtle showmanship. We could use a crafty artist like him in our new performance-based steamrolling of the well-heeled fat cats."

Lester and Rollo, startled, could only jump up and gaze quizzically at their incoherent partner. "He's shitfaced, Lester," Rollo explained.

"Is the man capable of accompanying us into that horse barn is the larger question," Lester harrumphed.

"Why do you always have to ask the larger question?!" Rollo snapped.

"Why do you always have to ask the obvious question?!" returned Lester.

"Chop Chop!! Jockamo Chop Chop!!" Zeke cried, still caught in that time. "You left me in the tank, Daddy! Drowning in here while you two laugh and ride away. Nice!"

Lester slapped him hard with his open palm across his cheek. Zeke took it in stoic silence, only uttering: "Again!"

FOUR

And Lester slapped him even harder, and Zeke called for more. Four more increasingly harder slaps followed until Lester was the one tiring. Finally, Rollo took charge of the striking by coming over Zeke's dome with an extirpated immense weed root, which sent the drunken wrought-up Borshellac reeling backwards into a pratfall ironically on a thicket of stinkweeds. He sat in abject stultification atop the smashed weeds, their swelling effluvia surrounding him in a cloud of foul vapors and for a moment he thought he was on the toilet of the old outhouse by the abandoned mineshaft he explored as a boy, thinking perhaps the rickety wooden structure had been blown away leaving him exposed to the elements. But he soon recalled the equine task at hand and pulled himself together and declared to his doubting partners: "Do not lose one jot of faith in my fortitude, fellows. I have emerged from an irrigation tank all those years ago, bitter but stronger, a better singer even, especially on railroad ballads, and now I stand before you humbled and ready to sneak into that barn and look a horse in the eye before appropriating him."

Lester eyed him skeptically as he moved close and searched Zeke's gaze before pounding on his shoulders with his palms, nodded and said: "Let's go get your horse. That's all behind you."

Zeke turned around looking for what it could be when he realized Lester meant his deep-seated fear of horses. Rollo approached him and said he hoped he remembers how to ride because they will be covering a lot of ground. Zeke thought about that practical consideration now and worried that it had been many years, the old saw skipping through his mind about getting right back on your horse when you fall off and coming to grips with the fact that he never really did. But he smiled at his becoming a bicycle rider, particularly on the challenging penny-farthing he inherited from an uncle named Frollinger taken into custody for bank fraud in Toledo, Ohio. "Riding a bicycle is actually more like riding a horse than riding some horses," he sought to expound with scant elucidation.

Now it was time to enact the plan. Under the moonlight Lester and Zeke scampered low through the high grass of the valley, veering sharply towards the horse barn off a narrow dirt path. They easily slipped into the barn and were very circumspect not to startle any of the horses as they quietly passed by each of the many stalls. A lantern glimmered lambently from the far wall, affording them just enough light to look over the resting equines, and Zeke moved gingerly but struggled mightily in his deepest recesses to maintain control of his pounding intensity and the old horse terrors that tormented him for so long. He stood in front of each stall and gazed upon the reclining horses in their sleep and told himself they were good and splendid animals that he would befriend and partner with in the great adventure ahead. But his breathing felt labored and the fetid stall smells left him shaky, anxious, diffident, the beasts' occasional muffled exhales triggering dark harrowing sensations in him and he was certain he would have to quit and flee the barn. He glanced towards the small side door through which they entered and Lester, noticing this, admonished him in a stern whisper: "If you skedaddle like a mutt through that door you will run from everything that you encounter for the rest of your life."

Zeke thought his partner was being a bit dramatic over one damn glance and he tossed off an aphorism of his own: "Relax, Confucius. Running away from life and running away from death are really the same thing. I don't appreciate the innuendo about turning heel like a mutt."

Lester was growing impatient now and implored him to make his selection so they could start moving the horse out. "C'mon, already! Pick a goddamn horse and let's beat it! They all look good!" As Lester exhorted him in his raspy whisper Zeke had fixed his stare on the only horse not lying down in the barn, a magnificent, enormous steed upright and kinetic with jumpiness, peering out at Zeke from his hay-laden stall where he apparently had been watching over the other horses, and now horse and man locked eyes for a good minute. Lester quickly sought to kibosh this one. "Hey, listen! This here one you're eyeballing seems too tempestuous, like he's trouble . . . and the size of the son of a bitch!"

But Zeke remained locked in a stock-still eye-to-eye gaze with this imposing unusual horse and began to understand the true nature of the restless fierce equine and it horrified him now. He desperately wanted to bolt for the door and scram into the darkness, but it was too late, the horse held him spellbound, this monstrous horse that neighed like a demon screaming from a sewer and whinnied like it was calling out for storms and destruction, it sucked Zeke into its vortex of living madness—the young man recognized something awful and disturbingly incontrovertible. Here was the massive beast of Caleb Borshellac that ran fast enough to inflict damage to any man's mind and struck murderous fear into young Zeke throughout his formative years. Now here was Scunj, raging violent Scunj—named by his father for savoring conch fed him by debauched sailors, or scungilli—back from the dead it seemed and as berserk as ever in disaffection for folks in general, Zeke in particular. The angry horse now kicked his front legs high and made roaring agitated horse noises and Lester became panicky: "The son of a bitch is making a racket, let's go!" Zeke would not move and Lester pressed. "What's the matter with you?! This crazy bastard will kill us both!"

Lester then bolted for the door and the new Scunj crashed the wooden gate of his stall and came charging at Zeke who sidestepped his path while managing to latch onto his neck and pull himself up and astride bareback and somehow ride the furious steed into the night without any notion where they were going. Lester was running for the high grass valley and Zeke spotted him as they steamed past in a wild gallop. "No stopping! No going back now! We are going wherever the hell this ride takes us and that is very likely hell itself!!"

"It will kill you, you moron!" Lester yelled, but Zeke never heard him. He was laughing harder than he ever had laughed and felt all the liquor in him and was glad about it and let out wild goat cries and guffaws that have no more cares at least for the nonce and Zeke knew he found the right horse, the only horse that would provide him such a chance. He imagined this was how his father must have felt riding breakneck at full tilt all those nights while looped and the idea of Caleb Borshellac occurred to him in a singular unprecedented manner. Here was a maestro of wanton harum-scarum phenomena projecting marvel and dread, or mostly stark unvarnished pure fear incarnate in his horseman, perhaps he was an artist hurling action imagery and a profound pathos around his virtuoso drunken rider and violent crazed misanthropic horse. Scunj the Second raced like the hellhorse broken out of some netherworld and never let up his reckless screaming pace penetrating ever deeper into the remote forest and Zeke held on for his life, astonishing himself with his well of horsemanship tapped, and through the woodland night across moonlit streams and primordial clearings of preternatural beauty and the quarreling wee folk he thought he glimpsed playing an unknown game with sticks and long colorful sheets and high bounce balls and the momentary fleeting respite they shared at a burbling stream, rider and his captor horse quenching their great thirsts together, Zeke knew his bond with Scunj the Second was unbreakable and possibly dooming into an underworld of the drunken wild outlaw acclaimed in his way from afar, enshrined in the myths of time. He drank the cool tasty water no one had drank before and thought of the tragic life of his father, so accomplished on horse and as an authority on all matters equestrian, yet tormented by the everyday components of salubrious living and he went the other way, the booze and madness road to another kind of end or anti-salvation in his dark nameless legacy. "The way I see it Scunj the Second," he said to his horse, " is you and I were destined to join forces in the name of the old man and reroute the unbalanced, but nonetheless serious, vision quest or dream he and your predecessor Scunj the First were riding like maniacs all the time looking to find. Something drove them beyond rebellion and anarchic defiance of societal realities, Scunj, cause they were forces of nature on a larger mission they likely couldn't glean a scintilla of, and you and me and our new band of highwaymen are going to double down with this outlaw idea until we get there. My mother never stopped loving that crazy bastard and she used to say he trafficked in fear and retribution and madness in dealing with people. No wonder he turned to the company of horses, unbroken wrathful ones in particular. Now it's you and me, Scunj."

The horse jerked his head with an agitated neigh and Zeke chuckled and stroked his side. "You're a pip for sure, Scunj! You're in charge of course, but if you throw me keep me near brush to cushion the fall, will ya? I can't wait to introduce you to my pup, Balt."

He worried about Balthazar's whereabouts and well-being under the aegis of his partners, but once mounted and racing again through the black of night woods all such misgivings lifted as his mind scudded forward with a gallimaufry of notions and concepts to consider in establishing their highwayman band and the identity they wished to create. While he and his partners had already laid the blueprint for Wild Man Riders of the Reckoning, Zeke found galloping at full speed in the natural wonders of the forest night the finest muse for plotting their artistic attacks on aristocratic travelers. He eventually traversed a field of wild strawberries and reached the banks of narrow river and followed its flow for a few miles until coming upon an outpost of a few scattered buildings and a tavern. Zeke had the hardest time coaxing Scunj into slowing down but the promise of a growler of creamy beer seemed to finally convince the volcanic steed to take a blow. "I'll be right back with the brew," he told him before entering the old-timey saloon with swinging doors and wooden floorboards. Several hoboes sat around solo nursing mugs of beer at tiny tables, pensive souls alone with their nocturnal musings. A couple of dwarves in bright checked suits were engaged in a game of backgammon, one sneered at Zeke. The bartender was a pale beefy fellow with a handlebar mustache and throaty laugh. Zeke ordered two growlers and expressed his surprise that the place was open.

The bartender laughed in a manner which made Zeke uncomfortable. "We never close, young man. Drinking all night helps hoboes get through it." He soon sent the two large wooden growlers topped with foamy suds sliding down the long bar and Zeke went to get them.

"Can I run a tab, barkeep?" Zeke inquired good-naturedly.

The bartender moved with a chesty strut now towards Zeke. "You a hobo, feller?" he asked.

"I am a founding member of a group who's going to raise dough for the hoboes," he stated with pride.

"That ain't what I asked you, chief." It turned out the bartender had a soft spot for the plight of hoboes and let them sit with a beer overnight in the saloon now and then.

"Sure, I'm a hobo," Zeke then acknowledged, though it felt wrong to him. "When I make some dough, I'll pay you back," he added.

The bartender smiled knowingly. "I bet you will. Say, who is the other growler for?"

Zeke replied with a simper that it was for his horse. Everyone in the place now turned to regard this stranger. The dwarf who sneered now lit a huge cigar and snickered with his buddy. "He's a special breed of horse and he goes for brew, what can I tell you?" Zeke explained to the room. They all just kept staring at him and the bartender folded his arms and shook his head. "Why don't you all come outside and meet him? We will do our little show for you."

Zeke went out to Scunj and they drank their beer thirstily. Zeke never really expected the hoboes to come outside but soon they slowly began to appear, and Zeke realized with some uneasiness that he'd have to improvise something with Scunj. He asked if anyone played an instrument and one of the hoboes stepped forward with a beat-up harp and proceeded to blow some haunting melodies, among them old train songs like "Rock Island Line" and "Orange Blossom Special" and "Playing Thimblerig with Hoyt on the Night Train to Norfolk." Zeke cajoled and wheedled a performance of sorts out of Scunj with the lure of more beer, and the two pulled off a series of trots and ambles and curvets, all with Zeke on foot mimicking such horse maneuvers himself, and the splendid finale of a caracole crescendo and Zeke belting out the old folk number "Sleepin' Off the Sneaky Pete in Coal Car #3." And Zeke led everyone in a rousing rendition of "Woke Up in Wichita on the Cannonball When a Bull Clubbed Me Over the Head." Zeke would later cite this show as the watershed in which he and Scunj by dint of necessity laid the groundwork for all of the highwaymen performances to come, much of the early morning vamping remaining as staples of their road stick-ups. When he saw both dwarves singing in full-throated glee he knew with certainty they had themselves the foundation what constituted indelible highwayman performance.

And so in the gray mists of daybreak, slaked by brew and gratified by their impromptu show for the fine hoboes, Zeke and Scunj rode on into the forest recesses, only to within a few miles come upon a rag-and-bone man on his wagon with his pile of miscellaneous junk so high the poor work horse could hardly pull it along. Zeke halted to appraise the sort of goods the strange wayfarer was hawking with his raspy incoherent singing out of the sundry items. The wide assortment of clothing he carried among the pots and cutlery and jars and seeds were what attracted Zeke, as he had been ruminating while horseback on the presentation decided for the highwaymen, in particular the outfits they would wear. Zeke described to the rag-and-bone man the nature of the toggery he was seeking: full chaps, shaggy like the cowboys wore, and the buckskin jackets with long cerulean fringes on the chest and arms and embroidered with a hobo toting a bindlestick on the back, the handkerchiefs of course with the dancing skeletons used as dust protectors-long flowing scarves to trail them as they ride, and the top hats.

The rag-and-bone man rubbed his chin at length before he spoke and coughed and blew his nose in a vile display. He was on old grotesque man with few teeth and a dirty gray beard. "I got some raincoats and sailor pants back there. Why don't you forget about all that hodgepodge of attire and buy more practically? You'll never find exactly what you're looking for, mister. Let me fix you up in a nice jersey and sailor pants back there and be done with it? And the raincoat is made in Hungary."

"None of those articles are even close to what I am seeking," Zeke replied. "Any jackets resembling buckskin with fringes? Skelton handkerchiefs? What about top hats?"

The old man snickered derisively. "You're only fooling yourself if you think you'll find such things. A bird in hand is worth a whole flock in the bush, son. I'll give you a good price."

Zeke looked at the old man seated on his wagon with his ancient workhorse and he took a mite of umbrage at his attempt to dissuade him from his visual image of the group. He resented his tone of compromise and settling for anything less than one's true and complete artistic vision of their enterprise. "You, sir, should not be trying to sell folks on anything they do not want. You have no business offering unsolicited advice on what one should wear in the representation of one's craft. I therefore must denounce you and everything you and your sordid wagon represent. I will not back down from what is right for me and my movement. I do thank you for reinforcing this conviction in me."

And Scunj and Zeke rode on with ever more speed and zeal into the forest commencing the new life as highwaymen and it took another whole day but they came upon the campfire of his partners as they roasted carrots they filched and it was a grand reunion, especially when Balthazar awoke to see his master jumping from his new fine steed and soon scooping him up for a hug and introduction, and then they were passing around the gin bottle and planning, oh the planning!

The cool night air was still and scattered above with glints of stars and smelled of early spring ripening on this momentous night of birth for the hitherto inchoate band of highwaymen. Now they all had horses of their own to ride on their heists and were eager and galvanized to make their marks and emblazon the times with their singular brand of robbery. Zeke exulted in the challenge ahead and felt certain the stick-ups, descending on night travelers like lightning bolts, followed by the shocking presentations of the shows would attract widespread notoriety in the newspapers and make them into famous outlaws. His confidence as a bold leader had grown a great deal already since appropriating Scunj, a wild violent horse well-suited to the task ahead and, more importantly, a fine steed Zeke believed to be actually his father's horse in some preternatural manner. A furious, disturbed horse, Zeke sensed the beast had mysteriously anticipated the arrival of Caleb's son to come and snatch him away and ride off breakneck into the forest. Scunj knew the son was coming, Zeke believed, and that he'd adopt Caleb's authoritarian audacity and unalloyed fevered ferocity in resuming the father's incomplete mission, whatever exactly *was* that mission Zeke would have to first figure out.

They hit the gin hard celebrating their reunion and with crocked ebullience entertained one another with improvised performances they would thereafter hone and shape into standard segments of their act. Zeke drank more than ever that night and it eventually rendered him wobbly, but he kept summoning the energy to push always forward with artistic ideas. They were, after all, artists who dabbled in crime, not the other way around, they often reiterated, a refrain which seemed to help crystallize the odd nature of their purpose. Ostensibly, they were out to make a modest living while raising funds for the plight of the hoboes. But to Zeke, the performance of the highwayman attacks represented an original, adventurous new foray into the very definition of what constitutes Art. He said that sloshed night of reunion to his partners: "Out at sea on the fishing trawler I was a prisoner forced to find an act on deck to entertain the fishermen, in the interest of my own self-preservation. Now the tables have turned, and we are the figures of coercion making our victims take in our shows right before we fleece them." He wondered about the new dynamic they would be springing on their prey, mugging the unsuspecting travelers of the night while at the same time providing quality unique shows, almost as if compelling them to attend like a troupe performing in the hoosegow for convicts. It was then on this drunken delirious night noodling around with notions and raw sketches of ideas the highwaymen began to build the very components of what would become their act. While it seemed quite desultory and slapdash at times the essence of their performance could have been broken down to four constant components: horsemanship, song, dance, and dramatic skits which were skewed towards a bleak anthropomorphism rooted in despair and loneliness.

Rollo once again got up on his horse and rode off standing upright and facing backwards, galloping in a series of dazzling crazy-eights around their encampment. After completing his ninth eight he broke into song, one of the old train songs that Zeke recalled, "There Ain't Enough Clumps of Coal to Make Me One Lousy Meatball," and he surprised his partners with his melodic command of a deceptively complex number. The refrain bridge in particular required a sophisticated tone modulation and nuanced phrasing to truly allow the tune to swing, and Rollo responded like a seasoned crooner. "Say, feller, are you goin' to scarf that meatball? / Cause if not it would suit my palate plenty well / You say it ain't no damn meatball? / And all we got is a load of coal in this here living hell."

Lester and Zeke were very impressed with Rollo's heretofore secret vocal talent and ceded the song almost entirely to their partner, except for joining in the chorus with full-throated voices and the filigree yodeling added by Lester at various silent intervals. Among several inventive beginnings that materialized this drunken night was the Salzburg Circus skit, which loosely takes place in the Austrian city where almost everyone is engaged in espionage. Rollo played Klaus Cloverleaf, the animal trainer undercover for the Kaiser, Lester was the trapeze artist Chan Charcutlier, who reports to dark Iberian fascist powers, and Zeke was Rube Doolittler, the blithe daredevil who gets shot from a cannon nightly and is spying on behalf of President Grover Cleveland (first term). The spy circus premise worked splendidly with the three principal characters as good friends but each operating as spies for vying world powers, as much comic and satirical material grew from the fertile confluence of politics and workplace situations. The one in which Klaus Cloverleaf trains an ibis to dive-bomb Charcutlier and bite his fanny as he attempts a triple somersault jump had quickly acquired classic status and became central to the comic nature of the Salzburg Circus Skits.

FOUR

Zeke worked hard that night of the reunion, a new urgency and focused stamina in getting the robbery performances right. Scunj was proof enough his father's mission was now his own, and he could feel his father's presence within guiding him and transforming his very persona with that of a bold, forceful leader who would not hesitate to take risks to achieve the ultimate vision. That slippery, still enigmatic endgame of Caleb Borshellac would at length reveal itself to him and such a revelation would prove the grand impetus to its very accomplishment, Zeke wholeheartedly believed. The highwaymen, giddy and boozing that night strove to set down the rudiments of their act—and they managed to churn out many enduring ideas—but inevitably such rip-roaring wassails leads to loss of consciousness and that's what happened here, they passed out, bombed. Zeke spent the night on his back beside the dying flames of their campfire, his faithful pup snuggled against his side, and the others were strewn in similar somnolent fashion with Rollo's sporadic snoring splitting the still night air.

Not long after the first shades of morning light Zeke, still half-sleeping, reached for Balthazar and noticed his absence. He rubbed his eyes and sat up to look around. He called out to him and heard something rustling in the woods and quickly rose to head over there. The puppy soon appeared and barked once, bidding his master to follow him through the trees and brush until they came to a promontory from which a long valley could be seen. A lone rider on a charging steed was in the distance seemingly heading right at them. They watched him in silence for a half-minute until he was close enough to be made out better. He wore a strange get-up Zeke couldn't entirely identify, but his attire flowed in his wake and he had a shotgun slung around his shoulder. "C'mon, Balt, this fellow could be our first robbery mark," he said, and they scampered back to the camp to awaken the others.

"But we're supposed to lay for our marks off road and surprise attack 'em!" Rollo objected upon hearing Zeke's plea to stick up the approaching rider. "Since when do highwaymen loiter in a conspicuous clearing awaiting a lone horseman to find them!?" he queried.

But Lester sided with Zeke, emphasizing the simplicity of doing nothing until the rider showed up, and they sat on a fallen tree trunk, facing the direction from which Zeke and Balthazar observed the charging horseman. The puppy seemed jittery to Zeke, dashing around in circles and whimpering some, so he bade him lay by his feet and scratched his belly the way he liked it. "There's nothing to worry about, Balty. We're going to roll this lone rider and leave him with something he'll never forget!"

The three men began to become impatient and Rollo even questioned Zeke's initial sighting of the rider. "Maybe you *thought* you saw this horseman? It had been a long night, the mind can play tricks," he needled him.

"Shut your goddamn mouths, both of ya! He'll be here soon enough, already. Now have some hooch," Lester barked, then downing some of his corn whiskey before passing it to Zeke. They drank in silence for a few minutes, watching the puppy sitting up staring at the woods. "After we hold this son of a bitch up and shock his system with our show, he will become one day renown as the first victim of the Wild Man Riders of Reckoning. There will be all kinds of stories written about this stiff," Lester predicted. Zeke couldn't tell if Lester was being facetious or meant what he said about their outfit's destiny as legends. They all seemed to stew in their own cogitations now for several minutes, passing around the corn whiskey, until a sudden burst of galloping hooves and whinnying and the raspy incoherent yell and guffaw of the rider all came roaring up behind them, the rider mad with shotgun drawn and generally aimed at the startled highwaymen. Even Balthazar went quiet after a few barks, seemingly perplexed by the nature of their marauder. The rider brought the agitated horse up high on his hind legs and he laughed and screamed about "old Mulligrubs, knew the hell I'd find ya," and he cut a strikingly lunatic figure for he was indeed the lone rider coming from the other way towards them. He now fired his improbably large shotgun into the air and spat a wad of apparent chewing tobacco at the highwaymen's feet. "I'm here to take my Mulligrubs back you goddamn horse thieves, and I'll see that you hang high on a tree for it, you stinkin' bastards!"

Only now did it occur to Lester and Rollo that this indeed was Simon Grackler, the unhinged Grackler cousin who lived in a tree and rarely had been seen outside the farm acreage. "Ahh, look at ol' Mulligrubs over there! I missed you, boy! I wouldn't let these shitholes take you away. Ain't gonna happen on my watch." He motioned with his shotgun towards Rollo. "You! Tubby! Bring my horse over here!"

Rollo gingerly approached and untied his lead, which Zeke had strung around a skinny tree, and the volcanic great steed seemed to smolder as he followed his path back to the men. Simon smiled as he stroked the horse's side with reverence and a weird giggling grin, showing his shotgun barrel here and there lest his captives thought about rushing him. Zeke's heart raced and he could hardly collect his thoughts as the magnitude of the predicament kept occurring to him. He couldn't decide if he was mad at himself for participating in the horse theft or for not being vigilant enough to stave off losing his fine new horse. He knew this Grackler cousin waving an outsized shotgun in front of them was some kind of lunatic hotspur the likes of which he'd never encountered. He wasn't very tall or burly but moved around in bursts of manic agility, which suggested he wasn't as old as he looked. He had a weathered face and crazy eyes and bad teeth and a mop of dark scruffy hair. He wore a full-length sleeping gown and night cap, so he must have been awakened suddenly, Zeke thought. But he managed to throw on an oilskin vest and was shod in high jackboots. The maroon and periwinkle blue taffeta extra puffy regal ruff he sported around his neck like some 18th Century earl completed the ensemble, as inexplicably silly while dementedly wistful. He let out a squeal of delight in spotting the bottle of corn whiskey. "I could use a little taste of that," he exclaimed, commanding they bring it to him. Rollo did so hastily, and he gulped some right down. "I'm gonna march you miserable crooks right over to the sheriff's office and see they lock you up. Now throw your firearms on the ground or I'll blast yez straight to hell!"

Rollo and Lester did as asked, but Simon fixed his barrel on Zeke when nothing came from him. "I don't have a gun, mister," Zeke explained.

"What kind of a horse thief don't carry a piece?!" he asked rhetorically.

Zeke answered him with a tinge of pique. "Well, I'm no horse thief by trade. While I did participate in the stealing of your grand horse, there was a very noble, altruistic cause which made it necessary. I don't own a gun and never have," Zeke maintained.

Simon glowered at each man and concluded: "Now that's effrontery in the most shameless manner. As if anything could justify snatching 'ol Mulligrubs. I ought to just plug the three of yez!" He moved around them slowly, thinking, and finally demanded to know the cause behind the thievery. Zeke was quite glad to provide him with all the details of their plans to become notorious highwaymen and donate the vast majority of their spoils to the Rambling Hoboes of America Fund, underscoring their credo of being artists first and criminals only as an ineluctable means to their overall raison de'tre. Balthazar scooted beside Zeke when he finished, as if to support his master if what he said went over badly, or so Zeke thought.

"Is that so?" was all Simon returned, after a space of thinking. He swigged some whiskey, petted the puppy, and mumbled that he really ought to just shoot the bastards, but instead garbled something about their essaying their goddamn show right there, and he spat out some more tobacco. It became fast evident that Simon Grackler liked to drain large quantities of hooch, and whiskey seemed one of his favorites for he hit up his captives for another bottle, which Lester fished out of his horse's saddle bag. Simon was in his cups, waxing rowdy and sportive, and fixated on the show he heard Zeke mention they would put on for their robbery victims. He reclined on a boulder with his bottle and shotgun and horse, ensconcing himself for the command performance he ordered. He soon called for Mulligrubs to join him as an

FOUR

adjunct critic and now Simon seemed ready to take in the entertainment. "You larcenous goddamn four-flushers better have something with this shtick," Grackler razzed them with a baleful warning before snickering.

They opened with the Salzburg Circus Skit, improvising new twists such as Rollo's Klaus Cloverleaf singing "Oh Tannenbaum" for the Kaiser during a flashback scene at the poulterer's coop, Lester's Chan Charcutlier failing to catch the daughter of William Jennings Bryant in a capricious attempt at the triple on trapeze and the famed orator arguing for Chan's execution notwithstanding the young woman emerging unscathed except for the inability to properly enunciate many words, mostly adverbs and compound nouns (concussive sequela). Zeke's Rube Dolittler, shot from a cannon culminating a twenty-one-gun salute honoring President Grover Cleveland's appearance at the Indiana State Fair, suffers a crash landing and the conk on the head leaves him convinced he's a cook from Juarez, Mexico, who is late for work and winds up teaming with Cleveland in a rousing song-and-dance duet. Simon sat engrossed in the show, sphinxlike with nary a sign of his appreciation of it until the very end of the final scene, and then everyone waited in silence for his assessment.

"You fellas ain't the dopey bums I took yez for," he began, "for I gotta admit the Circus stories there sort of pulled me in." He rose and paced with the whiskey bottle and a large stick he used to gesticulate in emphasis of his critique. "You missed an opportunity with the Kaiser at the big top—have him pop his cork and beat up a few clowns and sing a Sturm and Drang existential war song. Show him as a flesh and blood figure! And Charcutlier ought to spite the gasbag Bryant and do another triple with his daughter—this time sans a net. And you should have President Cleveland go to Juarez to give an address on US Mexico comity, maybe a song and dance with the cook *and Rube.*" He paused to knock back some whiskey and deep in thought he concluded: "You fellas are still lowlife horse thieves, but to be fair the show ain't all garbage . . . *if* you make the changes I'm recommending." He whispered for a while in Mulligrubs' ear and guffawed, slapping the steed's side before visiting the horse he rode there and appearing to share some unintelligible exchanges with him and another guffaw. He reached into that horse's saddlebags and found an onion which he began to devour ravenously. "The Grackler farm puts out the finest goddamn onions on the planet!!" he cried. And in a flash he pulled out another onion and hurled it at Rollo, pelting him smack in the chest. "Go on, Tubby, chow down on that big yellow sweet baby! I know you're hungry, fella!" and he broke into crazy laughter. Rollo groaned and grimaced but picked up the onion and slowly peeled back a couple of layers as everyone watched and took a bite out of it, nodding his approval as he chewed. "You're damn straight it's good, Tubby boy," Grackler said.

Zeke had been thinking and he sensed in Simon an outlier in every facet of existence, even in his confined farm life, and yet there appeared to be a yearning in the man to connect with a greater good of theatrical showmanship. His ideas were actually constructive, albeit a tad subversive, and Zeke intuited a creatively suppressed individual seeking an outlet for expression. While he would rebuke his notion of Cleveland, the cook, and Rube performing together in Mexico, he nonetheless would explore a way to extricate the Wild Man Riders from his capture by tendering an overture. "My partners are acquainted with the excellent onion crop the Grackler farm is known to produce," he began. "But let me state a bold observation: Providence may have guided us to your barn to snatch that magnificent steed Scunj—I mean, Mulligrubs—" Simon bristled at the mistake.

"What of this despicable name Scunj? You loathsome dogs sought to recast my Mulligrubs?" He moved towards Zeke now with his shotgun.

"No, sir, we have done nothing of the kind. The horse has a preternatural quality that communicated to me through generations and I believe he possesses the spirit of my father's horse, Scunj. This enabled me a bonding with my father that I never experienced while the man was alive. I truly believe that I am now riding on the path of destiny meant for me and he is there with me."

FOUR

Simon listened intently, his squinty eyes opening and his shotgun receding to his side. He swigged from his whiskey bottle and spit tobacco and bit into the remains of his onion. "Never knew my old man," he mumbled. "That's a pretty tall tale you spun there, fella, but I can see ol' Mulligrubs inspiring a lost sort of lowlife such as yourself. When you swing from the tree I hope you feel it was worth it." He let out a derisive chuckle.

Zeke pressed on with his pitch. "Well, hopefully it will not come to that. Providence, sir, brought us together I believe now. For your insightful critique could not come from someone without a desire to conquer grim reality through Art. You declared our capabilities satisfactory; we would be that much more potent with the likes of your direction at our backs. Opportunities to join an artistic movement are rare, rarer still on an isolated farm, and I see in you someone who probably has creative ambition beyond the soil. Why not join with us in robbing for the hobo fund and leaving our marks with life-changing performances in the bargain?"

Simon swigged and spit and pet Balthazar, who sidled up to him now, and he stroked Mulligrubs, his head down in thought. "You fellas familiar with that German highwayman from way back?"

Lester now piped up with eager optimism. "Dieter Schrampenkrieg! Of course. The Bashful Sandblaster is our loadstar and Muse. He was a great man whose teachings we follow."

"The Bashful Blaster . . ." Simon muttered and deliberated with a frown. "I read about him. Quite a fella. Well, I tell ya what I'll consider with all this. There will be conditions. Terms that I dictate that must be met. Then we'll see."

Zeke knew his hunch had been right and Simon was indeed a discontented farmer who harbored a hankering to break away from the simple life and ride into the iconoclastic adventure of the Wild Man Riders of the Reckoning. But, Simon held all the cards insofar as he had his shotgun loaded and could have taken them in for horse stealing. So he made demands which left the highwaymen no choice but to embrace. First, he insisted the name of the band be changed to

The Simon Grackler Riders of the Reckoning. Zeke, instantly recognizing an opportunity to inveigle Simon, led him to believe that he won something quite dear to the highwaymen by appropriating their name when they really could not have cared less considering the circumstances. Simon's second demand was unequivocally a bitter pill for Zeke and the band to swallow, ceding him creative control and final arbiter over all dramatic performances and comic skits the highwaymen presented to their victims. Zeke in particular winced with apprehension in as much as he saw his own strength and cardinal contribution to the enterprise the performance areas, but of course he had to subdue his personal disgust while putting on a façade of acquiescence. He would not constrain or inhibit his ideas one iota, he told himself, but would exhort, cajole, and convince Simon to concur with the storylines and scripts he whole-heartedly believed in. And it was only a matter of moments before he found himself at loggerheads with the unbalanced onion farmer, as the aforementioned trademark outfits the highwaymen had already agreed to acquire and don were not the sort of togs Grackler would even consider. The more he expressed his discontent with the image of such an ensemble for a man of his sort, the clearer it became the getup he intended to wear and envisioned as part and parcel to his role as lead rider: the very peculiar collection of clothes he was already wearing. "I want the bastards to know who the hell I am," Simon proclaimed, strutting around with a provocative insouciance showing off his sleeping gown and cap, oilskin vest, jackboots, and maroon and periwinkle blue taffeta ruff. "The raiment you see here smacks them over the head with the persona of Simon Grackler. No one else could ever approximate my garb."

Zeke asked what seemed apparent to him and his partners. "So the night we stole your horse we must have wakened you. You've been searching for Mulligrubs since in your sleeping gown."

Simon broke into a resonant belly laugh which he ended abruptly and declared: "I will not dignify such twaddle. This here feels right and projects me accurately. You mugs wear your goddamn own outfits, but don't think about tampering with my togs." And so that is how the image projected by The Simon Grackler Riders of the Reckoning became finalized. Simon with his sleeping gown and jackboots and shotgun and harum-scarum horsemanship was the front man, his odd mutterings and sudden lightning crazy legs moves and demented interminable howls of laughter all underscoring a loopy soul at the helm. The outfits Zeke and his partners decided upon were not so easy to procure, time would prove, albeit the shaggy cowboy chaps, buckskin fringe jackets, the long flowing dust protector handkerchiefs, and top hats were scared up for all and became the signature elements of their look. They did stumble upon an itinerant artisan of some renown in customized apparel and engaged the old fellow, Otto Milkwood, a senescent rumdum well past his prime but contracting for dirt cheap rates. Milkwood was a drunk and hard of hearing so it shouldn't have been such a surprise to the highwaymen when he embroidered on their buckskins an anthropomorphic oboe holding a candlestick instead of a hobo with a bindlestick as they ordered. An acrimonious dispute ensued between the highwaymen and Milkwood, who maintained with bitter rancor he only produced what he was told, and the highwaymen lost all patience with the surly rummy and slapped him around until he agreed to fix the work. Only as far as Zeke was concerned, the problem was only compounded by the resulting "Hobo Jack" leaping over the candlestick as he appeared more "Jack Frost," and the anthropomorphic oboe did not transition well into becoming a hobo on a train, looking more like Johnny Appleseed atop a pagoda. Lester and Rollo were more tolerant of the Appleseed on a pagoda transformation, valuing the arcane oddity of the image. Simon stayed out of it, stating he didn't care if they wore barrels, but somehow took a shine to Otto Milkwood and enjoyed bantering with the old-timer over shots of corn whiskey, and Milkwood even painted a picture of the onion farmer as a hobo on his steed leading a regiment of hoboes into battle.

FIVE

T HE SIMON GRACKLER RIDERS OF THE RECKONING soon began to blaze their way with a startling and strange sort of notoriety into the zeitgeist of forests far and wide. Their first robbery was so shocking the crazy band of highwaymen in their unorthodox attire grabbed everyone's attention and accounts of the crime were reported in newspapers everywhere. They bushwhacked a fancy brougham carrying a count and his family and their attendants in a second coach, the sudden subduing and overtaking of the wealthy nobleman from Bucharest was accomplished by a swift coordination of horsemanship and a fearsome display of violent capabilities via resounding gunshots fired into the dark skies. While there were hysterical cries from the countess and a bejeweled fat old woman and desperate aides of the count's attempting to negotiate a way out of the ordeal, the highwaymen remained stolid and somber in their directing the travelers to the roadside clearing designated for the show. The victims eventually quit their blubbering and begging as they realized this was a very different kind of robbery happening to them and mayhem and battery or worse did not necessarily appear to be part of their fate. Of course, the highwaymen opened with the Salzburg Circus skit and all went as contrived and performed in several rehearsals until Simon interjected himself into the drama. Rollo was in splendid form hoofing in unison with his horse a slow sweet soft shoe routine, then belting out as Klaus Cloverleaf several rousing Teutonic marching songs for the Kaiser at the poulterer's coop, where hitherto the poulterer remained an unseen figure of suspicion and treachery. But as the Kaiser tears up to the patriotic numbers, especially "The Rain That Falls on My Head Strengthens My Resolve and Trickles Off My Helmet" and "We Move Forward Together With Carbines and the Will to Kill the Enemy," Simon, waving an ersatz assegai he fashioned of metallic cans of corn, burst into the scene and declared himself to be the poulterer Jarland McCandlemas. "How dare you warble like a madman in my coop frightening my chickens!" he bellows, setting off a violent confrontation between the Kaiser's high command and the strange poulterer. McCandlemas is soon subdued and rendered a bloody groggy wreck, nonetheless managing to whistle for his "fighting cocks" who swarm the coop and claw and peck the unsuspecting Germans into a hasty retreat. General Buck Masterson, the cunning cock who led the attack, was quite ably played by Balthazar, certainly no stranger to chickens in his nomadic life before finding Zeke. The victory is Pyrrhic, however, as the Kaiser strikes back with a merciless onslaught of artillery and missiles which utterly destroy the Candlemas coop and all the fighting cocks as they are celebrating with cigars and much champagne. Yet McCandlemas and General Buck Masterson, out strolling the grounds while planning fortifications of the coop and compound, are spared, as is Klaus Cloverleaf who fled when the crazed poulterer was wrangling with the Germans. As the scene shifted and an interlude supervened, Zeke kept close watch on the Count and his wife and the fat woman (now stripped of her jewels) and their retinue all strewn across the craggy forest stretch and brooded over what could happen if the subjugated nobleman and his party were to rebel and not cooperate. He did not think he could ever shoot them, or anyone else for that matter, even if the pistol he carved out of an oak branch and imbued with blackberry juice were real. But regarding his highwaymen associates he knew differently, they meant business in a heist, and Simon, well, he seemed so bananas and volatile the potential for murderous rage could not be ignored. He wanted to believe it would never come to that, maybe Simon Grackler was just a harmless goofball and the others were lacking the brutality the most successful highwaymen occasionally have to display. Now he saw the Count sitting beside his wife, appearing quite relaxed, apparently very much enjoying the show as they were conversing and laughing together in their tongue. Throughout the show a gangling subaltern in a tight Alpine woolen suit and a multicolored beanie had been translating into High Rumanian for the Count and his inner circle the highwaymen's dialogue from the rotund cook's Latin, which he understood but not the English spoken on stage. The cook, a Flemish epicure dressed sharply in crisp white linen and three-foot high starched baker's hat, was a jolly rascal pickled stinko and relishing his importance by attempting some version of pirouettes that usually landed him on his keister. Notwithstanding, his Latin was flawless. It was the way the Count's retinue communicated, as they were a Babel of languages tenuously connected by assiduous attention to multiple translations determined by who understood what. As a testament of their equanimity on stage, the highwaymen did not react to the frequent interruptions from all the translating in the audience, but instead slowed down their delivery and timing to allow the Count and company to get caught up.

For some reason this crowd delighted in the forbidden flirtation between Lester's Chan Charcutlier and the marble-mouthed daughter of President Cleveland who was still recovering from the trapeze fall head injury which many blamed on Chan for dropping her, thus his moniker "Butterfingers." Lester played to the Count and pitched enough woo to canoodle the Cleveland lass to second base and then honeyfogle himself on over to third, and the nobleman tittered and sighed like a moonstruck schoolboy. But Zeke as Rube Doolittler came riding in on Mulligrubs (Scunj)—and after they stomped around in a synchronized cakewalk in which Zeke breaks into the sorrowful cowboy ballad "Seven Frolicsome Tumbleweeds Scudding in the Gusts, Mocking my Lonesome Despair, Until I Set Them On Fire." Very quickly he was in a telegraph station sending a secret message to Grover Cleveland who was still in Juarez, warning the president of the clandestine hanky-panky occurring between his daughter and the fascist-agent trapeze master Charcutlier.

The highwaymen were not very concerned upon noticing during the next scene change the Count was nipping a jug of grappa, and though ebullient in his horseplay with his translators, he seemed louder and shakier on his feet. Then he was yelling with vicious intensity at the highwaymen and the rangy subaltern spun his inflamed words into Latin for the cook, who then filtered the diatribe into English for the troupe: "Enough frippery, you wastrels, let's have the Kaiser and Grover Cleveland square off once and for all. And the trapeze artist and the beautiful President daughter dance the rhumba!"

At some point Klaus Cloverleaf is revealed to be the mysterious benefactor of the renegade clown association of greater Salzburg and their bruising brand of slapstick at the expense of their more ethereal traditional gagsters is shown as purely a mercenary tack. By the time Rube Doolittler is shot out of the cannon a martial harbinger hangs heavy over the big top, as Jarland McCandlemas and his unswerving stalwart, the indomitable little rooster General Buck Masterson, have gathered with a ragtag battalion of stray fowls and marching wee folk from their underground tunnels. A great battle scene ensues and much clown and fighting fowl blood is shed, but Masterson will not relent nor regroup, instead exhorts his troops onward. The Kaiser drains a flask of schnapps and wades into the fray, knocking out a string of ethereal clowns with one blow apiece before being pecked in the groin by a unit of desperate guinea hens. As he heroically extricates himself from the birds and slowly rises to his feet he breaks into "My Kaiser Blood Lifts Me Up to Lead Us On to Conquest (and Eleven Thousand Kegs of Pilsner Beer!)" But now it is Cloverleaf's turn to be projected out of the cannon and he not only lands on the singing Kaiser but both men are set upon by a frenzied band of bully clowns who really go to work on them. The marching wee folk who McCandlemas and the little general macabrely summoned from the earth, while battling valiantly with their truncheons and dirks, were marginal at best in the execution of Masterson's "Flank Left, Bombard North Coordinates" plan as life underground stunted not only their growth but sense of direction. Most of them flanked right and tumbled into a regiment of the Prussian Army who were taking a break in a splendid copse speckled with joe-pye weed and riots of yellow monkeyflower. Smoking cheroots and guzzling liters of lager, the Prussians hardly noticed the falling little figures crashing their verdant sanctuary. Aside from one vicious brute named Uwe Schnitzler, who had to be restrained from rounding the wee ones up in a large sack he intended to toss away, the Prussians were charmed by the whimsical little soldiers and they all got drunk and sang German drinking songs such as "Prost! Schnell! More Beer, Madchen Before This Soldier Meets Herr Schrapnel!" and "Beer Runs Through Me Like a River and I Run Through Mortar Shells Like Uncle Otto." But then all of a sudden the audience learns the war is over and The Kaiser and Klaus Cloverleaf, Buck Masterson and Jarland McCandlemas, President Grover Cleveland and Rube Dolittler, and Chan Charcutlier with Cleveland's daughter beside him, all declare victory and start dictating terms of formal surrender to one another to no avail until they become exasperated and fatigued and decide to start drinking and come together for the grand finale song and dance number: "We Are All In This Together Unless We Decide Not To Be Anymore."

 When the rousing beer hall style belter came to a close the Count and his retinue remained stock-still in silence for a good half-minute before dimly recognizing some reaction from them was expected. By this time they were so amused and fascinated and utterly perplexed by the performance no appropriate audience reaction occurred to any among them. Simon, stepping out of his Jarland McCandlemas character, glowered at the Count as he moved slowly towards him, his jackboots on rocky earth the only sound, his hands tucked into the pockets of his oilskin vest, his sleeping gown billowing behind him in the wind. "We're the Simon Grackler Riders of the Reckoning and you lousy swells better learn how to express appreciation of a goddamn good show!" The cook began translating into Latin for the subaltern but Simon shut him down with his index finger across his lips. And then he began to slowly clap his hands and met their eyes one by one until they seemed to figure out he wanted them to join him, but they struggled with timing and volume control of the palms striking one another, producing a dissonant, unpleasant noise that suggested they had never clapped before to create applause. Irked but undaunted, Grackler persisted until they were able to sustain a semblance of an ovation that he could live with, and he bade them to continue as he turned and mounted his horse and rode off into the night with the highwaymen who'd been waiting for him. They rode like the apocalyptic demons their name implied, rode with breakneck abandon for what seemed hours penetrating the forgotten recesses of the forest and Zeke felt a rumbling thunder building inside him, an exhilaration and fervor delivering him towards his true destiny, his father's mission subsumed in his soul. The bulletless bandolier he crafted from junked vulcanized hoses flapped wildly against his chest, while the propulsive power of the preternatural steed Mulligrubs beneath him made him believe something else was at his back beside the blowing wind. It felt so right and staunchly inexorable to be riding with his confederates deep into the night that he began to believe he had found his calling and the sensation of being ensconced in the sweeping nimbus of Caleb Borshellac was hurtling him at once towards his father's and his own ineffable incandescent fate. Zeke held a bottle of corn whisky and swigged as he rode, boozing like the old man, and he equally grew drunk with exalted visions of achievement, as was the father's wont as well, lofty ideas of accomplishment all in the cards on the path he now followed to who knew where, a path they now shared.

Lurid tales of the Gracklers spread throughout the forest and beyond, shocking, eerie accounts of their singular brand of highway banditry. Not only do they strip you of all your money and valuables, it was bruited, but they force their iconoclastic performances upon their marks and break down their minds with such volcanic desolation no one experiencing such anarchic catharsis and evisceration of sensibilities can ever emerge the same person. What are they truly after, these demented fiends of the night? newspapers pondered, what dark purpose can be behind such fury and artistic madness? After the success of their maiden robbery the highwaymen struck again only days later, bushwhacking two coaches of metaphysicians en route to a weekend of contemplation, crumpets, and croquet at the rustic retreat Ducky Paluccio's in the hills. After swiftly directing the eleven heavy thinkers and their two drivers to a grassy glade replete with profusions of gumweed and goldenrods, stripping them of whatever cash they carried and other perceived valuables such as scholarly volumes, the highwaymen prepared for the show dismayed by their victim's lack of much moolah. Still, the pale long-bearded, bespectacled group appeared to understand English and after the last debacle the ability to communicate sans translation gladdened the bandits. Among the metaphysicians was the eminent author of *Sniveling Mopes Languishing in the Root Beer Paradigm*, Windsor Adair Frappe, whose later monograph on the shameless delight he found in the coerced attendance of the Gracklers' show remained in print for many years. His observation that the highwaymen were "on some binge bent on skewering all rational thought and everyday reality with an indefatigable subversive zeal" became an often-used quote by bohemian wastrels populating the dingy coffee houses of Montparnasse and many exile outposts such as parts of Lower Silesia. Perhaps inhibited by the intellectual heft of their metaphysician spectators, the Gracklers began the performance tentatively, engaging in the snappy, trenchant dialogue of the Milkmen Guild's Wildcat Strike skit. Zeke, portraying the earnest, combative apprentice Emmett Stoaglmire, delivers a blistering rebuke of the dairy industry to a group of peasants on their way to clambake. The peasants bristle at his doggedness and the one with an odd arrhythmic gait bellows that he cherishes eating cheese every day and the militant stance the union is taking will shut the dairy down. "Is that all you care about? Filling your belly with their cheese? What about our ability to earn a fare wage?" The peasant turned surlier: "How dare you castigate me for a love of cheese! Your struggle is not mine, mister." Zeke's roughhewn quixotic milkman Stoaglmire seemed to connect with the metaphysicians and a couple of times they blurted incomprehensible words of approval, which sounded like, "free will bolsters your moral imperative," as Emmett entered the stage. "Collectively we wield power over those who exploit and oppress us," Stoaglmire begins, soon launching into a philippic on the "milk cartel" and the terrible subjugation of the modern milkman into automatons divorced from their very humanity on their routes, precluded from all the small talk, persiflage, and general flapjaw they traditionally engaged in with customers that made their vocation a desideratum to mornings in a civil, congenial society. "Change involves matter, not just form and privation," he thunders at the peasants as they disdainfully hurry away to their clambake. "I hereby condemn and indict the mendacious and malevolent dairy tycoon Hexton Torborg and we will prevail if we stick together!" With that the picketing milkmen roar their staunch commitment to the cause and Torborg is seen lighting his gigantic cigar, scowling, and burning his fingers which impels him into a St. Vitus' Dance which the metaphysicians simply ate up with delight. Once again Rollo, as Torborg, infused his character with a remarkable verisimilitude and his dulcet voice was in fine fettle as he broke into "Hexton's Hot Finger Romp" in which he sings of his prosperity and power in his industry often being undermined by his proclivity for painful freak accidents. Next he calls for his dutiful Pinkerton strike-breaker, Lieutenant Orion Skeens, a thuggish doglike brute portrayed with disturbing revulsion by Balthazar, and the crass tycoon and mangy psycho cur launch into a winsome square dance together as bluegrass notes waft over them.

During the first scene change break the metaphysicians, apparently enjoying the show, began talking shop in bandying about whether Hegel was a drinker and inveterate craps player and soon they were squaring off in debating the better thinker between Spinoza and Kant, which grew heated until the avuncular dean of the group, Windsor Adair Frappe, whipped out a mahogany carved pipe and stuffed it with, as he announced, "the Big O, the good old poppy tar, boys!" and took a hit before passing it around. Tooting the hop stick diverted the thinkers from their quarreling and quickly cast a mellow mood over them as the Gracklers began to launch the second act with a kinetic gusto.

Lester appeared as the Gaucho Gomez Gabbro, a lone Uruguayan cowboy vainglorious in his fierce solo rides across the pampas but his purpose and connection to the real world are tenuous and mysterious, a complex character who says little and, as the metaphysicians saw him, a contrapuntal Camusian figure. They were quick to project meaning in the Manichean dilemma posed by milkmen solidarity and a horseman galloping on the open grasslands in the valley of the Andes. "Neutralize yourselves, gringoes," Gomez snarls to the wind, "your insipid economic battles crush your will and spirit to rise above the quotidian quicksand which is sucking you under without so much as a whiff of the divine afflatus, the transcendent soul." Hexton Torborg is shown in his office arranging a contract to be put on Gomez' head, imploring several goons he doesn't "know much about the fellow, or truthfully, why he has to go, but he just needs to be taken out." Stoaglmire is more torn about the significance of the provocateur gaucho thousands of miles away and maintains in a milkmen rousing rally that he would not be lured into a clash with Gomez unless his insults went beyond the pale. "Even then I would seek to engage this strange Uruguayan in a colloquy to explore whether common ground can be found." In other words, Gomez posed no threat to the strike effort of the milkmen and while Torborg and his ilk might lash out with violence at something they cannot fathom, that is not a measure plied in solidarity campaigns. Again the spotlight is on the Gaucho Gomez Gabbro racing on his fine steed across the vast pampas of Argentina, attired now in a black Zorro hat and red neckerchief streaming in the wind and a kaleidoscopic, ornately brocaded balmacaan, singing/declaring his manifesto on the human condition: "Unfathomable estrangement from living humans invisibly seeps in and seals one away. I succumb to an unutterable loneliness, bleak beyond anything ever imagined, I am sliding into the black maw. I want to fade into nothingness, that is my anodyne, yet some mad beast stalks me now!" The metaphysicians were so entranced by the cryptic significance of the dark plangent form of Gomez they furiously took notes throughout the performance of his spectral manifesto. No one delighted in their zeal more than Simon, insofar as he wielded final cut of the skits and it was he who had remained implacable in the belief the show veer to the intellectual and philosophical to further engage the sensibilities of this audience. And now he was coming into distant view upon the pampas horizon, cutting a crazy rug akin to the mambo on peyote, and we soon behold him striding with a mighty gait and squinty glare, eyebrows overgrown wild thickets, the defiant toughness and power and hardy ruggedness belonging to but one individual: the labor giant of the miners and Congress of Industrial Organizations, John L. Lewis. And while remaining in his usual sleeping gown and cap, ruff, oilskin vest, and jackboots, Simon with only the classic unbounded beetle-brows animating the great man in such spooky vivid realness the metaphysicians recoiled with fear and nausea. Transfixed with consternation, several found themselves maundering existential conundrums which defied their investigations. "Are we pieces of one soul, or do we all have our own little souls?" asked Laszlo Phlyzzic, the stout one rather demonstrative in his desire to know. "Is it like other organs, such as the kidney or appendix? Consider the spleen and postulate the soul. Both possess form, of course." Phlyzzic spoke in a cadence betokening his dismay, and his colleagues had no responses for him. They too were riveted upon Simon's stunning characterization of John L. Lewis with only thick unweeded bushy brows evoking the legend, his sleeping gown and cap injecting the macabre. Archibald Spanko, the wiry scholar who favored corduroy overalls and thick Turkish turtlenecks of umber quasi-check patterns, began a soft insistent query, "What is the sphere of incontinence? Who is the incontinent man?" Simon's John L. Lewis frightened the bejesus out of these men while also extracting involuntary work from them. A fine and noble performance, here he came now on horseback dazzling everyone with harum-scarum riding acrobatics around the metaphysicians as they barked theories and soon he was showboating some extra fancy horse high-stepping while shooting off his .44 and howling to the heavens. Simon further showed off his horsemanship by featuring one of his most dazzling stunts, persuading his horse through a series of enigmatic serenades to trot backwards, accelerating into a swaying zigzag reverse gallup while continually introducing himself as "the one and only great John L. Lewis" and rising to stand and acknowledge the imaginary applause while he began his speech, only to be thrown off balance and bounced back in the saddle. He repeated this exercise six times before striking up the very lively and belligerent old mining song, "Desmond the Brave Parrot Hopped the Twig and Now It's Our Turn, Gents." He was singing another minors' rally anthem, "The Lung Turns Black and We Tip Our Hats and Burn the Company Store to the Ground," while creating the illusion he was marching on his horse's back when he was just shaking himself like a maraca, and then on the crepuscular horizon there appeared the faraway figure of the Gaucho Gomez Gabbro. The two horsemen of such stark antitheses who embodied deeply opposed philosophies of life now slowly rode towards each other as sundown approached on the vast sprawling pampas. Gomez trotted at a steady pace with his torso bolt upright and his chin elevated, evincing a valiant resignation to duty and destiny. Only once did he find cause to pause, when he felt chilly and searched his saddlebags for his poncho. As he pulled the blanket cloak over his head the opening proved too small and became stuck just above the eyes and Gomez suddenly found himself in a frantic struggle to extricate himself and his vision from the garment. Sensing the panic and instability from the man astride him, his horse went bonkers and threw Gomez off his back into a copse of needled chaparral. Aside from multiple contusions, he emerged relatively unhurt and eventually mounted his horse to resume his course towards the labor stalwart, who by now almost gave up on their rendezvous by dismounting on the rolling grasslands to light up a panatela and test his model sailboat in a meandering streamlet he came across. By the time the adversaries finally squared off on their horses with their firearms the night had fallen and visibility was very limited, so while they shot off numerous rounds all night at one another the pitch-black mantle engulfing them ensured neither man was hit. A rather anticlimactic ending to such a crescendo of tense drama that seemed headed for an epic bloody duel, but the metaphysicians ate it up, lauding the conspiracy of inadvertent factors railroading the outcome. The epilogue was brief but efficacious in use of lasting images: here is Hexton Torborg skulking amid stinkweeds on a hill watching from afar the striking milkmen burning him in effigy over a bonfire outside his dairy, while fireworks scintillate the nightscape; dawn heralds a lighter mood as the milkmen are deliriously performing the hokey pokey under the direction of their strike captain, Emmett Stoaglmire, all giddy over the six cheesemakers who walked off the nightshift to join the dance fun and likely turned the tide in the strike.

The metaphysicians were enthralled and transported and intellectually galvanized by the Milkmen Guild's Wildcat Strike skit and they remained focused on the denouement and its meaning long after it was over. While the more aggressive of the group importuned the Gracklers for answers in the immediate aftermath, Simon really spoke for the highwaymen when he exasperatedly told them: "Hey, you boys better back the hell off if you know what's good for you!" Of course, they still saw him as John L. Lewis and thought this utterance was fraught with significance to the skit. The Gracklers at this juncture were simply exhausted and occupied in packing up their props and scenery apparatus before riding off to pitch their tents and light a campfire to fry some fish and crack the whiskey.

It was Windsor Adair Frappe who posited the first interpretation of the allegorical meaning behind the Milkmen skit. John L. Lewis seemingly triumphed over the Gaucho Gomez Gabbro, indicating the one big collective soul usurping the upstart audacity of a little independent soul, while Hexton Torborg was vanquished in his ruthless rapacity as a capitalist. It is the everyman Stoaglmire who is left to dance with his fellow milkmen and inherit a world without their oppressor—but who will assume the helm going forward? Lewis? He leaves it nebulous but rules out Stoaglmire as "an oaf unfit for symbolic utility."

Notwithstanding Frappe's eminence as an existential thinker, excepting Lionel Grayson Blundor who as WAF's protégé had yet to break with him on anything, the bulk of the group found his exegesis simply too pat and glib and roundly derided the interpretation. Spanko went deep and heavy when he declared God and the Devil and the Archangel Gabriel and Horace were all out on the pampas with Gomez and John L. Lewis, but the milkmen ("unmoved movers") were the noble and just ones who won their demands and would "savor their substance as eternal and far removed from prudence." By eschewing prudence in their bold conflict, they "transcend the molecules of their corporeality and celebrate like children," which was the appended crux of Phlyzzic's explication which also identified Lieutenant Orion Skeens as the "simulacrum of canine evil" and John L. Lewis as a "hotspur nihilist flamethrower," raising the hackles of an increasingly vexed Archibald Spanko. The two men had some harsh words before nearly coming to blows, and they continued bobbing and weaving around one another shadowboxing, neither prepared to concede defeat despite no punches even close to being traded. The eleven metaphysicians all had their own strong ideas about the skit and could not let it go, increasingly the vehement verbal exchanges turned ugly, and it wasn't long before a full-blown donnybrook broke out. The rabid violence the men were inflicting on one another was merciless and appalling and Zeke voiced whether it was their responsibility to stop the senseless fighting.

"Let them knock themselves silly," Simon declared, "maybe the eggheads will wake up and get real jobs."

Zeke chafed at his philistine dismissal of such intelligent robbery victims who so thoroughly embraced their performances. He tentatively approached a bloody scrum of six or seven, seeking a way to short-circuit the free-for-all when suddenly a leg thrust out of the pack and caught Zeke in his private parts. Instantly and out of nowhere came Balthazar rushing in to bite the possessor of the aforesaid leg, Lionel Grayson Blundor, on the labonza, and he shrieked like a wounded alley cat. As Zeke collected himself doubled over, the largest metaphysician, Ethan Scuffbarrow, a beefy disciple of Schopenhauer who was being treated for a nameless brain disorder which made him powerful and prone to flamenco heel tapping when enraged, bum-rushed him and lit up his head with several hard blows. But Zeke managed to tie him up in a clinch and Balthazar sunk his teeth into his thigh while Simon smoked him on the forehead and nose with a couple of onions. Rollo and Lester were already on their horses waiting for the slowpokes when they realized the brawl the others were caught up in, so they shot off their pistols into the air and laughed when everybody scrambled with fright, and a few moments later The Simon Grackler Riders of the Reckoning were riding like hell through the cover of the nighttime forest where they would make camp after so many miles and have their fish fry and hit the hooch.

As Simon had been accustomed to sleeping in a treehouse on the Grackler farm, he missed the elevation and had begun climbing trees to grab his shuteye, tonight choosing a suitable spruce. Zeke spotted him monkeylike ascending a bough and called out a question: "We ought to be sending some of our loot off to the Hobo Fund soon, don't ya think?!"

Simon sat on the thick branch and looked down at his cohort, a thin spread of moonlight revealing his shadowy form. "Aw now don't you go stewing over the scratch, Zekey. Ol' Simon's got it in this baby at the higher altitude all night," he reassured. "And those good hoboes up against it will have their scratch hand delivered." He rose and raised the outsized leather pouch that held their loot from the holdups. Zeke hadn't known it had been decided Simon would protect the loot overnight by sleeping in trees with it. He thought he would ask Lester and Rollo if they had been consulted.

"Well, we ought to think about mailing the loot to the Hobo Fund cause it may take a long while before we locate them," Zeke returned.

Simon, higher now as he had resumed his climb, paused a moment to rejoin once more: "Don't you think our poor peripatetic brothers are foremost on my mind in our venture?! Why, I'm thinking about the improvements we'll bring them, like the fine chow they can take on them trains with 'em. Like that German highwayman, that fella the Sandblaster." "Dieter Schrampenkrieg?" Zeke proffered. "Yeah, him.

Shampeekleeg," Simon confirmed over his shoulder continuing up the tree. "He started what we're gonna see through all the way."

The Gracklers quickly commenced their most prolific period of highway holdups, rattling off an astonishing twenty-seven jobs over a six week span, inaugurating some of their best remembered skits and introducing a string of their finest song and dance numbers. Among their eventually grateful victims were coaches of noblemen, blue bloods in phaetons, grandees and grand dames in cabriolets, regional magnificoes in convoys, industrialists in caravans, the rubber magnate Elson Flidgette, the Ottoman Lord of Chancery, the Maltese tapioca heir playboy Carlo Pussilini, the governor of Kentucky, Clement E. Charkleman, and the calvacade of four-wheelers carrying the International Society of Osteopaths, Phrenologists, and Ameliorists which turned into a two-day jamboree replete with impromptu musical plays, bare-knuckle boxing matches, and gin-fueled blank verse poetry marathons. The Gracklers had largely achieved the widespread notoriety they sought and the newspapers dutifully documented every one of their highway heists, often in lurid accounts of the fierce brutality coupled with the peculiar, at times aberrant, nature of the performances put on for the captive audiences. A great fascination with the Gracklers burgeoned across all strata of populaces. Who were they and what did these strange menaces want? What did their outfits say about them, the cowboy chaps, the buckskin jackets with the hobo woven on the back, the dust protectors scattered with skeletons, the top hats? And the apparent leader of the Gracklers and his outre get-up, the sleeping gown and cap, the oilskin vest, the jackboots, and that most disturbing ruff around his neck? These are dangerous men, violent armed hoodlums whose mere name evokes dread and alarm, but a tempered fear for they too are recognized for their utterly singular dramatic performances interspersed with their own style of song and dance and horsemanship. Some reports recounted their putative pledge to the cause of hoboes, evidenced by that bindlestiff on their backs, and their avowed emulation of a lesser-known Robin Hood figure from Germany called Dieter Schrampenkrieg and the pecuniary succor that suggested. All of these elements of the Gracklers made terrific copy and the newspapermen could not write enough about them and engage their readers in all manner of insights, eyewitness accounts, reflection and speculation on what were they truly after, what did it all mean?

Many nights after a triumphant robbery and having had a hearty meal, Zeke sat by the campfire with a bottle of whiskey and thought about the whirlwind furious campaign they were on and wondered himself what did it all mean. He had long concluded the Gracklers do not owe their victim audiences any explanations or figurative answers as to the secrets and connotations lying behind their performances, and not just because they really had no idea themselves. Even if they did know, he reasoned, it would do the spectators a disservice insofar as each one of them must find their own meaning to the content if they require it to be there. But at this point, having come this far, Zeke was pondering the very meaning of The Simon Grackler Riders of the Reckoning and whether they have remained true to their original aim and purpose. Had their manifesto to become famous highwaymen in the spirit and principles of the great Dieter Schrampenkrieg been waylaid, the noble commitment to raising money for the Rambling Hoboes of America Fund (RHAF) through highway heists in the forest darkness, while stunning and beguiling their victims with original performances? Zeke knew the answer all too well, albeit the cold bitter truth is often too hard to digest and people like Zeke will not accept it until all measures to make it right have been exhausted. That is why at this juncture none of their now quite abundant loot had yet to be sent to the RHAF and was still stored with Simon in his saddlebag, a new enormous one he obtained from a tanner, which he slept with in trees every night. Simon had been demurring and remonstrating to Zeke's steady insistence they send the loot directly to the RHAF, maintaining hand delivering the donation would be safer and guarantee it actually made it to the hoboes. Sending such a large package of money and jewelry through the mail was too risky, and besides he always added, the RHAF headquarters were just a few more days travel to reach. Lester and Rollo were in complete agreement with Simon as well, echoing all of his arguments and assurances of their arriving at the headquarters any day now. He remembered they told him it was located in Passaic, New Jersey, but now maintained it had to be moved around a lot to throw off potential thieves. But the exact current location wasn't very clear to Zeke when they answered his inquiries, always at the place where the prairie grows hilly by the city of Slaughter Bends where the river splits into tributaries and the old train trestle has toppled. Well, it sounded like they knew where the Hobo Fund was, but they never seemed to be near any of those landmarks, and it just became increasingly frustrating for Zeke until he stopped asking about it. But he didn't quit thinking about it, in fact, it had been occupying much of his cogitations. And while he mused on their losing the real meaning of the Gracklers, he also began contemplating meaning in a larger sense, much larger, like what does anything mean anyway? He would look at Balthazar lying beside him and ask: "If the loot ain't going to the hoboes, what good are we, Balt? Supposed to be artists first, bandits second . . . don't seem that way anymore somehow." He would reflect on his harsh oppressive days at sea on the two ships where he was forced to perform in order to survive, and how what he was doing now as a Grackler had much the same benighted ruthlessness to it, only they were forcing their victims to watch their performances in order for them to survive.

    By the time the evening of their planned robbery of the Flemish plutocrat, Anders Stupenier, came around the Gracklers had been camped amid dense trees for two days preparing the attack and practicing the skits. They wanted this one to have a panache and quintessence all its own and took pains to produce something very special. By the same token, the heist itself would be their biggest score yet and it had to go just right because Stupenier was one of the wealthiest men in the world and was known to travel with untold amounts of his great fortune. The Gracklers decided they would curb the length of the performance as Stupenier might prove a rougher customer than usual based on the sheer size of the loss he'd be facing and he could lash out before they were done.

"Not only would our show be ruined and likely disparaged by his folks to the papers, but we'd have to shoot the bastard," Simon noted.

"We can't have that, too messy," Lester agreed, shaking his head.

"Not very Gracklerlike, popping a fella like that," added Rollo.

"That's why we're keeping this one short," reminded Simon.

"And sweet!" Zeke absently completed for him to the irked stares of all three.

The hold-up was sudden and lightning fast and flawless in execution, ending in a few minutes with several large bags brimming with money and valuables stripped from Stupenier and his retinue of four coaches. The plutocrat and his family and attendants were rounded up and taken to a moonlit glade just over a rise into the forest where they soon realized with uneasy gratitude that indeed these were the renown Gracklers and there would be a show. Anders Stupenier cut a striking figure in his tailored three-piece woolen suit, gold pocket watch visible, his pomaded hair parted in the middle, monocle over left eye, his jowls fleshy and overall portliness befitting a man of great wealth and leisure. He appeared distraught, muttering to himself as he sat in one of the chairs the Gracklers had set up for them in advance. They opened with the Johnny Appleseed on a Pagoda skit they had been working on for weeks, a riff on the hobo emblem embroidered on the back of their buckskins which some thought resembled Appleseed atop such a Far Eastern tower. We meet Appleseed, played by Zeke, caught in a rainstorm in the hot fields of Central America where he is leading a legation to study the banana plant. He is still simply John Chapman and his infinite love and understanding of bananas is known only to a small circle of family and friends. Earnest and indefatigable, Chapman is hell-bent on finding species of banana plants which can be grown successfully throughout the United States. Zeke was a natural in the role of the driven young fruit seeker doomed to disappointment, but profoundly intensified the character's appeal by imposing a recurring facial tic of his mouth opening and closing involuntarily, alternating with rapid shoulder shrugging. A risky decision but by all accounts it worked, and Anders Stupenier was seen himself once or twice sampling the movements. The ruling junta's Agricultural Secretary, Raoul Mendoza (played by Lester), resplendent in yellow military uniform and a crow perched on his head, becomes increasingly frustrated in trying to convince Chapman that plantains are not suitable for Eastern Kentucky and begins jumping up and down while grunting. Chapman shrieks that he is an American citizen and demands to see the American Ambassador of Quito, claiming his human rights are being violated. Soon Ambassador Marlon Flubbleman (played by Rollo) appears to flounce about and inflame the squabble into an international incident, though at length realizes Chapman is suffering from severe nervous strain and orders confinement in a Nepalese pagoda under the care of the allergist monk Lam Luiloo (brilliantly played by Simon). It is here Chapman accepts that he will never become Johnny Bananaseed and cultivates a tolerance for apples, from which he formerly would suffer extreme pathological reactions for even so much as walking near an orchard. Lam Luiloo patiently helps him overcome his fear and soon he is downing seven or eight apples a day, and between the two of them a good fifteen to eighteen, including baked Romes. Crocked on applejack in the belfry one night, Chapman is thunderstruck with the idea to flee with thousands of Luiloo's seeds and just roam and ramble all over the states planting them like his life depended on it. But he is grabbed in Burma by a bestial thug who works special ops for Luiloo, Muck Dooka, another dark portrait by Balthazar. After a short prison sentence, Chapman confronts Luiloo in the pagoda and kicks the vile monk's ass despite his showy jujitsu moves. Chapman eventually boards a steamship in Bangkok bound stateside and we last see him drunk and seasick strewn on the deck, but we know well how the story ends as he does have his bag of seeds in his hand.

 Though he struggled to rise his ensconced ample form from his chair, Anders Stupenier gave the cast a standing ovation and bade his retinue do the same. They applauded wildly and everyone had to take multiple bows and even reprise the showstopper number in an encore, "Cold Cold Plantanos, No No Grow," and they went on to do another three songs that the plutocrat's party particularly loved: "Yes, I am Johnny Bananaseed," "Monk, Pagoda, Apple Anyone?" and "Muck Dooka and Digging Deep in the Pagoda Dustup." Afterwards, Stupenier was so exhilarated by the production he hustled his massive frame towards the stage and the Gracklers, caught off guard, worried that here comes the big man's irrational charge and they were about to take him down when he only whipped out his gold pocket watch and presented it to Zeke. Expressing appreciation, Zeke declined the offer, but Stupenier pressed and Zeke redoubled his demurral, and very quickly this in itself escalated into a heated altercation until Simon stepped in and asked aloud "how the hell did we miss the watch?" and he snatched it from the plutocrat's hand and that was that.

 The haul that night was enormous and the fish fry wing ding was the most jubilant the Gracklers had yet to throw themselves. They got drunker and nuttier and sang songs and gave exuberant speeches and wrestled one another and talked about all the fun stuff they intended to buy, which is about where Zeke had just about heard enough and now had more than a sneaking suspicion they were sandbagging his efforts to locate the RHAF. Now Zeke had himself a good snootful of whiskey and he wasn't having the stringing along anymore and he threw cold water on their mirth when he suggested in a dead serious tone that it was high time they took that goddamn loot over to the Rambling Hoboes of America Fund. There was a momentary silence and they resumed their party, ignoring him, but he only made his demand louder and reminded them why the Grackler Riders of the Reckoning came about and the altruism of their mission, that they were artists first, criminals second. He invoked the spirit and principles of the great Dieter Schrampenkrieg, whose inspiring legacy was always their abiding lodestar. They tried to stonewall and temporize as always, but that wouldn't appease Zeke this night.

 And then they were shouting and Zeke was crazy hot liquored up and he started shoving them and they pushed him back harder and in all the screaming at one another it was Lester who finally yelled in his face: "You stupid son of a bitch!! There ain't no goddamn Rambling Hoboes of America Fund!! Not here or anywhere the hell else!"

Zeke just stopped, went stock-still all of a sudden, like the truth he'd been gnawing at just clocked him on the nose. But soon enough he saw they were striking the camp and were going to move out and he made a beeline for Simon loading all the great bags of loot.

"I'll deliver that myself to the hoboes!" he yelled and was maniacally strong in his fight for the bags, but three was just too many, notwithstanding Balthazar's biting their legs drawing some blood, and they worked him over until he lost consciousness.

And when all packed the three Gracklers looked back once from their horses as Balthazar barked and barked and Simon called: "The only thing he'll be delivering is himself to a hospital, that's if he wakes up." And they let out guffaws before riding away.

SIX

WHEN ZEKE opened his eyes again it was still night, the utter blackness of forest night, and all the ache and soreness and perfidy his partners had meted out before vamoosing now came back to him in spades. It was the breadth of their bamboozlement and the depth with which he swallowed it that pained him the most, the self-reproach and sinking regret unbearable to his consciousness. He closed his eyes and slipped back into an uneasy slumber. He dreamed he lassoed Simon after a horseback chase and, seeing his head was an onion, sliced it with his shiv and made the crazy headless Grackler prepare the famous Grackler onion stew using his own erstwhile noggin. He wakened in a fit of consternation, sitting up in the gray faint dawn light, until his good pup rose from his own slumbers to lick and slobber excitedly all over his master's face. Of course it was Balthazar, his one true pal in the world, who persuaded Zeke in short order to rise and keep going despite the setback and the injuries. He was barely ambulatory, willing himself around the campsite in an excruciating halting shuffle, nipping at the bottle of whisky they forgot to take, talking to Balthazar, not knowing his next move. He shambled later that morning over to the stream past some rolling hills and beheld a gladdening sight in the equine form drinking from the burbling waters beneath the shade of a fine oak beside a gauzy field of seamilkwort and foamflower. "Scunj!" he cried as if the splendid steed had returned from the dead, and Balthazar too barked with happy recognition of seeing their old friend. They made their way to the stream and Zeke hugged and stroked the great horse and they all drank the cool pure water of their stream. "The sons of bitches had no use for an extra horse, but you could have bolted free and left me—I'm sure grateful you didn't, Scunj!" Zeke pronounced. Convalescence would be necessary before Zeke could ride on from the campsite and the time would also be useful, he thought, to plan his next course of action. Having Scunj for transportation his desire for retribution strengthened and swelled in him as he could not shake the sense of betrayal he felt over their absconding with the hoboes' rightful monies. This notion of vengeance would marinate and simmer in him over the two days he spent swimming and fishing in the stream with his puppy and horse, relaxing around the fire with his whiskey bottle, and preparing and cooking the smelts and perches he caught for the evening supper. He realized again and again how fortunate he had been to have his two animal buddies with him during this low period and that he could not have mustered the fortitude to come back without them. In the early morning of the third day Zeke, though not fully recuperated by any measure, decided it was time to leave in pursuit of the Gracklers and deliver the substantial loot himself directly to hoboes everywhere. He presented to Balthazar the corncob pipe smoked by Simon the night they split, a stick Lester had whittled and used as a backscratcher, and the dirty ripped piece of cloth Rollo plied as a napkin during the fish fry as items to implant their scent in the canine's powerful smeller. As the new day broke with a gray drizzly rawness Zeke mounted Scunj and with a fired up resolve declared: "All right, fellas, let's go find the sons of bitches who stole the hobo fund!" And off they rode into the vast forest depths, Balthazar nestled in a saddle pouch with navigational responsibilities invested in his snout, which peeped out every so often to seek his bearings.

    Into the furthest reaches of the primordial verdure galloped Zeke Borshellac on his gloriously berserk horse, a fine beast he believed to be of mythic stature, and through the narrow muddy trails he flew that first morning with an abandoned, unburdened will to root out the miscreants who swindled him into an irredeemable banditry. "Onward, Scunj! Forward we shoot until our double-crossers are overtaken and the loot is distributed the way Schrampenkrieg would!" the

SIX

lone charged-up horseman cried amidst the vast wide woodlands, a voice unheard by people. He rode wildly at a breakneck pace with hardly any letup, save for the occasional pause for sustenance such as berries and hardtack he had packed, and he began to feel as he had months earlier riding Scunj alone and searching for his partners before they became the Gracklers. Now he again grew more convinced of his tremendous stamina and power, cocksure of his newly ignited mission, of his joining forces with the singularly exceptional horse to chase down the rats who may have been long gone, but notwithstanding, soon to be in his crosshairs. By the early evening of his first day, he knew again his horse had manifested to him through his father Caleb, and here was Zeke once more becoming more and more like Caleb. The second and third days the sun was spotty and the wind howled like a spectral fury all its own and Zeke opened whiskey bottles (his own remained in Scunj's saddlebags) and thought he was going to find his father deep in those woods while he knew now how his father saw the world, that view from the tumultuous road chasing ghosts and fraudsters, that is how Zeke felt him within once again. Soused and pushing Scunj relentlessly at full pelt, he was that invincible young man who nobody could thwart from achieving the amorphous altruistic greatness still incubating in his soul, the humanitarian efforts that would improve lives and secure his place in annals of famous and sundry stalwarts. Zeke and his animals discovered hidden brooks and rivulets of pure waters and they drank and splashed during short breaks for berries and hardtack and wondrous small sea creatures consumed raw with wild tarragon leaves. He knocked back whiskey like a man lost in the desert downing water and it hardly made him drunker, only more animated, alive, impassioned for the road and payback and finding his old man inside him. He gobbled mushrooms and mint plants and a most peculiar congeries of those tiny sea creatures that he nibbled like peanuts, sprinkling them with salty clover and sprigs of dewy dill weed. The horse rode like the splendid thoroughbred of all-time Zeke understood him to be and knew the presence of his father was with him through his mad beautiful steed and the harum-scarum thunderbolt they were together. Never had he ridden so far and so fast and so dangerously, while he had also never been so in charge of his capabilities, his resources, his sense of sublime and a uniquely exquisite destiny. Cognizant that he was in pursuit of his betrayers, even if nary a whit of their trail had been caught in Balthazar's nose, Zeke was very pleased that he was not the one being chased this time, not fleeing from the ship or the burning house or anything else.

He rode for days now, climbing lost hills of stark beauty luxuriant with riotous vegetation and spread thick with a rococo explosion of wildflowers like the rosemallow, broadleaf cattail, and yellow bell, and with a sneaking joy he swigged whiskey and assured Balthazar every so often when he stuck up his head with a sheepish look that he did not blame him for their being so far afield, their prey simply got too good a jump. As the drizzle started and swept over them in the gray bluster that persisted in those hills a reassessment insinuated itself in Zeke's mind about who was truly being chased, or fleeing, and he recognized in himself the revulsion of his resorting to the use of force, the threatened violence as a Grackler in their theater antics. And he was running away from that fiasco to begin anew and find the connections, the right individuals to turn him around and beat down the loneliness bedeviling him. It rained harder as he came down a rocky hill littered with charred trees and the ashen acridity was thick in the air and Zeke pressed forward, leaning on the whiskey more, as now Caleb Borshellac appeared to his thoughts as the flesh and blood flawed father he barely remembered. The image on the horse he had formed of him from the blurry fragments of memory was one of the hell-bent lone brilliant equestrian on a secret mission of monumental importance tragically marred by mysterious drunken demons within. But the more limpid image emerging drew a stark contrast with the boozing force of nature and at first it shook and disturbed Zeke and he wanted to avert it, halt and dismount Scunj as if the fierce horse was carrying him into some brutal truth. His mind's eye had preserved and enhanced the simulacrum of Caleb, the fervid wild horseman riding into the abyss of dark human deficiencies with an eye to rally and exhort those not yet doomed to hold on and fight it with every fiber of their teetering beings. But how in heaven did the son come to ascribe to such a stirringly sanguine idea of the fragmentary father from so long ago? How did he and what was the motive for such semiconscious crafting of a potent figure, or perhaps the archetype the son desperately sought? Such searing inquisitions Zeke impaled himself with and he swallowed it down with whiskey as the rain whipped against his face. He incrementally suspected over time, in the penumbra of his deliberations, that his father's departure from him and his mother at the tavern had little to do with his rancor at his mother's licentiousness. He remembered the fear, the palpable fear of his youth towards the leviathan of beastly terror, the original Scunj, the ungodly freakish prototype with fireball eyes that his father rode through remote woodland nights with reckless frenzy, and Caleb, drunk and raging would come for his boy sleeping in the hayloft and gather him up on the horse and together they'd charge with breakneck fury into the mad dread of the gaping forest blackness. And several times father and son were thrown to the earth, the bush, as if daring the violent bronco to kill them, and the father bestowed the crazed bronco pony Jockamo Chop Chop upon his son and it immediately seemed bent on murdering the boy and finally threw him so hard and far that he landed in that irrigation tank where young Zeke spent three days struggling not to drown, screaming to no avail for his father to help. Zeke stewed on the horror of his near death in that tank and the flimsy apotheosis of his father he had constructed through the years, and he realized now tearing through the muck and soak of thick vast forest atop Scunj II that he was searching for his father all that time in the assiduous assemblage of proper imagery. And the emulation began when the second Scunj manifested, the self-assured sense of grandeur, the booze-fueled cryptic mission of magnanimity, the relentless interminable quest for purpose when such putative noble chasing of his father's really was daunted and dismayed retreat, running away from the most elemental of responsibilities in the taking care of one's family as Caleb rode wilder and deeper, howled louder in the woods, drunker and more tolerant of his own violence, he could not escape this unforgiving cold reality that tortured him at some unknown level. Zeke saw in the dense black forest trails that he can never find his father and it was his mother, perhaps a tavern wench, but also the loving protective mother who did all she could to afford him a semblance of a home and rearing to grow into the man he became and not succumb altogether to depravity and dark atavistic tendencies to survive. Zeke stared squarely into his fears and trepidations and vowed not to slide again into a murky compromise of ideals where violence, or the menace of its fist, can be deemed useful if deployed for virtuous and righteous ends. Zeke Borshellac swigged whiskey and made up a song about working hard as hell with all he's got to ameliorate and improve the human condition for the folks who have nothing in this world, the poor, the simple, the downtrodden and working common people who never make enough no matter how much their hands and feet ache and bleed with toil, yes, Zeke sang out with all the voice he had into the wet black forest as the mad beast below him charged like a bolt of apocalyptic lightning and he let out an ebullient howl of conviction that one day his voice and his song would be heard by lots and lots of folks cause he was in this all the way for the long haul to effect lasting change, or bust.

  Another week went by in his far-flung forest pursuit of the Gracklers and the hobo loot and Zeke, culminating a long craggy descent through increasingly thick, overgrown vegetation and towering tight trees, suddenly debouched into boggy lowlands of a sprawling delta region. Patches of marsh and mud spread out everywhere from the easy river rolling into a flat murky horizon, dense bulrushes and endless stretches of tall cattails dotting the landscape in all directions. A meager block of buildings suggested a trace of a town in the distance and Zeke steered Scunj that way through the sludgy silt and gratefully found one of the places to be an old ramshackle dive called Juke's. He tied Scunj to a post off the worn wooden sidewalk and left Balthazar in his saddlebag as he pushed through the creaky swinging doors to the darkness of the bar he had little hope of being open. All seemed desolate here in the lost delta he stumbled across, but the small chance of

SIX

a cold beer and talking to someone drove him against the odds. Stale beer and tobacco smells overcame him as he groped in the dark contours where he caught some fading afternoon light from a window to locate the long woody bar.

A raspy voice barked from a dark corner: "What'll it be, feller?" A roly-poly barkeep with a stubby stogie in his mouth and a broken bulbous nose appeared, shambling over to glare at the stranger.

"A tall beer," Zeke ordered with satisfaction, only now noticing he was not the only patron of the dingy joint. A dim figure sat on a stool to his left, a man hunched over a drink and smoking, and he now sensed he was being watched by him. A curious number played lowly from the darkness, possibly a march by Sousa, Zeke thought.

"Not many folks coming through these parts here, eh?" he said to the bartender, who was washing some glasses. "I mean, any chance you recall three riders in buckskins and top hats stopping in recently?"

The bartender puffed on his stogie and shook his head. "Ain't seen no jaboneys rigged out like that."

Zeke watched with anticipation as he poured his beer and set it on the counter before him. He let it settle and took a sip and withdrew into his beer introspection, trying to fend off the sense of futility in his search. He began to peer to his left, recalling there was another patron at the bar and after hesitating for a while he called out to the man, asking whether he'd seen the three riders.

Roused from his own musings, the shadowy figure answered with a tinge of petulance. "No," he returned, "but what if I had? What about 'em?"

Zeke thought that was a forward inquiry for the stranger to sling back. "I'm looking for them, that's all." Zeke sipped his beer and stared at it.

The stranger soon rose and sauntered towards his interrogator with his boilermaker and cigarillo in hand and gazed intensely at him for a good while before saying: "A loner out beating the bushes trying to locate three riders usually means he's looking to kill 'em," he said matter-of-factly.

"I'm no killer, mister."

"No, I suppose you're not, especially since I think I know who you are."

Zeke was now dumbfounded and really scrutinized the stranger, who he could now see was wearing a garish plaid suit, turquoise ascot and a white cornflower on his lapel. He was a foppish fellow with a severe bearing about him, a slim but substantial presence who moved in slow deliberate increments which made those around him wonder about his arrogance and cunning.

"You're the gee who burned down Ma Moody's house," the stranger said. "Ain't ya?"

Zeke didn't care for the query and shook his head. "What if I had? What about it?" he rejoined in kind.

"Two fellers who supervised you worked for me. They'd report on the demolition job you were doing down at The Jolly Roger. They told me you busted your ass back there." The stranger visited his boilermaker and dragged on his cigarillo.

"Who are you?" was all Zeke could ask.

"You never saw me, but I watched you one time swinging that sledgehammer like a maniac. You had something in that, a raging . . . crescendo." He paused in reflection. "The name's Stu Leapers."

Zeke was wary of his blandishment in as much as the house burned to the ground and anyone connected to Ma Moody could not have been satisfied with his work. "It was never my intent to destroy that house," he said defensively.

"Well, it is all a matter of the perspective one sees it from," Leapers explained.

"I bet Ma Moody wasn't too pleased from her perspective, and she's in charge which is what matters," Zeke opined.

Leapers puffed on his little cigar and appeared to be gathering his words as he sat in the stool beside Zeke. He now met his eyes as he spoke: "Nothing matters as much as you think it might. You'll find that out as you get older and you find out some of the people you thought

SIX

were your friends all those years really weren't. Better to learn this while you're young."

A sullen sense came over Zeke as he realized he really had no friends, unless you included Balt and Scunj, and the piece of sagacity Leapers gave him did not help insofar as he couldn't lose what he didn't have.

"So you're saying Ma Moody didn't care that I burned her house down?" he shot exasperatedly.

"Just the opposite. She cared a lot, but many of us not so agreeable to her establishing a gambling house out there were quite gratified by your handiwork."

Zeke took a gulp of beer, almost finishing it, and turned towards the door as he thought of his dog and horse. "Well, Mr. Leapers, it was good talking to you, but I am going to have to push on." He drained the last ounces and rose as Leapers uttered words that now caught his attention.

"These three guys you're looking for, in the top hats and buckskins . . . I may be able to help you there."

Zeke held his gaze now and sat back in his stool when Leapers motioned him to do so. "You've seen them? Where?"

Leapers smiled slightly with a pleased countenance. "Not me, the man I work for would know if they came through these parts."

Zeke asked if he can talk with him and Leapers grinned at such eagerness, glad he could accommodate such a palaver so important to the younger man. "Can I inquire why you may be searching with such intensity and fervor for these three men?" he put to him quizzically.

Zeke recounted for the hardnosed dandy how he fell in with a couple of tinhorn highwaymen and a lunatic onion farmer and formed the singular Simon Grackler Riders of the Reckoning, and how their artistry and banditry blended together superbly until he discovered his partners had duped him and the money was never intended to go to the Rambling Hoboes of America Fund cause there wasn't one and these Gracklers were just a bunch of crooks. "They busted me up pretty good and left me for dead, riding off with the loot," he concluded.

"You rode with the Gracklers?" Leapers asked with incredulity when Zeke finished. Zeke nodded and Leapers had to digest this information. "They're quite notorious. And you're tracking them down to deliver the loot to the hoboes? Is that right?"

Zeke nodded. "So could I talk to this man who could help me?"

Leapers smiled again and met his eye before jotting an address on a torn piece of paper he found in his pocket. "Come by tonight around eight. I'll introduce you to Mr. Flanoosler. Most people know him as The Moravian."

Zeke remembered Crimcastle and O'Connell talking about him. "Sure," he said.

While apprehensive about associating again with those who knew him as a demolitionist, Zeke was hopeful the Moravian would lead him to the Gracklers and he spent the rest of the day relaxing with Scunj and Balthazar and cooking over a campfire a medley of small sea creatures he pulled out of the delta waters. As the shank of the evening saw the remnant of light dwindle into a smoky swirl, Zeke came trotting on Scunj down a narrow dirt lane past vacant lots strewn with nameless piles and overgrown with vegetation, continuing by faceless stone buildings and a smokestack factory blackened by soot until a modest brick structure well-receded from the lane appeared on the left. "That must be it," Zeke said, and Balthazar's snout shot out of his saddle pouch and he began barking at the place. It was the business headquarters of the man they had come see and very quickly Zeke was sitting at long wooden table in a room with a shuttered window and a glass of whiskey in front of him and Stu Leapers and Fent Flanoosler, the Moravian himself, across from him. There were other characters Zeke glimpsed flitting about other rooms, preoccupied in their tasks. After the introductions Leapers began: "Mr. Flanoosler was very taken with your catching on with the Gracklers, Zeke."

The Moravian was a middle-aged, olive-skinned, short compact man, barrel-chested with a thick neck and thinning, greased-back graying hair. He wore a shiny sharkskin sports coat with comically wide lapels and a button down polka-dot silk shirt with the letter M embroidered on both sides of the collar. With a glint of amusement he remarked: "Like everybody else, I enjoyed the stories in the newspapers. I never thought the same kid who burned down the Moody house was one of those Grackler screwballs." He chuckled and then grunted abruptly as if to focus himself. "So Stu tells me they conned you before lowering the boom with the backstab. So you want the rat bastards, understandable. I'm going to level with you, kid. I don't know where they are, no idea. But my team is real good at locating rat bastards like these."

Zeke interjected now: "I can't pay you or nothing, Mr. Fanoosler. I'm just about broke."

The Moravian smiled and waved his arm dismissively. "Don't even think about any sort of remuneration. As far as I'm concerned, the work you did on the Moody house makes you part of our crew already, trustworthy, capable, resourceful. A young fellow with your abilities and experience riding with the Gracklers is the sort of individual I want to offer an opportunity in my business."

Zeke was intrigued by the Moravian's confidence in finding his double-crossers, but equally circumspect of his motive to obtain him as an employee. "If I can speak frankly, Mr. Fanoosler, I appreciate the overture but my days on the dark edges with Ma Moody and the whole Bluddenville dog-eat-dog depravity . . . well, I figured those days were long behind me. I want to make the world better for those that need help most, like the hoboes. Shoot, I'm almost a damn hobo myself." He swigged his whiskey and looked around. "I don't think I can do much along those lines around here."

The Moravian glanced at Leapers and drained his glass of whiskey before slamming it down. "I must take issue with you there, Zeke. Bluddenville is often regarded as a bad place brimming with lost souls and heartless gonophs but is that not the territory one can strive to lift the poor sons of bitches?! I know we do here with my crew. Most folks don't know the eleemosynary element to the Moravian. I don't go broadcasting the kind of alms we kick in to the destitute but rest assured Zeke you will immediately be assigned to our charitable contributions collections."

They kept talking and Zeke soon thought it all sounded good, but a dissonant undercurrent to the position being offered would not leave him alone. "So . . . you're not affiliated with Ma Moody no more then, or were you in the first place? Cause she's going to have her goons haul me into her as soon as they know I'm back. Here he is, the torch who burned your house down, Ma."

The Moravian chuckled and sipped and became animated: "She's got her little turf down by the wharves and we left the sea hag alone until she tried to build that gambling palace out here. But you sure took care of that problem. Her cretins will know that you're working for me, and they will lay off you. Ma Moody is a degenerate old bitch who only trucks in fear and turpitude, while we are the ones who do good and dole out a largess for the needy. And we can aid the hoboes together Zeke."

They talked about hoboes and the hard rambling lives they lead and how it was incumbent on citizens to throw themselves into boosting their prospects of finding jobs and becoming productive and fulfilled. They drank a lot of whiskey and Leapers then had a contract out for Zeke to ink up enlisting him as a rookie in the Moravian's enterprise to improve everything in the world, including hoboes' existence.

They were about to propose a toast with glasses raised when Leapers interjected an offhand remark. "I know a couple of hoboes who love being railbirds roaming all over and cooking beans over a fire in the jungle while getting good and liquored up. You don't want to be helping them out too much, cause they revel in the hobo life."

They all agreed on this point, that some hoboes ought to be left alone and not patronized with overwrought attention, and they first toasted them but after some deliberation decided to toast all the other hoboes too.

Zeke woke up in bed not knowing where the hell he was but was grateful to find Balthazar snuggled up beside him snoozing in heavy breaths, though the one-room musty old shack surrounding them was resoundingly alien. Still clothed, he scrambled up and dashed outside to a sunny daybreak and several clotheslines stretched at various angles around him with great white cotton sheets hanging by wooden clothespins swaying in a gentle breeze. And then he saw Scunj chewing on hay near a water trough and hurried over to him.

A lanky young fellow in a stiff blue shirt and vest and a trilby hat appeared to introduce himself as Andy, a sort of jack-of-all-trades employed by the Moravian. "He told me to check on you back here, Zeke. They're letting you stay in the shack for now, since it's close to the Moravian's building. After you get some grub they're going to show you the ropes."

Andy led Zeke and Balthazar to the back door of the Moravian's building which opened to a tidy kitchen where the Moravian, Leapers, and Cal Crimcastle sat around a worn wooden table with cups of piping hot joe and the delectable aromas of eggs, bacon and warm cornbread swirling everywhere. A pudgy Samoan man in a khaki tropical suit was busy at the stove cooking the breakfast and Zeke saw him flip some eggs with a nimble flourish that suggested the fellow was a first-rate grub slinger. The Moravian bade Zeke sit at the one empty chair and told Poco, the cook, to "pour our pal some java." Zeke began to ask about his winding up in the shack and the Moravian cut him off: "Hooch and fatigue delivered you to the Sandman, Zeke. You needed a bunk."

Crimcastle gave his old demolitionist a genial hello. "You busted that dump up, kid, you swung that hammer like nobody's business!" he called with fond recollection.

Poco served them a sumptuous breakfast and Zeke hadn't eaten so well in months, and a plate of meat was laid on the floor for Balthazar. "Hey, where's the guy with the red hair you were always with?"

"O'Connell?" Crimcastle replied. "He moved away."

They ate in silence a while, only the sounds of knives and forks and munching and slurping until Zeke asked: "Where'd he move?"

Crimcastle snickered and glanced at Leapers before answering: "Chattanooga. He's got a broad there."

Leapers now began reading the baseball scores from the morning paper and the others listened intently, the Moravian banging the table when the Athletics lost and Crimcastle swearing when the Braves won and Zeke remarked that they were "true blue fans all right!"

"It's a game of analysis, odds, kid," Crimcastle snapped.

The Moravian glared at his blurt and Leapers veered the talk into the art of bunting and being a contact hitter and good pitching beats good hitting until the Moravian finished his last bite and placed his coffee cup down firmly and said: "Today Zeke you're going to learn how to make the rounds, collecting."

Zeke was still savoring his breakfast and he nodded as he chewed and speared a piece of egg with his fork. The Moravian became very sober as he folded his hands on the table and held Zeke's eye. "These are people who own businesses and have expressed a desire to donate to the poor, or more precisely, the hoboes. But they have since wavered on their commitment."

Crimcastle chortled and interjected: "Reneged on their pledges."

The Moravian liked Crim's modification and said, yes, we can call it that. "What we have to remember is that these good folks want to contribute to our fine cause but they develop cold feet . . . maybe doubts about the charity, or cynicism in general, or maybe they sense something amiss about you, the solicitor, as unsteady and shady . . . well, Zeke, you want them do right by themselves, the hoboes, and you . . . the latter is most important because to close the deal you must project confidence and strength and they must almost fear you, because you are the truth teller."

Zeke now seemed somewhat confused. "If they fear me they won't contribute though," he demurred.

Leapers cut in: "Zeke, listen, fear may be too strong of a word, but you have to let them know a pledge is a pledge and they owe it to the righteous sides of their characters to follow through on the commitment to the cause."

Zeke thought about this for a while and nodded. "But what if they are short on dough? Can they donate some other time?"

SIX

Crimcastle glanced at his associates and said: "Are they going to give that crock of an excuse to the hoboes? Look, these folks have the money but tend to be tight with it. Your job is to ensure they stay on board with the almsgiving."

Zeke sipped more coffee and thought some more about this new job and said: "So, I'm thinking I could offer them some real stories of hardship and despair hoboes endure every day riding the rails. I can spend time with hoboes . . ."

The Moravian now spoke with a peremptory authority. "No, you don't need to do any of that, Zeke. We've done all the ground work on this and communicated it all to the business owners. They know the dire need for their donations out there. You'd only be gilding the lily and frankly that may be construed as offensive to these folks, who are our partners in the end. You just need to be no nonsense about their honoring their pledges and show them you mean business about enabling their beneficent sides to emerge . . . because they deserve to feel right about themselves . . . and people are depending on them."

Zeke recapitulated: "I'm reminding them of the largesse due, which they ought to pony up for their own good because being a noble and responsible citizen requires they do not forget the lost souls riding the rails in boxcars all across the plains!"

The Moravian squinted and nodded slightly. "Well, yeah, that's good . . . a good start. You don't want to bring in the boxcars and all that cause we did that already. Be more succinct and make it about them. They could be the lost souls if they don't make good on their payments."

Zeke tried to process this approach and the Moravian said: "Stu and Crim will work with you on this and soon enough you'll be ready to make the rounds, Zeke."

And they took him to The Jolly Roger for whiskey, cigars, and long skull sessions in which the older men schooled their protégé in the age-old science of putting the squeeze on merchants without any rigmarole, just simple straight collection. They told him what to say and how to say it, the importance of being terse and serious, and appealing to their better senses to do what's right for themselves or there would be consequences (heavy consciences, Zeke understood, though he needn't say this). He had doubts about Crimcastle after the Moody house fire episode, but he seemed to like Zeke and care about his learning the job, and Leapers was very supportive and made him feel wanted and a welcome asset to their program. Mostly, Zeke was very excited to have found likeminded folks with humanitarian bents in an established system built to raise funding for the hoboes. After several whiskeys and a barrage of lessons, Zeke left their table to visit the men's room and Leapers and Crimcastle spoke frankly about the potential of their new pupil. "The kid is a godsend once again, Crim!" Leapers remarked with an admiring smile. "When he walked into Slaughter's old dive, I knew it instantly. He's the earnest rube who'll be busting his hump for us cause of the largest angle he's buying."

Crimcastle laughed and lit a cigarette and took a deep drag. "Hey, I saw the guy swing that hammer! He's all business when he wants to be, and when these stiffs who've been pushing back on our payments get a load of his hopped-up intensity . . . let me tell you, they will fall in line. Once he lets it slip he's with the Moravian, they'll crack fast."

They shared a good guffaw. "He's got a psycho look when he gets worked up," Leapers added, "they'll be paying him for protection from his own dark side." After a minute he added: "The guy sure gets worked up over his hoboes."

They sent him at first to a few businesses located in a lonely section of Bluddenville out near the Skinny Old Otter River where the woodland edge is impenetrable, as here were the corn grist mill, the lumber mill, the blacksmith shop, the sugar factory, the tannery, and the dry goods store. No longer was Zeke attired as a Grackler, though he packed his top hat in a saddlebag, now the serious young man of the Moravian's wore a simple black suit and shiny brogans. He rode Scunj and left Balthazar back at the shack to roam as he pleased now, insomuch as he'd been outgrowing his horse pouch and Zeke had to acknowledge albeit wistfully, he was not a puppy any more but a young dog. I. C. Pekoe's Dry Goods became Zeke's first collection visit and as

SIX

he tied Scunj's line around a rail he felt confident and very ready to begin his work making a difference for those souls who needed aid.

No one noticed him as he entered and traversed the noisy floorboards, as a few customers, one a matronly lady in a pillbox hat, went about their fabric searches amid the long aisles. He strode to a register on the side and asked the bespectacled fellow with a protruding Adam's apple if he could have a word with the proprietor, a Mr. Isaiah Canterbury Pekoe, on a matter of most importance, and such a meeting was hastily arranged in an isolated sector of the floor. Mr. Pekoe was a large stout man with long white whiskers growing wild from his upper lip and a twinkle in his weary smile. He seemed distracted by other concerns when a clerk brought him over to the strange young fellow awaiting him. "Well, I'm told you have some business with me," he said good-naturedly, sliding each of his thumbs under his suspenders.

"Yes, sir, I do. That I do," Zeke stated without elaborating.

"And just what might that be?"

Zeke paused before breathing deeply and looking Pekoe in the eye. "I've come to remind you, sir, of a pledge you made to honor your commitments to a better life. I can tell you with utter conviction that evading what you know to be the right thing to do will have serious consequences for you at some juncture. A bad conscience can lead to serious sickness you know."

Pekoe wasn't smiling anymore and rubbed his chin in studying Zeke's mien. "Just what are you driving at, young Turk? I think I know, but let's be frank here."

Zeke remembered his training. "You've fallen behind in your contributions. These are hard times filled with desperate folks who depend on you. No telling what they might do."

"Are you threatening me, young fellow? I'll call a copper in, I will!"

Zeke squinched his eyes and recoiled. "Threaten you? Dear sir, I would never, unless the warning I pass along from my own experience is construed as such, that to live a selfish life without altruism is the most baneful path to one's own health a person can take."

Pekoe stared at the peculiar fellow lecturing him about good deeds enriching one's well-being and seemed utterly dumbfounded.

"You aren't with the sea hag's gang, are you, son?" he asked just to make sure.

"No, sir. I work for a good man known as the Moravian, who is dedicated to the welfare of our donors."

Pekoe let out a knowing chortle. "So the other one's moving in on the hag's territory."

"The Moravian wants you to know your generosity will be rewarded." He pumped his fist against his own chest. "Right in here, you'll feel it."

Isaiah Canterbury Pekoe hesitated in deep reflection and by the grave look upon his features he was not feeling it inside yet. He bade his interloper wait while he disappeared in the back for a while, only to come slowly shuffling back with an envelope he handed over with a dazed resignation.

Buoyed by his maiden collection, Zeke tucked away his haul and strode down to Thuckleman's Sugar Factory to see what hobo funds he could shake out of these parsimonious renegers. Into the small front office he came seeking Rolando Thuckleman, the proprietor known in the region as a crusty oddball skinflint who rode roughshod over his factory workers and was an uncanny player of faro who often wagered sizable stakes on his skill and rarely lost. Zeke was hardly noticed as he walked into the front office of the large sugar refinery with frenetic sweaty men slaving over paperwork at worn old desks, most of them haggard and bespectacled, all wearing white shirts with rolled up sleeves, loosened indigo ties dotted with lumps of sugar designs, and all were smoking tobacco in various forms, several even exhibiting unusually long clay pipes. The men were too engrossed in their work to attend to a visitor and there were a couple of ladies who Zeke thought might be secretaries, as they were attired in dresses and the like, but they too had their own agenda of hosting a rather baffling tea party for three long-bearded fellows who turned out to be naval engineers from the Rhine Valley in Thuringia. At length, Zeke inquired of

SIX

a lanky old-timer in overalls and a news cap mopping up some sweet-sickening reeking glop that spilled near the coffee area and was told to look for the one "with the great belly and greasy pompadour and deep voice snapping at everybody like a rabid animal." He soon found himself lost in a maze of narrow dusty corridors lined with frosted glass doors and engraved department titles such as Finance, Advertising, Pest Control, Psychological Counseling, Stationery, Porter, Nurse, and Sundry Ephemera. He gently knocked on a few doors and turning a few doorknobs found them bolted shut, but a smattering of murmuring voices were heard inside the one marked Indian Clubs and Kites, confused, anxious voices punctuated by groans of pain.

"Mr. Thuckleman!" called Zeke. "I must have a word with you, sir." Only ripples of laughter were returned. "I say it is rather urgent, Mr. Thuckleman! I come with a message of selfless dedication to ameliorating the lives of those who suffer." Suddenly the door swung open and a muscle man in an elastic tank-topped jump suit and sporting a handlebar mustache stood staring at Zeke, while a class of eight or nine corpulent sorts were in rows performing sophisticated synchronized movements with the Indian Clubs.

"I am not Thuckleman," the muscle man stated, "and if I were I would not deign to respond to anything you have to say to me." Zeke found this fellow quite obnoxious, yet in his way amusing with such gratuitous contumely. As the well-built figure closed the door slowly in his face Zeke heard footsteps somewhere in the corridor and a shrill unintelligible stream of words redolent of a soliloquist in a histrionic drama chockablock in anguish. Zeke thought that the shadowy figure could be Thuckleman and he hurried back through the corridors wanting very much to square up with the man so known for being loathed and deplored as an employer of exploited Sugar Factory workers. He stumbled onto the vast floor where the massive heaps of raw sugar were alchemized and refined into fine particles ready to be packed in great heavy burlap sacks and delivered to merchants near and far. Then Zeke heard an angry voice lambasting a group of vat men as they struggled with a monstrous slab of sugar canes, attacking it from several angles with giant pitchfork implements to no avail. "Bend your legs, Schmecker! Throw your body into the cane, man! We are not goldbricking here, are we Schmecker?" Now Zeke watched the gangly, shaggy-haired fellow Schmecker look quite indignant, shaking his head in disgust, even shrugging with his palms up as if to ask: "I am stunned by your vile query."

Zeke approached the vituperative man of authority, noting the great belly and flowing beard and understood that here was the owner who needed to be straightened out and brought to heel on the promised contributions. He introduced himself simply, asking if he could have a word with him. The sugar boss stopped for a moment to take full measure of the impudent stranger. "I've come here Mr. Thuckleman to remind you, for your own good, of your pledge to make regular payments as a means of support for the bedeviled souls who suffer, while at the same time protecting yourself from a guilty conscience."

Thuckleman suddenly burst into guffaws after listening closely to Zeke. "Where in hell did Moody and her thugs dig up the likes of you?!" he put to him, still chuckling.

Zeke was disconcerted by the association again. "I don't work for Ma Moody," he corrected.

"What, did the sea hag finally croak?"

"I don't believe so," Zeke said.

"I certainly hope not," he went on, "but I work for a fellow known as the Moravian."

Thuckleman contemplated this piece of information with a dour countenance. He folded his arms across his chest, massive belly supporting them. "So they are going to fight over who collects my envelope!?" he cried. "Tell them I will not succumb to coercion, young man. You will have to kill me."

Zeke chuckled and reassured: "It is only a contribution and you owe it to yourself to make good on it so you can reap the benefits of magnanimity and be healthier in body and spirit, Mr. Thuckleman."

SIX

This provoked Thuckleman more and he began yelling. "You can't buffalo me, goon! I've had it with you wharf rats trying to suck the blood of hard-working people like me!"

Zeke was quite taken aback by his ire, which burgeoned into potential violence as he started backing up Zeke with his belly. Nobody in the plant took much notice, as Zeke saw them all hustling about their duties and they were probably used to their surly boss yelling. "I'm going to intimidate you, goon boy! How 'bout that, eh?" he yelled, charging with his huge gut.

"You can't ignore the forlorn souls who ride the lonely rails in the night," Zeke countered.

Thuckleman now unleashed a haymaker that Zeke ducked, and he instinctually returned a hard blow to the sugar boss's belly that doubled him over and dropped him to the floor. He lay sprawled on his swollen midsection for several stock-still seconds before slowly moving his extremities in efforts to rise, though these struggles failed, and he was only successful in turning himself over to rest on his buttocks. Others, plant managers and a burly foreman arrived now to aid their loathed leader, but Thuckleman cursed their scarce presence when it was needed. "Here I am being beaten by a gangster goon and you chowderheads are pulling your puds somewhere!" When they now began towards Zeke, Thuckleman waved them off, declaring: "Leave the goon be! He's with the nor'siders, who are taking on the sea hag."

"You have me all wrong, Mr. Thuckleman," Zeke protested, "I am only interested in the succor sought by those broken by hardship who cross the moonlit plains in boxcars."

"The guy's a screwball prattling about train rides in moonlight! Hey pal, the cuckoo act is bugging me now, so let's just stick to business here." His aides helped him to his feet and he huddled with his team for a few moments, upbraiding them for all of the company's recent setbacks and concluding with: "Give this son of a bitch his envelope and get him out of my sight!"

The plant manager who lit up a long clay pipe during all this now asked what they all were thinking: "You are going to knuckle under to them, just like that?"

Thuckleman smirked and snapped: "Good question for a knucklehead, who would know all about knuckling under. Well, I am doing no such thing. The payments will be coming directly out of your paychecks as a necessary overhead." And so the Thuckleman Sugar House was thusly brought to heel and the encounter with Rolando Thuckleman was bruited and embellished upon throughout Bluddenville until folks were saying a Moravian goon pistol-whipped and stomped old Thuckleman into a comatose state, adding the insult of shaving off his beard and forcing him to eat it upon awakening. That Thuckleman never lost his beard did little to offset this scuttlebutt, explicated simply that the beard the sugar boss now wore was fake, and this unshakeable view of his beard bothered him more than anything else about the ordeal and he would frequently entreat folks to tug on his "sterling whiskers" to demonstrate their authenticity.

Seven

IN A FEW SHORT WEEKS Zeke had established himself in the rough-and-tumble old harbor burg as a fierce enforcer without both oars in the water and a brutal goon not to be dismissed if one valued one's well-being. And Zeke himself felt quite gratified in his new work, sanguine that he was finding his stride in eliciting funds for hobo relief and persuasively communicating the personal benefits his donors would derive from their charitable largesse. In those initial weeks Zeke had the entire Skinny Old Otter River section of Bluddenville and all the businesses operating along the woodland perimeter toeing the line with their regular payments, and he already brought his unflappable persistence and remarkable brand of idealism to several staple companies situated closer to the main hub of the seaport downtown. These included the tobacconist, the cooper, the teamster stables, the icehouse, the new construction builders, the apothecary, the luncheonette, the chophouse, and work clothing outfitters. Zeke truly believed he had found his natural calling now, so confident and enthusiastic he was in his early successes and renewed faith in the beneficence and humanitarianism of his fellow citizens. "It has been amply demonstrated that people do care about the hardship and distress so many others must face every day, and when you beseech them to help the cause they do respond with generous contributions," he asserted in a toast one evening dining with the Moravian, Crimcastle, and Leapers, a trio of associates who could not be more pleased with their unorthodox hiring of an outsider like Borshellac, someone not so acquainted with the niceties of their organization.

"Yes, Zeke," the grinning Moravian concurred after sipping his glass of Bordeaux, "the innate goodness of individuals, people who make up our society, is a core truth we believe in and is why we prosper in our efforts and makes all the work worthwhile." He shared knowing smiles and chuckles with Crim and Leapers before saluting Zeke as "a good man and a great asset to our enterprise!"

Zeke became a tad sentimental in considering his good fortune to have come across Stu Leapers and being introduced to the Moravian's group of fund raisers for good causes like the hoboes. "I found you and my faith in people is restored. I feel like you are my brothers in solidarity fighting for the trampled spirits of the night. After the debacle of the non-existent RHAF we are reaping some big donations from the merchants, and soon we'll have to present the whole haul of a caboodle to hoboes."

The Moravian glanced at Crimcastle, who snuck a look at Leapers, who now offered some idea of their plan to present the funds to a wise old hobo and his relief agency called Ridin' the Rails with Bread and Soup (RRBS). Leapers said they would deliver all the moolah they collected to this noble hobo called Rufus the Jungle Earl, but they had to wait until he returned from a visit to the Arctic in a couple months.

"There's nobody else who works with Rufus we could give the dough to?" Zeke asked, confused by the delay. They said no, it would be better if they waited for Rufus, and he'll bring back pounds of blubber they could roast over a camp fire and the celebration could be something special. Zeke understood this, albeit he was not happy about it and worried about all that cash sitting in their safe, impenetrable as it seemed.

The whole business began to gnaw at Zeke and he thought of a notion one day to address matters head on. He had a banner morning soliciting generous bundles of alms from a variety of shops and firms, including the cheesemakers, the cobblers, the opticians, the sweet shop, the lumber yard, the wainwright, the notary public, the pawn shop, and the taxidermist, and, well, Zeke began to exult in his newfound capability to draw donations and command the respect and fear (of disappointing him, he thought) from so many proprietors. He believed he was hitting his stride, coming into his own in the field of fundraising for fine causes, and after an afternoon collecting at several old nautical dive bars, including The Jolly Roger, where Zeke wet his whistle with celebratory gusto, he decided he wanted to experience some direct interaction doling out some of his tidy sums of capital. It was still only the waning afternoon when he wended his way to his shack to ply his beloved sheepdog with salted meat and mount Scunj to go galloping through the Bluddenville streets and into the woods in search of the lost hobo jungle, the one he remembered stumbling upon by the hobo tavern way back when looking for the Gracklers, before they became the Gracklers. But after charging through woodland paths winding into denser and increasingly darker forest Zeke became bewildered by his surroundings and found himself utterly lost. He raced with an urgency to the highest elevation of a hill to see if he could attain his bearings, but soon found the raging rapids and rocky stretches too daunting to traverse and so began to start back to Bluddenville. Only the crepuscular descent of a spent day was well under way by now and the lost horseman penetrated into a deeper forgotten recess of the gaping woods. Zeke's consternation and overall fretfulness only grew as it seemed he would be engulfed in wooded blackness all night until he picked up a tiny distant light and began riding towards it. As he traced a long decline of a trail it proved to be fortuitous in delivering him back to the tavern he patronized many months earlier with Scunj, still the lone establishment down by the river hub to show signs of life.

As he did all those months ago, Zeke tied Scunj's line to a wooden post, promised the thirsty steed a growler of cold beer, and pushed through the swinging doors of the old saloon to hear his footsteps on the tired floorboards in the dingy, cavernous place. He made out the shadowy forms of solitary hoboes sitting quietly at tables with pints of beer and he recalled the kind accommodation of the bartender in welcoming hoboes to spend evenings nursing a beer in the serenity of the venerable old tavern. Zeke noted there were more this time around, at least double as the room was packed, and a contingent of dwarves were present again, four in brightly checked suits engrossed in backgammon with sullen expressions and large cigars stuck in their mouths creating clouds of smoke around them.

The bartender, bulky, pasty, handlebar-mustachioed, remembered Zeke from his lone visit to the tavern and greeted him with his growly laugh and hearty welcome. "So you have come back to our end of the earth! I am not so surprised, friend. The hobo brethren never forgot you."

Zeke bellied up to the ancient wooden counter with one foot resting on the bar beneath and returned: "Nor have I forgot them, good barkeep! I am a kindred spirit, if not exactly one of them, and the forsaken nature of your location reflects the sensibility of the existential quandary dogging me wherever I go."

The rough-hewn bartender finished drawing a draught in a large mug and sent it sliding to his old customer. "I recall you favor brew," he added with twisted sort of smile.

"Yes, beer it is," Zeke affirmed, "and I haven't forgotten you staked me a growler or two last time." He plunked down a bunch of sizable bills and the barkeep regarded it with confusion.

"That was my treat, friend, and this is far too much regardless."

Zeke smiled at the barkeep's generosity and glanced at the room of solitary hoboes. "Please accept it as my gratitude for your kindness and send a round to everyone too." As Zeke carried growlers for him and his horse outside the bartender announced the beer he bought for his crowd and they let out an odd hobo cheer, a maundered snarl of some arcane significance.

Outside Zeke leaned against a rail quaffing his bucket and assisting Scunj in lapping up his own sudsy delight. The dirt road was desolate and lambent with gaslight lanterns lining it, the sun had recently set leaving a lingering gray mist of the dying day. He told Scunj he'd be right back and went for a stroll with his bucket just beyond the sole cluster of buildings, over the rise towards the railroad yard by the river where the hobo jungle was situated. He made out a few campfires and tents and men sitting around in groups, stark silhouettes supporting one another in their raw, impromptu way of life, an adventure in roustabout survival. There were quiet murmurs and soft chuckles among the many hoboes sitting on crates in small groups, standing around or hunkered in a squat, gatherings of three, five, six passing around bottles and roasting potatoes, or "mickies," over whipping flames from old empty metal barrels. Zeke was given a mickie to roast and was grateful to have it as he spoke to the men, telling them who he was and the mission he was on to improve their lives, for he was always one more bad break from enlisting in their numbers and riding the rails himself. Some recalled him from last time at the tavern and the song-and-dance numbers he performed with Scunj for them. "Say, pal! You here to put on another show for all of us?" a pudgy hobo in a tattered double-breasted pin-striped blazer, a pair of torn plaid knickers, and a beaten-up derby cried.

"Well, I wasn't planning on it, friend. I came on another sort of mission, one more important. But I can slap something together if that's what everybody wants." Several hoboes around him heard Zeke and they egged him on, whipping up the phalanxes of their cronies to swell the chorus of entreaties until he said he would, and they all began their way towards the tavern. "I'll need my horse for the show again," he explained.

While he and Scunj drained their growlers they came up with a singular show that expressed much of the harum-scarum unpredictability of the hobo life, as well as inviting participation of the more theatrical of the hoboes in the crowd. A wiry hobo in baggy trousers and worn-out shoes appeared out of the swarm with an old banjo and instinctually started playing the songs of hard times: traveling across the prairie, boxcar numbers, hobo tunes. A very young hobo with a mop of red hair and ripped overalls, his chest bare, whipped out his harp and played it like an old wanderer of night trains rumbling through sleeping towns and knowing well the lonely glow of street lamps seen for but a few moments as the main drag passes by. And Zeke bought a great wooden keg of ale from the bartender and set it up on the sidewalk for all to tipple and now the evening became about song, dance, ale, mickies on sticks roasting over flames, and more and more ale. When Zeke broke into "One Swiped Mickie Equals One Split-Open Head" the hoboes were roused with high spirits over the old train classic and held their mugs high between quaffs, kicking out their legs and smacking one another on the shoulder in an inscrutable scramble, which of course was an old hobo tradition. Zeke hopped up and stood on Scunj, leaning on a lamppost dramatically, and with great intensity launched into the haunting old ballad of the lightning Lackawana special that jumped the tracks and went soaring off the side of the Smokies into the Black Possum River, with everyone perishing except for six drowsy hoboes lounging in a boxcar. "Skybound locomotive / Your unmoored moment of flight / Had to end badly in the river / Why did you leave the mountain and the earth? / Taking tragic passengers with you? / And sparing six half-crocked hoboes who hardly remembered their miraculous survival two months hence?" Next Zeke scared up a snare drum from a hobo in the throng and slung the attached cord around his neck and began striking it in quick steady beats, marching with high steps, backwards, and Scunj started lifting up his legs with whinnies, now both moving backwards, and finally, the wiry banjoist and the young red-headed harp player struck up an old familiar tune heard around many railroad jungles across the land. "Hopped-up Hoboes at the Hootenanny Laughing it Up" was a very old elegy the makeshift band explored deeply and proved quite moving as the song tells of good-time hoboes who made fun of everyone but were beaten up by railroad bulls in the end so badly they spent four days in Bear's Paw General Hospital. Still, the irrepressible foursome continued their yukfest in the Bear's Paw patient lounge, where they performed a comedy review to great acclaim. The song's denouement reveals they indeed had the last laugh as the bulls who beat them up, penitent for their brutality, paid them a visit on the last day of their convalescence and the bitter bums blindsided them on their way to the lounge and went to work on them until all were laid out unconscious. "Now those bulls sons of bitches were the hospital patients for several weeks / and the mirthful hoboes went to another hootenanny," were the last lines of the number that invariably stirs the souls and dander of hoboes.

Zeke knew he had lucked into a very tight, intuitively inventive combo and they busted out several additional train tunes from the traditional songbook of hobo Americana: "The Farmer on a Tractor Waved as We Rolled By, Or Was It the Italian Salute?" "The Stumblebum and the Quaker," "Del Schmaug Turned Rat Fink," "The Corncakes Skunk Loomis Cooked Us in Muscogee," "Paducah Rain Tastes Salty, Mr. Entwhistle," "The Tiresome Preacher at the Jungle Outside Chi-town Wasn't So Bad," "Lost My Bindlestick, Found a Gladstone With a Suit Inside That Don't Fit," "Stu Bleavens Dropped Dead," "The Grub Klepto of Yuma," "Wheat Fields Swayin' While I Watch 'Em With My Whiskey," "The Old Bag Hangin' Wash Gave Us Soup," "Lefty Malzone Was Right," and "Living Off the Fat of the Land, Except Sheboygan."

Zeke and the hobo musicians rode a sweet spot of crazy rhythm and profound blues ballads that exhilarated and aroused deep sensibilities in the hobo audience and, as the impromptu concert caught fire and whipped up passions, the hoboes began chanting cryptic slogans like "Corn on the Cob and a Cup of Joe, Brother Farmer!" and "Riptide Over the Side, Come and Get Me, Slowpoke!" and "29 Shots of Popskull Ain't Enough, Hey Mr. Bull We're Calling Your Bluff!" and "We're Getting the Hell Outa Here, Ain't Time for No Bum Steer, Regardless There Better be Beer! Got that, Admiral Johnny? Do you read me, General Willie?"

The crowd caught on to Scunj's continued pattern of five steps forward, five steps back, a caracole turn left and right, and eventually the entire hobo assemblage was moving as one in this manner and as the deeply felt music poured forth the hobo swarm syncopated their steps and it all slowly crescendoed as the beer flowed freely and Zeke himself slaked his immense thirst with a river of beer and he sang with an intensity he never knew he had while he grew more and more pie-eyed and suddenly he stopped short, mid-lyric, as he saw a hobo towards the rear on the shadows' edges, a familiar face that left him in momentary shock, one with mad burning eyes and mien macabre in conjuring time past vulnerabilities, for this unmistakably was his father, Caleb Borshellac, there in the throng of hoboes, standing with his beer looking daggers at the tongue-tied singer, it was Caleb young again and strong in his prime, and violently drunk in looking like he showed up to settle the score with his son, or that's how Zeke absorbed it. The stark silence hung over the assemblage until Zeke leapt from the sidewalk bench he'd moved to the street to stand upon and dashed along the outer margin of the crowd towards the mysterious figure who transfixed him. The two musicians struck up a number on their own, "The Rock Island Line," as an instrumental, which cast a partial return to music while many followed the wrought-up singer to see what he sought. As Zeke got closer the Caleb figure began to recede with a smirk of scorn across his features and the son stepped up his pace to maintain eyeshot and the father slipped further away until Zeke was chasing him. "Daddy! Why have you come? Is it really you? Scunj is here with me!" he yelled at the fleeing figure who always seemed just a hairsbreadth away from losing his pursuer as they tore through increasingly pitch dark and narrow woodland paths. Zeke felt the vat of beer he drank but it only honed his mind on his prey and lent a swirling surreal dreamlike quality to his perception, and he told himself he knew what he saw in the stranger suddenly appearing in the throng who was a dead ringer for his father, exactly as he remembered the man from when he was a small boy. Whoever it was Zeke chased in the black woods tripped on rocky scrub clusters and tumbled badly in a hard fall and Zeke quickly was standing over the man as he struggled to breathe and rolled over on his back and peered up at the younger man. He wore an insouciant smirk and stated with a cocky tone: "You didn't catch me. I stumbled over that treacherous patch. Big difference." Zeke studied the stranger's face and could not see anyone else but the mad paternal horseman of his boyhood who rode with unmatched abandon and virtuosity, and here he was as his mind's eye recalled him. Yet a ballast of reason tempered his frenzy, a stubborn sense of reality calling on him to cede the undeniable truth of his old man much more likely being dead.

"Declare yourself, stranger! Who are you?" he demanded, deciding the resemblance must be a freakish coincidence.

"You know damn well who I am, son, so quit the twaddle. I finally find you and you question me like some hooligan?" The stranger pulled out a pint of corn whiskey and swigged it before extending the bottle to Zeke, who shook his head.

"You heard me call for my father, so you're playing along. You'll have to do better than that." They were amid the patch of rough scrub staring at one another in the weak shaft of moonlight, the crowd of hoboes who'd followed hovered around them but kept a respectful distance, and the great horse Scunj had now caught up to everyone and also watched from afar.

The paternal hobo rose and sized up Zeke with a disdainful grin and said: "You had me all wrong, Zeke. I know you've been thinking about me lately and you'll find out that eventually all we have left is our legacy. You shifted mine and now I'm shafted, son. But we'll set it straight."

Zeke took measure of the man before him and a shiver of consternation shot through him, a fright of not being in his right faculties in experiencing this strange man, while concomitantly recognizing beyond a doubt his father had returned to correct his changing memory in him. "You should have known that after you leave the world you continue to evolve or transform just as you did every day of your life. It happens in the minds of those of us who remember you." Zeke realized that this was harsh, as nobody much can lock in their legacy, and he rued his statement. The hoboes now murmured and an animal was heard scrambling in the brush.

The hobo father smirked and remarked: "So you acknowledge who I am?"

Zeke shook his head and said, "I'm just making a point."

The hobo father twisted his face and posed: "What happens when nobody remembers you anymore?"

Zeke shrugged, casting his glance down. "I guess then you're really dead."

The hobo father chuckled and gloated at Zeke. "Well, I still got you," he sighed.

"I am going to ask you something as if you are real," Zeke began, qualifying his approach. "What were you so desperately searching for or chasing on that monstrous horse? The mystery of it, the middle of the night rides you'd come to snatch me for in the hayloft, the fear and exhilaration I forever recall, what were you after?"

The hobo father grew pensive and swigged his pint of corn whiskey and squinted at Zeke with his head cocked. "You said a lot of it right there, boy. It's up to us to face down our fears and that is usually where exhilaration lies. So I kept pushing it with that juggernaut horse of mine and then I needed it and wanted you to partake in the phenomenon of the night rides, but it wasn't a quest for something specific as much as for a state of being and becoming inspired to pursue great paths." He paused and nodded as if satisfied with his speech before taking another pull of whiskey.

Zeke already had concluded that there had never been a concrete prize or abstract vision his father chased on horseback through dark forests, but the new hypotheses had occurred to him about the impetus of the rides on which he was invariably drunk. "There is another way of understanding it. You were not searching for anything but running away from something. You ever think about that?"

The hoboes stirred and murmured and the leaves in the trees fluttered in a stiff breeze. The hobo father looked up at the sky and smiled oddly and cried: "Scunj! My magnificent thoroughbred!" He turned towards Zeke with a flash of ire. "I never ran from nothing and nobody'd catch me if I did!"

Zeke looked back at Scunj and noticed the group of dwarves in the bright checked suits smoking stogies were playing horseshoes off in a field by themselves. One made a ringer just then and jumped with squeaky cheer. Zeke now caught his father's eye and held it before saying: "Well, it seems to me you were running away from Mom and me and being a father like you ought to have been."

The hobo father doubled over in guffaws and quickly snapped back upright in a paroxysm: "Scunj, my one and only ally! Treachery engulfs me!" He stuck three fingers in his mouth and produced an ear-splitting whistle and Zeke turned to the great horse and saw him standing at attention as before a race and his eyes glowed fire red.

"It was Mom who raised me and provided me with the wherewithal to surmount those humble beginnings in the tavern and the hayloft. She sacrificed and nurtured me to go forth with fortitude. All you did was terrify me and nearly kill me on those overnight rides in the woods."

The hobo father swigged a hard gulp and yelled to Scunj: "Ya hear the ungrateful lily-livered poltroon, Scunjy!? You and I showed the craven son of a bitch the meaning of cold vicious nights racing through the woods to muster some courage in his deepest being, and his survival until now is a direct result."

Zeke reacted with wrath. "Why did you not rescue me from the irrigation tank?"

"That tank was what you needed. I did you a favor. Jockamo Chop Chop was a splendid pony you were unworthy of!"

Now the enmity between the men had intensified to the level of violence and everyone knew a fight was ineluctable, as the hoboes had grown vocal in their excitement and a swelling chorus of rowdy huzzahs filled the woodland night as they encircled the combatants, who were squaring off in the clearing of rough scrub clusters. Scunj was trotting about in agitation, neighing helter-skelter, and the dwarves suspended their horseshoe game and climbed trees to gain a sightline. The bartender had made his way through the crowd and quite naturally assumed the role of referee, albeit the Marquis of Queensbury Rules seemed far afield from this encounter. The hobo father suddenly came boring in with a furious charge and landed a wicked right hand after Zeke caught him with a hard jab. Zeke exhibited some fine footwork and classic combinations, backing the hobo father up and hurting him with a sharp left hook. But the older man was an indefatigable cyclone of steady advancing and continuous punching and after chasing Zeke around in this manner, connecting here and there, he began to wear him down and seemed to be the stronger boxer with more stamina and overall generalship. It became a delirious battle of wills as the two men traded blows in a brutal exchange of roundhouses that sent blood splattering and their legs wobbling, and yet they kept throwing bombs and connecting in a toe-to-toe savage spectacle which riveted the vociferous throng of hoboes. The younger man was wearing down now, groggy and unsteady on his pins, clinching as a desperate way to catch his breath, still able to unleash a wing-and-prayer haymaker after separating and rocking the hobo father. But a wild uppercut buckled Zeke's legs and a succession of bolo punches kept backing him up and he was nearly out on his feet and when he saw Scunj in the crowd with blazing red eyeballs and an ominous ferocity and he was a boy again terrified of the original Scunj and the forest rides, and the murderous onslaught being dispensed by his mysterious opponent transmogrified him further to the cowering boy in the hayloft bed wakened by the mad horseman who was his father. He was beaten and barely conscious and daunted by the insurmountable old fear . . . and Zeke tumbled to the earth and remained strewn in a twisted heap, motionless, as the hobo father jumped and roared with great jubilance. The bartender ministered to the fallen fighter and threw water in his face and watched him slowly awaken and call out for his horse and dog, and the hoboes were in utter slam-bang pandemonium, clashing and rushing into one another in a demented hullabaloo of drunken fevered raw roughhousing and a good-time brand of horseplay that invariably led to full-blown brawling, while the dwarves resumed their horseshoes and the harp player struck up some blues gutbucket with the banjoist, who launched into the old hobo ballad "The Melancholy Hobo Ate Franks and Beans All Alone in the Alley in Muncie." Zeke struggled to his feet and the bartender and hoboes crowded around him became very quiet as they stared and gaped at their beaten advocate, some with quizzical expressions of uncertainty about the young fellow's identity and motives, though most simply curious and drawn to a combatant of such impassioned barbarity, and he once more cried out for his dog and his horse. There was a great welter of confusion and pockets of convulsion carrying on all around them, as mobs of lit hoboes roiled and raved in all sorts of singular acrobatics and nutty sports that only held some semblance of cogency in the buried beer-soaked blurs of their minds' eyes. Smashing into one another and hitting the deck and scrapping maniacally in sprawling scrums, yet always laughing like little crazy kids, these hoboes could not wind themselves down from the electricity of the fisticuffs. And the dwarves challenged hoboes to horseshoes and sang the most strident marching songs with a hobo tuba player joining them out of nowhere. The bartender scared up a roasted red-hot mickey and handed it to Zeke and he took a huge bite out of it and swilled the growler a good hobo presented him and woozy with cobwebs he waded through the tumble and surge of hoboes. He cried out for his horse and dog and the hoboes parted their mob for him to pass through and they all paused to gaze upon the one who came to their aid. He glimpsed a grave dwarf in a bright checkered suit nail a ringer and declare himself undefeated. And a bucktoothed skinny hobo jump off the roof of the ruins of an old barn into a water cistern and yodel like someone out of his mind. And a three-legged race that faltered into a free-for-all with sticks and the filthy sacks the hoboes pulled over one another's heads. As he came over the rise in the dirt road leading to the tavern and the few faded buildings, he was stopped with stupefaction at seeing the hobo father mounted on Scunj, guzzling a large growler, with the great horse kicking his front legs mightily with a powerful beauty, neighing loudly, the eyes burning crimson flames searing into Zeke's gaze. "Scunj!! It was your will and my destiny that somehow delivered us here to this cataclysm! You galloped through time and extracted my fear of you as it was back in the hayloft. And the dark figure who rides you—and knows you so well— seems to be Caleb!" The majestic beast snarled and neighed and bucked and jumped around like a wild bronco and the hobo father was yelling incoherently at Zeke while sluicing streams of brew from his growler down his gullet and sloppily all over himself. He drained it and stood straight on his stirrups and whipped the empty growler at Zeke, missing his skull by inches, and bayed and yowled like a madman, now pushing Scunj to ride circles around Zeke while he howled with piercing laughter and shouted: "We took it to the little rat bastard, Scunjy!. Showed him the divine order of things in this goddamn family! He spit the bit with fear back in that hayloft hiding from everybody like a yellow dog and cowering beneath the wench's skirts in that odious shit-dump of a dive they inhabited." He brought the great horse to a sudden halt and glowered at Zeke. "You had your shot to overcome the obstacles I carefully laid before you, character builders you might say, but you never found your stride and spit the bit—right Scunjy? . . . he spit the bit!" he shouted, stroking Scunj's side while looking daggers at Zeke. "You destroyed your pathway to a better life, while tainting my legacy in the bargain." And he grunted disgustedly and in one final dirt-flying burst rode the great horse straight at Zeke and tried to take him out, albeit the target was alert enough to dodge the charge and tumble to the earth where in a prostrate sprawl he watched the hobo father ride Scunj into the blackness of the woods.

    The bartender appeared out of the hoboes swarming around Zeke and helped him to his feet, and as the tumult and cacophony of the raving hoboes diminished a strange quietude settled over the mob as the beaten despair of the one who came to lift them up was truly a plaintive spectacle. The bartender propped him up on one arm and slowly they made their way towards the rise in the earthen road and the tavern just beyond. Zeke tried not to think as it only led to greater pain, but grim recollections lay in the bushes for him and suddenly one ripped across his mind, the reason itself he came to the hobo tavern and jungle. The big cash he made that week on his rounds in Bludenville and his desire to deliver the bundle of cash directly to the hoboes; the moment he remembered this duty he assigned himself he also realized that performing it now was impossible. The cash was sealed in its leather casing in the saddlebag hanging on Scunj's back and the hobo father just rode off into the black forest night with quite an adventitious haul. His setback deepened now exponentially, Zeke was devastated and mortified that he could not provide the financial relief to the hoboes he promised himself he would. He had not told them of the moolah he was going to give them, which now was spirited away into the night by a haunting dark figure. And he saw no point in telling them of their loss. In truth, he could hardly face anyone with so grievous a failure weighing on his conscience and only wanted to find a stool back at the tavern to drown his disappointment in beer, and that is where the bartender deposited him after patching him up with some bandages and an ice pack. And he guzzled beer after foamy beer on the stool alone with his brooding and bleak cerebrations and unforgiving second guessing, and they let him be, no one encroached on the time Zeke needed to himself, except the bartender who plied him his brew and occasionally offered a word or two of solace, such as, "Your courage in that bout was undeniable, son," and, "Horse thieves are hanged in these parts, and they'll bring him in." But Zeke knew better, even in his sloshed, banged-up condition. No one was bringing anyone in here. He stewed and smoldered over this fact more than any and tried to palliate it in beer to no avail, until he wakened just past dawn the next morning on a bench in the yawning dimness of the deserted tavern. A few sharp shafts of the new light penetrated the old wooden shutters and long cathedral latticed windows mostly hidden behind black blinds, but Zeke returned slowly and uncomfortably to consciousness and found the shafts welcoming. He smelled a fire outside cooking something and he gathered himself and ambled towards it, coming upon a ragtag congregation of hoboes roasting mickies over a barrel with keen attention. They were somber and staunch in their quiet perfunctory manner of holding mickies on sticks over the healthy wind-whipped flames. Zeke recognized a couple of familiar figures but nobody spoke, just waited on their mickies and swigged from bottles and kept their heads down, and Zeke did as much and wished he could wet his whistle with an eye-opener and then the bartender appeared from the tavern wearing a long white apron and a bow tie, toting a jumbo growler they now shared. "How are you this morning, Zeke?" he asked after several minutes. Zeke just nodded and guzzled another mug. It was a raw brisk morning, smelling like rain, and Zeke thought about his sheepdog back at the shack behind the Moravian's office, and he missed Balthazar, regretted the whole business of the hobo donation he never got to make, and mustered the will again to return to his dog and find a new beginning. He belted back beer and mused upon his next move, disenchanted now with being the donation solicitor on behalf of the Moravian. He wanted to show the Moravian that he could eliminate the middleman and deliver the alms straight to the hoboes themselves, but he flopped, falling flat on his butt. The notion to let it all slide and simply stay put there at the tavern where the beer flowed continuously and the railroad jungle where he could roast mickies and sing old railroad songs and become a hobo . . . it tugged at him now and he saw himself hopping a boxcar for the western coast. But the preoccupation with his self and the licking of life's wounds this encompassed subconsciously precluded his foray into hobo land.

"Hey Zeke, you must feel stranded out here with no horse. I think I might have something for you," were the clipped bracing words of the bartender that broke his sullen trance. He pivoted and surveyed the thickset pale fellow with the handlebar mustache and was startled how burly and cross he now seemed, yet was truly a kind, caring soul who had stuck by Zeke. Maybe I'm similarly mixed up about my own predilections and natural abilities, he pondered with self-doubt, and I'm really more of a hobo than the sort of fellow who believes in helping others and improving the existence of all of us! Misperceptions abound in how we see others, so they surely are just as rife in how we think of ourselves, he put together, when the bartender poured more brew in his mug and said with some insistence: "Let me show you something you can ride home."

Home, he thought, is where others go, not Zeke Borshellac. The bartender seemed nonplussed by Zeke's indifference. "You live in Bluddenville, ain't that right?" he asked.

SEVEN

Zeke nodded and thought of that shabby old shack behind the Moravian's offices, and of course thought of Balthazar, and how much he missed the loyal sheepdog. And just like that he decided he wanted to go back more than anything. "What have you got for me, friend?" he answered the bartender now with some vim.

The bartender led him through the tavern and a back room chock-ablock with old books and wooden toy sailboats and farm equipment and old furniture and down a steep sticky staircase into a cool dank dark cellar, where he lit a kerosene lamp and poked their way towards a corner where the illumination revealed the outline of an old-time bicycle. The bartender had Zeke hold the lantern as he moved it from the wall for a look, the dust taking flight, and he wiped it down with a rag from the floor. "A stranger rode in with it a few years ago, had himself a few ales, and took a coach to some Masons' convention. He never came back for his bike, and I don't see him ever coming now."

Zeke liked the singular, time-enchanted aura of the large fat tires, thick steel construction, royal blue and copper trim, with high handlebars and a long red-and-white striped seat. The bike immediately drew him in, and he wanted to ride it. "That's a unique bicycle. Can't remember when I last rode one," Zeke remarked.

"I want you to have it," the bartender said. "It has been down here all this time waiting for the likes of you, Zeke. I don't want to see you marooned out here with my hobo pals and me. Something good is waiting for you out there."

"I can think of worse places to be stuck in than your four corners back o' beyond out here," Zeke answered, as the bartender wheeled the old bicycle towards the stairs. Outside Zeke took it for a test run down the bumpy dirt road and around the faded buildings constituting the one road of the tiny settlement, and a number of hoboes grew curious and watched him as he gathered impressive speed and fell into a fine rhythm, and Zeke felt an inexplicable power gliding the wheels and boosting the pedals, the fat tires leaving the dirt surface for seconds here and there gave him an uncanny thrill. The hoboes murmured with excitement as he sped by and others gathered for Zeke's second pass by, as he continued riding and finding new rhythm and velocity in his pedaling the singular bike, launching off bumps into airborne flights that seemed fantastical to all eyes riveted to the laps he was completing. Zeke stood straight up as he went by the large assemblage and he waved and pledged his undying support, promising he'd meet up with them again somewhere with the wherewithal to help them in their struggle. As he pedaled away he accelerated with a great thrust of power and the bicycle seemed to have a mind of its own as his pathway proved jagged and swerving and the uneven road lent itself to short airborne trajectories. Once he turned to look back and saw the distant crowd of hoboes all assembled to watch him vanish from their view, and again he felt a sense of belonging back there with them, envying their utter acceptance of their fate and ability to find small joys in the hobo railroad life. But there was duty to a nameless calling yet unknown to him, a vocation he sought to discover somewhere on the road ahead. The solidly built bicycle, royal blue with the fat tires and high handlebars melded with its determined rider and over country dirt roads Zeke steered it and then the crazy eights all over the forest glade and the rapid ascent of the sprawling verdant hills seemed to draw him towards something on its own, and Zeke let his legs pump gladly to see where it was taking him. The highest of the hills, covered in honeysuckle and dogbane and sweetflag with jutting spikes of yellow and red proved a severe challenge in the afternoon sun and he barely made it over the top when his toughest obstacle confronted him, a steep sheer cliff edge with magnificent fields of softly swaying black-eyed susans waiting below for as far as the eye could see. Zeke could turn back or go over the side and take his chances with the wildflowers, and he hardly stewed on it as the bicycle did not seem inclined to balk at the bold option. But he understood intellectually that he would never consider such a jump if not for the instinctual faith in this bicycle and the desire he felt to propel himself through the air and land in those black-eyed susans. He had no fear as he rode with all he had in the approach to the sharp edge and with an extra burst of velocity he went soaring over the crags and brush of the steep side and began an arc of descent that put his wheels smack in the midst of the sea of yellow-orange flowers with the dark brown centers that stretched endlessly towards the horizon. He took a hard jolt that shook him badly, but the bicycle absorbed the impact easily and he kept riding through the fields without halting and at a remarkable clip. It was a stunning phantasmagoria of big blue sky and wildflowers that imbued in Zeke a great buoyancy and belief that he was on the right course to fulfilling his destiny, whatever it may be, but he still harbored the idea that a great mission awaited him somewhere. On that glorious ride back to Bluddenville he vowed he would discover the right people and conditions and place to make his mark and take his stand and he saw it all unfold in his mind's eye as he pedaled and sped through the fields and forest on his special bicycle.

By the time he rolled into his city it was late in the evening and the streets were empty save a few unsavory sorts here and there. Wending his way through the cobblestone darkness he went to his shack and leaned his bicycle against a rain cistern, noticing for a moment the splendor of moonbeams reflecting on it in its repose, before rushing inside to his dog whose barking he gently muzzled as Balthazar instantly recognized it was his master. It was a fine reunion as Zeke was humbly joyful and Balt could not restrain his supreme happiness in having his beloved pal suddenly manifest in the dead of night and the sheepdog licked his face until the harried fellow could but only grin and laugh and, at least for the moment, feel cathartically alive. His sense of reassurance was short-lived as Zeke knew the Moravian and his crew would be looking for him and the collection money, and the shack had to be the prime place they'd be watching. So he packed up his few belongings and strapped Balthazar's burlap sack (used to ride on Scunj) to the high handlebars of his bicycle and under cover of the wee hour darkness the pair lit out, uncertain where to go. But they barely made it to the street when the clopping of horse hooves on cobblestone signaled someone was following them, and Zeke knew it was the Moravian's men and his adrenaline kicked in and he pedaled with a maniacal urgency. But the clopping hooves he could not escape, as down several lanes and turns into byways the chasing horse continued coming and seemed to be closing in on him, and this frantic retreat went on and on zigzagging through back alleys and deserted sections of the city as Zeke found himself bearing towards the lowlands and the wharves. As he came barreling out of a narrow footpath onto one of the hillside cobblestone roads that led straight to the wharves the ominous horseman was there waiting for him, and Zeke's only option was a sprint downhill for the old wooden piers and the dark sea beyond. The deafening report of a firearm resounded and Zeke cursed in a mad holler and pushed Balthazar's peeping head back in the burlap sack, and more shots followed in quicker succession and Zeke expected one to hit its mark as he steered towards the nearest pier and zoomed down it as a bullet struck an iron capstan right beside him with a stark resonant ping and he felt his fine bicycle surge with another thrust of speed in launching him high into a full revolution and, finally, the sea.

Eight

HE PLUNGED DEEP into the dark waters until his bicycle separated with its own descent and Zeke continued to sink as sea creatures were all around torturing him with their baleful regard, like they had been waiting for his return to them, the former fishhead fellow now the prodigal son dependent on their generosity of spirit in leaving him alone. They were great grotesque formidable fish with lowering dead eyes and menacing mouths chockablock with layers of long irregular razor-edged teeth, and one seemed to swim at him that looked just like Larry Skompis, the fish he grew to love from the Fish Story Free-for-All during his tenure at sea on the fishing vessels. He smacked into a giant sea horse and mounted the crazy creature and it bucked and threw him off violently and he was unable to hold his breath much longer and panicked at the inescapability of a watery grave and thought of his dog and was stricken with nameless terror . . . until a great propulsion of swimming force came up under him and guided him upward in fits and rhythms towards the surface of the sea. Before reaching the top for air, however, Zeke gave out and he took in water and lost consciousness and seemed for all intents and purposes to be a victim of drowning as his rescuer climbed out of the briny deep with him draped over his back and laid him out on the old pier and his soaked sheepdog, also somehow back from the sea, barked furiously but Zeke could not hear as the rescuer, a very large ursine man with a powerful frame and thick neck, a mammoth beast of a man, now pumped his back with both hands and water spouted from Zeke's mouth, and the hulking figure kept it up as Balthazar barked his snout off and another stood throughout watching silently, though with keen interest, the desperate fight for life. She wore those old-fashioned black-rubber rain boots with buckles and a threadbare skirt with slats that resembled the sort of dull-gray curtains never replaced in the fleabag hotels she knew so well, and the salt-and-pepper beehive hairdo she wore so redolent of a Prussian soldier's helmet, all of it together too familiar to the denizens of the Bluddenville wharves as the strumpet hag who ran the rackets down there with a ruthless hand and an army of goons to do her bidding.

"Work 'em, boy! Push that water outa him! Ma knows this louse of a lug you fished outta the briny. Well, welly, let the bastard live so Ma can settle his hash for him!" She unleashed her shrill horselaugh and jumped in a sudden little kick and spun around, as if in glee over the payback to inflict. Her hard-nosed indomitable manner evinced a singular force despite her meager size, and her quickness, revealed in short spasms, belied her apparent years and she possessed a raw strength that surprised many. All of which, coupled with the element of being the initiator of fights, enabled her to take out a few jaboneys on her own over the years.

And she let out her distinctive cachinnation once more as Zeke now was coughing and somewhat conscious again (he mumbled "Larry! Is that you Larry?" the Skompis sighting still in his befogged head) and the big goon was helping him to his feet and Balthazar was barking and yowling with excitement and the woozy master and dog embraced. Zeke was upright but unsteady in his steps before the goon propped him on a shoulder as they followed Ma Moody down the old wooden pier and over the cobblestones towards her shanty off the water. "Well, welly, since our last tete-a-tete you haven't shown Ma much loyalty," she scolded, "but I'll nurse you back again . . . cause I want to make you pay for your firebuggery!"

The goon swaddled him in a warm thick blanket and laid him on the same bed he spent a night fraught with Ma Moody's carnal visitations many months earlier, and his dog curled up beside him and licked his face and Zeke felt grateful for Ma Moody again coming to his aid in a time of dire need.

"Gunther! Prop him up so I can feed him some furmity and talk to the fellow. We will have ourselves a little chat, yes we willy." The rough-hewn behemoth slid their patient back toward the headboard and braced his upright position with several pillows of piscatorial motifs.

"How's dat?" he asked gruffly.

Zeke was unsure if he meant him or Ma Moody. "It's fine, thank you," he answered after a pause.

"Listen up, Gunther," Ma addressed him now, "I want you to go up to the Red Harpoon later tonight and see if Cal and some of those rat bastards are around. Take the Bottle and Freano with you. No beatin' 'em up now, Gunther! Let's see how you showin' up goes first, ya hear me?"

Zeke now truly appreciated the strapping immensity of the monstrous hulk who saved him from the sea, a solidly built giant with a fearsome aura who standing next to Ma Moody seemed beyond human, and who took orders without a smidgeon of resistance from the diminutive boss who dealt with him in a brusque overbearing manner.

"I'll be there, Ma. Crim may want to come back I'm hearin'."

"Well, welly, ol' Crim may be in for a surprise."

The gargantuan man turned to leave and Zeke called after him: "Gunther!" And as he turned, "Thank you for saving me."

"Think nuttin' of it, chief. Ma and I were taking some air when we saw ya racing down the pier and flyin' into the drink. The least I could do to pull ya outta dere!" As intimidating as he appeared Zeke sensed an affable side to the bruiser.

"The horseman bearin' down on you," Ma cut in, "struck me as one of Snozzler's acolytes and I couldn't tell it was you, or I might have held Gunther back (here she chuckled nastily), but I will say this, any poor bastard on the outs with the Old Snozzler and his scumbags is somebody we want to help."

Zeke was puzzled by the name Old Snozzler but suspected it was someone with the Moravian and asked. Ma laughed in her usual way and said simply: "Oh, that is what some of us who know him long still call the Moravian, the bastard was snozzled on hard hooch back when he first came to town. And when he wasn't he seemed even more snozzled."

Gunther had turned to leave but called back once more. "Ma, are you gonna be all right here with this hoople?" he asked with solicitude.

She stood taller with her head back and moved closer to him. "Whatch you sayin'? Ya big lummox always lookin' to cast me in a decrepit light, or more like throw a pall over me like I'm already in the goddamn box!"

The wary giant glowered at their bedridden patient and wagged a minatory finger. He said nothing, but Zeke felt the sincerity of his threat. "I am too weak to do anything bad you think I may do," he averred, "and I am too grateful to both of you."

Ma now had a thick pair of old leather work gloves in her hand and exploded, shouting "You're as dumb as you are big! Always trying to make his Ma look like some kinda hoddy-doddy gink!" She struck him hard across the face with the work gloves, whipsawing back from the other side for second nasty slap. "If anybody ought to be crapping himself with worriment it's this one here in the bed . . . afraid I may pop my cork over his heinous deed torching Ma's fine old house out near the forest." She looked at Zeke with somber reflective eyes. "And I still might," she added gravely before bursting into her shrill laughter.

Gunther finally withdrew, maundering something about everybody knows she can take care of herself, it's more about "the debaucheries" some of them knew she was equally capable of . . ."I hope you ain't up to some tricks, Ma." He glared a moment at Zeke again and shook his finger at him and disappeared.

Ma Moody grimaced with umbrage and moved to the window to watch him recede from their shanty, and it seemed like she was about to yell something after him but did not. With her back to Zeke she said: "Nobody could beat that boy up his whole life, except the big oaf won't mess with his Ma. I can still take him cause I got too much up here." She tapped her temple with her finger, squinting. "And a will . . . I got a will that outlasts them all. Like the Old Snozzler, he'll get his from Ma goddammit! Snozzie gonna go down, ya hear?!" She held Zeke's eye with a devilish sneer showing her crooked teeth before breaking into stark howls of laughter as she went to fetch her piping bowl of pungent furmity and sat beside her patient to feed him a heaping spoonful of her unique concoction of meat and beans and fat gristle and tripe and scallions. And Zeke found it a hearty stew that warmed him all over with its robust flavors, which he sluiced down with a tankard of mead Ma kept refilling for him. The taste was sweet and effervescent with an unsettling, malted turnip quality that left a puzzling but rich piquancy. She wore a satisfied sneer as she spooned her charge furmity and plied him with mead and Zeke was quite cozy and contented with his unusual victuals and grog, surprised at himself for such a reaction, even a tad guilty over it, but he was weakened and beaten-up after nearly drowning so he rationalized it accordingly. Ma was intermittently sipping a mug of her own and she shivered a moment with a pinched tickled face and a squeak after every swallow.

She began to talk to Zeke, telling him how astonished she was when word got around that he was back in Bluddenville and latched on with the Old Snozzler. "I knew about it; Morris Topsails told me. He sees you with that great big horse of yours and I don't believe the crumbum. Then he spots you in Lazy McGonnigle's dive making the rounds for Snozzie—" She squinched up her features in irritation, availed herself of her drink, and met his eye: "That big oaf of mine would have broken you in half and left you someplace for the jackals had I told him to." She poured him more mead and saw that he took a healthy gulp.

"Well, I do appreciate your clemency," he assured, "and your hospitality again." He recalled through a haze of fragmentary dreamlike memories the strange night he spent in her shanty those couple of years earlier and the truth of the experience eluding him, and a presentiment of Ma Moody's intent and purpose with him darkened his mind.

"Well, those louses Crim and O'Connell blamed you for the fire, and while you may not have both oars in the water, I held them accountable since they were overseeing the project. That's why neither of the bums are with Ma anymore! But here you are, Zeb, back in the very bunk Ma tended to your rejuvenation! And now there's another comeback for me to hasten, I'll be pulling your chestnuts out of the fire again!" She sent three heaping spoonfuls of furmity into his mouth before allowing him to speak.

"I can assure you the fire that destroyed your house was purely accidental, but I confess to losing myself in the demolition process and it nearly wrecked me in the bargain," he said. "My name is Zeke," he added.

Ma Moody looked him over with a pensive glint in her eye and ordered him to drain his tankard of mead and said: "Well, welly, Zeke you say? Pshaw! Ma's got you pegged Zeb, and you're smack back in Ma Moody's bed, now ain't ya?" She let out a sick chortle. "You listen up, boy, we could use some fresh blood in pursuing our business interests, so we will see, we will, well welly. Right now you knock a nod with the sandman—" She pinched his chin so hard Zeke flinched, and she held his eye and now had gravity in her gaze when she warned: "Snozzler's horseman ran you into the sea, which says plenty. But Ma is gonna want to hear all about your association with Old Snozzie and the goddamn upshot of your fling with them bastards . . . and then we'll see, Zeke, we'll give ya a looksee, we will, well, welly. Ma took somethin' of a shine to you at first, but you did burn down my house no matter how we mitigate that fact, you torched Ma's joint."

And she laughed her mad laugh and waited for her charge to fall asleep or become groggy enough to properly accede to the masterly carnal manipulations of the strumpet hag of the wharves. Like a renown surgeon famous for extraordinary skill with his hands she artfully roused her patient, who shifted position with smiling slumberous alacrity to better receive the ministrations. The sea hag's tongue was a formidable instrument of concupiscence and she wielded it with utmost precision and virtuosity and its subtle and surprising deployment elicited more than a few moans of pleasure from her subject. She brought the half-conscious Zeke along slowly and steadily, like a shower picking up steam and rain becoming a deluge and the confluence of rivers overflowing in a great cataract; Ma Moody worked the sleepy young man into a quivering body mindlessly ecstatic and fixated only on extending the delight, as evidenced by his primal groan sounds direct from the brain's libidinous zone. And she finally jumped on him and took him inside and rode him hard and long and gloriously in a way only the strumpet hag could. She might have been a fearsome figure who ran the rackets down by the wharves, a maniacal scrapper who climbed out of the gutter to become the hoodlum Ma Moody, but she never lost her pride and passion for her first trade. And that was because of her nonpareil prowess at the harlot's arts, in spite of an exiguity of beauty and the rough-hewn manner of a wharf gunsel. They all knew Ma Moody as a wizard, a mechanic who invariably knew just how to coax and stimulate the best out of a fellow's equipment and pulled it off with wonder and panache, and she was one who cherished a challenge like Zeke Borshellac. The inexorable succubus devoured the happy, pliable dozer and he had indefatigable stamina for one lacking so much consciousness; but the succubus could go the distance herself and no one ever outlasted her. And her record remained easily intact after she finished with Zeke, after she somehow got his rocks off thrice, as the exhausted and plain worn-out semi-conscious ward fell hard into a deep chasm of true sleep. She paused a moment to gaze at him before withdrawing, his muffling respirations of serious sleep moving up and down breaking the silence now. She patted his head and grinned in an unutterable way which seemed to show Ma Moody had stoked some of the old fires of great daring ideas of rollicking slam bam fun with no limits barred in bed.

 Zeke opened his eyes again well into the morning and the strange bed and surroundings reminded him of lying awake in his bunk at sea, fearing he had become the fish fellow he portrayed, or wakening suddenly in the hayloft as a boy by his father on the original Scunj, provoking an old terror. But he soon remembered Ma Moody and how she and her thuggish son brought him here after Gunther fished him from the sea. He had soreness and aches throughout his body and his breathing was labored, and one by one Zeke felt ambushed by the cavalcade of images flitting across his mind, the bout with the hobo father and the loss of Scunj and his money, the malevolent horseman who chased him and Balthazar on his bicycle into the sea, and Gunther coming out of nowhere to save him. Balthazar now whimpered in excitement upon seeing his master awake, sidling over from his reclined comfort to greet him with his tongue. And woolgathering lingered from the long night past of many images of wild and woolly carnal romps in which he was being overrun by a volcanic succubus connected to the wharf shanty, but he couldn't say for sure whether it really happened. Then he remembered Ma Moody feeding him furmity and a strong mead and how his consciousness began to ease up and give way before landing in slumberland.

And now he looked up and Ma Moody was standing over him smiling with her arms folded across her chest, her eyes glinting with waywardness, and she said: "You caught good shut-eye and I can tell your second recuperation in that bunk is on track as good as the first." She laughed in her way and Zeke replied that he was feeling much better.

"I could not express my gratefulness for your saving me and the care you have given me, but I don't want to further burden—"

She laughed in a full-throated howl, cutting him off with a suddenly solemn: "Ma ain't done with you, Zeb. There is some water under our bridge, you'll recall, and let's not forget that tryout we palavered upon last night." She sat on the bed beside him and held his eyes in a disconcerting manner before stroking his hair and asking: "Your night of sleep . . . you seemed so at peace. But was there pleasure in your repose? Or the in-between place when you weren't sleeping, do you know of it? It is a good place Ma likes to visit herself." She chuckled and her crooked teeth moved up and down with her head.

Alarmed, Zeke understood what she was intimating and desperately sought to refute it in his objective reasoning, holding out that such a traumatic event in the sea must have resulted in a crazed release of his libido, inasmuch as the illusion off coitus was more in line with onanism. He pondered all this, such a frightful notion adumbrated by the strumpet sea hag, her dominating the semi-conscious patient in the most violent of sexual romps, while she let fly her signature string of cachinnation. Now she fetched a large steaming bowl of furmity from the kitchen, a fragrant gruel replete with fried scallions, spiced calf brains, gigante beans treated with chutney and tequila, and fatback saturated in grain alcohol and infused with bitter kidney tallow. Zeke was hungry but he attempted to resist the furmity, despite its acrid aroma whetting his appetite, insofar as he suspected the contents of the strange stew were far removed from the kind of breakfast one consumes without consequences. But it was no use because when Ma Moody whipped up some furmity for a patient of hers she would not brook abstainers and very quickly Zeke found himself opening his mouth for a loaded steaming spoonful. Many more of course followed and then she declared his throat dry and thirsty and she was pouring him glasses of mead and the bestial succubus enveloped Zeke once more that morning, riding roughshod over him in every imaginable way in his dazed stupor so when he later reawakened from the half-sleep state he understood that there may again be more to his wet dreams.

    He spent three full days in that bed subject to the same routine of procedure with the furmity and mead and the succubus manifesting to have her way with her young convalescent, but his mind could not bear the terrible strain any longer and he forced himself to rise one early morning and sneak out and wander about the pier alone before anyone was stirring except the gulls. As he was sipping a strong coffee he purchased from a stand an uncouth brute in a blue serge army shirt and a gleaming shako hat sidled up beside him to expostulate with him the practical reasons for "staying put with Ma." This quasi-military figure was none other than Gil Taggert, better known as the Bottle as he heard them state his moniker, one of Gunther's crew whose duty was to "watch Zeb, make sure nothing happens to the guy."

"Little did we think you'd be running out on Ma!" he exclaimed in puzzlement.

"I wasn't trying to leave, just to breathe," Zeke explained, but to deaf ears. Back at the shanty, at least he was officially recuperated and out of that bed and he and Balthazar really did have no place else to go, certainly not with the Moravian out there looking for him.

Not long after Zeke was back on his feet Ma bade Gunther to deliver their house guest to her private veranda on the shanty's side overlooking the sea. Zeke knew this was the tete-a-tete she had alluded to in which they would talk about his association with her enemy the Moravian. She had blackberry brandy and pigs' knuckles as surprise comestibles for him to enjoy, and she poured a snifter and served him three porker's feet and waited until he began gnawing at the pork. "You like 'em, 'eh boy?! Well, we got a load of the porkers' hooves for ya." Zeke now began feeling queasy and thought he might vomit, wishing he could when he couldn't. Throwing up, apart from the mal de mer variety, usually made him feel better about himself, sort of like crying, the catharsis of processing the inherent gloom of the human condition into quotidian life, he would tell himself. They talked about the house and how Crimcastle and O'Connell were treacherous backstabbers and how Ma learned not to trust anybody with something that means a lot to you.

"I had preserved that bay window you liked so much, really a fine fenestration until the flames . . ." Zeke confided to her.

She gazed at him sternly for a while before speaking. "You didn't wind up working for the Snozzler until a couple of years later. You ran off somewhere . . ."

He took the opportunity to tell her all about his fortuitous foray into forming a band of highwaymen and the Simon Grackler Riders of the Reckoning unique approach to forest robbery in highlighting the artistry and performance of the work, not the criminality.

She lit up a cigarillo and swigged some bourbon and raised her eyebrows gazing at him. "I know about those boys, Gracklers. Showmen,

EIGHT

scourges . . . I don't see you riding with 'em, Zeb." She exhaled a blast of smoke his way.

"Well, I was . . . a founding rider in fact. But my partners deceived me and stomped me when I confronted them and then took all the loot we were supposed to donate to the hobo fund . . . I rode through the forest looking for them for weeks and ran into Stu Leapers in a tavern, and that's how I fell in with the Moravian."

She squinted and fired up another cigarillo and chuckled hoarsely. "I don't know half of all that screwy chronicling you just laid on me when you were riding through the forest with your pals, but I can see you only latched on with old Snoozzie as an expedient of desperation." When she pressed him about the collection of protection money she thought his making the rounds among merchants meant, as everyone in Bluddenville imputed, Zeke reiterated his unshaken belief that he was picking up their contributions to the hobo fund on behalf of the Moravian, who was deeply committed to the cause, or so he thought at the time. Ma Moody listened with a gathering sense of delight and marvel and sheer hilarity to her ward's story and when he finally finished, she howled with a wild and shrieking laughter that shook her hard. She leaned over still chuckling and stroked his cheek gently and said with amusement: "The Snozzler exploited you, Zeb. He took advantage of your good nature, well, welly, he did! But with me, you'll know where you stand." She smiled awkwardly and her jagged crooked teeth seemed to Zeke threatening and he squirmed, but Ma Moody slithered her slight frame into his lap and now he was holding her like a child as she met his eyes. "You'll do well with Ma, Zeb," she said, "cause Ma runs the numbers, has the finest working girls, and ask any hophead who's got the hop joints they frequent here, and they'll tell you me."

Zeke didn't like having Ma Moody strewn across his lap in an intimate manner, planning his career as part of her illegal enterprises, but he felt he had run out of options and had to cool his heels with the strumpet hag for a while. And when he did have moments of chagrin over the next several weeks in which he pondered skedaddling Bluddenville with his dog in the cover of pre-dawn hours, he was daunted by Ma Moody's unwavering insistence on money he owed her for lodging and the copulations attending the near nightly visits of her succubus. Of course, the latter remained nebulous to Zeke's half-conscious, hooch-plied grogginess and seemed to him more a matter of gouging prices for a place to bunk. Nonetheless, the opportunity with her crew Ma had been alluding to shifted into work Zeke owed her to pay down his debt. "You may be broke, Zeb, but you're able-bodied by God and Ma will put you to work to square us away! You remember that, boy, or you'll find yourself back at the bottom of the sea without Gunther pulling you out!" is how she put it. Zeke deliberated on his options incessantly, but it was no use. He would simply make the best of it until the chance arose for him to bolt Bluddenville once and for all. He would wait and watch and be ready. On this night he could but look down at the sea hag strewn over his lap and down blackberry brandy, munch on a pig foot and stare out at the shimmery moonlight dappling across the choppy sea.

"Ma, is that the lummox Gunther pulled out of the sea?" was the interrogatory whisper that emanated from the shadows behind them in the shanty, and Zeke knew it was not meant for his ears. The strumpet hag pivoted and rose to address the murky form and Zeke noted a sudden softening of her demeanor, an almost tenderhearted brightening of her countenance in regarding the questioner.

"Why Cyril, I'm so glad you came by to see your Ma. You were composing today and must be spent, but a poet must be among society too. All is grist for the mill, son!" she concluded with her trademark cachinnation, albeit a much-muted version.

"Who is he, Ma? Gunther doesn't think he's a sea creature, just a man who had to be rescued." Ma laughed hoarsely and stepped towards the figure and slowly coaxed him to emerge from the darkness and reveal himself, all of which took several minutes until the lanky, colorfully attired individual squinted in the outside light and stared at Zeke for a full minute seeking to glean a sense of him. "Why were you in the sea?" he asked, breaking the long silence.

EIGHT

Zeke was standing about ten feet from him, and Ma was beside her son regarding him with a beatific smile. "A man on a horse was chasing me on my bicycle and I went off the pier."

Ma rubbed her son's back and said softly: "The horseman was the Snozzler's, my dear, and he wants to give Zeb the business."

Cyril considered this explanation and said quizzically: "All so temporal and redolent of our sordid world of the wharves . . . I preferred the more unlikely fanciful notion of your springing naturally from the sea like an amphibian creature." He laughed a most unusual laugh that struck Zeke as almost a frantic yodel. He found it impossible to accept that the slim, brooding figure attired in a tight green paisley silk suit and a polka dot navy ascot, congress gaiters, and a wild shock of red hair to be the brother of the powerful brute who rescued him from the sea. His features were handsome and princely yet possessed that indefinable sum of parts to produce a distinct strain of detached Weltschmerz, supercilious introspection, and a twinkle of loopy mischief that seemed to Zeke plainly at odds with the world of the wharves.

"I've been to sea on fishing trawlers and believe me, I am not naturally therefrom," Zeke assured affably.

"Cyril is a poet, Zeb, and is renown throughout Bluddenville for his verse. He will one day take his place aside the Romantics like Wordsworth and Coleridge and Keats, but he has to work hard every day, isn't that right, my dear?" Ma beamed proudly, although in the last part she darkened and became dour in addressing her son.

"Of course, Ma, composing is intrinsic to the process of lyrical creation. But the muse can be fickle and strikes at its whim. And as we agreed, Ma, a poet needs to immerse himself in the grist of everyday life," Cyril declaimed.

Ma seemed to ruminate as Cyril's words resonated through her and the result was skeptical observation uttered in a very gentle manner. "Yes, of course. But every great poet eventually had to buckle down and put words on paper. Every poet must produce a stanza here and there."

The fishing boats docked outside could be heard heaving and shifting in the breezy night air and several fishermen were swearing and quarreling over the finer methods of their craft. A fat man in lederhosen and a teal fluted turtleneck was selling strips of meat cooked over a fire, tossing off nonsensical remarks the fishermen were growing exasperated towards. "The hot gristle sizzles and the aromatic smoke made the woodcarver cry. His supper was on the table back home waiting for him through time, but he was lost." The fat man in lederhosen said this twice and the fishermen were apoplectic.

"See, there is a piece of existence that cries for poetic filtering," Cyril commented, breaking the silence now.

"Go on, son, find the profundity down there!" Ma exhorted, but the young man held back.

"It is more important what we don't say than what we commit to paper," he mused aloud. He paced a bit holding his head. "So, by choosing not to compose it I am making a choice and the poem is what is not written," he decided.

Ma Moody chortled in a most equivocal manner, not wishing to stir her son's ire, though it was plain she did not concur with his literary conceit. "How then would we judge such a poem's value against another's poem also not written by choice?"

Cyril now drew a pinch of tobacco from a pouch and placed it between his cheek and gum and began snorting and snuffling as he padded about in rumination with his hands behind his back. The row outside with the fishermen and the meat cook grew louder now with hysterical hollering and Cyril listened for a few moments and frowned. "Those men must be avoided as the subject of a poem at all costs. Knowing such a truth is more important than the verse one may hammer out."

A horselaugh that sounded painful escaped Ma's mouth and she seemed to struggle for a moment to keep her cool. "What about you, Zeb? Are you going to pipe up and tender your take on my son's extreme concept of less being more?" She announced almost as if to no one in particular: "Time for the arson drifter to stand and deliver!"

EIGHT

Such a characterization as "the arson drifter" stuck in Zeke's craw, but her continued referencing of him as Zeb eclipsed it in overall pique. "Who is Zeb?" he asked wryly. They looked at him warily and then met one another's gaze in exasperation. "You are Zeb," Ma retorted with a snicker. Zeke started to correct her when she sharply cut him off. "You are who Ma says you are, Zeb. I like Zeb, ya hear me?"

Zeke was puzzled and irked by the old strumpet's needling of him. "Well, I like Zeke cause that's who the hell I am," he asseverated, adding in turning to Cyril, "and I don't think deciding not to write a poem is poetry. That is nothing, nada, diddly squat."

While Ma did not appreciate his belligerent tone in addressing the Zeb issue, she chose to acknowledge his support of her censure of the notion of not writing a poem being a poem. "This one here was one of them Grackler boys riding wild in the forest, so he knows something 'bout art, Cyril," she remarked, adding after a pause: "I should say he claims to be a Grackler."

Cyril eyeballed Zeke up and down with a skeptical squint in his scrutiny. "I remember the Simon Grackler Riders of the Reckoning. They were a magnificent combination of robbery and theatrical performance, the likes of we may never see again." He paced a few moments, his face twisted in reflection as he concluded: "Honestly, Zebulon, I don't believe you were one of them."

Zeke chafed at the incredulity of the son and his use of the full name Zebulon in addressing him. "Frankly, what you believe doesn't matter," he retorted.

Cyril's face flushed at the insult, and he ran his palm over his features as if grappling with his response. "You are the jackanapes my brother yanked from the sea! You should be grateful we call you by any name!"

Ma Moody had heard enough now. "Shut it, both of you—ya hear me?! Zeb will show us who he is in short order now that he's with us. And if he ain't who we think he is . . . well, he will end up being nobody."

Cyril grunted knowingly, muttering, "Like that miserable Bert O'Connell . . . when that bum let us down we no longer had his back with the Snozzler. And that was that for him."

Ma took her sons and Zeke the next evening for supper at the Hong Kong Palace, a run-down chop suey joint on the wharves that was still a mainstay with well-connected locals. The place had a gaudy but cheerful quality that appealed to Zeke, particularly the hundreds of grasshopper and beetle-shaped lanterns hanging everywhere that lit up brilliantly at all various junctures and seemed to be chirping lowly in a steady undertone. He found them relaxing and the view over the harbor sea was quite stunning with the resplendent eatery's spectrum of colors reflecting onto the river. They sipped black tea and gorged themselves on chow fun, lo mein, and of course, the famous chop suey of the joint, and somewhere between all that eating Gunther, on his third plate of chop suey, commented that it seemed subpar to him. "I guess the old dump is slippin' from its chop suey heyday. Seems more like slop for the sows."

Cyril bristled, skillfully lifting with his chop sticks a dripping portion of chop suey high for all to view as it traveled the arc towards his mouth before he swallowed the gooey gallimaufry in a gulp. "I am of the notion that the Palace still holds its own as the chop suey champion." He grinned with a cocky insolence and speared another collection of meat, sprouts, and rice and turned towards Ma, who was tucking into her own plate of chop suey.

"Cyril is right again," she declared as she chewed, "the Palace still has the best chop suey anywhere."

Gunther seemed deflated with defeat as he clenched his teeth and squinted at his brother and mother. Zeke was not consulted on his opinion, albeit he deemed the dish quite tasty, and he was not about to volunteer it as the tension escalated. Gunther's sulk spilled out into his muttered mimicry of Ma: *Cyril is right again* . . . He studied his mother's face with consternation on his own. "What do you mean by *again*? Are you saying he's right more than I am?"

Ma broke into a sharp laugh. "Gunther, you are a big, strong moose of a fellow who everyone fears. Why can't that be enough for you?"

Gunther brooded and drank black tea and clenched his jaw as he said: "It was always about Cyril the poet for you. I'm the *other* brother."

Ma snickered and gobbled down some chop suey before responding: "Cyril is a poet who exists on a rarefied air, Gunther. You should be grateful to have such an artist in the family."

The owner of the restaurant, Funton Fong, who'd been apparently eavesdropping, now appeared at the table with a broad smile and outstretched arms. Fong knew the family for many years and had always been anxious about somehow offending them, mainly Ma, and incurring their wrath, so he often interjected a preemptive measure of ingratiation that almost invariably backfired into contretemps. "Cyril . . . our esteem*ed* poet!" he called, slapping the skinny son in the silk paisley jacket and polka dot ascot on the back, which clearly perturbed him. He proceeded to pat Gunther on his brawny shoulder and jocosely put up his dukes as if to tussle with the fearsome bruiser. "Gunther! C'mon, ol' Fong take you on!" The older restauranteur laughed awkwardly and Gunther smiled in a cavalier manner, while Ma inquired in a sober tone: "Tell me, Funton, is there anything you are doing differently with your chop suey?"

Fong hesitated, now visibly anxious as his signature dish has been called into doubt. "Anything Ma Moody not like about her chop suey?" he rejoined.

"Just answer the question, Funton!" she snapped. Fong deliberated, finally settling on the least provocative response: "No, never Ma Moody, chop suey same as always."

A satisfied grin now came over Ma's mug and Fong too smiled again with a big sigh of relief. "Ya see, there, Gunther, Funton corroborates that Cyril indeed did have it right. Now finish up your goddamn plate like you used to." They watched as the big fellow sneered and looked around perhaps gauging his options before slowly grasping the chopsticks and polishing off the remainder of his chop suey. Fong patted him on the shoulder again and smiling broadly, though still apprehensive, withdrew. Ma now pulled out a bottle of bourbon and took a big swig before passing it around to the boys, then lit up a cigarillo and passed around panatelas for them. "All right then, hear me out. Saturday at The Oilcan Conclave we're putting on a reading of poetry to show the bastards in this burg what genius sounds like." She turned to Cyril, who was blowing smoke rings with his cigar, and addressed him sternly. "You've had months conjuring your Muse, darlin', but Tennyson became Tennyson for a reason—"

Cyril took a serious hit of bourbon and snickered disdainfully. "And what would that be?!" he asked with a smirk.

"He composed verse! Don't be a dummy! With your talent, it's a crime to be so goddamn lazy." She paused to puff and survey the table. "Zeb, you will be his handler and chief aide. Make sure he captures it all on the page. Gunther, you'll run the security over at the Oilcan and sweep those hopheads into a cordoned off section, like usual." Gunther nodded with a look of resignation and resentment and Zeke felt a pang of empathy for his secondary status in the family dynamic.

"Nobody has mistaken me for a bard of any sort," Zeke said to Ma, "but I will do my best to help Cyril harness the poetry inside him."

Ma smiled darkly and squinted in her glare at him. "Well, Zeb, if you are a Grackler as you say you are, I would expect nothing less than you inspiring my boy to produce his finest poems yet! The Gracklers were true artists of their time and that ought to translate into coaching a raw visionary like Cyril. I'm depending on you to bring it outa him, Zeb."

NINE

It was a week until the Oilcan Conclave reading and Zeke took his role as Cyril's poetry advisor seriously. He arrived mornings at his spacious quarters above the quality clam bar known as Barnacle Stubby's, as well as one of Ma's more high-end cathouses, Barnacle Ruby's (Stubby and Ruby were married). Cyril lived with three of the most prized prostitutes in Ma's entire stable and frequently dined and drank in the clam bar, where he built up a monumental tab he had no intention of paying off and, as Ma Moody's privileged son, Barnacle Stubby would not dare to mention the mounting sum. After a few days of mostly futile efforts to rouse the young poet to the task at hand, the work of creation, the capturing of sound and vision and great mysteries in verse, it was clear to Zeke Cyril either could not or would not listen to him as a coach or motivator. He would without fail find him in bed with his courtesans deeply engrossed in the most licentious and wanton of sexual relations, occasionally involving demented role playing and depraved animal noises, and he would avert his gaze and quickly withdraw to the main parlor to wait for the poet to present himself. Zeke only ventured into the hidden rooms at the urging of Cyril's bellowing to join them, and when he did locate the orgy they all let out chuckles and entreaties to dive in—before he fled. Late in the morning the poet would design to appear in the parlor, bedecked in a fine satin robe with an embroidered likeness of himself flying with wings and holding an ice cream cone. While cordial to Zeke, he was cavalier and dismissive, quick to note his gifts were uniquely attuned to the muse—and his muse was extraordinarily fickle—so he saw no point to rushing into matters. "You have to relax and savor the fruits of life, Zebulon. Only then the muse will speak to you."

Zeke took his often trotted-out maxim in stride as the knee-jerk defense mechanism of an unregenerate libertine. "Well, let's hope she addresses you before Saturday," he said, "because your mother is expecting some luminous poetry out of you at that Conclave joint."

Cyril laughed and shared a murmured observation with his courtesans and none could contain their howls. "Fear not, Zebulon," he proclaimed in a theatrical manner, "my mother is not the cold-blooded, tyrannical Ma Moody the newspapers are always writing about, particularly if you become part of her inner sanctum, our family, and . . ." he grinned and chortled as he caught the courtesans' eyes, "and Zebulon, the old girl has taken a real shine to you, judging by the early morning assignations I've heard about."

Zeke grew exasperated and simply rejoined: "I'm not concerned about your mother, Cyril! I mean reprisals if you bomb. She has been good to me and the least I can do is try my best with you. Why don't you show me some of your poems, so I have an idea of the sort of work you do?" And the debauched poet snickered with a condescending nod before herding his entourage of hookers for the walk below to the clam house for lunch. Zeke soon ascertained the apparent unsettling reality that Cyril was not turning over any poems to him for one inescapable hypothesis: he had not written any, or any that anyone not so drunk or opiated could make any sense of.

Each night over furmity and mead Ma Moody grilled him about how the composing was going, the nature of Cyril's subjects, and Zeke could but fumble with vague replies, such as "it's a nonlinear process that emerges cryptically."

Ma found this answer amusing. "Ah, now Zeb! There you go with your fancy poetry lingo! I want it in regular terms on the boy's verse."

Zeke wondered what poems of the young rake's she may have read, and asked: "I don't know if you're ready for his new material. Very daring, searing vision."

NINE

Ma fixed him with a cognizant look, and returned: "Now how would you know what Ma is ready for, Zeb? Is Cyril telling you things?"

Zeke paced with his hands clasped behind his back, thinking, and simply putting to the old strumpet: "Quick, name your favorite Cyril Moody poem!"

She froze after a fleeting visage that appeared to appreciate the revelatory intention of the inquiry, albeit she would never outwardly recognize a misplaced belief in the younger son as a man of letters, an artist, a visionary bard of stark raw poetic imagery. "Well, welly, Zeb, you can ask some impossible questions. Why not ask my favorite tadpole from the summer when I was a little girl in Halifax? All I know is it ought to be one of these new poems he's working on for Saturday! And if it *ain't* among that batch, I'm holding *you* responsible, coach!" She let out one of her trademark cachinnations that invariably captured the observer's conclusion, even for a few moments, that she indeed had lost her mind.

Wednesday night came and Zeke had nothing out of Cyril, not one old poem even, and his suspicion that he never had written any verse at all was only deepened when Ma Moody prevaricated around the issue. He thought he would take a walk shortly after dusk to the tap house Johnny Junco's on the old pier over the water, but Ma squelched it, only to relent on the condition that Gunther joined him. "The Old Snozzler has his thugs imbedded in every alley and corner of this town. And he's coming after the one who jumped ship on him. Gunther will watch over ya, Zeb. Ma has grown too accustomed to having you around, especially in the wee hours"—she murmured the last phrase in a sotto voce aside fashion—"so I ain't gonna play it careless with Snozzie."

They enjoyed cigars on the stroll, presents from Freano who just returned from a sojourn in Dover, New Jersey, where he had stumbled upon a secret roller of broadleaf offering bargains. The men smoked in silence, Zeke brooding upon his predicament with Cyril and the pending reading seeming darker now. The fine cigar was such a sensory pleasure it helped him cope and contemplate the pickle in which he found himself. "It was really thoughtful of your friend Freano bestowing us with his excellent stogies," he remarked.

Gunther hesitated before responding. "It is customary to buy something for friends on a trip. In fact, cigars have become Freano's standard gift, so if he stiffed me there would be a problem." Gunther pondered this for a moment and laughed hoarsely. "So do you believe if something is expected of you it diminishes the task and, in this case, devalues the act of cigar giving?" Gunther stopped now to complete a long puff and exhale of a cloud, leaving his lineaments surrounded in haze from Zeke's view, the swaying creak of fishing boats and a few wharf shavers skipping rocks on the water the only noises betraying the stillness of the harbor. The hulking figure seemed to Zeke dejected and cynical in the pale moonlight, the second banana status hard to take he figured, and Gunther asked suddenly: "Doing what's expected of you should not render it meaningless. Because I'm big and strong why should beating up some louse for good cause not be seen as worthy?"

Zeke could feel the big fellow's bitterness and deep torment. "I think you have a point, Gunther," Zeke acknowledged, "but with great strength comes responsibilities too. I believe the weaker ones rely on you to rise to certain occasions to take on threats from bad eggs. You know, they look to you for that protection."

Gunther puffed away and chuckled to himself. "I guess somebody has to keep Snozzie and his goons in line. Not sure how noble it is or how much I'm appreciated. But at this point in my life, a career switch ain't in the cards, Zeke."

Later at Johnny Junco's, knocking back tall glasses of German black lager, Zeke saw in his drinking partner's pensive expression a man who felt he gave up on himself and went with the flow of his life's work as Ma's enforcement boss, that he capitulated into her vision of him in her empire. It was only a hunch, maybe true on some level, but Zeke empathized with the man who rescued him from drowning in the sea and sought to elicit from him what his alternative existence might have involved. Honing in his mind a way to broach the idea, he finally asked him: "Say Gunther, had you not become the strong arm chief of ma's operation, what vocation do you think you may have pursued?"

Gunther reacted almost as if he didn't hear the question and flagged down the barkeep to order two glasses of single-malt scotch, and he raised his glass to toast the poet Edwin Arlington Robinson, "who captures in verse all sorts of folks who live in a town like most towns, and we come to know 'em in a way only poetry can achieve."

They clinked glasses and drank the fine scotch, the boggy peat echoes resonating with exquisite heartiness in Zeke's palate. He thought it a curious toast of Gunther, about an obscure poet he had never heard of before. He didn't really answer the question, he thought, albeit within the toast it probably lay. "Are you a secret poet, Gunther?" he asked.

The outsized bruiser swooshed some scotch around in his mouth and he relished the swallow. "I've always kept art close and inside, private and inviolable. It is locked in my mind and cannot be expressed—not after Ma made fun the one time I tried to tell her she may have two poets on her hands. She laughed so loud I felt shivers down my spine. *'You? C'mon, boy! A galoot like you ought to stick to cleaning punks clocks!'* was what she said once the convulsions of laughter died down."

"Could it be she thinks you're hornin' in on Cyril's craft? Would you even have thought of poetry if not for Cyril?"

He slanted his head looking upward, as if ruminating on Zeke's attempt to explain Ma's mean treatment of his poetry interest. "It ain't about who is first, Zeke, it's about capability and caring about the work."

Zeke knew how deeply earnest Gunther was in his divulgence and instinctually wanted to help him. "I would really like to see some of your work, Gunther, and offer my critique. Maybe we could use you Saturday."

The big man finished his glass in a hurry and slammed it on the bar. "I don't think so. I haven't fooled around with it for years. That ship sailed, Zeke."

"What sort of material did you write about?' '

"I thought I would show people, in a town, like Robinson's I got my own. I like a poem penetrating everybody's veneer, like 'Cliff Klingenhagen.' But it's too late now."

"Who's Cliff Klingenhagen? Is he a real person?"

Gunther thought about Zeke's questions before answering. "Yes, Robinson wrote the poem about a man in his town. A fine man who sacrificed for others. A humble fellow who would throw himself over a cliff into a rock quarry if it meant one hungry baby would be served a bowl of oatmeal. We need to waken the Cliff Klingenhagen in us all." Gunther guzzled a fresh large lager and rose to recite the Klingenhagen poem, becoming teary with sentimentality by its end.

Zeke was impressed by the big man's utter depth of tenderness in experiencing the poem, but at the same time thought it implausible Klingenhagen would take his own life to provide a bowl of oatmeal to a baby. "While I admire Klingenhagen very much based on his serving his friends good wine while restricting himself to wormwood, I believe you are overrating his stature as an altruist."

Gunther bristled with indignation. "I believe you are overrated as a slumbering fancy man my mother devours early mornings." Zeke was perplexed by the acerbic pronouncement, though subconsciously he was starting to put together the full nature of his role working for Ma Moody.

Later after leaving Johnny Junco's, traipsing along the narrow cobblestones amid the midnight fog from the sea, Gunther disclosed that he was indeed at work on a poem. "It's a poem about you, Zeke. Rescuing you from the sea inspired me to follow up now and explore the person you truly are. I only have a couple of stanzas written, but so far I am excited to go deeper beyond the veneers and tap into your dark side. I want readers to know you, Zeke, to understand that while you say you want to devote yourself to engendering well-being and goodness in the world, there is baggage that comes with the Borshellac package."

Zeke reproved him about the baggage line, snapping with a hint of jocosity: "I always travel light, Gunther. Are you referring to my beloved dog? I will forever pack him along on my travels."

Gunther smirked. "If I was speaking about Balthazar I would have made that plain. But, come to think of it, his ferocious jealousy of you is growing tiresome to all of us."

Zeke was piqued by such a caustic comment, but he patiently held back on escalating the tension. He did not want to engage in a quarrel with the big fellow and risk losing his trust and budding friendship. He may need his aid yet with the Moravian crew seeking his whereabouts, he considered, and he couldn't blow the haven Ma had been providing him, notwithstanding the strange wee hour dream state activities that seemed to be happening to him. "I don't think you know my sheepdog very well, and he has been available for games and petting, but you show no affection for the canine. It is not Balt's fault you are impassive towards him."

Gunther bit his lip and looked down. "I haven't given him the time of day, have I?"

"Let's not dwell on it. I hear people down that alley, folks playing something," Zeke blurted, pausing beside a long moonlit tight lane of cobblestone between backs of row houses and an old shipyard of grand retired vessels mostly rent into parts. They decided to check it out and came upon a group of somber hoboes engaged in a serious game of horseshoes, all sipping from bottles of cheap wine beside several fire barrels over which they were roasting potatoes, or "mickies." The game was set up amid the old shipyard parts in a clearing surrounded by gigantic propellers from long grounded ocean liners, and Zeke found the pale beams of moonlight cast an enchanting hue over the otherworldly scene. To get there Gunther and Zeke had to climb a rickety fence and wend their way through the yard piled with enormous remnants of boats, strewn like sculptures for no one to see, and much clambering hither and thither. When they emerged out of the propellers no one noticed them, and they moved towards the hoboes who were intently watching the competing hoboes who were pitching shoes. Zeke and Gunther quickly were embedded among the mickyroasting onlookers and passing their own whiskey supply back and forth. A lanky hobo in frayed overalls and a weather-beaten top hat grinned oddly before pitching his horseshoe in an underhanded looping motion that landed wide of the stake. There was a murmur of disapproval from his supporters, as his opponent, a short cocky hobo in a battered derby, T-shirt and old vest from a three-piece suit, began warming up for his delivery with great intensity. His pitch was high and as it hovered in the night sky a hobo yelled: "It's gonna find the stake, Captain, coming down a ringer!" Zeke wasn't sure if the hoboes were wagering on the horseshoes contests, but the partisan rooting was striking, and when the "Captain's" shoe returned to the earth a clanging, wondrous leaner several of the onlookers erupted in hobo cheers. But the lanky one with the misshapen top hot now set himself upon a ritual of squatting up and down, spinning around and beseeching the heavens before kissing his horseshoe and whispering to it, and as he began his pitch a hobo voice called out: "Ring it, Joke, show the bastard who's boss here!" And as the shoe followed its trajectory another called, "Joke, like you rung it back in Topeka! Clutch, baby!" A harsh resounding clamor followed as the shoe entered the propeller area, disappearing into the surrounding darkness with a series of cacophonous clanks until utter stillness supervened. Everyone paused, motionless, perhaps trying to process the aberration of such a wild, errant pitch. Zeke was skeptical of its authenticity, suspecting the lanky hobo they called Joke was staging some kind of drama through which one incredulous inept pitch would lead to curiosity and mystical musing once his subsequent pitches found the general propinquity of the stake. Joke was the first to move on from the stillness as he walked with sullen tentativeness towards the propeller populated shadowy fringe and everyone watched him fade from sight and become lost out there somewhere. And then there was nothingness among the hoboes and Zeke and Gunther watched in consternation as they formed in loose rows with their bottles of hooch and the Captain called them to "inattention." He pulled out a harp and began playing "St. James Infirmary," much to everyone's delight, stopping after a while to recognize crickets in full sound before a tapping horseshoe from the grove of propellers started a metallic percussion riff of splendid rhythmic syncopation. It was Joke and he soon reappeared in a happy gambol, swaying and twirling, and the group of hoboes chuckled softly, as if his act were familiar to them. And Joke cried out in a voice of unloosed conviction: "I want a ringer, I need a ringer, I . . ." and he skipped forward in his herky-jerky promenade, swinging his horseshoe around like a whip until he let it fly high into the darkness above and suddenly it came crashing down around the stake, hooking on to it. " . . . I made a ringer!" he declared. A roar went up from the erstwhile solemn hoboes as they yelled out Joke's name and a few broke into the same happy gambol of their hobo pal, as they toasted him with whiskey. It was as much Joke's showmanship as his making the ringer that made it all such a memorable moment, Zeke reflected, and he took note to remember what such beguiling imagery can mean one day. He would remember the strategies and elements of Joke's ringer in exciting a crowd from that day onward, though swearing never to compromise the true message of a performance through manipulative frippery.

Gunther now was holding a horseshoe and smoking a fat cheroot, knocking back whiskey from a new bottle, and he moved towards the near stake while gazing upon the riveted hoboes who seemed inquisitive about the big fellow's ability to toss a shoe. In their genus of hobo, throwing horseshoes was a skill intrinsic to their ethos, as some of the legends of horseshoe champions came out of their very ranks, including "Sheppy Ring-Rang Plepper," the four-time Lackawana Railyard champion and known for unorthodox pitches that often struck inattentive onlookers. As an outsider, Gunther emerging in the pit with a horseshoe in hand was an act of provocation, insofar as a solid throw would be taken as a challenge to their natural superiority at the game. But his shoe was far and wide of the stake to the palpable relief of the hoboes and embarrassment of Gunther, who mostly had forgotten about their hypersensitivity to outsiders pitching. He had something else on his whiskey-slackened mind and that was an irreducible lyrical vestige long lying dormant in his innermost being. The palaver with Zeke uncorked the remains of the poet manqué, stifled square in his dithyrambs and rhymes by a prepossessed mother who valued only his brute strength and ability to project menace. Now he stood in the center of the shoe pit and used the silence to build intense anticipation before he began: *"Hoboes and Horseshoes and Whiskey / Pitching and Huddling in the Lonely Moonlight / the Joke's Shoe Falls Triumphantly from the Night / Wonder and Jubilation Ensue / That Ringer was for All of Us Because / We were Here to see it / And Remember How Joke Made It / And Ringers Await Us All Somewhere / Don't They? / They Goddamn well Better be in the Cards for me!"*

At first Gunther's poem was greeted with silence but soft applause began, presumably as they digested the words, and this cascaded into robust clapping and huzzahs. Zeke, impressed by the big fellow's verse, soon stepped into the moonlit pit and seized upon the moment by stating that Gunther Moody will be reading at the Oilcan Conclave Saturday evening, along with the "illustrious Bluddenville bard, Cyril Moody, the very brother of Gunther."

The big man met Zeke's gaze now with a dose of pique therein and said in a low voice to him: "You've conscripted me back into poesy, my sea monster, and I will return the favor with a work about you! Beware, for I am known for revealing the darkness that lurks in otherwise decent folks' hearts."

Zeke found his warning amusing and chuckled. "Well, my rescuer, I assure you nothing will turn up in your expedition, but I invite your scrutiny." And the hoboes were abuzz about the poetry reading at the Conclave, mostly because they knew the joint was always good for complimentary victuals and a shot or two can usually be cadged, and now they called in raucous cries for Zeke to pitch a shoe too. Visitors to their isolated realm hidden amid the propellers, when deemed to be kindred allies, were sometimes urged to pitch a symbolic horseshoe of concordance and amity. Unlike Gunther's uninvited throw, seen more as a challenge. Zeke now lined his up with much concentration before stepping into his slow delivery and sending his shoe into a steep arc that somehow returned to earth with a clangor that proved to be a leaner. Applause swelled along with a holler or two for the impressive newcomer to say something, speak to the lost gang of tramps with their unrepentant love of hooch and horseshoes, and perhaps do so in verse and make it somehow count to them. At least that is what Zeke inferred was being elicited of him. *"I made a leaner tonight / my horseshoe performed almost as envisioned / as it crashed downward remaining upright / on the stake it reposed with indecision / The leaner spurs me on towards ringers / Since its closeness presently ever lingers."* His effort was met with dense stillness that hung over them like a Euclidean algorithm, until Zeke proffered hints of interpretation, i.e., the failure to make the ringer only inspired him to work more to achieve one.

"Why the hell would a leaner be better than making a ringer?" a particularly weathered hobo with a red bulbous nose and a pinstriped old vest shouted in rejoinder for all of them.

"The ringer/leaner here is figurative," Zeke said, "in that we always want more ringers or something else just out of reach."

The red-nosed hobo scoffed with a snicker. "As long as I'm liquored up just right and throw enough ringers to win the goddamn game, hell, that's good enough for me!" And everyone broke into hearty laughter, including Zeke, although he joined the yuckfest late and not as robustly as the hoboes.

The next morning Zeke, after once again reconciling himself to the carnal mysteries overwhelming his nightly slumbers (incognizant of his whiz-bang succubus), he sat down for breakfast of fatback and whortleberry furmity with an eel-infused, brine-fermented mead and began a conversation with Ma Moody, sipping mead herself and smoking a peat rank cheroot while regarding her charge with a prideful but patronizing grin. "Cyril seems determined to shun my services as advisor and consultant to his reading Saturday," he stated flatly. "You bade me to impose discipline so his finest verse can be harnessed; it is a mission I find unachievable." The strumpet hag swigged some mead and puffed her cheroot wearing an infernal amused smile. "While he may have lyrical gifts, he seems more bent on playing the dissolute lothario surrounded by multiple harlots," Zeke added.

Ma Moody would have none of it. She glowered with disdain before ordering him to produce the results she demanded. "The effulgence of genius is often encased in the base animal low-down and dirty needs of certain individuals. You hear, Zeb? You best get on with the business of getting the poetry out of that boy! You'll have some answering to do should you flop, Zeb! Yes, you will, well, welly!"

Zeke tried to move past this attack, scarfing his furmity and sipping mead in silence before responding. "I have enlisted Gunther in the festivities Saturday. It is with him I have made strides, starting with the discovery of his being a poet manqué long dormant. His voice too must be heard. Your strong-arm brute who inspires fear is also a bard with exquisite meter and imagery, profundity even."

The sea hag boss' eyes narrowed as she regarded the young man she welcomed into her inner circle, albeit with a good measure of suspicion still, his update jarring to the firmly established order of the Moody hierarchy. "The big lummox is starting up with all that again, eh? Thought he gave up the ghost on his drivel ten years ago, more . . . are you putting bugs in his ears, Zeb?!" she demanded.

Zeke shook his head. "Gunther has something unique and deeply felt inside him and it must be expressed."

Ma Moody snarled derisively, "Pshaw! Goddamn galoot is deluding himself again. You listen here, Zeb, the boy needs to knock it off!"

Zeke was puzzled by Ma's visceral reaction, suspecting there was more to it than he knew. So what if her bruising enforcer son—many would say the most fearsome thug of the wharves—harbored a hankering to dabble in poetry? But the blood among the Moody triumvirate ran hot with history and old rancors and assiduously applied arrangements of the order and standing, Zeke apprehended, and in that context her ire did not seem so dissonant. "I've already announced that Gunther would be on the bill. Cyril of course is the headliner, but the brothers both reading only enhances the card."

NINE

Ma Moody puffed on her cheroot and blew billows of smoke in Zeke's face, before draining her mead and slamming it on the table. "Why would a man feared in every quarter for his brute force and killer instinct and fighting greatness not be content with that? Why would he want to become a joke as a half-assed hack poet and endure the torrents of mockery sure to descend on him?"

Zeke only replied with: "He is more than a brute and I don't believe his poetry will be ridiculed."

Ma stood up and threw her chest out, glaring at Zeke. "Don't push me, Zeb. You don't know my boys like I do. Normally I'd break in half any hoople arguing bunkum with Ma, but you don't know no better. So we'll let the galoot read on Cyril's night and you'll eat crow, yes you will, well welly, crow will be shoved down your gullet, Zebby."

Zeke made his appointed round later that morning in calling on Cyril in his rooms above the brothel and clam bar and found him in utter disarray, as usual, though his sprawled unconscious form wrapped loosely in a feathery boa with three naked harlots snoozing around him was the most debauched scene he encountered yet. The women, buxom lovelies tricked out in tight shiny dresses (in varying stages of dishabille) and undone lavish coiffures, snored in an odd mixture of syncopated sound that surprised Zeke with its raw musicality. He began to withdraw from the premises but stopped as an obligation to check on the troubled Moody son's condition. What if he never woke up? Zeke considered. He would carry that failure to provide aid forever. So he walked past the snoring entanglement of bodies, though Cyril was still and silent and quite pale which sent a shiver through Zeke. He proceeded to the kitchen and filled a large bowl with water and poured it over Cyril's head. By increments the soaking stirred him until he rose to his feet and surveyed the pretty snoozers before regarding Zeke. "So the sea monster misses the water. Well, chief, I don't want your damn water. I didn't pull your ass out of the big drink! That would be our Goon Squad Honcho."

The harlots continued to snore, sogginess notwithstanding, as Cyril stepped over them and invited Zeke to the lounge for a snifter of cognac, albeit the reigning poet of the wharves was wobbly on his feet and his eyes struggled against closing. Cyril poured two glasses and fell into the davenport where he appeared to Zeke an unregenerate wreck in unbuttoned white shirt with immense puffy sleeves, lame toreador pants and olive patent leather loafers with no socks.

Zeke stared at the spectacle of his self-destructive pupil until Cyril mustered the desire to address him. "I still don't know why Ma sends you over here every morning . . . I am an artist with my own goddamn vision." The harlots had stopped snoring all at once, as if they were a musical group, and now were stirring slowly. One called: "Where are you Cyril, sugar?" Cyril smirked cavalierly, "I'm over here, toots. Talking to my poetry advisor." He snickered slightly and the women chuckled with exclamations of puzzlement. "Nobody can tell you nothing about poetry, Cyril honey! The audacity of that is beyond me!" the same harlot remarked. The three moseyed their wasted way towards their libertine and plopped around him on the davenport. The one with a mass of blonde hair and a striking curvy figure looked Zeke up and down and concluded: "So this is the one who presumes he can teach you something about poetry?" She shook her head with a laugh. "Don't look like he's got much going on!" They all chuckled. The brunette with the wild bouffant chimed in: "Let's see what the big man has got!"

They all entreated Zeke to recite one of his poems to demonstrate his own mastery, but he steadfastly declined. "I've never promulgated myself to be a poet," he stated. "Ma enlisted me to motivate you and offer my experience as a former Grackler to help with the word craft of poem structure." He spoke more for the harlots as Cyril heard this before.

"Well, as I see it, Zebulon," Cyril said, "you got nothing with which to help me, and you won't even do a poem of your own to build a modicum of credibility."

Zeke burned with umbrage. "I'm not in the habit of making up poems on the spot."

NINE

"Ahh, c'mon, Zebulon!" the women pleaded derisively. "A little spontaneity never hurt anyone, Mr. Poetry Man!"

Zeke just sat there with his cognac for a long silence until he decided he had nothing to lose. Many of one's best decisions are made when there is nothing left to lose, he noted, and he was curious what his aversion towards the impromptu would produce when so compelled. And the words he spoke the night before amidst the massive propellers for the hoboes did not come out too badly. He downed the rest of his snifter and rose to a position across the davenport to address his audience. He awaited the full force of his fortitude and boldness to spread throughout his form and find voice in issuing forth with the following: *Would you rather be a true artist that no one recognizes but yourself and couple of others / Or a widely recognized artist who is a really only a charlatan? / The fruiter has mangoes but no more gooseberries / Little Oggie Norstratch ate a plantain with salami and blubbered like an infant / Everyone felt it was the fruiter's fault for running out of gooseberries / Old Si Stuggelbahn never tried a lichee / Old Si Stugglebahn lived in his shack with remorse and anguish / Over what he did with his life / And failed to do / But the lichee never concerned him / Despite his contention with the fruiter / A grizzled Flemish fellow with freakishly large ears and a penchant for anthropomorphizing his fruit / He boxed a pineapple and took a TKO / On a lark he traveled to Malta with four red pears and nine apricots / And during a tropical sabbatical he married a honeydew melon / Little Oggie Norstratch ate a papaya with bologna and shrieked like a banshee.*" Zeke maintained an inward gaze as he breathed with great intensity in collecting himself from the tempest he conjured in his deepest recesses. When he looked up his audience was staring at him, silent and, he thought, searching his eyes for more. But he had nothing else for them, the words sprang forth from somewhere in him and he was not exactly sure they understood them or valued them. He was not certain how he himself felt about them, only that he was relieved and wrought asunder with their emission.

Cyril lit a cigarillo and poured himself a cognac and sipped it. "Well, Zeb, my sea creature, you drove at something there with old Stugglebahn beating himself up in his shack, but it was Little Oggie who, for me, and I only speak for me, qualified the human condition with his screwy grub pairings."

The brunette perked up and clucked her tongue jocosely, wagging her index finger at Cyril: "I'd have to take issue with you on that, Cyril! It was old Steagglebak who spoke to me! I understood his pain of regret when it is too late."

The blonde weighed in with another tack: "You're both missing the point. The fruiter was the one who blazed his own path, despite the acrimony of his patrons, finding companions and love within his world of produce." The other harlot had dozed off again and was snoring a lively sea chantey rhythm, or so Zeke thought, while the blonde and the brunette and Cyril now engaged in increasingly fractious badinage with respect to the meaning and preeminent character of Zeke's poem. At first, Zeke felt somewhat flattered that his impromptu verse affected them with such ardor, but it left him roiled after a bit that they dug in on their opinions without consulting the poet himself. Not that he would have definitive answers for them, he realized, rendering his input otiose. The escalation of their polemic into raucous, coarse shouting coupled with slinging explosive personal insults replete with the vilest of profanities caused Zeke serious concern of the situation's volatility. The slumbering strumpet, a beauty in scanty black lace and lustrous auburn mane, found great amusement in her mates' fracas, which by now had a physical element to it of extremities waving and shaking for emphasis of point-making, and she began emulating them with caricatured mimicry and peals of her own laughter. Soon Zeke found humor in the debate through her mockery and could not contain his own hilarity. The tide soon turned and everyone was laughing so hard they were crying, and before long Cyril guided the cathartic merriment into the lascivious and carnal and just like that in hardly a jiffy the group became immersed in a full-blown orgy of satyriasis, sans Zeke of course, who quickly withdrew from the company once the erotic nature of the shift in tone was apparent.

Composing poetry was beginning to gain a toehold in Zeke's consciousness, streaking towards status as a *sine qua non*. It was not that he craved laurels or renown through his verse, but that in summoning from his turbulent depths words of potency, words wrenched from the dark abyss within, he thought he could affect the lives of a few miserable souls who suffered in silent resignation. He now understood the power, the raw incendiary inspiration packed in certain words spoken a singular way together, and what it meant to be able to tap that mightiness inside and let it come streaming out. He would go deep and shake and tear and wrestle the words from his very bowels in the idea that hard-earned verse could save people, illuminate their thinking and embolden their wills to get back up. Zeke roamed the wharves and the narrow cobblestone lanes of Bluddenville the remainder of that increasingly wet and windy day, hearing the sounds of verbs and nouns and consonants and sibilants emanate from within his chest and scud up through his gullet like invisible animals all making their own utterances. He bought himself a cheap corncob pipe and fired up some peaty tobacco and steadily hit the whiskey as he surrendered to the sounds and images of his words sluicing up through their conduit, the sudden bard who saw a possible path in his quest to do some good. He wandered into a dim narrow cave strewn with seven-foot piles of books everywhere, an archaic bookshop from another century, and he smiled with exhilaration being among them, smelling their pungent old hides beckoning with adventure.

An ancient proprietor with a long beard and spectacles and suspenders holding up his oilskin trousers on his gaunt frame shuffled from the shadows towards the strange customer. "May I assist you, young feller?" he asked in a wheezy but determined voice.

Zeke regarded the old-timer with kind amusement, apprehending that here walked a figure of another time, a man of books enveloped in his old world of lasting hardcovers where tales and insight awaited one. "Nothing in particular," he answered him, "though I'm partial to poetry."

The old-timer smiled inwardly and nodded knowingly. "You strike me as a poet, son," he said. "Poets have that look in their eye when they come in here."

"What look is that, if I may inquire?" Buoyed by the proprietor's curious remark, Zeke wanted to believe in it.

"It is a look of hunger and unease and loneliness mingled with a soupcon of amusement."

Basking in the blandishment a moment, Zeke felt that maybe the old-timer was right, who was he to say otherwise? And now he felt obliged to buy a book, a volume of poetry of course, and he asked him if he had anything by the great Edwin Arlington Robinson. A glint of approval appeared in the proprietor's eye as he bade Zeke to hold on a minute, which for his slow ambulation meant twenty, but he returned with a sizable leather-bound tome and a faded notebook with lined empty pages and a couple of pencils. "Read the wondrous master carefully and learn," he counseled, handing him the book, "And write in here, son. Fill the pages in a hurry. It's in you, and it's got to come out. Let it out now."

Zeke took the notebook and pencils and met the old-timer's gaze, a shaft of dust-particle twilight from the opaque window faintly illuminated the man's otherworldly features. He forked over the few coins the old man would accept and thanked him in plain words he felt were inadequate. A sense of bestowal of duty filtered through Zeke before he returned to the cobblestones and the wharves and now a night of capturing the words, sounds, memories as they arose in him and came forth, he wrote them down in his notebook, between pulls of whiskey. Through the stiff winds and later the hard rain he trudged along the agitated dark waters off the piers and observed the bleak seaport imagery of harbored ships and the noises, buffeting, grinding, creaking, squawking, the swirling unmoored nautical detritus airborne whooshing balefully. His words came in bunches, staccato blasts, and cascades of expression he could hardly keep up with. He contended with the precipitation in trying to preserve his notebook's dryness and chanced upon a pale light in a window of a meager ramshackle structure overlooking the sea that seemed uninhabitable. But he lurched his way towards it and soon found shelter, stark and shaky, but nonetheless a place of retreat to put down his poems.

NINE

It was a fishermen's hidden den of some depraved maritime underworld, and several weathered ruminative fishermen, some in slickers and long fisherman hats still dripping, sat alone at places along lengthy wooden tables. An old hunchbacked man wearing a dirty long apron shambled towards Zeke, grinning dementedly. Disconcerted initially, Zeke quickly realized he came to take his order. "Rum," he told him, and the old man giggled while nodding, which Zeke took as an approval. The fishermen drank in silence, stock-still and brooding it seemed to Zeke, but then there would be sudden interstices in which they'd engage in fierce vituperative debates about arcane nautical matters that Zeke could hardly understand owing to their strange seaman's patois. Fascinated by the fishermen, he began to sketch some impressions of their mysterious presence and inscrutable manner of interaction. "They appear angry and disgusted by the life at sea that spits them back out to dumps like this one, while at the same time they cannot escape their inviolable quintessence of being fishermen. Yet a few strike me as poised to move on to vocations available ashore, such as butchers, masons, cobblers, and constables. Then again, there is no empirical evidence to buttress my hunch and it occurs to me the notion is rather silly," Zeke scribbled in his notebook before a couple of arguing fishermen paused to regard the self-contained stranger writing away in his little realm. When he looked up, they averted their glances. Now Zeke could not stay focused on his composing and kept glimpsing their way but when they met his eyes he turned away. He began to fret that perhaps they remembered him from his own days at sea and wanted some kind of retribution. *Could the stocky cross-eyed one be Devilcake? But he has no cummerbund* he wondered, relieved the seaman was without the fancy frescoed rubber midsection sash the thuggish fisherman known as Devilcake favored. His mind now became mired in his harrowing past as a fisherman trapped on a trawler among dangerous, foreign mates and his desperate struggle for survival through his on-deck performances, predominantly in his Fish Fellow character. *They will see to it that I am unconscious and then shanghai me into one of their dastardly voyages . . .*he suddenly felt nauseous from the dreadful sensory memory of donning the fish head for long hours of demanding shows. His panic saw in their faces a conspiracy to capture him, and he wanted to bolt but knew that would only force their hand faster. He remained motionless, fearful, watching them drink and plot his imminent shanghaiing on a lost trawler of rogue fishermen. They oscillated between rowdy, profane rows in their curious patois and inexplicably abrupt breaks of sullen, bitter silences. Zeke found them utterly mysterious and enigmatic but unequivocally menacing, and he decided upon rising to his feet to simply saunter out the door as if nothing whatsoever was out of the ordinary. And that is what he did, and no one appeared to even notice him. Outside he speculated whether he had overreacted and after tramping along the piers in the hard rain for a while he wended his way back to the godforsaken shelter and after considerable hemming and hawing he thrust open the door and met their eyes as they all turned to the door. Zeke stood in the rain and held their collective glower for several fraught seconds and felt all the darkness and despair and doom baked into human existence in those moments and was finally able to shake himself enough to hightail it into the wet winds of the night.

He hit the whiskey hard now and roamed the rainy cobblestone byways of Bluddenville with a boozy madness of stark bleak poetry stewing within and shouted with full-throated fury. Only a random hobo or lone rumdum were within earshot of his tumult-borne, raging verse and on this tempestuous evening Zeke discovered the grit and guts and emancipating madness laced in his voice, and he let it rise and rip. He stumbled upon a small office building almost nondescript with its red brick and box glass front, a place he sensed he knew somehow and perceived a faint light inside. In his liquored-up febrile momentum he followed his impetuous urge to enter through the front door, which opened and soon Zeke was engulfed in smoke and the steady beating of bongos and kerosene lamps forming the most incandescent of lights, to which he was drawn toward the rear where he now heard a man's steady voice, a carefully cadenced voice that struck Zeke as familiar, reciting what appeared to be poetry. He advanced through the increasingly dense haze and flickering brilliant lamps where he now beheld the lineaments of a gargantuan figure pounding the bongos with a primitive skill as he declaimed poetry to no one, certainly unaware Zeke had entered. The hulking shadowy figure wore a driving cap with a visor, dark glasses, and a red union suit. Zeke could see he was barefoot, his intensity of recitation and percussion also made him dance and shake his body. His verse was addled and muffled at times but Zeke thought he knew that voice. He strained to understand the words, their inflections, the sound of every syllable exploding with a nameless recognition that he could not quite place until it became apparent the refrain in the bridge was: "*Hurtling on a fleeing bicycle he came on a bleak dead of night / And the sea swallowed him whole / Until I figured it was worth a fight / In I dove and back from a watery grave our sea monster I stole.*"

"Gunther!!" Zeke shouted at the entranced poet. "For the love of God, what is this?! You are speaking about me, are you not?"

"*I hear him now / the creature I saved / the one who is determined to do good / yet the sea creature flounders and flops not knowing where he once stood / or why he believes he is someone who can deliver the goods for anyone else.*"

"Gunther!! You've gone over the edge! What have you done to yourself, man?!" Zeke implored frantically. He watched the hulking form spasmodically shake and swing his limbs and twist and jerk his body in the most disturbing manner while he maintained a martial tattoo that invoked demented visions of drunken fevers. Zeke accosted the much larger man attempting to jar him back towards reality, but Gunther adroitly stepped aside of his rush while jutting his foot out to trip the one he saved. Zeke hit the floor hard but pulled himself up, shook his head in disgust, and acknowledged the big fellow had every right to do some cloistered marathon sessions in preparation for the reading. "You are woodshedding in here, right? I mean, I guess I could understand that to a degree. But good Lord, Gunther, you've worked yourself into a fugue state of some kind where you seem dispossessed from your body and persona."

"*The sea creature cannot fathom the stark uncertainties of existence, so he lambastes and longs for his return to the dark waters / The sea monster is not thankful for his time on dry land / all he can muster is a predilection to flee from every perceived threat / back into the inky moonlit sea so calmly awaiting its big fish's dive."* was Gunther's comeback in verse. The outsized burly poet appeared to break for a pause between stanzas, his wrought-up intensity, nevertheless, found expression in his pommeling the bongos in a violent dissonant manner that seemed to Zeke like the man simply snapped. Then he conjectured the vicious display of anger related to the perceived lack of gratitude in him for the doughty rescue effort by the big fellow, so Zeke squared up with the inflamed fellow and forced their eyes to meet somehow and he told him in straight heartfelt language the gratefulness he would always carry for him pulling him out of the dark sea that night. Gunther grimaced and slowed his drumming as his face now grew somber. His beats became soft taps and his frame ceased to shake and shimmy, and then he seemed to glower at Zeke in an unhinged way and just as the smaller man began to seriously fret whether he could make it out the door before the dour beast could catch him, Gunther erupted into great boffolas of laughter. Stunned in an uneasy speechlessness, Zeke could only wait until his mirth had dissipated and the big fellow told him in all earnest profundity: "It is you *I must thank,* Zeke! You encouraged me to write poetry again, after all these years. I realize now how much I missed it, how much I need it. Zeke, it was you plunging into the sea on your bicycle that led to my return to poetry."

 Zeke slowly absorbed the startling declaration of gratitude from the capricious giant and allowed a smile and a pull of whisky, albeit Gunther engulfed him just then in a bone-crunching bear hug that sent his flask into the air and spread enough momentary pain throughout his torso to cause him concern of serious injury. But after some tense, awkward minutes in which Zeke had to collect himself, catch his breath and lie down briefly upon a teak divan laced with hand-carved rococo seraphs, he was fine. He even was persuaded by the big man to hang around for a few more stanzas of the epic Homeric poem he was composing about him and his rescue from the sea. But it was too much for Zeke to process in his condition and with the volatile dynamics of the impending reading pitched over his head like a gleaming assegai, the expectations of Ma and the performance of her golden boy Cyril, the peculiar insertion of Gunther into the program with his personal journey of poetic narrative catharsis, the pressure to pull the evening together as master of ceremonies in a raucous violent drunken den of Bluddenville iniquities, it all swirled balefully in Zeke's snockered mind and he quietly left as the big fellow's lyrics of his epic titled *Zeke Borshellac* receded behind him and echoed in his ears as he lumbered over the puddled cobblestones in the rain back to the Moody quarters on the piers.

Ten

THE RAIN PERSISTED into the morning with nor'easter squalls blowing in and thunder cracking over the heavens, rattling Balthazar under the covers at Zeke's feet in their bed. Zeke comforted the sheepdog with lavish petting, a crumpet and turkey leg he scavenged from the icebox in the kitchen, and smacked his lips against his warm snout before leaving him snuggled in bed as he ventured out before anyone else had stirred. He downed a pot of java and eggs at the little diner run by the irascible old Greek Lignose. He took a long ramble along the piers watching the new inclement day dawn and turned inland, now sipping his whiskey again, as he pushed towards the outskirts and the edges of the forest until he came upon a tiny tailor shop squeezed between a tannery and a blacksmith. He sipped his whiskey under an old thickly leaved ailanthus tree and gazed across the muddy road at the shop and its proprietor's name prominent upon the signage: Beppo Malzone. It occurred to him that while the evening presented challenges to surmount with the rivalry of the brothers, it also represented his public debut as a poet in his own right. And his garb should reflect the new image accordingly, he decided. So he entered the little shop and explained to the ancient fellow he aroused from a nap, a bespectacled codger in a fedora and wide-fluted pea green corduroy suit too snug on his chubby frame, that he was becoming a poet, a "full-fledged poet whose verse would help people understand the human condition better and fortify and inspire them to move forward in their lives without fear."

The old-timer, still sleepy as he stirred, now tangled himself in the tape measure he had slung around his neck and exploded in Italian imprecations. But he rebounded soon enough and moved from the counter towards Zeke who he sized up for quite some time, adjusting his glasses to increase the magnification here and there. "You poet, ehh?" he repeated, nodding, considering.

"Yes," Zeke replied, with a trace of equivocation in his voice. "I think I can extract the words in here that will prove meaningful to folks," he awkwardly tried to amplify, tapping his chest.

Beppo Malzone now tapped his own chest in a similar manner, nodding and chuckling. "All of us have words here . . ." he observed with a trace of an accent.

"All of us . . ." Zeke agreed, also chuckling.

"Mine is spoken through the finery I make. You have come to the right tailor to rig you out as a poet," Beppo Malzone assured, and began taking numerous measurements of Zeke's form. The old man seemed excited by his work order, his first in several months he confessed, and told Zeke he would have it finished in a few hours and invited him to wait on the veranda out back where he could work on his verse. And that is what Zeke did, suddenly feeling buoyed back there overlooking a brook threading into the forest as he nipped his whiskey, glad to be on a path towards a life of the mind, a poet others can draw strength from when down. When the hoary old tailor finally emerged from his shop onto the veranda, he was glowing with pride in the suit he fashioned for the young customer who declared himself a poet. It was a pea green corduroy suit with clownishly wide lapels and bell bottoms, with wide fluting laced with yellow threads, very close to the very suit worn by Beppo Malzone himself save for the more extreme flourishes. It also was a tight fit on Zeke as he tried it on, and Malzone insisted on a starch white shirt with ripples of ruffles overflowing and an ascot of silk in ivory and violet checks. The old tailor allowed himself a slight smile upon seeing his work on the young man, but he was a craftsman rigorously devoted to his work and held a critical gaze upon Zeke for several minutes before directing him to saunter past the perimeter of the forest towards the brook so he could "evaluate the costume in the natural verdure of the forest." He asked again and again that Zeke recede further into the denser bush so he would "fade into the lush landscape until it seems you are engulfed by the woods so you can emerge new and luminous in your impressions."

It so happened that Zeke somehow actually got lost and had a conniption over failing to find the right trail back and stumbling wholehog into the brook. Finally, Beppo Malzone went in the woods himself to pull his customer out and was not dismayed at all. Rather, he saw the matter as nothing more than a foofaraw that actually benefited the new poet by adding a wrinkle to his image, the dirty poet of the earth unafraid to confront the muck and mire in his explorations. But there was one accessory Malzone felt was missing: a felt fedora such as his own except for the realistic stalks of corn he created to reach for the firmament in a dazzling show of mindless optimism. "Now you look like a real poet, son!" Beppo declared, carefully disposing the new felt lid upon his head.

"Well, now I think I feel like a real poet," Zeke affirmed. But as it was time to leave it became clear to Malzone that the new poet could not pay him quite yet, as Zeke inquired about the "prospect of a jawbone purchase." Malzone flew into a fit of Italian oaths while smashing a stick torn form a branch into a rainwater cistern set beside his veranda. The old codger really let loose swinging the stick and Zeke was impressed with his ferocity and stamina before the old tailor whipped out a wooden match and lit up the stick for them to simply watch burn. After a while Zeke said good-bye and promised to return with cash one day to pay him.

"You already paid me plenty, son. You gave me the chance to make one more suit and it turned out to be my best." Zeke smiled and began his way back to the city, once stopping to call back that he was still coming back to pay him. "Forget it, I'll be long dead by then," he said, waving his arms.

The Oilcan Conclave had been a foreboding, notorious nightclub jutting like a jagged cluster of weeds from the seedy far edge of the wharves for well over a hundred years. It was once a favorite haunt of pirates where they would raise hell and party like the rowdy soused degenerates they all were, as pirates always felt at home in Bluddenville amidst the ever lurking threat of violence on the streets, the bustling depth of its prostitution trade, the gambling joints and betting parlors, the bare-knuckle pier boxing, and the high-grade opium invariably available to the hopheads languishing around the harbor alleys. The rain finally lifted during Zeke's hike back to the wharves and he delighted in the early evening post-storm freshness of the wet earth and twilight air. He arrived at the Conclave before everyone except the owner, a barrel-chested old salt with sailor skeletons riding whales tattooed all over his arms, and a few burly bartenders who doubled as bouncers. Zeke shook their hands and the owner, whose name was Mogler, said, "Ma tells me you're pulling in a good crowd tonight. That so? Cyril brings 'em in, I guess."

Zeke swigged a mouthful of whiskey and replied, "She expects a full house. Some of 'em want to hear Gunther read too, you know."

Mogler chuckled derisively, the bartenders grinned knowingly. "So it's true what we're hearing," Mogler said. "That slaphappy brute is going to embarrass himself!" Zeke took stock of the cavernous dive, padding around as snippets of his own verse streamed through his mind, musing upon the long worn wooden tables, the bars on both ends stretching into dark corners, the filthy warped floorboards, the unadorned raised stage lit eerily with a smattering of candles. He began to feel anxious and his whiskey offered relief, as he now sat upon a stool near a dark recess and watched them come drifting in. Fishermen straight off their vessels, slimed and looped already, hoboes out of the alleys and jungle, ripped, looking for the complimentary pigs' knuckles and hard boiled eggs, a legion of off-duty strumpets, many of whom could be enticed into a trick regardless, the usual country contingent of sodbuster yokels freshly paid, an aggregation of wayfarers passing through looking for an evening of amusement, a few members of The Maritime Laborers and Sail Riggers Guild, representatives of the Bluddenville Poetry, Phrenology, and Pipe Carvers Society, Oliver Oogenschtupp and his entire shop's roster of scrimshaw artisans, hopheads manifesting in several pockets, some already nodding, a battalion of The Moravian's gang strutted in, led by Charlie Crimcastle, and they found their perch on barstools in a dim corner, and then came Ma Moody herself, an unavoidable presence of blunt formidability that sent a shiver of silence through the floor as she slowly made her way to her table on the far right not far from the stage. Before she sat, she remained upright a moment to survey the room with a grave gaze, Freano, the Bottle and two other thuglike sorts beside her, and all eyes were fixed on her. She wore her signature ensemble of that dull gray skirt with slats, a drab cardigan loose on her skinny frame, and of course, the shellacked beehive holding her salt-and-pepper hair up high. Her only gesture to a night on the town was the silky white blouse she had on under the cardigan, and the neckerchief depicting a long needlefish tied around her neck. She met the gaze of Charlie Crimcastle across the floor and shook her head with a derisive chuckle, remarking to her associates, "There's our turncoat, boys, smack in the mix of the Old Snozzler's humps!" She sat in her chair and leaned back, crossing her legs and exhibiting her trademark black-rubber rain boots with buckles, fixing her steady glare at the crowd and the stage with her hands joined behind her head.

A local hobo band known as the Lackawana Freeloaders soon took the stage and struck up a rollicking set of good-time gutbucket rhythm and blues numbers, as the weathered tramps, a trombonist, a flugelhornist, a drummer, and a stand-up bass player, were all recalled by Zeke from the other night he and Gunther played horseshoes at the shipping parts dumps. Zeke could feel the perilous tensions running through the heterogeneous factions now seriously tanking up as the Freeloaders really tore it up with their hard-partying sound. He sought some quietude to prepare once more for his master of ceremonies duties as well as running through the poems he had earmarked to recite, and while pacing in a back chamber he espied the hulking ursine form of Gunther through an ajar door as he sat on a bench swigging a bottle and looking over notes of his own. Zeke felt relieved that the big fellow had arrived on time and was taken unawares by his sudden presence as he had slipped in the back entrance inconspicuously. But he also became concerned as he approached him and got a load of his garb and the profound soul persona he appeared to be projecting. He wore a resplendent smoking jacket of silky silver and crimson gloss, a black and yellow polka dot silk scarf skillfully wrapped in pleasing folds around his neck, charcoal fine slacks led to argyle socks and deluxe suede loafers, and upon his dome tilted at a slight angle a finely woven cinnamon beret. Zeke now could hear him rehearsing his poem and paused before addressing him, his voice sounding affected and stilted, not the speech timbre he had been accustomed to from the massive Moody. " . . . he went whizzing by me / Straight into the wine-dark sea as it devoured him and his bicycle / And his dog / And I mused about these speeding creatures and their identities / Who is this man on a bike? / Where is he from? / What is his purpose? / And what can I do? / For one thing, I dove into the water off the pier and pulled him from that still sinking bike / And back up to the still air of wee hours darkness / I saved him and resuscitated him on the pier / While his dog found us on his own / And I saved him because that's what you do / This young man named Zeke Borshellac / Let's hope he does good with the new life he now has ahead."

Zeke already had heard some of Gunther's epic poem about him, but listening to him practice reciting it now in such a stilted manner caught him off-guard. It irked him to be a figure encapsulated in verse, as it afforded him no control over Gunther's Zeke Borshellac while at least he had a modicum over his own. Mainly, however, hearing the big man utter those lines about him, or the entity this bard manque deemed him to be, made Zeke delve deeply into an introspection with some hard truths to stare down about the direction of his life and whether he was on the right path to help improve the existence of other people. A soupcon of dubiety snuck into his conviction of poetry being his vehicle to deliver his best to the cause, an infinitesimal wisp of uncertainty slipped into his cerebrations via his gut, and he told himself that even those who achieve greatness had to wrestle with the creep of misgivings. So he doubled down in his belief in himself as a poet to effect positive change, and now, bearing secret witness to Gunther rehearsing his poem about him, he soon was overcome with gloom in the huge fellow's use of his name as a heroic figure. It did not feel right to Zeke as the daunting road ahead to become a poet of consequence with memorable work seemed beyond him and impassable. He was perusing his own poems and grappling with the noxious strain of self-doubt, unaware even when the raucous sounds of the Lackawana Freeloaders ended and only the coarse clamor of the liquored-up crowd continued to amplify.

"Hey, chief, it's about that time we get this hoedown under way!" came the voice of Mogler jarring him from his pages and looking up, the burly owner with the skeletons riding whales tattoos all over his arms was bearing down with a coercive mien. The maddening din of drunken vociferation seemed to crest as Zeke looked Mogler in the eye and felt the manifold pressure of the master of ceremonies job awaiting him on that stage. He nodded and slowly followed the Oilcan Conclave coarse owner through the back hallways towards the bar area and the raised platform with a kerosene lamp throwing a stark spotlight in the center. A gulp in his throat made him rue his willingness to accede to Ma's assigning him the MC role, and he felt the tension manifest in beads of sweat on his forehead as he clasped the pages of his verse in his hand. And then he was standing in the lambent spotlight peering out at the motley crowd of customers encompassing working stiffs and underworld and demimonde alike, all shrouded in dimness and dense billowing smoke, and he went utterly blank, frozen in a lost panic, and the crowd became more and more quiet until a dead stillness underscored every long painful second. Then he thought of "The Tender Heart of Clyborn Wankus" and spent a while crinkling through his pages until he found it. He hesitated as fear gripped him. As a Grackler stage fright never visited him, which vexed him all the more now albeit he realized back then he had his fellow riders with him presenting the shows. Here he was all alone up there in front of a fierce crowd. He turned to the Lackawana Freeloaders sitting on the side by their instruments and motioned for the stand-up bass and bongos to accompany him, by pretending to play them. And this aided Zeke in finding some composure, as he grooved in herky-jerky fits to the bopping percussion and steady undercurrent of bass, and he now began his poem about Clyborn Wankus, who everyone believed was a notorious gunfighter but was actually a clerk in a department store. "Don't shoot me, Clyborn Wankus / As if telling you not to shoot me would dissuade you if you felt like it / Shooting me that is / With a mad dog renegade such as yourself the best policy is to eschew you / Without provoking your umbrage or high dudgeon / Cause then you'd probably shoot me in the head or heart / Or more likely both." He went on to describe a bad man with a deadly shot who wore a black hat and black buckskin jacket and walked with measured intensity, glaring at anyone in eyeshot, great gleaming pistols hanging in holsters on his sides, every move he made, every corpuscle living inside him, was intent on striking fear into the hearts of every person who came his way. They obliged him by avoiding him, steering clear, so in a way he got what he wanted. Or what he thought he wanted. He really wanted was respect and admiration, but he only seemed to get fear, odium, and loneliness. He mostly was dealt loneliness and it nearly destroyed him, but he was able to rally in his later years and embrace his job in a department store with an open fervent vigor, where he was the happiest in his life. When Zeke finished the bass and bongos accompaniment continued as he moved in syncopated twitches and twists, allowing the resonance of Clyborn Wankus to hover over the crowd until he suddenly crossed his arms and slashed them outward signaling silence. He remained stock-still for several moments, still so wrought-up in the verse, and an uncanny stillness held sway over the crowd who were riveted but puzzled too. He sensed he piqued their interest and wanted to follow up with an even better poem, but the dizzying panic inside was ever a threat and he could not refrain from looking towards Ma Moody and her goons appearing none too pleased with whatever he was pitching. He shifted into MC mode and told them his name, introduced the Lackawana Freeloaders, and thanked the crowd "for turning out for what we promise will be a great evening of unforgettable poetry." They stirred some now with murmurs of restlessness and Zeke sensed losing this crowd would not only be a merciless proposition but possibly a physically painful one. He frantically searched his pages for a proper poem that would cast a spell over them. He came up with "Anton Brooks Cornflower." As he crinkled his chaos of papers the fear stung him and he had to dig deep again to begin: "Anton Brooks Cornflower was a wealthy magnate who lost everything / But continued to believe he was the same man who owned factories all over the world / Until he could not pay his debts and was forced to live on the streets / And shout furiously to strangers that a mistake had been made / That Anton Brooks Cornflower was a self-made millionaire who would not let the indignity of their petty jealousies stand / He would come back stronger and wealthier and more powerful than before." Zeke went on to tell the tale of Cornflower's struggles to secure loans and start new ventures in lumber mills, glassblowing, spices, and goose-feather greatcoats, all of which showed initial promise but failed atrociously. "In the end Anton Brooks Cornflower never got it back / Never recaptured that early success that deceived him into thinking it easy / Never again felt that invulnerable glory and ebullience of living / Never again thought himself worthy of his own respect / Never again was capable of savoring the rich bounty of existence that was all around him the whole time." Again, he let the accompaniment go on before slashing out his arms to stop them, and another uneasy silence supervened.

 He saw Ma Moody now visibly agitated and upright, gesticulating to her goons, and a sharp fright shot through him as he now picked another poem randomly from his pages. It was clear she wanted him muzzled and removed from the stage as he launched into "Quincy Quentin Kensington," and Mogler was shouting from the wings for him to "wrap the crap up!" On one side of the stage was Freano, the Moody moose waving an enormous wooden pole with a three-prong hook on one end, and the Bottle, the beefy Moody bruiser with a bad temper, on the other side with a hook of his own. "Quincy Quentin Kensington was a man who commanded everyone's respect and admiration / As a banker and ombudsman and father and bassoonist

TEN

/ Until he embezzled the profits of a Turkish Taffy manufacturer / And decamped to Eurasia where he assumed a new identity / as a mute laborer who tap-danced on street corners for donations / And played the bassoon in radical political salons with a world-weary enervation and a large fake mustache / Until Baroness Lilah Shempski publicly shamed him by calling him 'Shorty' and slapping him many, many times in the face." Zeke struggled to recite these words as the Moody goons stalked him with their hooks, and they grew bolder and more determined to hook him by chasing him at times around the stage. The Bottle actually snared his neck in the great hook and for a moment it appeared Zeke was done for the night, but he was able to grab onto the pole and pull back, now holding his ground. And just as the Bottle was yanking with all he had Zeke slipped his neck loose and let go of the pole, propelling the oafish brute backward with such velocity he crashed into the brick wall near the Lackawana Freeloaders. Zeke could not restrain a chuckle at his handiwork but had to duck the thrusting hook of the furious Freano, which he did with a nimble pivot and fancy footwork bordering on showboating. He motioned toward the freeloaders to strike up the bass and bongos again, now accompanying the wild slapstick of his dodging the desperate onrushes, and Zeke's confidence in eluding Ma's bullyboys only grew. The crowd by increments embraced and rooted for the nutty MC, roaring soon with rowdy laughter and drunken cheers every time he scrambled, feinted, or swiveled to deceive their advances. And to underscore his victory he picked up "Quincy Quentin Kensington" where he left off and in a sonorous proud voice, he recited the washout banker's grim tale of lost prestige and elusive redemption. "Quincy Quentin Kensington forever chased that fleeting span of time / In which he was banker big bucks and an ombudsman / Who cared about public parks and was a father devoted to his children / Whom he'd regale with selections on his bassoon."

They roared with merry gusto over Zeke's remarkable moves to remain on the stage, all while reciting his best received lines of the lost banker Kensington, and the very last phrase, *selections on his bas-*

soon, suddenly sprang up as chant volley after Borshellac unwittingly spoke it twice, the crowd parroting it back in a deafening giddy manner, SELECTIONS ON HIS BASSOON . . . and Zeke, sensing a moment, going softer, *selections on his bassoon,* and they only grew louder and crazier, while Zeke decided to come back with it as a question: *selections on his bassoon?* And the wild mob quickly pivoted with STUPEFACTIONS OF THE BUFFOON, which is the way it went for a while, Zeke employing a myriad of tones, inflections, and accents to the original *bassoon* line (miming playing a horn towards the Freeloaders, and the flugelhornist began to provide notes for his improvisation) while the unhinged full-throated lunacy of the crowd stayed pat with STUPEFACTIONS OF THE BUFFOON. But Zeke had achieved what appeared to be the impossible, he survived the hooks of Freano and the Bottle, who at some juncture during all the vehement hilarity of the chanting back and forth, recognizing the forceful will of its singular mindlessness, simply had to accede to its sweeping power. Even they chanted with the crowd eventually, Freano and the Bottle, and Ma Moody failed to find their participation in the least measure humorous and screamed oaths of derision at her two top goons, albeit no one heard her with the din prevailing. She stormed to the bar to order a tankard of port laced with tequila, and she peered across the room at another not involved in the chanting hullabaloo, reclined stolidly in his chair surrounded by his own hoodlums. "Well, Snozzy, you too are not having it . . . but we'll get the buffoon before you do, Snozzler old bastard!" she muttered, inaudibly amidst the blare. She watched Zeke bounce around in a frenetic free-form romp, playing a non-existent bassoon that blew flugelhorn sounds, and he soon suddenly stopped and slashed his arms out again, and let the stark silence again linger and charge the air, before concluding with: "Quincy Quentin Kensington never got it back, my friends, but there was so much more all around him everywhere that he ignored. Aren't we all a little like him? Whatever we had wasn't as great as it seemed, and recapturing it is a futile quest, and living so each day, each moment, so it counts, never seems to happen."

TEN

Silence greeted his finale until they apparently processed it, and one looped pirate sort blurted a heckle of "Bunkum! Twaddle! The Bastard Oughta be Beaten!" and one of the young Turks from the farmlands bellowed "the jamoke is jerk-off!" and one of the fishermen cried "Fraud! It's some sick trick!" and he pulled a live trout from his bag and whipped it at Zeke, catching him smack in the chest with the wet slime splattering all over him. The force stunned him and as he backpedaled collecting himself he was transported to his harrowing days aboard the lost trawler as the Fish Fellow. A rage swelled in him, an all-encompassing fury at the indignities he had had to endure and the awful injustices baked into the human condition in general. He felt too a crushing otiosity at the pointlessness of it all, which scared him terribly, employing such despair in the greater juggernaut of anger towards a reality that oppresses and defeats the collective cognizance by creating the schisms, strife, and discords. He began to read from his unfinished elegy, "Micah Ferguson Gargletoppe," which fit the unfiltered mad conniption of his ire insofar as it carried an unintelligible but wondrous rhythm to its eloquence. "He came from the mountains where folks were good and simple and kind / The fellow known as Micah Ferguson Gargletoppe descended to the lowlands to seek the adventure for which he pined / But he only met deceivers and miscreants and those who enabled them / And Micah Ferguson Gargletoppe grew bitter and frustrated and soon a bleak darkness colored his theorem / Which began to fuel his modus operandi in viewing the people of the lowlands with suspicion and cynicism / So back up in the mountains returned Micah Ferguson Gargletoppe where once again he experienced joy and love and amity and altruism." As he read he broke into a marching histrionic flailing, first depicting Micah's descent from the mountains and his visage infused with hope and exhilaration and curiosity, the final return ascent showing a dejected Micah, slumping and sagging and eyes dead and downward in a very slow ponderous march. Zeke sensed the crowd's confusion and impatience building as he started his march towards the rear of the stage, from where he espied Gunther sitting quietly in the shadows of the hallway. He was studying his pages of verse, practicing a phrase or rhyme sequence intermittently, and Zeke gazed upon him a few moments with a bleak sense of the reception the big fellow would be dealt. In his poet's garb of silver and crimson shiny smoking jacket, polka dot silk scarf, charcoal slacks, argyle socks and deluxe suede loafers topped with his cinnamon beret, Gunther seemed so sanguine in his trying to turn to poetry again—yet Zeke darkly foresaw the dejection he would feel upon his pending debacle. He moved closer to him now and got his attention, nodding and the big man nodded back, acknowledging the time had come. Zeke returned to the soft light of center stage and proceeded to introduce Gunther, although there was a palpable sense of impatience through the crowd, a pent-up excitement starting to boil over in anticipation of the main event, Cyril Moody. Zeke announced the next poet as "someone you all know, a stalwart individual who occupies a position of the highest command with the Moody Conglomerate, the older son of the estimable Ma Moody, a man who harbored an affinity for poetry many years ago but sacrificed a potential career for the sake of the family business."

Now the cries from the restless crowd, still increasing in number with standing room allowing a late influx, began coming from all sectors, voices rises from the smoky floor: "We want Cyril!" "Cyril! Cyril! Let Cyril read now!" "Cyril is the Moody Poet! Not the Big Goon!"

Zeke ignored them and continued: "I am very pleased to say he has embarked on a comeback and is here tonight with a new epic poem, from which he will read choice selections. Here he is—Gunther Moody!" The big fellow strode towards the light with buoyant verve, and as Zeke relinquished the center to him the crowd reacted with a medley of titters, whistles, and murmurs regarding his striking attire. Gunther remained silent long enough to make the crowd uncomfortable, perplexed, and as he surveyed the faint figure obscured in the dense smoke he found the one whose presence was most disconcerting, even daunting, his mother's sketchy form upright with glowering eyeballs and folded arms, and he locked eyes with Ma Moody momentarily until he had to avert his gaze, and then he began to read from "Zeke Borshellac." "Hooligans on horseback chased him on his bicycle through the cobblestone lanes / Zeke Borshellac pedaled with desperation and fear and raced faster and faster / Yet he could hardly shake them despite all his pains / And down the hill he barreled at a clip that was breakneck / His sheepdog Balt so shaken in his pouch the poor pooch was a wreck / Then they hit the pier and continued straight out high over the sea / For into the windy night they flew, sinking soon enough into the shimmery dark waters of desolate wee hours." He paused and slowly sauntered about the stage, the overflowing crowd now hanging on his words. His mother was vexed they were not rowdier and stood on her chair now and motioned for the boo birds to vent their disgust by holding her nose with fingers of one hand and thrusting the thumb of her other hand down. Now Gunther watched his mother do this and shook his head in chagrin, gesturing to the band that he wanted some accompaniment and with an ease of motion conveyed it to be the cymbals and a train whistle's lonesome blasts out of the flugelhorn, the bass and bongos completing the severe dead of night sound he sought. He recited the breathtaking verses of his dramatic rescue and their taking Zeke in as a lodger and patient and began the middle stanzas speculating on who Zeke Borshellac is and where did he come from and what is his purpose here. "Have I indeed done a good deed in pulling him out of a watery grave?" he asked rhetorically. "An otherworldly being who appeared in Bluddenville out of nowhere who no one thought too much about / Though he came shrouded in mystery and a deeper unknown calling, which he strove to discover / And we struggle to know whether he is good and just and righteous / Or someone best left alone to plummet to the bottom of the sea / Where he would surely be now if not for me / One day we will know the truth about Zeke Borshellac / And whether I am a savior feted or fiend reviled." Zeke was spellbound with the chiaroscuro postulate Gunther describes in presenting his journey to find his raison detre, his altruistic mission, and the potential that he could be quiescently dangerous and destructive despite all magnanimous intentions. It made him think about his will and capabilities and the ambiguities ever embedded and laced through all matters of existence, the deep-seated doubts and dismays that will undermine one's ability to be of use to others. And yet it mustered a second wind in him to move forward in his quest to help people and become a better person. He was anxious and eager to find his calling, as a future in poetry seemed dim, but as he lost hope for his own poems he was completely riveted by Gunther and his namesake poem's existential explorations. And the crowd was eerily quieter too, the hecklers and boo birds muted, save the distinct timbre of listeners hanging on every one of Gunther's words, and the haunting undercurrent of flugelhorn, bass and bongos.

That Gunther had turned the tide and worked the crowd into a new open amenability towards his verse was unequivocal to Zeke, as their attentive quizzical faces attested and the soaring words proved irrepressible. "Zeke Borshellac" quite simply was a fine epic poem in the Homeric tradition that seemed to find a ripe audience for its debut . . . but an agitation stirred in one section off to the side, a hurly-burly of antipodal rebukes and oaths led by the fearsome sea hag who could not brook her muscle boy's play for reinvention. She wanted her Gunther the only way anybody ever knew him, a brutal bruiser who protected his mother and her interests in whatever way it took. Flanked by Freano and the Bottle, Ma Moody stood on her chair and gesticulated with a raging vengeance as she split the poetic intense stillness with cries of vituperation. "Ya big dopey galoot, think ya on yer way, ya do ya do, well, welly, no sir, yer going down the crapper cause ya got nothin' NOTHIN', AND MA IS WATCHING ALL YOU BASTARDS! Taken in by the phony ass claptrap!"

And so her diatribe fouled the place, left a vile vicious slime of execration throughout the dive and stole the night from her son's inchoate efflorescence, mostly because no one wanted to buck the sea hag boss and be subject to her wrath. And then Freano threw a turnip at Gunther, clipping him on his chest and backing the big man up, silencing him mid-line of verse. He collected himself and squinted his eyes scanning the smoke obscured crowd, soon locking eyes with his

TEN

furious mother, who shouted with shrill derision: "What's the matter, ya' lardheaded palooka?! Lost yer place on the damn page?" Her shrieking guffaws reverberated throughout the place like a possessed chicken in a funhouse, while Gunther struggled to steady his focus again. "Hey, clodhopper, my pal Bottle here has something that will wake your ass up!"

With that The Bottle, smirking in his belligerence, suddenly whipped an oversize tomato at Gunther and caught him flush in the face, fast following with another plunking him on the neck. Gunther snarled and groaned and tried to wipe the splattered tomato coloring him red, and defiantly he clutched his pages and commenced to read again only to now be bombarded with tomatoes by the entire crowd, who were chanting for Cyril with a raw frenzy, and Gunther raised his arms in an attempt to cover up and lost his pages in the bargain. "We want Cyril! We want Cyril! The Poet of the Wharves! Gunther is a piss-poor palooka!" the rabid crowd screamed in unison as the white paper floated like giant confetti around the big fellow, and he slipped and slid on the tomato slimed stage until Freano sprang closer to clock him smack on the side of his dome with another turnip, and Gunther hit the deck hard and remained on his back motionless as tomatoes pelted his fallen form. Zeke rushed towards him to provide aid and succor, but a Freano turnip clocked him flush on the chin and he dropped, followed by a fusillade of tomatoes to which he succumbed in a supine grogginess. The crowd's attention shifted on a dime before anyone could notice bouncers dragging Gunther by their huge hooks across the stage and dousing his face with buckets of water until wakened and able to sit up. No one paid the least concern or curiosity for the big man's welfare, he was completely forgotten. A giddy buzz of anticipation rose as a commotion manifested in the last rows and beyond towards the Oilcan Conclave's entrance. Word spread swiftly among the wrought-up drunken patrons that Cyril had indeed arrived, and even the most hardened, depraved murderous miscreant now hollered with happy animal exultancy, for here came *their guy*, or more importantly, *Ma's guy, Ma's favorite, Ma's true poet son*.

They were all on their feet straining for a look at the Bard of Bluddenville, or the Poet of the Wharves, and glimpses they stole through the chaos of their roiled ripped swarm and smoke and madness was a skinny staggering form barely conscious, unable to stand if not for the stable of several strumpets propping him up on their bare shoulders (unabashedly in their scantily clad lacy frou-frou slips with Cavendish pom-poms), this disheveled debauched rake with a shock of red hair and a fey profligate handsomeness in a paisley silk suit replete with fancy ruffled shirt and sleeves, orange ascot, and two-tone pointy brogans, arduously moving through the aisle towards the stage with the wild mob parting for him, cheering and shouting praise and even singing drinking numbers of grand welcome, the band striking up swelling swirls of triumphant, if unhinged, marching songs of local tradition and allegiance. As Zeke picked himself up he gathered and reoriented his sensibilities to the new mood of full-throated jubilance and victorious greeting of their prodigal son, their fair-haired boy, *their Poet of the Wharves, Ma's true poet son!* And he could but watch from his cast aside perch in the darkened wings as Cyril lumbered forward to stage, the crescendo of acclamation accompanying his every shouldered step, Ma Moody upright in a seat of prominence between her thugs, looking on proudly, perhaps pinched some over her boy's condition, the singing, the chanting, the band's rousing rhythms all building to a feverish pitch as Cyril now teetered amidst his strumpet underpinnings, battling himself within, steadying, steeling himself to stand alone and deliver the vaunted verse they anxiously waited. After a number of attempts at releasing him—only to have to quickly catch him from falling down—the strumpets finally were able to arrange his stance so he balanced, uncertainly but enough for them to recede into the darkness, ceding the center spotlight to the revered poet son. His eyelids were heavy as he strove hard to keep them open, his legs were wobbly and he tottered precariously, once lurching so he had to right himself at the last second before tumbling. The crowd nervously murmured approbation of his efforts to stay upright and afforded him utter silence as he sought his footing up there. They knew Cyril Moody

TEN

was an unregenerate rumdum whoremaster, the pampered princely son of Bluddenville's underworld boss, and they had no choice but to like him, but they embraced him as one of their own, one of them, *their wasted preposterous poet.* And now he came to the moment, after clearing his throat elaborately and taking a few more fortifying swigs from his flask, when he dug in his stance and began to recite his poem. "I'm so tired of waking up to the world . . . and people wanting pieces of me . . . it is preferable to fall down and sleep . . . give me good whiskey . . . a pipe full of opium . . . and my bevy of fine harlots (he turned to them and stumbled) . . . and old Cyril is good . . . and *you people need to* (he pitched forward now and nearly went down, but righted himself to continue, wagging his finger) *leave me alone and compose your own goddamn poems . . . yeah! That's right!* (realizing he hit on something) *Write up verse for yourselves and leave me the hell out of it . . . cause I'm tired of waking up to a world that ain't mine . . . and has no way out . . . look, I got nothing for you . . . nothing ever changes 'round here . . . I'm gonna lay down and die one of these days and sleep off all the garbage . . . thank you."* And when he reeled this time he could not outlast it but crashed down hard onto the stage and lay in a sprawled still heap.

A long pause of silence followed, as the enthralled standing crowd seemed to process the truncated appearance of the Poet of the Wharves, apparently bewildered for the moment by the caustic unorthodox nature of the performance. Ma Moody cast her glower around the place, borne in her seat of salience between her goons with whom she whispered now, and then breaking the quiet tension gripping everyone (as the strumpets administered to their fallen chieftain) bellowed the loud bark of Freano: "He still has it, our Cyril has! Only a great poet could level us with blunt truth like that!" Now the Bottle broke in: "Genius! The Poet steers us to our own souls for poetry!" The crowd started murmuring and roiling in pockets of emotion as Ma pronounced: "That's right, ya humps! Find it deep in your own stinking selves! My boy is still brilliant as ever, yessir, well welly! My boy Cyril thrilled every one of ya sons of bitches, he did!" And the place all at once erupted in pandemonium, a good-time ebullience of hard partying song as the band struck up the stirring traditional numbers of Bluddenville yore, such as "Gut Ten Pikes and Call It A Day, Uncle Nobby," "Sea Legs and Scurvy, Ain't That a Pip!" "Sturgeon Smoking, Jonus Jumped In," "The Scrimshaw Swindle of Guy Schmutzie," the putative anthem, "The Seines of Skeleton Isaiah Jammed With Stinkfish," and the rollicking paean to the lam, "Shrovetide Dusk Skedaddle." They sang together in thunderous jollity, expansively and passionately and increasingly rough-and-tumble with all the back-slapping bonhomie for their unifying poet son, and the exultant jumping and spinning started breaking out, spirited smashing and crashing into one another by the more sloshed patrons who seemed to savor the violence.

Zeke got caught up in the jubilant jostling scrums entangled throughout and could hardly penetrate a pathway away from the mayhem, finding himself circumscribed to the thin halls and small rooms behind the stage and here he glimpsed, beyond the welter of nearby agitators, Gunther Moody, sitting on a bench slumped forward with his head down, an abject figure of despair to whom he called to no avail. He waded through the delirium somehow to make it to the big man and hesitated a moment, recognizing his profound personal pain. "Gunther, I thought your poem was splendid. It said more about me than I could have. While you were reading, I was so spellbound nothing else mattered. Time stopped while I listened. You had everybody. It made me contemplate my existence."

He did not look up and only answered: "Don't give me that. You heard them."

"No, they are wrong. It was transcendent, and that's something rare." Some rowdy drunken hoboes caught up in some kind of roughhouse brawl now came careening close and Zeke put his hand on Gunther's shoulder. "C'mon, you should clear out," he urged him.

Gunther now bristled with ire and rose to snarl: "I wish you scrammed a long time ago. Before I let you bamboozle me into believing I could take another shot at verse. You duped me, Zeke. You flat out snowed me into trying again and now I'm ruined cause of it." A burly fisherman crashed into his side and the gigantic Moody enforcer flared in pique, grabbing the poor fellow by his shirt and throwing him to the floor like a sack of millet.

"Don't say that Gunther!" Zeke rebutted. "I meant every word, and tonight hearing you read proved that you are a true poet of great gifts."

Gunther clenched his teeth and narrowed his eyes as he peered out into the raucous revelry raging on the floor, his tree-trunk neck taut with sinew, straining to see someone, Zeke thought. And he knew who it was that he sought. "Don't give up, Gunther. It's in you and it has to come out." Zeke recalled the book shop proprietor's words. "You can't make it here. You'll always be the same. You have to go out on your own, Gunther. You have to get away from Ma."

But Gunther saw her now standing with her arms crossed, the boss of the night, glaring at her massive son, and he could not avert her eyes.

"You know it was Ma who turned them against you!" Zeke cried.

The big man began towards her and Zeke shouted again, not sure if he heard him as Gunther threaded through the rowdy mob. But he knew it didn't matter, as Gunther was broken, and Zeke felt sick. In a daze of dejection, he wended a path behind him and watched with a lumpy throat as the vanquished gargantuan neared her steely pose and obeyed her stiff hand gesture aimed downward by dropping to his knees before her. And she cracked the side of his face hard with a backhand before swinging back with a stinging open palm. Her jaw jutted in clenched anger and she suddenly began hollering about "that son of a bitch Zebulon who was supposed to coach the boy with the poetry goods and not you, boy, cause you are my killer, always will be, boy, no sniveling snake rat bastard like that Zebulon can change that!!"

And Gunther had leaned forward on the floor to hug her ankles as she spoke this tribute to their bond, her trademark black rubber rain boots with buckles soon shaking and kicking to break free of his humbled form. Zeke deplored the disgust in her face and could not stifle his voice: "His poem was great. What you did was depraved and selfish. You know it was evil, Ma. Tell him, tell him he is a poet!"

She fixed him with a deadly glower and her eyes bulged and veins throbbed with loathing. "You neglected poor Cyril, ya rat, let those broads nearly ruin him. And I trusted you to coach him. Then you go after this one here."

Gunther moved to a crouch as Ma jawed viciously at Zeke. "I'm gonna make ya pay, Zebby. You owe me quite a sum, yeah ya do, for the bunk and the poontang that's been visiting upon your deep shuteye. You owe well-nigh a small fortune. And Ma intends to collect it, yes she does."

The band had launched into the beloved Bluddenville old tune, "Flotsam Trunks and Jetsam Shoetrees, Who Jettisoned My Chiffonier?" and the merry celebrants now sang the well-known lyrics together without easing up on their boisterous and bruising brand of roughhousing. The good-time drunken hilarity had spiraled into a rowdy violent spectacle all across the Conclave's floor, albeit Ma's immediate orbit remained the eye of the hurricane as the ruckus revolved around them. Zeke, vexed and indignant at Ma's threat, could not restrain his retort: "I'm broke so you can't collect dough I don't have! I got nothing, Ma."

The sea hag boss let out a loud, shrill laugh, her well-known creepy cachinnation. "Well, welly, Zebby boy, ya gots *other* attributes I value! And you'll just have to pony up through some honest work, won't ya, Zebby!? And while the *visitations* overnights will just keep addin' up, well, welly, we'll be in'ertwined together for quite a spell, wouldn't ya say?"

Zeke felt a harrowing chill pass through him as he thought of the bizarre raw carnality that had been descending upon his dreams, and he began to recognize the disturbing force behind the erotic rampages overwhelming his slumbers, recalled only in fragments. He saw the look in her eyes, the knowing smirk, and he began backpedaling in revulsion, when from his peripheral vision he now picked up several figures, burly menacing men he observed earlier who were seated with the Moravian.

TEN

The bad blood with the Moravian seemed inescapable now, the bag of loot ultimately stolen by the Hobo Father had to be accounted for by his former collector. The Moravian suddenly appeared out of the shadows with his men, Cal Crimcastle and Stu Leapers among them, and he glared murderously at Zeke. Just then Gunther rose from his haunches with purpose, the pages of his poem "Zeke Borshellac" in his hand. He ripped them up into little pieces with a flourish of finality, meeting Ma's pleased gaze then, knowing what else she wanted from him. He turned towards Zeke and lunged for him, but his former poetry coach nimbly dodged the bruiser, pivoted, and bolted at full pelt. But he very soon found himself snarled in a swarm of crocked wharf hooligans engaged in a fierce form of horseplay and now turned around and caught a glimpse of Cyril shambling about unsteadily but mostly conscious with his band of strumpets vigilant. He had his own group of admirers crowded around him as he managed a few laughs, like he was a king mingling with his subjects, and it appeared to Zeke Cyril would always reign as the harbor's self-destructive poetry prince, or at least as long as Ma reigned. Here he was with a bottle of whiskey in one hand and an opium pipe in the other, and living like that Zeke wondered how long their poet would be around. The Moravian and Crimcastle and Leapers and two unknown thugs now ambushed the momentarily distracted Zeke and yelled for the collection money he never turned in. "You better think this one through, Zeke," the Moravian himself exhorted him, "cause your life will fall into chaos before the big abyss, if you don't pony up!" The thugs made a beeline for him but the welter of roughhousing roisterers, many of them rube farmhands and overwrought wrecked fisherman clashing in good fun, proved too much blockage. Instead he skewed towards the shadowy back end and was headed off by Freano and the Bottle, who frantically maneuvered through madcap revelers in seeking to snare Zeke.

He heard Ma's raw shrill bark upbraid the Moravian somewhere behind him: "You best leave Zebulon be, Snozzy, cause he's mine, ya hear! He owes me the moolah, Snoozler, and he's my feller come the wee hours under the covers!" The crowd surged and ruptured into scores of frenzied scrums and Zeke desperately tore a path through as the Moravian's gang followed and fanned out, while Ma herself gave him chase and he could hear her hollering: "It's no use, Zebby, we gonna get ya! Might as well give up the ghost and come home to Ma! I ain't gonna bite ya, Zebby!" And she let out one of her trademark cachinnations, followed by: "But I may eat ya up, I just might, like I eat red hots with mustard!" And more of her disturbing laughter before he heard her yelling for Gunther to "get the son of a bitch, your Ma needs to descend on the boy in slumberland!"

Zeke crashed into a wild foofaraw going on between the Maritime Laborers and Sail Riggers Guild and Bluddenville Poetry, Phrenology, and Pipe Carvers Society and wound up flipping head over heels only to catch sight of the menacing figure of Gunther charging towards him tossing bodies out of his way. A terrible panic tore through Zeke as the killer behemoth appeared like a raging deadly cyclone out to destroy him. He knew Gunther desperately wanted to earn his way back into Ma's good graces and hauling in "Zeb" for her would more than accomplish that. He also knew the big man blamed him for the debacle of his poetry reading comeback, despite all of Zeke's subsequent encouragement and praise for his work. He heard Ma whistling and laughing her demented laugh somewhere behind her storming son and he threaded through a pack of hopheads puffing opium pipes and then was out a door and racing on the wet moon-shimmering cobblestones down a crooked back alley. It was raining and the streets were slippery but Zeke ran faster than he ever imagined he could run and he heard the brisk footfalls of his pursuers behind him, gaining on him every time they seemed to fade away, and this was debilitating to Zeke's belief that he could shake them, as was the incomprehensible hollering from the chasers, Gunther's deep guttural voice the most recognizable, as was the endless winding narrow streets he barreled down fleeing them, and the rain coming in sheets now, and hearing once Gunther yelling "You duped me you rat bastard! Made a jackass out of me with the poetry angle!" And he ran until his feet bled and his legs throbbed in pain and they kept coming, Gunther was inexorable, a roughneck juggernaut, and Zeke ran until he couldn't run anymore and he tumbled and fell forward hard, remaining stock-still, prone.

ELEVEN

WHEN HIS EYES OPENED to a squint in the gauzy lingering darkness of morning he was supine, under the covers of the same bed to which he'd become accustomed. He felt the strewn weight of his beloved sheepdog pressed against his leg and glanced upon Balthazar with appreciative affection as he wondered about waking up in Ma Moody's guest bed after the tumultuous events of the previous evening's poetry reading. His jittery consternation over finding himself back here was incongruous with the delightful sensuousness passing through him at the recollection of the powerful sexual force that descended upon him and rode him into wanton unrestrained passions of saturnalia. And he quickly understood again the true nature of such a force and the succubus who visited him. He flinched at the half-dried stains all around him on the bedsheets, and a gooey sticky discomfort suffused his loins while a sense of being violated undermined the post-ejaculatory glow of the slumberous night. He sprang up and anxiously looked every which way around the room and after convincing himself no one was watching, he leapt from the bed, scooping Balthazar up in his left arm. He knew enough not to make any noise and sat petting his dog's fine coat hoping Balt would remain silent as well. A solemn sense of defeat usurped his every breath, so utterly vanquished and debased he felt right then. A good part of him died in Bluddenville over the years, he knew, and what was left of him could not survive much longer in the old wharf city. Zeke knew he had no choice but to scram and do so in a hurry without any notice or fanfare, only quiet decamping and continuing until far, far away. He looked around the first floor to which his room was connected and was glad to find it empty. Where had the succubus gone to? he pondered. Having been around her for so long did nothing to make Ma Moody any less inscrutable. She could have been anywhere, he recognized, and by the wharves her long foreboding shadow hung over everything, but he was glad she was not present at that moment on the first floor of her pier house. And just as importantly, her zealously recommitted enforcer Gunther was likewise nowhere to be found. "Well, Balt, it is high time we hit the road," he said, and hugged his dog, kissed his nose and showed him his index finger across his lips to signal that noise ought to be kept down as they split.

Into the pre-dawn diehard night they came, a fellow walking his dog along the piers as the kerosene harbor lanterns cast shifting shades of pale luster over the lapping unrest of the waters. As he trod along the old wharves and heard his and Balthazar's footfalls on the worn wooden structures he gazed upon the many docked fishing vessels undulating gently in the sea, creaking and rattling. It was before the vast majority of fishermen began to stir when a lonely quiet still reigned, the last solemnity of night a strong curtain holding back dawn's arrival. There was a humble dingy beauty to the gritty cobblestone square, the great fountain sculpture of the fiery fisherman astride a giant seahorse spouting streams from his mouth, ever the focal point of the harbor, and Zeke recalled his mad dash past it from the schooner of his confinement that fateful morning long ago. He espied the scarce scattered fishermen busily moving around their boats in preparation for a day trolling deep waters, a couple others working the ropes and anchor of an old barkentine rigged out for long voyage. A light rain now began to fall and Zeke wished he had a hat. He maintained a good pace along the wharf front with Balthazar trotting right at his side, their flight from the old wharf city appearing to be on track and inconspicuous enough when they spotted a group of fishermen lose control of a lowering trawl of fish and subsequently scramble to gather them again. Their trawler had been out all night apparently and now all of their trawl—vast mounds of myriad varieties of the sea's fish—lay dispersed everywhere on the wharf area around their vessel.

As Zeke and Balt approached this chaotic scene another pack suddenly manifested, a bunch of hooligans emerging from a just closing tavern across the street, a sodden crew who very quickly saw an opportunity to appropriate the fresh flapping catch of the evening. And in an instant they struck, making a stealthy grab for the trawl itself still containing much of the fish and bolting with the lightning speed of drunken crazed thieves cocksure in their strides. Zeke watched all this from a safe distance and fully intended to stay his own course and skirt all the commotion. But such was the mess of spilled and strewn yield of the sea that Balthazar jogged towards the farthest afield fish and lifted a porgie in his mouth to bring to his master. "Thanks, Balt," he acknowledged in receiving his present, "but I don't know about . . ." He surveyed the nearby cluster of shiny flopping fish and thought to himself that having a few for their supper later would not be a bad idea. In his frock he had a long scroll of brown paper he had been using to write poetry and now he hastily began picking up several porgies, wrapped them tightly and jammed them into his frock's long pocket. He felt fortified with fresh fish on him now as he kept moving but a terrible shrill voice, a familiar fearsome shriek suddenly rang out piercing the early morning's fleeting repose. Instantly he knew the succubus hovered somewhere, lurking in the hidden recesses, onto his escape with his dog, and a frightful violent shock shot through him and stuck in his stomach like a hot dagger.

"Well, welly! Look who we have here strolling with his goddamn mutt! And after such a satisfying night in the hay, I'm a tad insulted, Zebby!! You ought to be back there with the Sandman, Zebby! Don't get any ideas on ditching ol' Ma now!" By shaft of moonlight he now could see her sitting on a mooring capstan out by the old decrepit pier, whittling a gnarled hunk of branch with a sizable chiv, a cigarillo hanging from her mouth.

The fishermen by now were all bunched together angrily debating who was to blame for allowing their trawl to be stolen. Ma now began shouting out to them as Zeke was passing by closer to the cobblestone square abutting the wharf. "Hey fellers! Hey fishermen folk! There's your thief right there with his dog! He was working with them that's glommed your trawl, and he's got a load of fish on him! The dopey-looking feller in the dark frock with the damn dog! He's the one lifted your fish!!"

And of course as they instantaneously shifted their wrath from one another to the man in the frock with a dog, unifying and focusing that fury into a single all-encompassing desire for vengeance, running at him with the acceleration of murderous rage, Ma Moody let out an unrestrained earsplitting cachinnation, that chilling vicious trademark laugh that invariably unnerved Zeke and this time added considerable dismay as he bolted with Balthazar. He made out one last shrill cry of hers: "Come on back, Zebby! Give it up and git your butt back where it belongs—right here with Ma! You can't leave Ma, boy! I want ya and Ma'll git ya, I will willy!!"

The rain picked up and was coming down steadier, the wet cobblestones reflecting gleams of the occasional kerosene streetlamps. He ran like his very life depended on it and it probably did, for the gang of fishermen chasing him were vicious unsavory characters who valued vengeance above all else when someone disrespected them. A glance over his shoulder showed there were more than he thought, at least ten of them, and they appeared more like pirates in their rough ragtag zealotry. And they were coming after him with some hard charging serious acceleration as Zeke and his speedy sheepdog coursed their way through a byzantine route of winding, crooked cobblestone lanes leading further and further into the deepest bowels of Bluddenville. Now and then a stone hurled by the pursuers whizzed past Zeke or skipped past his legs. Here and there he would pass denizens out and about in the early morning dark, noting the chase with keen interest, even agitation, but they remained observers only. Zeke felt the bundle of fish jouncing in the long pocket of his frock and thought about tossing it back at the fishermen, perhaps call out to them that it was all a mistake, he did not intend to steal their fish. But then he heard the menacing holler of a voice he seemed to recognize, a deep husky voice with a raw disturbing timbre: "*I will gut you like a hammerhead with my shank, you gutless gonoph!*" And the man's deranged chilling guffaws resounded and Zeke turned as he ran and knew the lineaments of the one leading the chase after him to be indubitably those of Devilcake, the cross-eyed burly fisherman who tormented and tortured him on his first berth aboard a fishing trawler years earlier. He thought that might have been him in the fishermen's tavern some weeks back on a night of hard rain. But it wasn't. This time it was Devilcake, all right. The grim identification sent icy spasms of terror through him, intensifying even more the stakes of his escape, and now he recognized that he was approaching the outer rural purlieus where he once worked on Ma Moody's house as a demolitionist, which meant the woods was not too far away and therein lay his best chance of losing his pursuers under cover of the pitch-black timberland.

Into the wet woods he and his dog ran pushing through the density of tall trees and penetrating overgrown pristine wilderness of scant pathways and nearly zero visibility and Zeke increasingly sensed the fishermen had fallen farther and farther behind until he suspected they had given up altogether and turned back. And just as this gladsome thought entered his mind he crashed into a great oak and went down to the wet earth with his head ringing, half conscious. The smell of woodland wet in early spring momentarily cast his mind into a reverie of boyhood, but as he regained full cognizance to find Balthazar licking his face with excited concern he slowly rose, wobbly but determined to resume running and weaving through the trees. *How his pursuers would have enjoyed his accident,* he thought, and he cursed them for causing it. He moved through the dark woods with a groggy resolution, grinning with a wounded satisfaction that he had filched the porgies and felt them with pride wrapped in his frock. He now even wished he *had* stolen the entire trawl. His only mistake was being seen by Ma Moody, the ubiquitous strumpet sea hag! *What in the name of God was she doing on the wharves whittling at that ungodly hour!? Summoned from Hell to bear watch on her fleeing captive?* He cursed Ma Moody and her jaboneys and cried aloud in unshakable defiance: *I will cook their fish and savor it tonight!* And just then as he paused he heard rustling and distant footfalls and he feared it was them and began running as fast as he could before smashing smack into an immense tree and once again falling on his back mostly unconscious. Balthazar again was agitated with worry and licked his face, nudged it with his snout, and brought him back once more to get up and continue his way through the woods, tottering, reeling, scrambling, staggering, pitching, but pushing forward. Faraway guffaws of a madman now barely made his earshot and he thought: could it be Devilcake? No, the staccato shrieking and raspy gurgling of the troubling laughter signaled to Zeke a foreigner of some sort, a Burmese perhaps. Zeke and Balthazar just kept running and running and covered good ground. And Borshellac was clocked by other trees just the same and he kept rising off the wet earth, each time perhaps a skosh slower, but concomitantly with that much more will to continue running. Yet he was chagrined and tormented by his enduring propensity to land himself in precarious predicaments that ultimately require extrication only through fleeing angry mobs of violent maniacs who want to kill him, or at the least, beat the bejesus out of him. *Why must I always flee for my life, run away and start anew somewhere as a stranger?! he cried into the black woods. When all I want is to live a life of the mind! And live righteously! And for the love of Pete, to eat well . . . a fine cut of meat or a slab of Wensleydale cheese or a slice of shoofly pie with vanilla custard once in a while ain't so much to ask!* Zeke thought about past aspirations that have degenerated into dark mad pipe dreams, hopes that would transmogrify into protracted failures, and a wellspring of fervor for new ideas and visions twisted and distorted by despair and desolation. His loneliness was an unyielding condition that deceived him at times into thinking he was used to it, he could handle it, right before lowering the boom. Through it all his one unswerving steadfast aim was to do his best to help people and effectually dedicate himself to the task of making life better for everyone he came across, but too often, he knew, he had had the opposite effect on folks. Now he slowed to a halt as the rain picked up again and he and Balthazar took shelter under the thickness of trees, a peculiar bower bastion, and he rested upon a large rock. Here he ruminated on the direction of his life and took stock of the experiences and travails that brought him to this very moment in time. He understood for a while now that he was lost in the forgotten backwaters amidst the lurking snares and shadowy webs of far-flung ruination. All his dreams of work and friends and love, *the elusive idea of true love he somehow never soured on,* were all eventually met with disappointment and disgust and culminated in his bolting alone, chased. He thought about the hobo father showing up out of nowhere and their fight and the aberrant figure riding off on Scunj with Zeke's collection money still in saddlebags of the great steed. The hobo father forever would remain mysterious and daunting as the harum-scarum whirlwind of a distant boyhood spent in a tavern with his mother who happened to be a wench and a barn from which his father roused him for breakneck nocturnal drunken horse rides in the forest. Zeke reflected on matters such as these for a long time on that rock, indifferent to his sopping state, at one point searching his frock for a pint of rum he figured he still had and pulling it out of a crowded pocket. He took a good swig and it went down just right and he smiled a bit now knowing that Ma Moody and her sons and the Moravian and Crimcastle and Freano and the Bottle and Devilcake and all of them back in Bluddenville were behind him. After a while he came out of it thinking that being Zeke Borshellac ain't so bad, and he wasn't in the box yet. His heart still pumped blood and his breathing kept coming in and out the way it always had. And he was happy to have Balthazar at his side, who reclined close to him now and Zeke stroked his soaked, matted sheepdog fur as he reflected. How Zeke loved that dog! "Balthazar, as long as I have you with me on this journey I know everything is going to turn out all right and go our way," he stated as an indisputable fact, and he hugged him around his shoulders and nuzzled and kissed his snout. "You know," he observed after a space, "maybe we're not running *away* from places, but *towards* new ones with folks just waiting to welcome us. At least that's a better way of looking at it." And they hung around there on the large rock under the thick trees that protected them from the rain, which during this meditative interlude ceased falling, and then the first pale light of dawn appeared and slowly strengthened into the beginnings of a beautiful morning.

The isolation and singular silence of the forest felt soothing to Zeke, and he basked in the wilderness verdure as he and Balthazar began their ramble through tall trees and over hills rife with all manner of budding vegetation. He found a contemplative stride that lingered over the gurgling wonder of a winding stream and savored the sounds of hidden tiny birds buried in a round dense tree. A family of otters were busy with some unknown project near the stream and Zeke admired their presence of attention. Only as dusk seemed near did he think about making camp and resting, and the porgies promised to make a fine supper. He cooked them over a fire in his small weathered pan and as they sizzled in their own juices he gazed at the sunset sky over the hills. He found his whiskey bottle, which he left alone since morning, in his frock and took a sip. He petted Balthazar and soon placed a bronzed smoking porgy in front of him on a rock and chuckled as his dog slowly came around to grasping it in his mouth and devouring it. He gave him another one and began himself to sink his teeth into the succulent tasty fish. "Yep, Balt, it was worth being chased by those sons of bitches to eat this fish," he remarked with a smile. They slept side by side for warmth as the chilly night air grew breezy, tucked under some brush next to a cluster of spruces, and before he fell asleep Zeke stared at the stars above and felt at peace with everything, though he knew it could not last. Change was ahead in his journey. He wanted more than the life he had known, and he knew he was ready for it. "We're going to find it, Balt. Whatever is out there for us," he said.

He hiked through the pristine wilderness for several days like this, rising at the first light of dawn and pushing onward at a measured easy pace that allowed full appreciation of the majestic surroundings. Early morning mists cast the wooded pathway in a mysterious shroud and Zeke would call out for his sheepdog, who had disappeared into nearby dense bush, and Balthazar always reassured him with a bark of his presence. The forest sounds of busy animals going about their days amused Zeke and connected him to it all, unless the volume bespoke of larger, more fearsome creatures. He mostly lost himself in the luxuriant refuge of the forest and its stark otherworldly clearings and the rolling hills that invited the wayfarer to the other side, beckoning of unknown secret marvels. Here in the forest oblivion Zeke could simply explore moment by moment and experience the virgin land in dreamlike wonder, cogitating upon the great ontological questions of famous thinkers, such as who whipped it all up in the first place and split without formally taking the credit? He drank the pure cool water from the rushing streams and caught a wide assortment of tiny unearthly sea creatures to cook up for their supper each night, assiduously monitoring their simmering slow roast with huckleberries and oat grasses. Since he was a puppy Balthazar had not appeared so exuberant and spunky to Zeke and he found himself smiling often at the sheepdog's gambols and explorations in the endless woodland. This is the place for a dog with Balt's heart, he understood, and felt a pang of remorse at the itinerant way of life he had only shown him, often fraught with severe volatile milieus. In the quiet recesses of remote forest a dog can do as he pleases, he mused, run amok if so desired without anyone around to tie him up. They both found their own serenity and a healthy balm of freedom, albeit evanescent, by simply being open to the great natural world enveloping them. But as much as Zeke savored these exquisite days of hiking through the virginal forest with his beloved sheepdog, mulling whether to settle in such a lush hidden world of discovery, he could not deny a yearning for human connection and yet finding a larger purpose and place in life. Oh, he pondered long and hard about disappearing in the woods for good with his dog and living the natural existence of a woodsman off the fruit of the earth, or at least endeavoring to continue the journey open-ended and see where it led. And he had managed to convince himself a few times that this was the right path for him now, living free like a frontiersman in the woods and beholding all of its vast splendor. In the wilderness Zeke found his spirit healing after the dark insidious events that befell him in Bluddenville, once more he felt a modicum of joy inside as he passed through trees and the inextinguishable faith he carried now stirred and rejuvenated. He anticipated wondrous happenings coming his way somewhere ahead in the unknown pristine forest, for he knew such a venue already existed and those who were there already would welcome his arrival and adapt to the permutations his presence would put them through. He could not envision the place in his mind's eye, but he had ancillary glimpses in the fine tree leaves gently swaying in the wind and the honkers soaring in formation and squawking like loony loons and the doe and her fawns pausing for a drink in the burbling stream. He felt an incipient exaltation at witnessing these fleeting vignettes and believed he was on the right course and would stay on it until he got there, wherever that may be.

One late overcast morning, after Zeke had been rambling along meager sinuous trails through thick, overgrown bush for several hours, an abrupt rise in the woods made the trek quite arduous. He tore into the challenge and upon reaching the apex he was all tired out and envious of Balthazar, who rather insouciantly trotted his way to the top with nary any effort. The other side met them with an almost impenetrably tight morass of wildly branched trees and underwood, but the declension was longer and much less steep with a deep narrow brook rushing near the bottom. And Zeke could make out through the diffracting shafts of light guiding their descent that beyond the fast-flowing water and its misty spray the bottom opened into a clearing, which became a stunning green expanse once he caught a good vista. It had been two days since he came upon open land and he saw in its long grassy inclined plane that stretched to the cloudy horizon an excitement and tingle of curious anticipation. He hastened his way to the brook's white misted pool of foment, the repository of its rapid cascades, and he and Balthazar drank its fresh water, crossing at its lowest, narrowest, and debouching into the illimitable realm of yawning grasslands. Glimmers of sunlight peeping through the clouds greeted them, as if exhorting them onward towards the zenith where the sky appeared to sport a steadier blue. Balthazar raced and romped about pell-mell at the dramatic new environs to which they'd shifted, and

Zeke felt the same canine merriment in his chest and after throwing a stick several times for his sheepdog to retrieve with happy alacrity, he simply joined him and cut loose himself in abandoned sprints. It was as one such sportive dash slowed when he first noticed the faraway lineaments of a small farm, a faded white silo, rust-red barn, a modest clapboard dwelling, and with a wave of astonishment at such a far-flung farm and sanguine stirring at the prospect of meeting people after so much time isolated in the woodland, Zeke gravitated towards it. Among the chief expectations spurring his interest was the idea of warm hearty meals for him and Balthazar, as the fare of the wild had its limitations, and his gustatory fancy made his mouth water. And then he spotted a lone distant figure at work in the fields, a cluster of large animals, cows he thought, nearby. As he advanced he soon discerned the form to be a dairymaid tending to the herd. She was engrossed in her work, stroking their hides and evaluating them, Zeke thought, and she apparently did not perceive the stranger approaching from the lower end of the pasture. She wore a long white dress that fluttered in the breezes, a canary yellow top with a wide round white collar, and a white puffy bonnet with a small brim. Her straight golden brown hair hung down her back and seemed to Zeke a most beautiful color. The closer he and Balt drew the harder at work she appeared to be, darting about the cows with a myriad of arcane tasks with which she vigorously applied herself. He thought maybe she had become aware of him at some point but chose to continue her duties and ignore him. It was hard to tell.

At about twenty feet away Zeke called out to her: "Hello there! How are you this morning?" When she did not respond, he moved closer and addressed her louder as she seemed preparing to milk the black bovine with the white patches.

Now she turned and glanced upon the striking personage who seemed to manifest from nowhere, his sheepdog near his side watching her. She recoiled but quickly steadied herself to ponder the stranger looming suddenly like a stark specter who at present continued, or so tried: "I've been traveling through the forest—" his mind went swirling into speechlessness as he gazed upon the radiant aura of the dairymaid, the most beautiful woman he had ever seen, and he could not look away and remained simply gaping. "We've been in the woods and—" he stammered out before again going silent. Balthazar barked softly and stuck his snout into his leg until Zeke averted his eyes and caught the dog's quizzical look, one that sensed his master's awkward faltering.

As Zeke now snapped out of it the dairymaid assessed the encounter with her wayfarer. "You're a hobo, aren't you? We haven't seen any hoboes out these parts."

Thunderstruck by his primal attraction to her Zeke was still speechless and incapable now of rational thought. He had never seen such lovely, lustrous eyes and fine ruddy cheeks and a simply enchanting face and the breathtaking overall figure she cut before him proved too overwhelming for Zeke to handle and immobilized in his daze, he groped for words, any words, to further their introduction. But they would not come, despite Balthazar poking him again with his snout and barking lowly. The dairymaid regarded him closely, as though she were studying him, and Zeke thought her expression betrayed a portion of scorn, even repugnance, but perhaps a dark curiosity with the odd creature she mistook for a hobo.

"No trains run anywhere near these parts, so you must be quite lost," she determined aloud, as if she were addressing two dogs, not one.

Zeke knew right then and there he loved her utterly and forever and felt himself breathing heavy and growing light-headed with a swooning vertigo, and eventually stammered out a garbled "I'm no hobo" that the dairymaid interpreted differently with a somewhat patronizing smile.

"Of course you do, you must know lots of 'em! But you're all alone, way out here. Don't you roam around together?"

It took some of the air out of him as he absorbed how she perceived him, but part of him understood it as he'd been around hoboes for years and did share their roving independent searching spirit, as well as a predilection for whiskey and foraging off the land wherever. And not only were hoboes his object of succor and alms but he generally found them earnest, good-natured souls with a tincture of lunacy that invariably produced laughter. Notwithstanding, he had never thought of himself as a hobo and her seeing him as one sunk his reverie of flirting with her before he could get a sentence out.

The dairymaid discerned the chagrin stalling a response from Zeke and allowed a slightly skeptical sigh before tendering a kindly overture: "Well, I suppose you are spoiling for a good meal after traipsing through the woods for so long. I can fix you up a nice plate of farm fresh victuals if you like."

A warm rush of joy suffused Zeke at the notion of such a meal and time yet to spend in the dairymaid's presence, though it was tempered by the offer emanating from pity deigned as a sense of duty. And she hadn't mentioned Balthazar, which he pointed out. "Thankya," was his terse reply, "my sheepdog could use a plate too." And he quickly cringed inside at his words, fearing their forwardness.

"Of course, he will eat well with me!" the dairymaid affirmed, as she knelt to pet Balthazar fondly. She rose with a smile of compassion in regarding Zeke and asked him his name. When he said it she told him hers, "I'm Lavinia. I know these are very hard times and I have much empathy for those wanting." She paused before adding, "I never met a real hobo before and we'll do our part to sustain you for your rambling around." And then she switched back to her cows and sat upon a wooden stool and went about her chore of milking them in the most efficient manner, clearly to Zeke like someone who was a professional in her trade, and he watched with fascination, figuring she'd come across with the grub once she finished. He admired every facet of her aura and did so with a mooning gaze. He could tell she cared about the cow she so carefully worked on by the manner she grasped its bag and squeezed and pulled down, holding it tight between thumb and forefinger until every drop trickled out. "I'll take you over to the house as soon as I'm done with Flossie," she said while she milked, "but I have to draw her dry or she may quit making enough for tomorrow."

ELEVEN

He had misgivings over not completely disabusing her of the misconception that he was a lone lost hobo who wandered far from the railroads and jungles, but being near her and the fine meals she was soon to bestow on him and his dog was too good to jeopardize with gratuitous particulars.

Once she finished milking she began across the pasture with two full pails in tow, but Zeke quickly insisted that he carry the weighty pails for her. Reluctantly she consented and considered him with a quizzical but sunny expression. "I must say, Zeke, encountering a hobo who came out of the forest is a prospect that formerly would have caused me much consternation. But I have no disquiet being out here with you, as I don't sense that kind of desperation or character about you."

"It would pain me to think my presence may cause you the slightest distress. I am a harmless wanderer," he assured in a low garbled manner, such was his jitteriness.

Lavinia stopped by the chicken house on their way and Zeke saw the little stove in there keeping the birds warm as they gathered around the light emanating from it. She inspected their feed bins and turned some of the pullets' eggs and the whole gaggle of them clucked and flapped around making a ruckus. One very large rooster remained perched on a crate beneath a window and only moved when the others began to settle, hopping down and marching towards Zeke with a raised beak scowl. Zeke quietly with bemusement awaited the chief chicken, or so he ascribed to him, strut his way over until he paused but a couple feet away.

"Now, Hooper, don't blame him for your being disturbed in here, it is my fault," Lavinia admonished the bird. But the rooster attacked Zeke by pecking him all over his ankles until he shook the creature off him. Balthazar broke into a barking frenzy as Lavinia hollered for Hooper to stand back. It was all over very quickly and in the protracted calm afterwards Lavinia and Zeke both began to chuckle at the crazy chicken's truculence.

"I guess he doesn't care for me," Zeke remarked.

"Hooper doesn't care for anyone," she said, still laughing quietly.

Once more they began across the pasture in the crisp breezy air with spotty intervals of sun and Zeke felt a blithe wonder over the idyllic secluded farm with the fetching dairymaid. There were moments when he could have very well believed he was in a dream, the kind you do not wish to waken from too fast. And now suddenly Balthazar bolted like a mad demon hound towards a rolling expanse of grassland that rose to a hillock and Zeke tore after him in a frenetic anxious state. He had never seen his dog race away so precipitously, so hellbent.

The dairymaid spun around and called: "What's wrong, Zeke? Is he all right?"

As he cleared the hillock Zeke perceived the irresistible allure Balt ran towards, as the dog had glimpsed from afar what he saw now. The indelible image would forever stay with him as he descended into the vast valley and beheld Balthazar barking and scrambling to and fro as if possessed on a tactical mission to herd the sizable flock of sheep that had been tranquilly grazing until his disruptive arrival. In Zeke's utter astonishment he watched Balthazar work with maniacal fervor in rounding them all up into one tight regiment and begin driving them forward. It was a riveting exhibition of natural know-how and efficacy, and Zeke now halted and remained gaping on the spectacle with arms crossed.

Livinia caught up to him and stood beside him surveying the fine display of herding and observed: "It is wondrous the way the instinct is in his nature and comes alive upon seeing sheep."

Zeke started towards Balthazar and the sheep, but halted after a few steps, and called back: "I guess it's in him and had to come out. Wondrous is right. We all have something like that in us, I would think."

He continued towards his dog to coax him from his trance, pondering what natural instincts may be lying deep within his own recesses. After shouting to him to no avail Zeke swooped in on Balt to hug and pet him and provide an interjection of affection for the dog to come out of it, while lauding his stunning display of shepherding. As they began towards the dairymaid Zeke could feel the collective gratitude from the shell-shocked sheep staring at their withdrawal.

At the modest red clapboard farmhouse Zeke and Balt waited outside sitting under a maple tree while the dairymaid said she would be right out with "a good meal for each of you." And she was good to her word, plying them with a large picnic basket stocked with bread and cheese and meat and fresh vegetables and her two guests tucked into it like the hungry wayfarers they were. Zeke savored his food with a singular gusto in the splendor of the fine morning, albeit he maintained his pace and manners as Livinia sat across from them on a stray bale of hay watching them with keen interest. Balthazar had no such qualms about devouring his grub with a ravenous intensity befitting a wild beast, and her first remark, after a long space of silence as they ate, came with a warm smile: "I'm glad our eminent shepherd finds his food so appetizing!"

"Your meals are a cut above what we are accustomed to chowing down on," Zeke said. Sunlight suffused the farmland around them and the breeze in the trees lent a soothing note to their picnic. But Zeke could hardly relax as he was quite bewitched by the strange, beautiful dairymaid who had been so kind to him and seemed intrigued by his journey. Except she deemed him to be a hobo, an identification that piqued her curiosity for sure but concomitantly relegated him to freak or oddity or worse, pitiable status, hardly the way he would have truly aspired to meet such a lovely young woman.

She asked him where they last came from before trekking through the forest and he told her Bluddenville, to which she visibly recoiled. "I have always heard it's a place full of depraved hoodlums and blackguards and danger lurks everywhere," she said.

Zeke finished chewing before replying. "It is a grim and wicked city but some folks there are decent skates who are up against the brutish clout of the underworld. I am fortunate to get out in one piece."

She studied him for a while and he could feel her mind speculating about him while he continued gorging himself. "I suppose they had one of those hobo jungles there and that's where you found shelter and enough to eat," she drew as a conclusion.

A dizzy sensation passed through him with the humbled realization of what the hoboes he had known must have thought about being pegged unmistakably as hoboes. You can exist in a certain classification of life without ever knowing it, or for that matter, not even fall within the parameters of such a classification while remaining clueless about others seeing you as such. "Hoboes will always treat fellow railbirds with great hospitality. Jungles are open to all comers," he said generally, leaving himself apart. "They ride the rumbling boxcars over the moonlit plains and look up at the stars and dream their wholehearted hobo dreams. In solidarity and song they find faith that better times are coming down the pike, for their numbers are growing and they will be heard one day."

Zeke surprised himself with his florid oratory, responding with an involuntary instinct that seemed to fit the moment. Livinia appeared to enjoy his speech, almost succumbing to laughter as she digested the gist of his remarks, laughter Zeke knew would have been in a gentle, fond manner. He wished she had broken into laughter, how even more beautiful it would render her.

"Your words make it sound like such a grand and noble adventure. I suppose they pack more power when spoken by someone who has rode the boxcars over those moonlit plains. Where are you and Balthazar traveling to this time, if I may inquire?"

Now Zeke was gazing at the dairymaid as she said these words, but he heard them in a way you might hear a stirring song that moves you deeply, and suddenly he knew where they were traveling to, an isolated enchanted farm with a dairymaid he loved from the moment he saw her. He wanted more than anything in the world the chance to work on that farm, yet he hesitated in asking her for fear she may dismiss the notion outright. Why would they hire me? he thought, realizing he had no experience on a farm and Livinia took him for some rambling hobo beating the bushes. "I don't know," he finally answered, pausing to regard the rolling pasture and the distant stream and irregular edge of forest, and then meeting the glorious mysteries of her gaze once more. "But I'll tell you what. I've been searching for some work for a long time and not having much luck. But something tells me that maybe you can use a farm hand here to help out. While I don't know much about farming, I'm a fast learner and about the hardest worker you ever saw and I've got good stamina to finish what I started." He looked over at Balthazar who was now lounging languidly with his full belly. "And you saw for yourself what my sheepdog can do for you to keep those sheep in line."

The dairymaid smiled and chuckled some as she considered Zeke's overture. She explained that such a decision of course would not be up to a dairymaid but the farmer who owned the land, her Uncle Phineas, who she added was not her real uncle but a fine man her father trusted like a brother when he enlisted in the French Foreign Legion. "I have lived with him and my Aunt Abigail here on the farm since I was a girl and my mother was taken to the sanitarium and my father wanted to fight for liberty with the Legion."

Upon hearing her hardship Zeke felt very sorry for her and asked if she had seen her parents since and if they were well. She breathed deeply before answering and said, "No, but I have faith Providence will lead us back to one another and we'll be together again. The doctors told me my mother's mind had to heal before she could come back. After my father is done fighting wars for the Legion he will come back. Until then I have my family here on the farm and am grateful for that."

A long silence passed and Zeke thought the notion of working on the farm with Livinia, a prospect just then he wanted more than anything in the world, seemed a cruel illusion. He rose and was about to bid the beautiful dairymaid adieu rather than press her about working for her uncle when she said to follow her.

He waited with Balthazar on the porch of the farmhouse and after a while Livinia emerged with a lanky, dour man with an aquiline nose, wire spectacles, and muttonchops. He wore heavy oilskin overalls, grasping the suspenders, and a checked flannel shirt underneath. He surveyed Zeke from pit to dome and fixed his gaze on Balthazar.

"I'm not in the habit of putting hoboes on the payroll, but a first-rate sheepdog, as Livinia attests you have here, would be most welcome." He then moved closer to Zeke and asked him if he'd consider selling his dog. "I'm sure you can use the money."

Zeke stood straight and met the farmer's eyes as he declared: "Sir, I'd rather part with my life than with Balthazar, so please don't insult me. He is my bosom buddy and the most trusted partner one can ever hope to have." Zeke noticed Livinia frowned at her uncle's offer, before he said: "Thanks for your time," and began away.

"Now hold on there, feller," the farmer said in a slightly lighter tone, "I respect a man who loves his dog and that comes across with you. I didn't expect you to sell him."

Zeke hardly believed his reframing of it but heard him out as he continued about farmhand work being hard and doubting whether a hobo can handle it. "Son, I'd like to provide opportunity for the likes of your ilk, but it appears a futile exercise."

Livinia now pulled her uncle aside and whispered in his ear and he nodded. Zeke felt the ambivalence in the farmer's face as the stern figure stared at him before saying: "Insofar as next to nobody ever comes passing through these acres, somebody ought to beat nobody, and that there is the kind of canine shepherd we can use. Well then son, I will give you a chance to show me what sort of farmhand you are. If you wash out, no hard feelings. Livinia will show you where you can bunk in the barn."

A surge of gratitude overcame Zeke as he sought words to express it to the farmer uncle, Phineas Von Klobbert, though he managed only a garbled thank you as he and Balt followed Livinia, herself visibly pleased, to the old barn where a hayloft to occupy awaited them. After settling in a few minutes Livinia took them to meet Aunt Abigail in the kitchen of the farmhouse, where she was busy preparing cherry, blackberry, and strawberry preserves while baking a rhubarb pie. She warmly greeted Zeke and petted Balthazar with a smile as she made a pot of tea and spoke of challenges the farm faced to maintain a semblance of solvency. "We've never hired a hobo before," she once noted, "but all of the Lord's people are worthy of working the soil so long as they work it hard and with the dignity it deserves."

Zeke sipped his piping hot tea with a cinnamon stick in it and averred with utter conviction: "I revere the earth and welcome the opportunity to work with it and learn from it."

Livinia now recounted the dazzling performance of Balthazar herding sheep to her aunt and Abigail listened in wonder, gazing admiringly upon the dog. A hale, matronly farm wife, Abigail appreciated the sheepdog's talents and said: "We can put to fruitful use the abilities of such a fine canine."

But Zeke perceived a hesitancy too in her tone and mien, one that betokened broader concerns and challenges. At that moment the sound of a screen door creaking open and slamming shut caught their attention and heavy footsteps across adjacent wooden floorboards were heard before a very tall, rangy fellow in dungarees and a long canvass brown coat entered the room with squinty eyes and a startled expression. He had a long bushy mustache and a weathered face that seemed pinched and glum and exasperated, that of a sullen farmer who imbued the room with an awkward tension.

Livinia anxiously introduced him to Zeke. "This is our longest serving farmhand, Zeke. Mr. Horst Schtuckgloo. He can make anything grow."

Schtuckgloo looked at her and corrected: "Anything except a dead man I can cajole into springing from the soil." His voice was rough and raspy and his intense glare struck Zeke as freakish. When Livinia told him Zeke and his dog were going to work on the farm with him he nodded without saying a word as his eyes bore into the younger new hand.

"We could use new blood," he said, "but don't you get all caught up in your own method of farming. We have a way of working the soil out here. Ya hear? We've grown what nobody has ever grown out here and we will continue to do so."

"I assure you I am here to serve the vision of the farmers who'd laid claim to this magnificent acreage in the forest wild, yourself and Uncle Phineas," Zeke enunciated clearly.

Now Horst Schtuckgloo gazed at Zeke as he circled him to his left in wide strides. "What makes you declare such docility to your superior sodbusters? It ain't that you don't care about the soil, is it?"

Zeke rubbed his mouth and reflected downward a moment, frustrated by the peculiar farmer's line of inquiry. He held his composure as he replied: "I already told you that I revere the soil."

Horst shook his head with confusion as he cupped his large right hand around his right ear. Livinia knew he was playing with Zeke and tried to intervene. "Horst, I think we've gone far enough . . ." But Zeke was well past miffed by now and shouted very loudly at the loopy farmer: "I REVERE THE SOIL!"

Horst chuckled now, delighted that he got a rise out of the newcomer, and he quickly launched into naming the crops and livestock on the farmland he would have to learn everything about: *turnips, beets, potatoes, parsnips, eggplant, green beans, peas, onions, asparagus, strawberries, corn, wheat, and rhubarb.*

Zeke asked if anybody knew Simon Grackler, a former farmer from the Grackler Farm where they grew the finest onions anywhere. Nobody responded, except Aunt Abigail who mused about the Grackler Riders of the Reckoning and Zeke nearly divulged his history as a highwayman, albeit decided what was the point as Horst jumped in again to name the livestock they had: *chickens, cows, sheep, and pigs.* Abigail had heard enough of him and announced they would "bring Zeke out to Booth Booley in the corn fields and get him started." And they began moving away but Horst had a smirk on his mug as he extended his hand to shake Zeke's, and once they clasped he squeezed hard and began pulling and yanking around Zeke's arm. Unable to disengage, Zeke held his position while tugging back on the strange farmer's arm, and now it became a bona fide contest between them as Livinia called to Horst to let go and Balthazar began barking. Zeke quieted him, however: "It's ok, Balt. Just a game he's playing." A game he was determined to win and their struggle intensified as Horst Schtuckgloo now started quoting Scripture vociferously, at least Zeke thought that was what it was, before the older fellow began guffawing as he suddenly released his grasp on Zeke whose momentum carried him into the credenza with a crash.

"Horizontal is our hobo, closer to the earth and nearer the sanctity of benefaction," Schtuckgloo declaimed.

Zeke picked himself up from the floor and shook off the jolt as his dog provided canine solicitude. He assured the dairymaid and Aunt Abigail that he was fine and was ready as ever to commence with his farm work. "Don't mind Horst," Livinia said, "he's not used to meeting strangers and perhaps he felt threatened by you."

TWELVE

LIVINIA DELIVERED the new hand to the great corn fields abutting the north forest where a few farmers were engaged in ploughing the land, one far away with a great wooden tool which he powered himself, the attached steel blade digging up the earth in his path. "That's Mathias Edgecomb out there," Livinia pointed out. "He's a resourceful agriculturist who has interesting theories."

As they gazed out on the sun-streaked horizon the small distant figure doffed his wide-brimmed hat and hollered: "How's Lady Livinia this morn'?"

Livinia chuckled and waved with a shout: "Brought some help for you, Mathias."

Now drawing near them came two massive draft horses pulling a plough with two long wooden handles held by a big fellow with a long black beard, close-cropped hair, dark glasses, in overalls and flowing scarf. He was caught up in his work and seemed to only notice his visitors when Livinia called to him. This was Booth Booley, one of the foremen of the farmers who greeted Zeke warmly upon introduction.

"Hobo, eh?!" Booley assessed. "Never saw one work the land, but we could use you, Zeke."

Livinia parted with Balthazar for the sheep pasture where the new star shepherd would be placed in charge, and Zeke hugged and kissed him good-bye for their first separation at all since Bluddenville. Booth Booley set up his new ploughboy with an old ox and a great iron-bladed cast iron heavy plough to be drawn through the adjacent tracts which were slated for wheat. "Now turn that soil like you mean it," Booley counseled before leaving him to himself. "Phineas wants more wheat this year, and he'll be looking to see how many rows you furrow through."

Zeke grasped the handles and felt the strength of Gomer, his ox, as he said: "With Gomer here we're going to rip through this field! I believe I can be a farmer, Mr. Booley." And he steered the massive plough straight ahead in fine deep furrows, the partial sun now emerging from clouds more and Zeke accepted the challenge of hard, physical work, lonely labor of long sweaty hours amidst the soil, so arduous and loaded with burdens that he wanted to quit many times to rest and reevaluate his foray into farming, but he pressed on with a zeal rooted in making the soil work, the attraction of the beautiful dairymaid ultimately carrying him forward. He spent the better part of the afternoon ploughing the wheat field with the old ox Gomer and he never worked so hard in his life, sweat trickling down his face and his muscles aching with strain, but he would not stop as the severe labor under the majestic woodland sky and the enchanting farmland surrounding him all fused with his attraction to the delightful dairymaid, and it became an almost spiritual experience. As the sun descended towards the horizon and its golden hue grew tinged with a gray darkening mist Zeke remained on the plough with Gomer, and only when summoned by the cry of Booth Booley to come aboard his and Mathias Edgecomb's horse-drawn buggy did he accept his day was done. When he related to the seasoned farmers that he completed sixteen long furrow rows with Gomer they were impressed to the degree of skepticism, but they had seen him periodically at the plough throughout the day and allowed that the tyro stayed on it without requesting a break. In barely sufficient light Booley eagerly inspected the wheat field ploughing and had to acknowledge the sixteen furrows were done while at the same time reproached the work as shoddy and deficient insofar as the rows were so sinuous in design that the zigzagging often crossed over one another and continued meandering into curlicue abstracts. Zeke would not speak of the mystical revelations, the powerful epiphany he came under in his ploughing, but he understood why the crazy quilt of rows resulted. How can a man plough straight when he was in love for the first time in his life? Or at least he believed he was with Livinia the dairymaid since the very moment he laid his eyeballs upon her pulchritude that morning as she milked her cows out on the lost ethereal pasture. The ride back he hardly spoke, so introspective he remained with his infatuation of her and the fine tiredness of his worn-out frame feeling good with a rest earned, and he slipped into some vague musings of a new life as a farmer with Livinia. Mathias Edgecomb and Booth Booley were pretty quiet themselves, only a little agricultural talk about the pasture fence needing mending and how they could use another ox and draft horse for the fields and that the stray animals were so bold now they better put together some formidable scarecrows this year.

They were good men, Zeke thought, and he was pleased that they gave him an overall promising appraisal at the supper table later with Uncle Phineas, Aunt Abigail, Livinia and a subdued, saturnine Horst Schtuckgloo. Also present at the table were an older dairymaid in a starchy cloak and a puffy white cap who seemed coarse and cheerless to Zeke, and two boys, one around nine with a mop of blond hair and weathered overalls who wore a steady smirk and the other a tad older, slender with a shock of black hair and crooked teeth ensnarled in a mischievous grin. "Aww, when can we have the rice pudding, Grandpa?" the younger boy, Ogden, pleaded.

"Well, now lad, you've barely dented those chunks of meat lying on your plate. Let's not waste good rabbit, Oggie."

Ogden grimaced at his food and said: "I know we hunt 'em a lot, but why should I have to eat 'em? I had lima beans, now the rice pudding!"

The older boy, Huxley, jabbed him on the shoulder with a mock command: "Ogden, hop to it will ya, all that tasty rabbit is gonna rot soon!" And he broke into uproarious laughter.

Livinia smiled upon young Ogden and said: "And you ate your parsnips and red cabbage. Rabbit can be an acquired taste, Uncle." She rose and brought the boy an ample portion of the pudding, and Huxley glommed onto a serving of his own.

TWELVE

Phineas watched bemusedly and shook his head jocosely. "You boys are spoiled by her, you know that?" he asked.

Zeke sat entranced by the strange farm folks who took him in as almost family, observing the singular way they interacted and presented themselves. He struggled not to stare at the dairymaid and wished he could come up with something to say to her, but his mind scrambled whenever he began.

Balthazar's status had become elevated, and he sat in front of the fire with a big bowl of rabbit stew and everyone crowed about his amazing prowess shown on the sheep meadows. "Those sheep would follow that dog to Timbuktu," Uncle Phineas remarked fondly. "It is truly splendid to behold a creature discover the natural vocation he was indeed put on earth to pursue."

Horst Schtuckgloo swigged from his tankard and began muttering Scripture, or so it seemed to Zeke, before he rose to solemnly approach the sheepdog as he reclined by the fire. "Easy now, Horst," Booth Booley urged lowly, "easy!" He met eyes with Mathias Edgecomb and Zeke now grew concerned as he saw their exasperation with the older farmer.

"We are all given life by the Lord for a grand purpose, a master design we often cannot perceive," Horst declaimed, kneeling to pet Balt's coat, and the dog seemed ambivalent, puzzled by Schtuckgloo, the whole table watching now in silence as Zeke rose to move closer. "We must sacrifice ourselves to the soil to grow bountiful crop," he spoke with his hands raised, looking above, "as we too are planted in the end and merge into soil." Just then a leftover lima bean soared through the air and plucked Horst Schtuckgloo on the head, and he grunted and poked with his petting hand Balthazar, who broke into a vicious growl towards the old farmer. And the pent-up tension in Schtuckgloo now snapped and he burst into biblical fulminations with the most cryptic of gesticulations accompanying his stentorian stew of portent and scripture aimed at no one in particular. Zeke had rushed to his dog's side and held him soothingly, yet firmly, so he would not attack the unmoored Schtuckgloo, but when a fingerling potato next clocked him across his features the preacher farmer recognized his assailants as the boys, Ogden and Huxley, who were hardly containing their laughter, and he lunged towards them—albeit they were already bolting out the door. The wild scene now over and the parties departed, everyone else broke into loud guffaws, except Zeke who was still comforting Balthazar and disconcerted by the whole situation.

As the laughter subsided Uncle Phineas noticed the new hand seeming disconnected and sought to explain their ways: "Not to worry, Zeke, the boys teasing Horst is a staple of our postprandial evenings and he really can handle their monkeyshines, because we believe behind his bombast he understands their juvenile brickbats."

Zeke pondered this notion. "You mean he accepts their antics? He did not appear so while chasing them." A murmur of chuckles and whispers followed this from the table as all eyes fixed on him.

"Not on a conscious level," Phineas replied grinning, "and if he ever caught the guttersnipes it would be paddywhacks for them! Which makes it such great sport, the stakes, son." The last words from Phineas *the stakes* stayed with him and he looked over at Livinia laughing gently now with Booth Booley and her image shone in a corona of resplendency just then, almost as if he were in a dream state of heightened sensuality, and he wanted to woo and win her love somehow and had to try against the odds, while knowing the stakes of failure could be devastating, if not fatal in one way or another. He knew in the inviolable buried depths of his soul that he would never find another like her, such chances come but once. The vision thrilled and scared him at the same time and he knew he had crossed into a new life, a more direct, immediate, intimate challenge, not an abstract concept of striving to help people but a chance to find love and become someone fulfilled and wiser and, consequently, better capable of doing good for others in the world. He struggled not to stare at her and never felt such excitement and fear simultaneously.

While Balthazar achieved exalted status among their new farm family as the finest canine shepherd anyone had ever seen, Zeke slowly earned their approbation by the indefatigable work ethic he evinced every day out on the fields and tending to the livestock. Even the skeptics such as Horst Schtuckgloo came to accept such a colleague, if begrudgingly, as his capacity for pushing himself through sweat and toil beyond all rational limits showed remarkable commitment to learning the rudiments of agriculture. The fervent zeal with which he attacked his days of duties frequently carried him beyond his circumscribed labors, and thus his inspirational enthusiasm would veer into comic relief, unless the foul-ups resulted in damage or destruction of some measure. Slopping the hogs, for example, might turn into a stampede of escaping swine as his frenetic style would unnerve the beasts and through the fence they'd bust. Or the surfeit of solicitude he occasionally applied to the chickens might trigger an uprising of the perturbed birds, who would turn on Zeke with a sudden viciousness that left him victim to their pecking assaults. And then there was his fortitude at the plough, a strength and stamina quite impressive with ox, draft horses, or by himself, yet he continued to struggle to maintain straight rows. They still crisscrossed, looped in crazy eights, parabolas, and the much admired but impracticable abstract skeins. Not only did Zeke find he had the ability to work harder than almost anyone, he also discovered how much satisfaction and gratification he derived from the long days of such diligent exertion. His inability to concentrate and fully focus on the chores at hand stymied his apprenticeship as a junior farmer and it left him chagrined at times, but he knew the reason for his stalled progress. He was utterly in love with the fair dairymaid Livinia from afar, and even a momentary glimpse of her among the cows as he wrestled with his plough and ox from a faraway field would reanimate his entire spirit and bring a silent goat-cry of exultancy soaring from his loins and suffusing his heart. It would suffice in propelling him with such a robust vitality through the rest of his work that all took note of his volcanic energy. But what he gained in might he seemed to lose in applying details of certain procedures, and such was not missed by Phineas and the crew. So Zeke was a farm apprentice in progress, while Balt was a bona fide star and accorded such deference. Everyone fawned over the sheepdog, petting him at every turn and his meals were exquisite fireside repasts with a heap of treats thrown his way from the table every night. He had to feel like he arrived in dog heaven, Zeke would tell him, quite content to occupy a status well below his dog's on the farm. They usually ate lunch together under a tree and had themselves a picnic of sorts, and Zeke would tell his dog how proud he was of him and how they'd always be a team. He was friendly with all the farm hands but they all seemed to have their bonds with one another and Zeke was fine with sticking with Balt as his sole buddy, and they bunked together in the barn, up in the old hayloft, and as he lay there in the darkness with a shaft of moonlight penetrating around them, he'd think of Livinia and how wonderful it would be to get to know her better. Of course, he would have to actually speak to her and have a conversation, maybe even share some laughs to do so, and he would resolve the next day to seek her out and address the dairymaid. Or at the supper table he'd direct a comment or two her way. But the next day would dawn and he would be pushing his plough out on the corn field and before he knew it the sun would be waning and he'd be back up in his hayloft lying there thinking about her again and his failure to get to know her. That very first day he met her he was able to converse with her and they had found humor together in the chicken coup, but that was before he began thinking about her too much and the unique attraction she held over him and how much he wanted her. Now he would fall victim to his own terrible jitters and willies and either clam up altogether or act in a manner that only reinforced her opinion of him as some screwball hobo who cannot shake the harum-scarum and peculiar ways of those legion of rough-hewn souls who ride the rails and gather in jungles over meager campfires. In fact, his farm identity as a lost hobo who they kindly enlisted became so entrenched it would have been nearly impossible to declare rightly merely a figment of their own perception that he so far chose not to correct. And being their hobo had, paradoxically, its own power of invulnerability in there were few expectations and parameters to meet, as a hobo and his dog emerging from the forest came enshrouded in mystique and a romantic image of a rough-and-tumble world of adventure and escapades of hard living. He was closer to Balthazar than the farm folks, it seemed, as if he were also another species of creature they could marvel and wonder over and express affectionate curiosity towards, while careful to subjugate dog and hobo in classification as beings invariably beneath them. And so Zeke's dilemma was overcoming the obstacle of being viewed as a hobo and the limitations accompanying that, while utilizing the mysteries baked into such label and transcending and transforming himself with such panache the dairymaid would begin to see his persona truly and take that leap of faith in him. A tall order for the fledgling farmer, but as he told Balthazar every night in their hayloft after another day failing to approach her, he had to find a way to her heart.

Aside from their constant pursuit of reckless, riotous hijinx, Zeke rather enjoyed the company of the two orphan boys, Ogden and Huxley, who had escaped confinement to a work house for children and, like him, fled for weeks in the woods before stumbling on the remote farm. Phineas and Abigail were touched by the plight of the young ruffians and took them in provided the boys pitched in with their share of farm chores. The latter part needed much improvement, but their juvenility bought them plenty of tolerance. They naturally were drawn to Zeke as outsiders on the lam and as kids looking for kicks, a hobo contained an aperture into an alternate universe of playing by one's own rules, emphasis on playing. More than once Zeke thought he could use the lads in bridging a connection to talking to Livinia as she milked her herd. By engaging them in some children's games strategically within eyeshot of her he hoped the fun would be contagious and the dairymaid might join them. But, for example, the afternoon he assembled the six Indian clubs in a geometric cigar shape and drove the eleven stakes of wood into the earth in an algebraic "loose disc" equation and mounted the four lit torches and, of course, the medicine ball (he used rolled hay in a sack) they contend over with sticks—the popular beloved game of "Harry Killed the Luckenbill"—of which they entered into a very rowdy game as Ogden and Huxley exceeded all boundaries of violence with the sticks and managed to set the fence on fire, and Zeke only attracted Booth Booley and others with buckets of water. On another occasion he again set the urchins up near enough the dairymaid in a slingshot and kite flying combat contest (the well-known boys' game of "Jake Shot the Bastard Dead!" Now the game called for eighteen gourds coated in lard, two with long lit wicks, a cudgel, and a "Euclidean grouping" of dandelions. Zeke could only find five gourds on the farm and availed himself of eggplants and a rubber souvenir that was originally from a carnival in Muskogee, Oklahoma. The game began intensely but in spirited good fun with the boys guffawing like hyenas as they attacked one another with the array of ammo, while Zeke maintained the kites aloft and captured some gourds and once he thought Livinia looked their way with a smile from her perch with Flossie over two-hundred feet away. It all came to naught, however, as a furious Horst Schtuckgloo came storming into their game on his horse-drawn cart and thundering incoherent scripture—as apparently it was his souvenir Zeke borrowed— he destroyed their carefully arranged components, except the souvenir which he held up momentarily to check on, while lighting the whole pile up in flames and giving chase to the teasing and cackling boys. "Schtuck Schtuck Gloo Gloo, we heard all the dirt about you, Schtuck Schtuck Gloo Gloo, Horst is cockeyed and cuckoo!" they chanted to the old farmer over and over in diminishing volume as Zeke watched them all disappear beyond the horizon. And Zeke was left alone to ponder what Livinia, who left herself, might have made of the disturbing scene.

    Thwarted at every turn it seemed, Zeke plodded forward in his attempts to talk to Livinia and hopefully court the beautiful dairymaid. Distance on the fields always seemed an impediment and he resolved to call out "good morning!" to her from his plough over four-hundred feet away and she finally heard something but thought he was in distress and sent a man working in the nearby turnip garden, Cy Undersnettle, over on horseback to attend to the stricken hobo. When Zeke insisted to Undersnettle that he was in good health and it was all a mistake, the brawny turnip farmer thought otherwise and the two men took to grappling in the mud from the earlier showers. Ironically, it was Undersnettle who threw out his shoulder and Zeke accompanied him to the house for an examination by Doc Hockers, the farm hand who learned some first-aid medicine back when he marched with the Minnesota Cavalry in the Second Walleye Campaign . At the supper table Zeke always thought he had his best opportunity to speak with her, but with so many around who would overhear him he could never get the words out. Once he managed, "Saw you out there with Flossie today—" but his train of thought vanished like meat in a wolf's paw, and he but nodded at the staring eyes and hummed a Sousa march nervously.

At some juncture during his time at the farm it became apparent to Zeke that a well-dressed man had been making visits to the farm in a well-appointed carriage for the explicit purpose of spending some time walking the woodland pathway beside the stream with the dairymaid. He couldn't remember the first time he even noticed them together, so little did it register any cause for concern early on. He thought he could be anyone, a courier bearing tidings, an acquaintance of her family back home perhaps, or a neighbor they all knew. The man did seem well-known to all on the farm and whether he had a romantic relationship with the dairymaid never occurred to Zeke. Perhaps there was some denial in his thought processes, but as the weeks wore on and the visits seemed more frequent he gradually made some inquiries and finally understood the gentleman to be the son of Lord Cumberland, who oversaw all the region, and that he indeed had such designs on Livinia, and this was a very dark day of despondency for Zeke Borshellac, who did not appear at supper that evening but went straight to his hayloft (as did Balt for his succor) with a pint of rum. The aristocratically attired fellow in the fancy carriage's name was Gerard and while everyone greeted him on the farm with bonhomie and cheerfulness it remained unclear whether they truly liked him for who he was or for the power he represented in his father, for Lord Cumberland alone could save the farm from the foreclosing lenders if Phineas and the farm hands could not turn the tide of descent towards insolvency, as it slowly and steadily threatened to swallow them all. Zeke could not but believe that the latter represented the predominant prism through which he was received. The glimpses of him which Zeke caught always were from afar, beyond the rolling fields and pastures, yet they always stopped Zeke cold and sent him into a swoon of nausea, and he fixed his sullen eyes on the tiny figure and carriage and felt as if here was Death incarnate slowly traversing his way towards him. He could not shake the persistent presence of Gerard Cumberland on the farm and the noxious effect it was producing in his mind, and the engulfing despair left Zeke increasingly lost. He began to drink more at night as sleep eluded him. That is when he started wrangling one of the fine horses they had on the farm, a powerful young steed not fully broken in called Catapaltus, taking him on long nocturnal rides in the woods as he and his father had done with the two Scunjs. With fevered mind craving breakneck speed through the dark mysteries of forest eves Zeke rode this beautiful black horse into the deepest reaches of pristine wilderness and it alone pushed him through the desperate nights. A superb horseman, Zeke savored these secret rides with such a fast horse on which he would penetrate the trees and bush in the blackness of cover at a hell-to-split clip and swig his bottle of rum at slower intervals. He could think and breathe again and come around to his true self of remaining committed to a cause and persevering until the end, and he would return to his hayloft and Balthazar believing he would somehow overcome the privileged advances of Gerard to win Livinia's heart. He found freedom and solace in the forest and recalled his weeks with Balthazar hiking over the remotest woodland and living off the land. He missed the natural wonders and peacefulness he found among the lost majesty of far-flung forest. And the idea of returning one day occurred to him, but that would mean a harsh sentence of loneliness now that the dairymaid entered his existence, if only peripherally. Such drifting thoughts of Zeke invariably came back to her, and the prospect of true love she presented for him to win or lose.

TWELVE

While the night rides reduced Zeke's sleep they did not adversely affect his performance on the plough. If anything, the madcap galloping proved therapeutic in working through the pain of his dimming romantic aspiration as he clung to an irreducible, inextinguishable sanguinity, which was committed to making something happen with Livinia. After one long day on the plough, he hitched a ride with Booth Booley and Mathias Edgecomb back to the barn and he took a few pulls on his bottle of rum in the back seat before he broached the subject of the dairymaid's wellborn admirer. "What do you fellows make of Lord Cumberland's son coming around the farm so often lately? He seems to spend much of his time in the company of Livinia."

Mathias laughed as he tugged on the horses' reins. "Well, you don't have to be a genius to see the Cumberland son is pulling out all the stops in courting our Livinia," he said. "And you don't see many of his class pitching woo on the farm, unheard of really."

Booth Booley weighed in: "I think Gerard's interest in Livinia is the sole reason we haven't been closed by the lenders. Will he throw the farm to the wolves if she sends him off? A good question, fellows!"

Zeke tried to be careful not to give his own attraction to Livinia away by following up on Booley's question: "Well, that would be a vile retaliation, lowering the boom like that just because a poor dairymaid rejected his advances! We must do all in our power to save the farm on our own and spurning any Cumberland largesse with strings."

Mathias Edgecomb laughed and remarked: "You're off target on both fronts, Zeke. A young countryside dairymaid like Livinia is not going to squander an opportunity to rise into the upper classes, even if she doesn't find the fellow to be the fair-haired boy."

Booth Booley snarled: "It's more about what his intentions are with her. I am wary of his motives, but they may be true."

Zeke now stewed with more anxiety as he contemplated the untenable situation and resolved to begin moving forward with his own plan to court her.

At the supper table that evening Zeke listened with new gravity to Phineas' discourse on more frugal planting techniques and equipment deficiencies and how much they needed a banner crop come harvest time. The very survival of the farm depended on a bounteous fall, and even that was no guarantee. It seemed every night now for weeks the farm's teetering fate at the mercy of the bank took on a darker tone. But when Phineas looked up with a quizzical half-smile across the table towards Livinia and said: "I noticed Gerard came around the farm this morning. How is he and Lord Cumberland? Are they well?"

As all eyes turned her way the dairymaid met their gazes with clenched jaw and nettled expression and quickly deflected any such talk. "Oh, they are quite fine I'm sure. I really wouldn't know more than you about their lives. Just because Gerard comes around now and again . . . doesn't mean anything."

Abigail glanced around the room with a smirk. "Oh, I think it does, Livinia. It means very much indeed. Let's not be naïve, dear." She chuckled and the others joined her.

Livinia now blushed and smiled, stammering as she began. "Well, he is a man who seems very confident and sure of himself, that I can say. I've never met anyone like Gerard who has the wherewithal to do so many important things at his fingertips."

Zeke broke the space of silence that followed by observing: "Born to the manor can afford one many fine possessions, but it cannot buy everything. Some things are not for sale."

There was a stark silence at his remark, with dumbfounded faces trying to process its intent. Zeke groped for words to explain himself as their eyes fixed on him, and Phineas put to him in an irked tone: "Surely you do not imply any form of sordid transaction between our Livinia and Lord Cumberland's good son?"

"I was merely stating a fact," Zeke replied, "said when I said it, you only heard it in the context of the conversation before it. I was actually quoting an old hobo pal of mine who was born into rich parentage but ended up riding boxcars with a bindlestick."

It seemed like a clever pivot but Aunt Abigail clucked her tongue in displeasure and declared: "Gerard is a fine gentlemen who happens to come from a noble heritage and to suggest such coarse mercenary design does him an enormous disservice."

TWELVE

Zeke again assured everyone that his comment had no bearing on Livinia and Gerard, and the boys Ogden and Huxley were unable to contain their laughter as Og blurted: "Zeke howls at the moon at night over Miss Livinia! We seen him on his horse!" Now everyone burst into laughter and Zeke tried to take the teasing in good stride, chuckling himself in concealment of the mortification he felt. He glanced at Livinia and saw she also seemed embarrassed by all the attention, and they met eyes for a moment before she turned away. At least *she* wasn't laughing with the rest of them, albeit she seemed bewildered in an uneasy way to him.

As the table eventually fell silent, Zeke felt compelled to deliver a bon mot to fill the awkward gap. "An old hobo pal of mine used to say that hoboes are immune to put-downs cause they are so down-and-out, but in such a free-wheeling, maverick way that nobody can put the knock on 'em and get their goats."

The remark was met with bafflement and indifference and as Ogden and Huxley began to leave, Horst preemptively rose to glower in intimidation in case they were planning some prank to spring on him. A Brussels sprout came flying out of nowhere with a trajectory that landed it precisely on Schtuckgloo's forehead, and his outrage flared for one outburst of "those little devils I will smite them down with a good larruping!!" and this was followed by a stream of tortured foul vituperation in which Horst vented all his stored fury and violence by shadow fighting with kicks and blows in a paroxysm of sick frustration. But then, all of a sudden, realizing all eyes were upon him, he quickly reversed course and steadied himself, carefully and laboriously proclaiming: "Nonetheless I have grown quite fond of our troubled young charges and only want them to grow out of their destructive mischief and turn towards the Lord to discover a useful vocation to pursue productive lives . . . I will expose the lads to Scripture and get them right with the Lord God our creator. I remain dubious, however, of their futures in farming." He said this after everyone at the supper table realized his outburst clearly went beyond the boundaries of civilized, acceptable behavior and a heavy interminable silence supervened his tantrum. But his attempt to walk it back proved moot when a red beet came hurtling from a side window with such speed that when it clipped him smack on the temple he dropped to the floor, though the old sodbuster rose quickly as he was really stunned more than injured by the beaning. This time the perpetrators were identified by their laughter, as the boys could not hold in their raucous glee before fleeing.

After all the hullabaloo died down Zeke mustered up his nerve to address Livinia as she was leaving the supper room. "I hope my remarks in no way offended you, as if in any small measure that is the case then I humbly apologize," he began in earnest.

She smiled warmly at the gesture and said she "understood" his comments "for what they were" and not to concern himself.

Zeke felt buoyed by her unaffected congeniality and thought he would mention his new splendid horse who was still quite wild and no one rode except him. "It is the awe-inspiring steed Catapaltus I have taken to riding in the wee hours through the distant secluded reaches of the forest. These are rides that have become indispensable to my mind's reconciliation with an infernal imbroglio that has me in a perpetual state of sixes and sevens."

Livinia expressed solicitude for his welfare in mounting the wild beast Catapaltus for such overnight rides in blackest night of woods. "It smacks of lunacy, Zeke, to risk your life in such a manner."

"The blackest woods are ubiquitous in my existence, and the only way out is to challenge the order of reality that currently leaves me lost and hopeless. The night rides aid my quest to break through to the other side."

It was just the two of them and Balt standing in the archway of the supper room and Livinia said: "I don't believe I understand you, Zeke. What do you mean by the *other side*?"

Now Zeke was simply too shy and afraid to come right out and declare to the object of his desire that *she* was the other side. He hemmed and hawed and even cleared his throat unnecessarily more than once, convincing himself she really did recognize his intentions towards her but was feigning ignorance as a form of flirtation. Of course, back in the hayloft with his bottle of rum and Balt at his side he knew better, that his fear of laying his cards on the table with the dairymaid once again undermined his woo-pitching capabilities. With Gerard not only being Lord Cumberland's son but apparently enjoying the support and encouragement of Uncle Phineas and Aunt Abigail and the whole Von Klobbert agricultural team as the lone, best chance of the farm maintaining solvency and holding onto their means of employment, Zeke withdrew again into a melancholy funk. "I don't see a way to get through to her, Balt," he complained to the reclining sheepdog. "A good part of me wishes we never chanced upon this farm because I would never have known the true joy life can be had I not met Livinia. Now I face a hard slog of sullen lethargy, devoid of all joie de vivre." The dog slowly rose to all fours and abruptly shook himself intensely, as if to rid his coat of an itchy build-up and to shiver away the querulous whine he just heard. He looked at Zeke in a singular long manner which seemed fraught with exasperation, as well as empathy and solace upon the apprentice farmer's dilemma. Zeke swigged more rum and moved to pet his faithful pal, but Balt rolled away and sprang into the air with the swagger of a dido that sought to convey counsel. "What are you pulling on me, Balty?" Zeke asked with a curious sober tone. The dog simply locked his gaze upon him until Zeke had to avert his eyes and then he seemed to understand Balt's communication. "I know, I know, you never heard me grovel in my own self-pity before and you're wondering who this fellow is who wallows in defeatism?" Balthazar barked in an affirmative manner, or so Zeke thought. "I think you make a point. It's high time Zeke Borshellac stands up for himself." He took some deep breaths as he contemplated his statement and his dog barked again in the same robust, supportive way. "I've been skirting the edges instead of moving forward in the desiderata of my existence, the aspirations of helping the poor souls of this world to better lives." Balthazar seemed to digest Zeke's words and he barked three times in a keener, urgent tone before he raced in a circle wagging his tail barking even more ardently as he now stuck his snout in Zeke's chest and poked him with his paws. Zeke chuckled at first at the dog's excitement but after a hit of rum it occurred to him his canine buddy was concerned over his understanding a fundamental truth about himself. "I think I know what you're driving at, Balty," he said, "you're saying that I need to give myself a break. I ought to look inside more and know who I am. Believe in myself more and then the rest will follow." The dog stared at him with his tongue hanging out, breathing heavily, and then he barked a single full-throated cry. "You know me better than anyone, Balt, so I guess you have something here. I'm not going to skulk around anymore like a lost hoople who doesn't know the time of day. I'm going to let rip the real Zeke Borshellac from here on in and lead with what really matters to him. I mean me." Balthazar ran in another circle and barked his loudest bark yet and Zeke smiled and laughed and said: "I know, Balt. Unless I believe in me I'll never win over a beautiful dairymaid like Livinia! And I'm telling you right now, while I may not be no son of Lord Cumberland togged out in foppish finery and riding around in a fancy carriage, I am still Zeke Borshellac and I got my own good points. They got me pegged as a hobo, well, I'll show them one truly unforgettable hobo!" The dog barked once more, a more restrained bark however, as if he were attempting to fathom the last resounding vow.

 Zeke went riding that night on Catapaltus deep into the forest, singing aloud hobo songs he half remembered and embellished with flourishes of his own, swigging his rum and newly alive with ideas on presenting his hobo persona to the Von Klobbert farm folk in general, Livinia in particular. He discovered a mysterious moonlit clearing covered in wildflowers and here he sang and began to imagine the sort of show that he would someday put on for his dairymaid. There was song and stories and journeys into the hobo culture that would carry into his important work providing them succor and support. Yet while his rides continued to prove deeply satisfying in bringing out his best work towards all his goals, his everyday toil with the plough in the fields did not yield many opportunities to begin anew with Livinia. He was far afield ploughing for corn, squash, beets, and bell peppers, fairly isolated with his reliable ox Gomer, an older beast who proved his stamina time and again to the new plough boy—when his chagrin over several days of this reached a breaking point. He decided aloud to Gomer, the only creature within a quarter mile, and to the blue skies above in a holler of conviction that he would seize any opportunity going forward, and shortly thereafter as he laboriously pushed his plough ahead with Gomer's help the dairymaid appeared on the distant horizon with a coterie of her cows. His heart swelled with anticipation as he began shouting as loud as his lungs would allow a simple, straightforward greeting. "Hello!! How are you this morning!!" He knew it had to be terse, insofar as the distance was great and it would take many attempts to convey the content of his cry. The fiasco of his last such distant salutation had receded from his memory, albeit the quarrelling and brawling with the turnip man Cy Undersnettle surfaced enough in his consciousness to cast Cy as the rowdy culprit who sabotaged those earlier efforts. He kept shouting the same plain greeting of "Hello!! How are you this morning!!" and it wasn't until the eleventh or twelfth time that she even seemed to pivot slightly in Zeke's direction. She recognized a sonorous voice reverberating from some faraway origin but could not yet register Zeke across the great expanse between them. He continued to shout until his voice felt the strain and cracked but he maintained the greeting, now jumping and flailing for a visual effect to flag her attention. When it appeared to work and she peered out his way, her hand over her eyes like a sun visor, he thought she was more confused if not concerned, and her faint cries were to an unseen form somewhere just over the horizon. Then she disappeared from Zeke's eyeshot, only her herd of cows remaining, as she apparently hurried towards the person she had been addressing. Disconcerted, Zeke continued to shout "Hello! Hello!!" until his vocal cords ached, adding "Hello Livinia!!!" after a while. As his heart sank in contemplating the possibility of such overt rejection, his mood suddenly brightened as a horseback rider became visible on undulating skyline. But very quickly he realized it was a man galloping towards him, not the dairymaid herself, and then he saw it was indeed the belligerent turnip farmer Cy Undersnettle once again sent on her behalf. And as before, Undersnettle came with an urgency in the understanding that Zeke was in dire need of medical help, having an attack of some kind, and despite Zeke's insistence that he was in fine fettle the turnip farmer would not back off. A vituperative quarrel ensued, and it wasn't long before the two men took to fighting, exchanging blows and scrapping in the muddy earth until they became entangled in head and scissor locks and simply agreed to desist in their aggressions.

    His chagrin only deepened as the isolation of his ploughing duties left his chances of engaging the dairymaid in conversation greatly limited. He tried to focus on agriculture and learning as much about farming as he could, and the hard work at the soil with Gomer did him a world of good. He knew he would get his shot and vowed to be prepared, deciding on a "hobo mystique" to adopt in courting her, one replete with songs and speeches and stories from the boxcars traveling over the prairies and mountains across the country. At the supper table he kept his remarks mostly confined to the daily farming output and anecdotes related therein, such as the natural parabolas his ploughing once formed veering into more traditional rows and his methods of injecting renewed curvature. Once he attempted a "hobo joke" he heard at late night horseshoes in Bluddenville, involving a drunken horse wandering into a hobo tavern and ordering sixteen beers with his pounding hoof, but after six or seven times Zeke slammed the table with his palm Uncle Phineas asked him to knock it off. Mortified over his indiscretion, Zeke refrained from all table talk for a week and could not even glance Livinia's way for longer. He rode longer and farther in the forest nights on the breakneck Catapaltus after that, swigging whiskey with a thirsty abandon, struggling to square his shortcomings with the striving demands he placed on himself. At times he could not shake the harrowing imagery of his drunken father riding recklessly through woodlands all night with no destination sought, no plan or control of reason, only speed and hooch and furious madness over a life gone off the rails, and Zeke would feel himself becoming the violent fevered rider that his father had been and yes, at times he *was his father charging drunk in the woods*, and he remembered the hobo father who stalked him at the jungle near the tavern by the river and their fight that left him defeated and without the second Scunj and the bag of money he was going to bestow upon the hoboes himself, directly. It was the taunting, baleful simulacrum of the hobo father now chasing him with murderous intentions, hunting him like a hellhound hungry for his soul, that frightened him to his bones as he rode ever faster and with hell-bent wanton dementedness, and he wished he could fight the hobo father again, wished he could confront him, challenge him one more time, but instead he was pursued by the rabid apparition of a hobo father who would pursue him with a bloody vengeance to the four corners of the earth. Such were the night rides upon the fearsome Catapaltus through the forest fueled by whiskey and rum and relentless anguish over his failure to connect on the even the most elemental of levels with the beautiful dairymaid. On such nights racing through the darkness Zeke understood his father and the seduction of self-destruction, but he mustered all he had to stave off such impulses. When his opportunity came, he vowed, he would be ready to make the most of it. He would present himself as the most interesting hobo she would ever meet. He would tell her all about his plans to provide direction and leadership to the hobo populace roaming the land by train, showing them the way to rise up and force righteous change through marshalling solidarity and coalitions with sympathetic movements such as the Farmers' Party, or the Grange Progressive. In the drunken dark forest rides Zeke fought off the doubts that would dim his vision and diminish his belief in himself to actuate his dreams, and the hobo father chivvied upon his heels with chants *"It is time to come home and concede defeat! It is time to accept your failure! It is time to let Papa take over! It is time I beat you up again so badly you will drink alone dazed and crushed like a little boy lost in the hayloft all over again!"* Zeke galloped all night as fast as Catapaltus would carry him and as dawn's first light broke through the trees he would thank the heavens he stayed ahead of the hobo father for one more night.

Thirteen

During this period Zeke found himself spending some time on the fields with the two mischievous shavers Ogden and Huxley, who would come out to visit their favorite hobo as he ploughed and cajole him into taking a break. The boys were drawn to his hobo tales of adventure and he was always pleased to ply them with a few as they sat under an elm tree and smoked their corncob pipes and played mumbletypeg with their jackknives. Zeke let them have their fun as he saw a lot of his own rough-and-tumble boyhood in the lads, and he relished concocting stories for them as honing his overall hobo persona for his eventual dating of Livinia, or so he hoped. Of course, he knew they were goldbricking from their farm chores, but a small respite in which they could imagine picaresque lives of excitement and camaraderie in traveling all over the country was perhaps something boys on a far-flung farm needed. He spun a tale of riding the rails across the moonlit prairie land and being chased atop the cars by the bulls with their long wooden paddy-whackers and how he had eluded capture several times from this one egomaniacal bull with a bald pate and black beard, and the man grew obsessed about catching his evasive hobo, so when Zeke dismounted from the boxcar roof onto the sloping brush-laden earth the bull did the unthinkable and jumped after him in pursuit. And after they fought and beat one another up, they were still in the middle of nowhere and realized they needed one another and became a team. The bull, a railroad veteran named Alton Ostertag, Zeke explained in conclusion, became a hobo and savored the journeys across the country and felt alive and free for the first time in his life. But then another course in which to employ his young pals struck him as on the distant horizon across the ascending fields he perceived the tiny figure of the dairymaid surrounded by her herd. "Hey lads, can you suggest one of your boys' games we can play? A very good one in which we can include Miss Livinia in the fun?" he asked them. "She looks to me like someone who could benefit greatly from one of your jolly pastimes."

The boys smirked at one another and snickered now. "Oh, sure, Zeke," Ogden remarked, "you're just angling for a shrewd way to swoop in and honeyfogle her off her feet!"

Zeke blushed with his annoyance at the younger boy and returned sharply: "That's an impudent remark to make, Og. I happen to admire Miss Livinia and would like to introduce her to one of your rousing children's games for some fanciful fun. She works hard with her cows and deserves such a respite."

Huxley puffed on his pipe and chuckled. "Hey Og, I think you hit a nerve. C'mon, Zeke, we know you hanker for the girl."

Zeke squinted at the flip urchin.

"Ahh, well, she may not go for hoboes, but she'd be better off with you than that high-toned stiff Gerard. That would be a damn shame if Miss Livinia went for that born-to-the-manor hoople."

Og seconded his brother's opinion: "A *God* damn shame!" He also took issue with him: "Who said she don't care for hoboes? She's only being friendly to Gerard cause he's Lord Bumblelard's son."

"You fellows seem to have it all figured out," Zeke smiled. "All I'm looking to do is engage her in one of your games, and you boys have all the pomp and circumstances of politics entered into it. But the moment is fleeting, so let's get going!"

They decided on "Shrike on the Fruitwood, Mr. Suggs," with "Gangway Galoots" placed on the back burner. "Shrike on the Fruitwood, Mr. Suggs," a.k.a, "Splatterbrain Suggsy, Whoa! Whoa! Whoa," an erstwhile coal miners' recreational divertissement at which the men would violently compete at picnics, union jamborees, in city alleys and deserted lots in drunken wee hours, grew blither and more sportive over time until morphing into the popular beloved children's game in largely pastoral purlieus. The game was famous for its fast-paced thrills and strategy wars in which teams vied to establish ownership of "cobblestone quadrants" in which they would install "ordnance garrisons" stocked with fruits and vegetables to launch as shells or grenades. For example, an ear of corn striking an opponent was a score unless the targeted individual caught it in the air, shucked and ate more than half of it before being tackled and pinned to the ground. Produce edible without being cooked, such as a tomato or apple, had to be completely devoured before the one who caught it was tackled and pinned. If such catcher successfully gulped the produce down and while still free hurled and hit an opponent with the inedible remains of the produce (i.e., the banana peel, core of an apple) then the struck party would have to run backwards for two-hundred and thirty meters and set fire to six of his team's "special elite janissaries" (stick figures of the front lines, forty-nine per team to start). An occupation of an opponent's cobblestone quadrant by at least a third of a team's human players or one-seventh of the team's janissary stick figures (seven out the forty-nine) for more than one minute and thirty-eight seconds (counted aloud in *mississippis*) meant a successful seizing of the territory, unless one of the other players lay supine in the closest "mucktangle," which were strategic declensions dug two feet down, sixty-six inches long, twenty-six inches wide, and was able to sing one of the eight roundelays ("Michael Row the Boat Ashore, Hallelujah," for example) agreed upon before the game by the end of the two-minute mark from the beginning of the occupation. The game flourished with farming children for many years and they were quite serious about the many complex rules and abstruse paths to victory, but no one could emerge winner without completing the most challenging and traditional part of delivering an uprooted corn stalk to a pre-selected chicken at the "Valhalla Palace," a mound of earth with an eighteen-foot circumference and tall pole with the flag of triumph (four symbols of equal sizes: a chicken, shucked corn, plough, and scarecrow) flying, where the stalk is replanted and circled with the chicken three times in an Indian rain dance. Zeke and the boys were setting up the Valhalla Palace, building the requisite mound and procuring a pole and flag and, most importantly, a chicken from the coop who'd be a good fit. The big rooster Hooper who seemed to loathe Zeke was available and sought by Huxley, but the compromise chicken chosen was the old speckled rooster known as Admiral Haggerty, and as they approached the dairymaid to invite her to play she made a big fuss over one of her favorite chickens, the Admiral it turned out, and embraced him.

As they continued to prepare the playing field (quadrants, mucktangles, janissaries, etc.) Livinia expressed genuine curiosity and amusement in the arcana and odd nuances of the rules, revealing she had always desired to play "Shrike on the Fruitwood, Mr. Suggs" but by the time she arrived on the farm she was already deemed too old, and as a female, not recruited for participation in any regard. So Zeke was buoyant that the dairymaid was eager to play and they chose up sides, Zeke pairing with Ogden, Huxley with Livinia, and then they had to run through the rules for her benefit which took enough time to preclude them from actually beginning a game before she had to return to her milking chores. "Well, we all really should be getting back to work, but maybe tomorrow we can play?" Zeke asked.

Livinia had already started towards her cows in the distant pasture, but she turned with a frolicsome smile and said, "Yes, I would like that."

Zeke glowed warmly with anticipation from that moment, lying in his hayloft that evening telling Balty all about the development, albeit the next two days they continued reviewing the rules with Livinia out on the field without having time to begin play. The next day it rained, and after that Horst Schtuckgloo snatched Admiral Haggerty to accompany him on a wagon ride to a conclave meeting of his Grange farm worker pals at the Mad Squirrel Tavern. Then Livinia did not appear on the horizon in any direction from Zeke for several more days, but one day she did, and the Admiral was out and about and Zeke and the boys were ready to play. Livinia by now had a rudimentary grasp of the rules and the game commenced with much excitement and genuine delight in all the tactics and brinksmanship evinced by both sides, resulting in airborne produce clocking one and all and roundelays sung from the earth and several torched janissaries. It was during the penalty round when Ogden called for a "Suggsentia," which each team can call but once and consists of one player performing a sustained whirling, tumbling and zig-zag darting piece, all the time avoiding being captured while a teammate circles the field's perimeter. If the Suggsentia performer remains at large throughout the teammate's runaround, they receive two scores. If the Suggsentian is captured and brought to one of the five holes on the field filled with water and borax (two-foot diameter, one-foot deep) and his left foot is completely submerged before his teammate makes it around the perimeter then two scores accrue to the capturing club. Zeke was the Suggsentian and proving a master of reeling gyrations and intermittent somersaulting and, most importantly, a very elusive target as Huxley and Livinia sought to catch or trap him somehow before Og made it all the way around the playing field's outline. A speedy runner, the boy turned it on in the last quarter as his and Zeke's triumph appeared inevitable, and he beamed and cried to Zeke to maintain his intensity and "don't get cute and blow it!" But Zeke's ulterior motive of engaging with Livinia and rendering a constructive dalliance with her from the game now seemed to find expression in his more subdued logroll-style tumbling alternated with paroxysms of shaking slapstick convulsions. He was unequivocally showboating and taunting Huxley to come and capture him, and while he was very cleverly and adroitly allowing the older boy to get near only to be faked out and fooled each time, he underestimated the quickness and will of the dairymaid who came at him in a flash and was able to trip him with a legs first slide and attempt to subdue and wrangle him towards the water hole. Og was not quite home yet when Zeke found himself wriggling, flailing, and grappling desperately to extricate himself from her holds and advances in the muddy earth. It was impressive to Zeke how much the beautiful dairymaid wanted to win, a true competitor he noted, and she clearly was having herself a good time as if she found her girlhood again, judging by her incrementally escaping laughter, but then from across the wide-open farmland came a booming voice of a man shouting. Zeke momentarily turned his head to peer over the rolling, slightly ascending green vista to glimpse a figure faraway driving the reins of a horse-drawn carriage just before he felt an arm wrap around his head from behind and was yanked backwards into the mire, a stealth attack by Huxley now buttressed by Livinia in her grasping his feet and thusly capturing Zeke, now dragging him to the water hole as Og dashed his final two-hundred feet—but the shouts of the distant man grew louder as he came barreling towards them on his carriage—and very quickly they stopped playing to watch and wait for him as they saw it was Gerard, the son of Lord Cumberland and frequent visitor of Livinia's whose romantic designs upon her were no secret. But no one ever saw the nobleman in such a state of vociferous rage.

 He pulled up to the dairymaid, who was streaked with mud, while Zeke and Huxley looked on beside her and Og kept his distance, suspending his mad sprint. Leaping from the front of the carriage before his horses even fully halted, Gerard rushed to Livinia, clutching her by the shoulders and asking her with great solicitude: "Are you well, my dear?! Have these crude louts done anything to harm you?" Then sternly sizing them up: "What in good heaven is going on here? Don't trifle with me, you hooligans! Come clean now."

 The dairymaid smiled at his overwrought concern and assured him all was fine. "Oh, Gerard, you have misconstrued our game of Shrike on the Fruitwood as some kind of strife between us." She moved towards him and hugged him, but he fast bristled and spun around towards her playmates again with a roiling ire. "You know, the boys' game," she went on, "it is so droll and fun—"

 "I know the game, Livinia! Unfortunately, it remains extant in my father's lands. And you should know it is beneath a lovely maiden such as you. The Shrike on the Fruitwood is a grotesque and imbecilic exercise relegated to the lower forms of juvenile country life who know no better, and revel in its coarse violence and escapist piffle."

 The dairymaid appeared dismayed by his denunciation and very matter-of-factly took issue with him: "I find the game enchanting and an uproarious lark to play, Gerard, so unpredictable and demanding . . . you ought to play yourself."

But Gerard was not having any of it and ignored her remark, as he was scowling at Zeke and now moved towards him and planted himself a few feet away. "You're a hobo, aren't you? Why does a hobo appear out of nowhere and start working on a farm? What do you want here, mister? Because I and others who care deeply about these acres are not pleased when trespassers come around, especially those of dubious character. We have been watching you and are very wary of who you are and what you want. And now I catch you out here roughhousing with our lovely Livinia in a degenerate game for savage guttersnipes. I will have a good talk with my friend Phineas about his judgment in hiring hands."

Huxley let out a low raspberry sound and a muttered, "Baby Bumblelard."

Gerard could not hear his words but the impudent tone came through and irked, he snapped: "And I'm not sure the Von Klobbert farm is the best environment for two delinquent lads to be raised and I will make some inquiries therein as well."

Now Zeke was seething with indignation already but once Gerard taunted that he would report unfavorably on the boys' farm status he could not control his wrath. "Sir, Ogden and Huxley are orphans who have found a true home here at the Von Klobbert farm. They have good farm folk who care deeply about them, and they are learning the agricultural vocation while young and full of high spirits. You can denigrate my presence on this farm to Phineas all you wish to, but I humbly ask you not to cast aspersions on these boys and jeopardize their continued standing here."

Livinia spoke in sympathy of Zeke's sentiments, noting "the boys have been thriving" as young farmers, albeit adding that Gerard "would not seek to undermine" them—but son of Lord Cumberland cut her off with a most contemptuous guffaw at the whole business and followed with a sardonic query of Zeke: "So, the *grandiose hobo vouchsafes that I can address his shortcomings with Phineas Von Klobbert! How*

THIRTEEN

generous and understanding of you! But his protective, benevolent nature commands me to spare the children, to lay off the poor lads." Now he wasn't laughing as his glower at Zeke grew grave and he began to berate him with invective and violent gesticulation, calling him "a depraved lowlife exploiting the altruistic nature of a fine, proud farmer in Phineas Von Klobbert," and his "deceitful wangling of a position working the soil is unconscionable . . ." He was about to say a good deal more and perhaps order him off the property had not Livinia interjected herself, moving in front of Gerard exclaiming that he was overreacting and walking him away where they then had an animated discussion of some charged emotions. Zeke could not make out much of their quarrel but "he's harmless and has seen hard times" and "a grassroots wayfarer who can work a plough" and finally, "he's got you in his hobo spell, but he is a wretched derelict who will remain unregenerate in his destructive, irresponsible way of living." She was looking at Zeke as he and the boys were gathering up some stray janissaries strewn around.

Gerard went on: "He's a hobo, darling, an itinerant coarse hobo who will continue to run away from all duty, all responsibility, indifferent to others struggling to make a living, but only concerned about moving on and riding away from it all to perpetuate his aimless freeloading excursions. Even if Phineas and I do not send him packing, he will *skedaddle* into the night soon enough and go *riding the rails* with his vagrant pals."

Soon she was walking with Gerard to his horses and fine carriage wearing a sad look, Zeke thought, and before she climbed up into her seat she called out to him: "You were right, Zeke. Shrike on the Fruitwood is great fun. I felt like the tomboy I used to be—thanks for showing me how to play." She smiled and he replied: "It was my pleasure, Livinia. Doing anything with you would be fun." And he and the boys stood still and watched Gerard take the reins and with a harsh yank propel the horses forward at the same fast clip with which they stormed in.

Zeke was so anxious the next several days waiting for Gerard's censure to Phineas redound to him and the boys that he steadily sipped his flask of rum on the fields. Livinia was nowhere to be seen and he nursed an aching pang of torment thinking he might have blown whatever chances he had in developing anything further than a friendship with the dairymaid. While she stood up for him to Gerard, there remained a patronizing air towards him as nothing more than a farmhand with a colorful hobo past, and of course she did leave the field that day with Gerard in his carriage. Once again he relied on Balthazar to help him through his melancholy troubles and self-doubt in their evening conversations in the hayloft, and recognized his honest and noble sheepdog was showing him that leading by example was a viable way to rebuild his farming persona. Balt was universally considered a paragon of effective herding and all-around dynamic foreman of livestock movement on the Von Klobbert farm, quite simply one of the most valuable workers Phineas had. Zeke would redouble his efforts pushing his plough and throw himself whole-heartedly into his labors upon the soil while picking the brains of veteran sodbusters like Booth and Mathias, and even the unpredictable Horst, to increase his agricultural know-how. At supper evenings Zeke now kept his table talk to farm techniques and soil assessments, though the constant drum of pecuniary shortfalls threatening the farm's very existence was disheartening. He wanted to say so much to Livinia and feared his silence now came across as cowed concession to Gerard's warning. But it just felt too awkward to launch into banter.

And then each evening her uncle and aunt would inquire about Gerard to her, whether he was well and was he by that day and, occasionally, if he had spoken to his father about their precarious predicament with the bank. Zeke could see they were investing much in her relationship with the son of the powerful Lord Cumberland and how this made her uncomfortable, but also wanting to please her de facto parents whom she loved very much. "I sort of mentioned it to him on Wednesday again, Uncle Phineas, but I'm not sure he listens to me. I don't know what he can do about it."

THIRTEEN

"His father can do a great deal, dear," Aunt Abigail answered.

Zeke could see Og and Hux cutting up with scamp eyes on one another and barely suppressed laughter after Hux muttering "Old Bumblelard slid his jib!" and Og following with "Bumblelard junior choked on his bib!"

"You boys watch your tongues!" Aunt Abigail scolded. "The Cumberlands will intervene on our behalf! Who else have we to save us?"

"Zeke Borshellac!" They cried in ebullient unison, and chuckled with rascally glee in bolting the table, and Zeke could not tell if he should have been flattered or insulted, but either way he relished their adverse spirit.

"I wish they'd curtail their antics," Phineas sighed, "because Gerard is just waiting for a reason to ship them off to that workhouse reformatory out by the smelting factory in Buglerton."

Livinia rose to excuse herself, declaring that, "Nobody is sending the boys to any such infernal place. I told him to lay off of them because they belong here."

Horst Schtuckgloo, no advocate of the boys as they've had their clashes, nonetheless snarled from his chewing on meat: "No Cumberland is to be trusted, got to be vigilant with the shavers around here."

Zeke nodded staunchly, "You said it, Horst. I will be watching over them. I trust us on the farm, not Cumberland and son." He left with Balt and they repaired to the hayloft where Zeke sipped whisky and cogitated on the many developments over the last few weeks on the farm before falling asleep.

Zeke woke before sunrise and when he saw Balthazar had already left the barn he rushed into the misty darkness and breathed the moist fresh earth and smelled the pungent country flora as he wended his way towards the yawning pastures where the sheep grazed. Along the way a pale thin light broke over the farmland and as he crossed the ploughed corn fields he caught pieces of the sun peeping over the horizon. From afar in a lower valley he saw Balt moving around the scattered sheep in a seemingly random, but very calculated, precise manner that mustered the livestock into a cohesive unit. Zeke watched with pride the fluid marvel of his sheepdog's artistry and control of his environment. It was evident that Balt had released them from their nightly pen all by himself, as he knew how to open gate latches with his paw, and herded the flock to the grassy pastureland which they now grazed upon. *Never would I have known such innate talent resided in Balthazar,* Zeke considered with wonder, as he watched him move with utter authority and stare at any sign of recalcitrance with a staunch eye (notwithstanding his shaggy mane) that appeared to intimidate such sheep. It was a quiet confidence, projecting strength, that enabled Balthazar to so efficiently and gracefully drive and herd his flock, and Zeke was fascinated by his dog's uncanny prowess out there, the sheer natural mastery he displayed, and he mused upon it at length as an enthralled spectator. Afterwards, Balt's game face faded as he exuberantly ran over to warmly greet Zeke in proper canine fashion, even fetching a stick or two, but when he returned to his sheepdog duties he was all business once again, driving his flock with minimal but calibrated effort back into their pen. Zeke soon hurried off to his own field to begin on his plough with the tough old Ox Gomer pulling for him.

 Despite his setbacks of late with Gerard such a presence on the farm, Zeke was grateful to be there working as hard as he ever had on the blackish umber soil, pushing himself past his physical limits in a feat of endurance some others were incredulous over, and he savored the harsh rigors and sweat streaming down which enabled him to feel formidable and the embodiment of perseverance. He worked long hard days with the soil and plough and lost himself thinking things through, pondering what natural ability connected to heart and soul lay deep inside himself. He took breaks by visiting Balthazar with his herd and watching the canine master work before they would picnic together under a tree for lunch, which is where on a couple of occasions they crossed paths with the dairymaid. Of course, Zeke had calculated that by joining Balt in pastureland his odds of encountering Livinia during their picnic seemed inevitable over a span of a few weeks, insofar as she occasionally milked her group of cows in the general vicinity, and she was truly very fond of Balthazar and cherished spending time in the sheepdog's company. In their nightly tete-a-tetes up in the hayloft Zeke's frustrated pining for the dairymaid, related in all its wrenching failure, clearly made an impression on Balt and, at least Zeke believed, the dog apparently decided to become his coach and advisor in the matter. To be sure, it was not as if Zeke could hear his dog actually talking to him, rather theirs was a more mystical relationship in which much was communicated through the eyes and snout and cock of the head and expression of the body and Zeke knew as much as anything he ever knew to be true, such as two plus two equaling four, that Balthazar wanted to help him fall in love and find happiness and he believed his special connection with the dairymaid could make a difference.

So one early bright sunny afternoon as they sat sprawled under one of their trees chowing on some farm fresh seasoned vegetables and bread and cheese Livinia saw them from afar and came over with a warm smile and bounce in her stride. "Hey Balthazar! How's our grand sheepdog doing today?" And Balt dutifully rose to race over to greet his friend and she embraced him with happy laughter and he licked her face as she squinted at his slobbering.

Zeke quickly invited her to join their picnic and she at first declined, saying, "I would love to Zeke, but I have to return to my herd and finish drawing their daily production."

Zeke normally would have replied that he of course understood work is work and all that, but this time he came back with: "Well, Livinia, let me point out that you are entitled to a break here and there, and I know Flossie and the others would be glad to see you take one, as they probably could use a break themselves. So you may as well break yourself with us, as we've got some fine victuals here."

Livinia smiled warmly at Zeke's earnest overture and she glanced back towards her distant herd and assented: "Well, I guess you're right, Zeke. A few minutes and a small sandwich couldn't hurt."

Zeke swooned with nervous incredulity and became caught up in an amorous reverie, and an awkward space supervened until Balthazar poked him in his side with his snout and shook him out of it.

"Oh, that is great!" he finally piped up, and began fixing her a cheese, onion, pickles, and peppers sandwich on rye bread. They sat under the old linden tree and Zeke felt the dairymaid never looked more beautiful as the mild breeze tousled her light brown hair falling from her white bonnet, her long yellow dress fluttered playfully, and the shifting shade of the leaves allowed sunlight to dapple her face in a most pleasing manner. "I want you to know how much we appreciate your giving us an opportunity to work on your uncle's farm, Livinia. Balt and I are in the best place we've ever been, and we owe it all to you."

Livinia seemed moved by Zeke's words, but she downplayed it: "All I've done is help hire two outstanding additions to the farm—" and she stroked Balt as he lay beside her—"and you Balthazar are a revelation to all of us as to what a great sheepdog means to a livestock farm!" Her expression quickly changed to a pensive inward one of uncertainty and she looked at Zeke and said: "It seems more and more like we're not going to make it, Zeke. It pains me to see my uncle and aunt so distraught and up every night running over the numbers. The farm is failing and we need a loan or someone to vouch for us for a full year."

Zeke saw the anguish on her face as she reflected introspectively a moment. He wondered whether she asked Gerard for relief, as her aunt and uncle had beseeched her to do, but she only spoke of the cruel bankers who were moving against them, not about the son of Lord Cumberland and his potential to importune his father to intervene and protect the Von Klobbert Farm. "Don't worry, Livinia. Nobody's foreclosing on this farm. We're going to have the most bountiful harvest ever this fall. It'll pay down the mortgage by itself, you'll see."

But she remained sullen as they started again to eat and after a long silence she said in a low wan voice: "You're probably speculating whether I brought this to Gerard's attention." He answered honestly. "I haven't," she said. "I should for my aunt and uncle because Lord Cumberland can help. I know he can."

Zeke looked at her quizzically, not sure of her reasons. "I don't want Gerard to think that I'm using him like that," she began.

"But if he is your only resource . . ."

THIRTEEN

"It will look like my motive all along was to enlist his father's support through him." Zeke caught her eye for a moment before he said: "If he truly cares about you he will want to help, and none of what it might look like should matter."

She hesitated, her lips pursing in avoiding his gaze. "I know, Zeke. I know that."

Zeke thought he perceived something in her unease. "Well, it may have been at mine and the boys' expense but Gerard seemed to care a whole lot about you at the Shrike on the Fruitwood game . . ." he murmured.

Now she became disconcerted and averred: "No, that was nothing but an overwrought embarrassment and I apologized to you and Ogden and Huxley."

He thought he may have had his answer about her and Gerard Cumberland, but so much was conjecture built on hunch and mirage. "You didn't have to, Livinia. I could understand his emotion."

She shook her head. "That doesn't make it right."

They finished their sandwiches in silence, savoring the gentle wind filtering through the leaves above them, and Livinia stroked Balthazar's fur and scratched his belly in a way he liked. As they began to stir and part ways for their duties, Zeke said, "Balt and I owe you, Livinia. We're indebted to you for seeing we got these positions here. I hope to pay your kindness back in some way someday."

She smiled and met his eye. "Having you here as my friends is more than I could ask for."

Zeke watched her stroll across the pastureland and wondered if she considered what Gerard would ask for if his father halted the pending farm foreclosure at her request. What Lord Cumberland's son would ask for, he thought, was what he wanted regardless and would pursue until he got it—or not—and that would be the dairymaid herself. And Zeke now pondered whether that would be too steep of a price for her, which it had to be, he concluded, because she did not love him.

While a burgeoning buoyancy began to slowly gather in Zeke's new romantic Weltanschauung on the farm, he was nonetheless chagrined by his failure so far to connect with Livinia in an amorous manner beyond the farm pals which they remained. Even if his intuition vis-à-vis Gerard and her were true, it did not mean that she would necessarily give him a tumble with a few dates. He started to lose sleep once more and mounted Catapaltus in the wee hours for long breakneck rides deep into the woods and across open range and towards hills and rivers, swigging a bottle of whisky and ruminating hard on everything, again and again thinking if only there was some way he could raise the money to pay Phineas' creditors. He lived in his head with such confounding ruminations, as when working the soil with Gomer and his plough he went as far as human endurance would allow, and it felt all good to Zeke, as he knew answers would come to him. He would see them from afar, Livinia and Gerard, walking together along the stream or across the meadows towards the edge of tall trees, and he could only remain stock-still and so despondent as if defeat taunted him in this way, reminding him that it would always be there haunting him that he did not measure up when it mattered most, long after he parted ways with the farm and the presence of the dairymaid. He had his plough and old steady Gomer and the blackish umber soil and the sun and the bottle of whiskey he relied on more and more, and he had the arduous work that stretched his sinews to the limits of exhaustion, but it wasn't enough to keep at bay the dolor of what he did not have. That mocked and tormented him from distant points on the farmland when he would look up from his plough, sweat beaded on his brow, or glance across the range while picnicking with Balthazar under a tree, or hitching a ride with Booth Booley and Mathias Edgecomb from the fields to the farmhouse, worn and dog-tired from a long day, and he would spot them off somewhere walking on the horizon, and the pain would come.

The tone and tenor of the suppers took a turn towards the grave and solemn and at times, the panicky, as the inexorable descent into foreclosure showed no signs of reprieve. "The deputy sheriff is going

THIRTEEN

to show up here one day and seize the land," Horst Schtuckgloo one evening foreboded. And Horst stood bolt upright and peered above at the ceiling: "Luke 10 says 'Thou shall love the Lord, thy God, with all thy heart, with all thy being, with all thy strength, and with all thy mind, and your neighbor as thyself.' Jesus replied to him, 'Thou have answered correctly, do this and thou will live." Horst gazed fiercely around the table and no one dared make a sound as he poured himself a glass of red wine and drank it down thirstily before commanding: "Let us pray! Love our Lord! We will live to till our earth!"

Ogden was chuckling now as he muttered something to Huxley, and Horst picked up on the exchange and riveted his glower upon the boys. "What is so funny? What did you say?!"

And Og felt the eyes of the table on him as he understood it was not a comic moment. "I said, 'What are we going to tell the earth."

Horst glared incomprehensively.

"You know," Huxley piped up, "you said we will live to tell the earth. Tell it what?" The boys glanced at one another with the whiff of a snicker.

But the eyes of the table had moved onto Livinia, who was expected now to provide an update on her connection to Lord Cumberland through her courtship with his son. "I do get the impression that Gerard wants to help our cause and appears ready to enlist Lord Cumberland on our behalf." She spoke stolidly, straightforwardly. "He understands how much trouble we are in, he is aware of the creditors and bankers who come around here, the straits we are in."

Phineas looked stern and disconcerted. "But he will not act yet? What holds him back, Livinia?"

The dairymaid could not find words; it was Mathias Edgecomb who said what had to be said: "Gerard wants Livinia to *ask him to save the farm.*"

Phineas now appeared puzzled as he gaped across the table at the dairymaid. "But I thought that happened weeks ago?"

Livinia locked eyes with her uncle and then her Aunt Abigail for as long as she could before her face contorted as if holding back tears.

"I couldn't ask him," she admitted. "He knows the farm is failing," she reasoned, "if he wanted to help us why wouldn't he just do so?"

It was Aunt Abigail, quite rankled, who answered: "Because without you caring enough to ask him, it is just another farm among hundreds in his father's territory. With you asking him to save it, his help becomes something much deeper and important because you are now the farm."

Livinia seemed to withdraw inside herself, reflecting in a sober, clear-eyed manner as if coming to grips with an inevitable reality. "I will ask him tomorrow, Aunt Abigail," she declared, meeting her aunt's eyes, "and he will therefore ask me something in the offing. And I will have no choice anymore. Maybe that is just what I need, Uncle Phineas." She softened her look and sighed with a deep breath.

"Well then, that is good to hear, Livinia," Phineas exclaimed, his face brightening. He either ignored or never heard the part about Gerard asking her something, as no one seemed to make too much of it. They all just assumed a dairymaid like Lavinia without any dowry whatsoever to her name would jump at the chance to marry a nobleman the likes of Lord Cumberland's son.

Only Zeke heard it so loudly and aggrievedly that his stomach began to burn with pain and he had to suddenly leave the table without a word, followed shortly thereafter by Balthazar, and up in the hayloft of the barn he went to drink whiskey and brood. "It's just ain't right, Balt," he lamented before taking another swig and wiping his mouth with the back of his hand. "If we saved the farm though, then she wouldn't have to sacrifice herself for him to do it." He thought about it and drank some more. "Eh, no small task, and I'd be doing it for one main reason, not unlike Gerard." He almost chuckled to himself.

His nocturnal rides on Catapaltus became more frequent, longer and deeper into unknown wilds, and ever intensifying in reckless velocity. His swilling whiskey during such outings only increased to the degree of entire fifths being drained before the beginnings of dawn. He needed the rides because they enabled him to think and reflect and contemplate on a higher plane and perceive the right path forward.

THIRTEEN

His whiskey-soaked mind churned and roiled in a volcanic kaleidoscope of fury and aspiration, his raging tangents of equity and rectitude as elusive ideals and the oppressions and hardships that were woven through every place he had ever lived goaded and provoked him. But his fevered ruminations were unruly and mad and breaking in a thousand directions, creating a sloshed skein of tempestuous ideas and dark memories, albeit Zeke believed there would be limpidity amid luminosity if he continued riding Catapaltus deeper into the darkest forest at ever more breakneck clips. And one such night riding at his most harum-scarum speed and bombed ferocity he thought he caught a whiff of some indeterminate viands cooking somewhere in the surrounding bush, and he grew curious of such evidence of life in so isolated a remove. He pulled on the reins of Catapaltus, surprising the great powerful steed who seemed to bask in his maniacal galloping, and they poked through overgrown trails and attenuated paths, crossed a forgotten stream and a moonlit dale of blue grass and whortleberries, before penetrating thick woodland again and catching sight of a smokiness emanating from a declension. It proved elusive to track, as thin dissipating smoke blown every which way would be, but soon Zeke brought Catapaltus to a halt as he came upon an edge overlooking a narrow bank of a creek with several fur trees providing cover to the fire and three figures, he counted, sitting around it below. Slowly he navigated his horse on a zigzag path down the steep descent towards the smoke and camp, careful to be quiet as possible, until he pulled up near them while still concealed in darkness behind trees. Here he eavesdropped on their colloquy to determine the identity of the men before interjecting himself into their private moment. He quickly recognized their talk as that of hoboes, especially the jargon of *hopping the cannonball on the slow track* and the mickies on sticks he gathered they were roasting over the flames. So immersed in their hobo world of hooch and fire-roasting were they that only when Zeke astride Catapaltus halted but a few feet from the fire did they finally peer up at the figure casting the long shadow over them.

"Good Lord in the High Heavens! Who the hell are you?!" the one hobo shouted after being thoroughly startled and scrambling away. He wore a battered porkpie and a rumpled, raggedy oversize gray woolen suit.

"I am a friend, someone well-acquainted with the cause of hoboes ... call me Zeke," he said, reining in a suddenly restless Catapaltus. "The nearest rail line must be a good distance from these woodlands," Zeke added, "I am curious as to whether you fellows may be lost?"

The one in the porkpie looked at his companions and rubbed his ruddy, stubbled features before replying. "Well, we ain't exactly lost, mister, but we don't know where we're going either. We aim to jump the cannonball down the line, until then we're seeing what's what, ya understand?!"

Zeke returned that he did indeed understand, mindful of the bit of defensiveness in the hobo's tone.

He dismounted to join them around the fire. A stick with a mickie on it was offered to him by the husky, curly redheaded one in a worn plaid vest over a threadbare striped pullover. "Welcome, brother," he greeted. The other one, a skinny fellow in an old soldier's blue jacket and a battered boater, not to be outdone in hospitality, thrust a fifth of rum into Zeke's hand. "Have a slug with us, pal," he said. The one in the porkpie, whose name was Spodio, now kept staring at Zeke, craning his neck closer from across the fire, and finally exclaimed: "I knew I knew you from somewhere, brother! I was there that day by the river some years back when you and that tough old hobo feller went at it hammer and tongs in a dust-up not to be forgotten."

Zeke swigged the rum and gazed into the leaping, crackling fire as it cooked his potato. A shiver went through him as the memory of his bout with the hobo father was invoked. "So you remember the fight?" he asked. "That mean old cuss got the better of me. And the bastard stole my horse and bag of loot I was planning to bestow upon the crowd of hoboes there that day."

THIRTEEN

Spodio lit up a thin cheroot and puffed in silence before asking who was the "snarlin' blackguard" he fought, adding none of the hoboes knew him and he had a "portentous mystery" to him.

"That's the worst part of it all for me," Zeke acknowledged aloud now, "this brutish dark nemesis appeared to be a version of my father who'd seen hard times and turned into a much more violent and angry and maniacal figure than I'd ever known . . . and even though I know better that the passage of time since I'd last seen him almost certainly translates into his death well before that day—I am not truly convinced the mean brutal gee who beat the hell out of me in that fight was not him."

"It was an epic fight to the death, what you call a death match," Spodio now explained to his pals. "We all thought that one of you would wind up in the box. If that feller was your pappy, then you have my sympathy, brother. A feller like that has the devil himself in him fighting to kill somebody."

Zeke stared at his mickie darkening above the swirling flames and reflected on the hobo father who seemed to stalk and haunt him and an oppressive consternation came over him. It was becoming harder now for him to discern the realities of his father and the hobo father through the receding prism of the past, the ugly opacity of the brawl with the paternal bushwhacker who appeared out of nowhere to goad him into a scrap, the shaken memory of the theft of his loot and horse. "It feels like my past is chasing me and ever nipping at my heels while my future confronts me with harbinger. I have right now and that is elusive, slipping away. It is the struggle, the fight that abides and cannot be ignored," Zeke muttered almost as if to himself.

"Yeah, you said it brother. You know the score," Spodio affirmed. "The whole shebang is out to get us . . . that's why I like to keep moving." The skinny one in the beat-up boater added: "All of us like to keep moving. Otherwise, you ain't no true-blue hobo."

The curly redheaded husky one piped up with a cocksure but affable smile: "And a hobo who's riding the rails can always tell who the phonies are! There's a fellowship in our ranks, chief, that will not brook the frauds. And the ranks of hoboes committed to greater good through solidarity is growing, chief. Growing all the time."

Zeke thought of the bogus Hobo Fund the Gracklers concocted to induce his unswerving service to the highwaymen's cause, noting the irony that the hoboes themselves may be mobilizing to effect a better way of life somehow for all the common folks. "Well, back where I work a plough on a fine farm where some wonderful folks took me and my sheepdog in, they right off the bat figured I was a hobo and now that I think about it, I never really disabused them of that notion," he said.

After a space the husky redheaded one let out: "Pshaw! I never would have taken you for a hobo! You don't have that combination of freedom and deprivation in your eye."

"I know I'm not one but I let them hold onto that about me. I've known a good deal of hoboes in my life and I see it as a kind of honor. I think I can contribute to the movement in a way that will improve the lives of these good folks."

The skinny one in the boater now took out his harp and began blowing a slow plaintive number as the men silently drank the whiskey they were passing around while downing their potatoes. Zeke was impressed with the hobo's playing and found himself ruminating upon his life on the farm and the struggles everyone faced every day in the hard work of the soil and the pending foreclosure. And his own romantic disappointment. The harp player's name he would learn was Vigalor, and the wistful sentiment of his melody and the whiskey had Zeke desirous of more hobo songs, the kind of spirited defiant tunes he remembered fondly from the jungles and the back alleys of Bluddenville. Soon after Vigalor finished his instrumental ballad Zeke broke into "The Moon Looks Mean When I Pass Through Moline," and was blithely surprised at the smooth baritone lent by the red-headed husky hobo, whose name he would learn was Hogan, as well as the rhythmic capability of their apparent bellwether, Spodio, and together they harmonized on the old hobo number. The surge in sanguine spirits Zeke felt throughout got him thinking about the challenges hoboes and farmers face and how paradoxically alike they were, the dependence

THIRTEEN

on fruit of the soil, their adaptability to the changing of the seasons, and their deeply felt grievances with government and the opportunities available to them to make it and not falter or perish. Hogan started singing another well-known hobo chantey, "Cornfield Confidential: Fourteen Ears, Fifteen Hoboes and No Damn Butter," and Vigalor soloed a complicated riff that was nothing short of virtuosic in scope. A sense of fortitude and faith swelled in Zeke as he sang the old hobo songs and a raw inchoate revelation came to him and it had to do with helping hoboes and farmers and marshalling their causes into a powerful united movement. He had no notion how they could work together, only that merged their strength would be undeniable. They sang a few more numbers, including "Coal Car Carl Cracking Wise Near Cleveland," "Hey Mr. Brakeman, Your Choo Choo Is A-Chug-Chugging While We Chug-A-Lug It!" and the southern classic "Boozing in Boxcars on the Way to Hobo Heaven." As a half-crocked Zeke finally emerged from the cathartic sing-a-long and mounted Catapaltus on the second try after first falling, he managed to murmur to his new pals that they'd be welcome at the farm should they come around for some of the fine victuals the farm folk would make available to them.

FOURTEEN

HIS NIGHTLY HORSE RIDES with whiskey were taking a toll on Zeke though he would not acknowledge it. His formidable will and the importance he placed in working the soil, the arduous labor and sweat of his strained sinews, all became the desideratum to his abiding belief in better times ahead. It enabled him to hie himself in the early morning mists to his plough and Gomer and rigorously rip up the earth in long narrow furrows. But his body was incrementally wearing down from the lack of rest, the whiskey, the deficient nourishment, and the lonely forgotten exile he increasingly suffered as an outsider on the farm who pined from afar for the dairymaid he loved. He would spot them far in the distance riding on that fancy carriage of his, and her resigned unhappiness at succumbing to his grasp deeply pained Zeke. He knew she surrendered to the inexorable force of reason, the practical, pragmatic pressure advanced every day in small measures by Uncle Phineas and Aunt Abigail and the exigencies of pending foreclosure, and the subtle shift in her demeanor at supper struck him as too sad to contemplate. Her laughter no longer came as often and the robust guffaw she sometimes could not control disappeared altogether, he noticed. It seemed everyone else on the farm just figured the inevitable bottom line of all romantic affairs just asserted itself with Livinia, wealth and power subjugating another relationship it desires, trumping love easily. Except Horst perhaps, Zeke allowed, as nobody knew what he was thinking. And Zeke himself knew it inside so indubitably that the dairymaid was selling out because she believed only she could save the farm by doing so, and they wore her down until holding out for true love seemed selfish and silly when prestige and protection were on the table. It was more than he could bear when he saw them together, which was more frequent now than ever, and he was forbidden to have any encounter with Gerard as per Phineas, as the son of Lord Cumberland did have that talk with the farm owner about Zeke's place there. He was a hairsbreadth away from being expelled from the farm, as were Huxley and Ogden who remained boisterous rascals full of pranks between their chores but were likewise careful to keep their distance from Gerard when he came around. Zeke felt like one of the urchins, relegated to the sidelines of the farm folks and ordered to watch his step around the imperious son of Cumberland, and increasingly incapable of even engaging the dairymaid in simplest of palaver. His dejection at seeing her in such a grim bind with the smug land baron who was born to the manor precluded his capability to talk to Livinia without extreme self-consciousness. After several times in which he began to speak and abruptly stopped, having gone blank and recouping by singing old farming songs, Zeke ceased trying.

But there was the one evening of the square dance they held in the great barn, and Livinia was there by herself and Zeke had some whiskey and made his way over to ask her for a dance. Horst had brought in a farmers' band he knew from the Grange Movement and they were a stark ensemble whose main style was chamber music, though they occasionally played some raucous drinking songs of the old countries from which they hailed. While they perhaps were not the best fit for a square dance, the farm folks adapted their regimental square dance movements accordingly, and the dance resembled a bunch of folks scrambling around like they were being attacked by a swarm of hornets. Most of those who actually knew how to square dance were disappointed in the music and were critical of the band, but Zeke was relieved to find such an aberrant band offering heavy somber notes punctuated by the spasmodic jumping around because he would not be exposed as being devoid of an elemental grasp of basic square dancing. Out on the barn floor, Zeke erupted in a wild kinetic mishmash of herky-jerky conniption and Livinia maintained a few dos-i-dos and spins and struts of traditional square dancing—while she seemed to find Zeke's antics amusing. When he glimpsed her chuckling from across the floor he did not realize she was getting a kick out of his moves, though he generally was delighted to see her in cheerful spirits. After a spell he realized she was focusing on him and he turned up the loopy dance steps, high kicking frenetically with vibrating arm wiggling and torso syncopated jerks in which he several times lost his balance and tumbled to the deck.

As he picked himself up once, Livinia was standing over him smiling. "You sure have a distinctive style of dancing, Zeke Borshellac! Do all hoboes dance like that when riding trains in the moonlight?"

The mysterious mercurial music of the Grange band blared on as the farm folks swirled around them in various forms of square dancing and improvised movement. Zeke took a few steps towards the dairymaid and felt suddenly the momentousness of the encounter. "Well, we're all different . . . you have to do what feels right for you . . . as an individual," he said, thinking how right it felt to talk to her.

Livinia chuckled. "It certainly stands out, the way you dance."

"I'd like to learn the proper way to square dance sometime," he mused.

With that the dairymaid grasped his hand and dragged him out amongst a group of dancers and directed his participation, which produced many slapstick moments and hilarity for all, and Zeke was a good sport about being the butt of it because he was *her* partner throughout and that is all that really mattered. Booth Booley, Mathias Edgecomb, Cy Undersnettle, and most of all, the hell-bent urchins Ogden and Huxley, all enjoyed the boffolas until their sides split, razzing the comic star of the dance floor with good-natured heckles. Horst Schtuckgloo sat upright in a shadowy corner and watched it all with a gladsome countenance, for despite their early quarrels he, like the others, were rooting for Zeke and cared deeply about Livinia, and something subtle and well-nigh indefinable transpired out on that floor, the old farmer recognized. When he heard a couple of his livestock hands wondering aloud where the Cumberland son was that evening, Schtuckgloo turned towards them and snarled: "The likes of that feller thinks himself above a square dance, only the peon pissants engage in such things." And Schtuckgloo let out a guttural grunt with a knowing nod.

The following Friday after a long day in the fields Horst pulled up in his horse-drawn wagon at the barn to be welcomed by Balthazar and poured a whiskey by Zeke, and afterwards the two farmers together went to the Grange meeting. Schtuckgloo had been inviting Zeke to attend one of the gatherings of the Farmers Party for a good while already, and tonight he hoped his new recruit would be open to their ideas and embrace the movement. Far into the woodlands they began to wind through a path towards a massive archaic barn at the top of a rising range, and Zeke was struck by the utter darkness of the remote land and the great torches of flames arranged in cryptic patterns out in front and visible from miles away. Many farmers were milling around outside, hard-looking men in overalls and long coats and whiskers and puffing corn cobs, everyone soon reacting with geniality at seeing their old pal Horst jumping off his wagon to glad-hand and introduce his younger farmer buddy.

"Hey Horst, whatchya have there, brother farmer? A youngblood who wants to do his part to save our way of life with the soil?" one man with a long speckled beard and straw hat and oversize overalls called out.

Horst was shaking hands with old pals evidenced in the manner which they backslapped and shared hearty laughter. "Feller's name is Zeke and he's got himself some real guts and flames deep within that no one can extinguish. I want him to know about our movement."

A large stocky farmer emerged from the shadows and adjusted his wire-rim glasses in solemnly looking over Zeke. "Your new pal, Horst, doesn't strike me as a farmer. At least the farmers we know from around here. Seems more of a nomad." He took a few steps towards Zeke and met his eyes: "You ain't some kind of hobo are you, son?" This brought some murmurs among the men before they got quiet awaiting his answer. Farmers deplored the proliferation of railroad tracks through the open plains and much of their land, so any association with the locomotive invaders did not sit well with them.

Schtuckgloo interjected: "Well, the feller's well-traveled for sure, but on a plough he's—"

Zeke exclaimed over him: "Yeah, I am a hobo. The kind that came upon a sweet farm concealed in the forest and was given an opportunity to learn farming. I love the soil and the work. And I'm looking forward to my first harvest in the fall."

The large stocky farmer paused a few moments to digest Zeke's words before approaching him with his hand out to shake. "Welcome to the Grange, friend." As they shook he added, "Now let's all get a draft of fine lager."

Inside Zeke was surprised by the cavernous hall with a stage, immense floor, raked seating, and a balcony. There were stands with wooden kegs of beer all around and portraits of founding farmers of the movement from generations earlier. The crowd seemed to swell in size now to Zeke as the seats began to fill up and the men were guzzling big tankards of beer and becoming very boisterous in their agricultural palaver. Horst knew everyone and seemed to disappear in the sea of sodbusters and pipe smoke and by the time the meeting got under way Zeke had downed about three liter tankards and found himself a chair near the front. The meeting was a violent crescendo of bitter passions expressed in rhetorical tones, but was curiously framed in very strict, abstruse rules that seemed absurd to Zeke at times. When a speaker declaimed a notion rejected by some, the naysayers stood up and began singing "Old McDonald," though substituting obscene pejorative names such as "son of a bitch" for livestock. Those supportive of the idea then stood on their chairs and countered with the old farmer paean "I Grew an Eight Pound Onion on a Banker's Grave" to disrupt and drown out their negative counterparts. But it never escalated into the rowdy free-for-all Zeke at first feared it might, as the byzantine rules of the Grange's constitution were held sacrosanct and violating the strict vision of the First Farmers would be tantamount to resignation and exile from the community. The farmers

FOURTEEN

were rugged and rough men inured to long arduous days of work, men who liked to blow off steam now and then, though not in a combative manner towards one another if possible. The disagreements among themselves may have been profound, but civil and professional they did their utmost to remain although lately this had become an increasing challenge. They had many demands of the government to assist their struggles in restoring agricultural prosperity during the encroachment of industrialization, albeit little relief was offered. The farmers had grown angrier in recent years and espoused more radical solutions, such as abolition of national banks, taxing the rich industrialists, and regulating the railroads. The turnip farmers caucus even introduced the idea of a habitat resort lodge built on the shores of an unspecified Great Lake and available as an educational sanctuary for failed farmers who refuse to give up without studying the great agricultural minds of history. Zeke listened to the fiery speeches and intense debates, often over the complex nuances of irrigation techniques and frost remediation, and he felt their call to arms and was inspired to embrace the cause even though the actual strategy and objectives seemed murky to him. His dutiful belief in helping people was stirred once again and he deeply wanted to aid not just the farmers, but all the poor souls who had nothing and were inculcated to blame themselves and feel defeated, lost. He wanted to help farmers and hoboes and every poor son of a bitch who was down and out. It was in him and had to come out, he felt, this natural desire to help the oppressed and distressed, it was simply who he was in a world he had now seen in all its tantalizing wonders and abject cruelties.

 He watched Horst stride upon the stage and recount a story of when he was a boy on a poor farm and how he caught a hare one day and it became his pet, Klaus, and he cared for it and loved it until his father snatched Klaus away for their supper one evening. Horst went silent at the thought and Zeke thought he was going to cry up there, but the old farmer instead bellowed: "If our crops were plentiful that year, Klaus would not have been killed. My father skinned him and made us eat him. That's why we need better farming laws."

A lanky farmer in a wide-brim hat and smoking an enormous pipe that generated great clouds of smoke around him now strode to the podium. "My name is Wyatt Plantwater and I stand before you, brothers, to declare the time has come to build our own stores to sell our crops. The store owners are fleecing us, and we are the growers. Let's build our own stores!" The crowd for the most part approved of his speech, but some "Old McDonald" singers vociferously struck up and of course were countered by "The Eight Pound Onion . . ." choristers.

"What baloney, Plantwater!" a stout farmer with a twisted grimace and in a canary yellow jumpsuit and sporting a driver's cap cried.

"Stick it straight up your butt, Macklemore! You're too dumb to weigh in!" Plantwater shot back.

But Macklemore ambled up to the stage and usurped the podium to declare "that will not work cause it costs moolah to run stores and we got none!" He chuckled at the Old McDonald singers and the Onion counter crooners. "What this body ought to do is show some balls and blast apart some of the damn railroad tracks cutting across our land and preserve our way of farm life."

Zeke was working on another liter of beer and lost in woolgathering on improving their lives, free-associating ideas of building coalitions, marshalling movements into concerted action, organizing folks who seem to be at loggerheads but really have more in common and can prevail in creating better lives for everybody. It felt damn good, he said to himself, to be thinking such grand and noble thoughts and an aura of optimistic strength came over him now. And as he further withdrew into this half-crocked state of glorious idealism the fellow fulminating again at the podium was Horst Schtuckgloo and he was quoting scripture and invoking the "great hell to be paid by the powers that be who have kept the heels of their jackboots on the necks of working farmers like us for far too long!" Schtuckgloo was fired up in a violent rage so much that Zeke worried he could collapse any second from such overwrought madness, and then he did just that but bounced back up with a laugh that he was just joking and was fine. Horst would do that to make sure he had one hundred percent of an audience's at-

FOURTEEN

tention. And the farmers grumbled and shouted in protest at such a childish prank, but then Horst went down again and this time they figured he was joking again so busied themselves with singing Old McDonald and others countering with the Eight Pound Onion song, until word spread that Horst had actually passed away on the stage and sudden quiet fell over the hall . . . until Horst jumped up full of laughs and Scripture damning everyone. The place was now a welter of raw drunken anger boiling and bellowing in an incoherent din devoid of humanity. Bedlam broke out in the form of many brawling factions, most hardly cognizant of what they were shouting and fighting about. Zeke almost involuntarily found himself climbing on the stage and moving towards the podium and finding the gavel pounded it louder and louder, yelling his lungs out for order and decency as the agricultural brain trust of a great movement requires dignity and unity, until they all stopped and looked up at him, quietude now descending over the hall. Zeke hesitated in gathering his thoughts as he felt their eyes burning through him with all of their skepticism toward a newcomer and all of their deep yearning for that one special farmer who would rise up from their ranks and synthesize, simplify, and amalgamate in powerful oratory their platform and prescription to preserve the good life of the soil, before it was too late.

"Farmers, friends, neighbors . . . my name is Zeke Borshellac . . . and I stand before you this evening as someone who has roamed around for years finding new callings over and over again in all kinds of places. Right now, I think of myself as a farmer cause I'm pretty handy with a plough, and I love the work, the soil." Most suspended their wrangling and were listening, watching him with wariness and curiosity, but some of the rowdiest were heckling and catcalling.

"Who the hell let this jaboney in?" one rock-ribbed burly farmer hollered.

Another one with big ears and crazy eyes bellowed: "Now we got hoboes lecturing us!? What kind of party are we here?"

"A bunch of numb-brained nimrods!?" another old-timer shouted rhetorically.

"You may call me a hobo in a pejorative manner, but I call myself a hobo proudly. I have traveled a great deal and tried my hand in many lines of work before I came to farming, which include fisherman, demolitionist, highwayman, fund collector, and poetry adviser. I learned some hard lessons from each of those vocations, insights through experience that can be applied to the dire state of affairs facing us here today as struggling farmers. We must overcome the bitter conflicts among ourselves and come together as a united force prepared to defend and preserve the agricultural way of life. I am here to tell you the most important idea advanced by the Grange Movement should be the conviction and commitment to helping the poor souls who are voiceless, the downtrodden who have nothing, the oppressed who live hand-to-mouth travails every day and traverse the land seeking a break wherever they may find it. The succor we provide them will enlighten and enrich us as farmers and individuals in ways that matter most and will stand as the heart and soul of the Grange movement as we grow and enlist folks to join us on our path to power. I have come to know and respect many hoboes in my peregrinations, I have been called a hobo myself, and now I am proud to call myself a hobo who found a calling in farming. I can envision many hoboes soon settling down and following me into farming, but we need to be open to their aspirations as the Von Klobbert farm has been to the likes of me. My fellow farmers, there remains a hobo in every one of us that is but one bad break or funk of spirit from hopping on that train to nowhere seeking warmth, nourishment, and camaraderie along the way. I say let us partner with those hoboes who ride the rails, and we fear trespass on our lands. We can feed them with our crops and fortify them with our grassroots principles of hard work and freedom while affording them opportunities to work the land, as I have been. If you talk to any of them, get to know hoboes as I have, you'll see that all they are really looking for is a chance, somebody to give them a shot. That somebody ought to be us."

A stark silence and stillness greeted Zeke's remarks at first, as it wasn't clear he had finished speaking. But even when that became

FOURTEEN

clear it took them a while longer to process his message and collectively decide on it, and the ensuing quiet seemed eerie to Zeke. But then all at once the great hall erupted in wild applause, a deafening raucous ovation of clapping, cheering, and shouting with every farmer on his feet and it went on and on, beyond all standards of a receptive audience evincing its heartfelt unanimous approval. Now they were singing the old farming songs with such passion and volume that the place seemed to shake and Zeke himself filled with an exultant surge of hope and confidence that he'd found the right movement of simpatico souls, and a young farmer ran up to present him a massive mug of beer, and soon they all were holding up gigantic beers and swaying together as they belted out their beloved agricultural anthems, and Zeke beamed as he thrusted his mug high and sang along with them. "Sodbusters Sockeroo" "Don't Eat Pegler's Goo Goo Crop," "Farmer Stroud and the Eleven Glommed Beets," "How Many Harvest Pecks on a Pontoon?," "Scarecrow Artie Used To Be a Yellowbelly," and the Grange's traditional number, "When the Bastards Bury Me I'm Growing Back as a Cornstalk," all were covered in full-throated fervor. By the time Zeke wended his way through the charged, won-over swarm of farmers to find Horst out front for the ride back he had become a new staunch and singular voice of leadership in the Grange Movement, and he remained silent on the wagon the whole way with sanguine musings of grassroots coalescing possibilities, while a half-crocked Schtuckgloo serenaded the hidden forest creatures of the night with a rousing medley of the aforementioned farm classics, mostly melding the joyous rave "Sodbusters Sockeroo" with the stark bluesy mysteries of "How Many Harvest Pecks On a Pontoon?"

Over the next several days those farming classics reverberated in Zeke's head as he pushed himself ever harder on the plough with Gomer ripping up row upon row of good earth. There were moments in his excited cogitations about a new symbiotic movement of farmers and hoboes in which it all seemed like a castle in the air, a mere figment he concocted through a fever or perhaps bad liquor, and he would suddenly lose hope until he caught himself and recalled it was real and he would sing the farm numbers in a soft voice to himself. He would tell Gomer about the forging of forces he envisioned bringing together to benefit one another and strengthen the overall united cause. He could hardly wait until the next Grange meeting when his new inchoate ideas would find form and conveyance and it all felt wonderful and gratifying to be at the forefront of such change and progress.

Sometimes in his isolated toil on the sprawling range of land it seemed daunting, even overwhelming, and he had to go on long rides once again in the dead of night on the powerful black steed Catapaltus. It was on one such ride in the deepest purlieus of pristine wee hours forest when he descried a distant glow and a stagnant gathering of white smoke among some treetops. Zeke was naturally inquisitive of such signs of life and steered his splendid beast in its direction, and after galloping through to a grassy glade he saw the kerosene lit windows of the wood cabin, smoke billowing from its chimney. As he trotted closer, he could tell the place was an inn which probably had a bar and victuals and the horses and carriages outside indicated some patrons were there. He was intrigued by the hidden nature of the inn and wondered about those who traversed the woods as he had to wind up there, in such a peculiar haunt shrouded amid the verdure. He tied Catapaltus to a post and went in to see for himself, sidling to a stool in the dark corner of the long bar where he could observe the doings while mostly anonymous. The folks struck Zeke as tradesmen, blacksmiths and coopers and lumberjacks with brawny builds and plain dress, except for one party at a table off the far end of the bar that was quite rowdy with laughs and cries, where one fellow seemed to run the show with his enthralled gang all around him, many young pretty women in décolletage dresses of taffeta and risqué flourishes in his direct orbit. On closer study Zeke could see the women were high-toned tarts whose only purpose that evening was to serve the grandee who had them enthralled throughout. He heard him laugh a mirthless howl and utter cranky piques and petulant aspersions aimed at his women, and Zeke thought he knew that voice. He circumspectly crept along the bar to get a better look at the man and once his head spun his way, as he was chuckling with his girls, Zeke glimpsed in his mien none other than Gerard Cumberland carrying on with his de facto harem. Once Zeke determined he had not been spotted, he settled in to observe and eavesdrop on the unseemly display that the other patrons distanced themselves from. Here he saw a lush of a rake in disheveled velvet suit and ruffled fancy shirt honeyfogling the bevy surrounding him, groping them at will as if he were buying fresh fruit, insulting them left and right with vile gutter talk, and swigging champagne with a lush's abandon. His guffaw resounded like someone whose primary purpose for laughter all his life had been mockery, like a nobleman whose coarse laughter was meant as a warning to others to back off and let him dominate the night. Zeke watched the spectacle of Lord Cumberland's son carrying on with the slap-and-tickle fooling around, a cocotte perched on each of his knees as he regaled them with tales of his travels and ambitious plans for his father's regions. They wanted a garrison built on the land to install an army regiment, and mills and factories were in the works to generate economic progress and more taxes, new towns and railroad stations and houses enticing new families to move there.

"The interminable acreage of agricultural debacle is going to transform into a thriving, profitable, new society of industrialized neighborhoods," Gerard boasted to his rapt audience, before adding with a peal of laughter: "And my poor father, the old Remittance Man exiled like a fugitive, can finally return to London, and I will remain in charge here with you lovelies and all my deeds and titles of landed ownership." That all said, the inebriated heir to the manor let himself slump into the smiling forms of his gorgeous gaggle, who as a professional group with great skill in the art of sexual foreplay and kissing and petting, got busy as their boss submitted to their ministrations.

Zeke had grown increasingly disgusted by the grotesque sybaritic decadence of this disdainful son of privilege, felt a fierce outrage of betrayal in his plan to build over farmland, while mostly wanting to protect Livinia from this debauched reprobate's clutches before it was too late. He could not understand what Gerard was trying to perpetrate upon her, but he knew it was not borne of good intentions or love of any sort, only of conquest and despoiling the dairymaid of the innocent beauty and kindness and glorious good nature and happiness she possessed in spades. There are those of bitter enmity and dark selfish visions who will desire possession of raw, natural beauty and purity and virtue, Zeke felt, because it so mystifies them, reminds them of their own sordid misanthropy by contrast and makes them feel threatened by such sublime embodiment that they simply are drawn to own and control such individuals and ultimately squelch their inner effulgence. Zeke left through the long shadows of the bar and mounted Catapaltus with a reinvigorated determination and urgency to prevent Livinia from succumbing to the pragmatic capitulation of Gerard's woo, and that meant stepping up his own so far largely ineffectual efforts to court the dairymaid himself.

Fifteen

BE RETURNED to his plough and trusty ox with a singular conviction that his opportunity would come and he was ready to meet its challenges. Zeke had a remarkable capacity to immerse himself in endless lonely days of arduous work in the fields because he had that belief intact, and of course, Balthazar as his boon companion nights in the hayloft for encouragement. He saw Livinia a few times from afar walking with Gerard by the stream and tooling along the distant horizon in his carriage, sightings that sank his heart with dismay and revulsion each time. When he first heard talk of the Pig Roaster Summer Picnic to be held at Redmond's Landing over on the Bockboxen Forest Isthmus, replete with music and theatrical performances of sundry sorts, kegs of beer, flame-cooked pork, beef, and mutton, and an appearance by the sponsor himself, Lord Cumberland, Zeke did not think he would even attend. He equated participation in such an event as support and endorsement of the Cumberland superintendence and could not abide such an association. Further reflection, however, allowed him to sense an opportunity. Livinia would undoubtedly be present and perhaps he could connect with her while exposing the dichotomy of ideals and values championed by his new Grange movement in contrast to the Cumberland brand of exclusion. He decided to spread word that hoboes everywhere should flock to the Picnic at Redmond's Landing on Bockboxen, that they too should enjoy a day outside of music and great slabs of roasted meat and kegs of beer. It would be a chance to demonstrate solidarity with their agricultural brethren. And so, on the big day Zeke rode out early with Horst Schtuckgloo on his horse and buggy, along with Cy Undersnettle, to enlist themselves in the construction of the makeshift performance stage and reviewing stand for Lord Cumberland. Zeke wanted to witness how the event unfolded from the very beginning and be prepared to launch himself into the forefront of any tumult that might result from the clash of contingents he set in motion. It went surprisingly straightforward most of the afternoon as he saw the smooth steady unloading of meat from horse-drawn carts to the various great fire pit grills where the aromatic smoke plumes shot high over all, the brass and wind orchestra played parade and patriotic songs loudly and unremittingly, and the burghers and farming folk of the region steadily kept arriving to eat, drink, dance and sing their hearts out, while their children ran wild with their own games and pastimes of amusement. One group even began a Shrike on the Fruitwood contest, which was rather quickly and quietly ended by Cumberland's attendant officials. It was a merry feast of roasting meat over great fires and rhubarb pie and blackthorn parfaits and figgy schnecken and watermelon and vanilla custard and tapioca pudding and a rotating orchestra playing inspirational marching songs, some long forgotten time pieces of baroque complexities, and many by the one and only John Philip Sousa that everyone had heard since they were knee high to mosquitoes.

Zeke was not convinced the blithe mood would endure, especially not after Lord Cumberland and his retinue of attendants arrived in a caravan of four opulent coaches drawn by strikingly large draft horses directly onto the fairgrounds with a flourish and majestic blare of a trumpeter as the distinguished riders disembarked, the picnickers now gathering to greet them. Among the coterie coming out to wave to the crowd was Livinia, looking ravishing to Zeke in yellow and white ruffled dress, on the arm of Gerard, who, Zeke thought, assumed an imperial air of arrogance even beyond his usual pomposity. He and his father were in their formal finery of navy double-breasted gold trim suits bearing their crossed poleaxes coat of arms, red cravats, spats, derbies, and white gloves, and there was much protocol and ceremony of walking stiffly and waving while local officials deferred to them with obeisance. Lord Cumberland was a large, bulky man with a permanent expression of exasperation mixed with disgust who seemed to Zeke to be simply going through the motions without enjoying one iota of his visit. Ogden and Huxley were in the back of the crowd sitting up on a branch of a tree when Zeke, right under them, heard them laughing and calling out "Lord Bumblelard and the clown prince of darkness!" He was relieved that their jeer fell short of most folks hearing it, yelling up that they ought to knock it off. While he certainly appreciated their sentiment Zeke did not want to cause an immediate ruckus, inasmuch as he could not keep his eyes off the dairymaid in her fine dress and thought too severe of a heckle would only embarrass her. She was on display and seemed quite uncomfortable throughout the shuffling about to some fey old punctilio. But the whole effect was quite ghastly for Zeke to absorb, such a vision of loveliness so utterly dominated by the overweening prince, or Baby Bumblelard as Og and Hux would say, and he wondered whether she even noticed his own figure of despair towards the rear of the throng. Eventually Lord Cumberland and his entire retinue were seated in the reviewing stand and were brought several platters of roasted meat and tall tankards of beer, as the entertainment portion began great guns with the afternoon sun shining brightly over the fine blue sky. Now came out the great farm combos with their oboes, bassoons, guitars, fiddles, drums, and violas, with farmers both jocose and pensive singing with the kind of earnest intensity that can only be born of the soil, or so the folks believed. "Cornstalk Hideaway with Wanda Purvey," "Haystacks and the Dead Swede," "Scythe Swaths, Width Eighteen Feet," all were capable of producing tears in the hardest sodbuster with even the most incompetent of musicians simply by virtue of the deep-rooted familiarity of the old numbers. Zeke saw Mathias Edgecomb singing the lyrics of "Scythe Swaths, Width Eighteen Feet" with such heartfelt sincerity he seemed like a little boy affirming his faith in living a good honest life, a farmer's life. He noticed Booth Booley with some farmer pals passing around a jug of wine and taking turns dancing a minuet with a discarded shredded scarecrow they surrounded in a circle. The bands were pure escapist nostalgic joy and the farmers delighted in the old-time music of their youths, the wafts of pungent heavenly smoke from the great spits of flame-roasted meats watered everyone's mouths, and the exuberant sounds of the swarms of playing children all was combining to produce a moment in time and memory when through that rarest of synchronicities all seemed right and beneficent.

And then the packs of hoboes started showing up, hungry hoboes who made beelines for the flame pits and succulent charred meat and great tankards of fine brew and at first no one questioned their presence, no one really minded hoboes from faraway worlds of railroad tracks and jungles had come to join their pig roaster picnic. They mixed well with the farmers in showing their penchant for good-time merrymaking and overall hail-fellow-well-met unpredictability, such as their sudden breaking out of horseshoes for a serious game, the random yelling of some screwball jive like "Scrambled eggs, Butchie! Flapjacks tomorrow or else!" as every last one of them hits the deck in an inscrutable piece of hobo culture. And of course they started singing hobo songs as they became more liquored up and demonstrative, which now was beginning to grate on the farmers who otherwise appreciated their robust personalities and fascinating, if disconcertingly peculiar, contributions to the gathering. While the farmers and hoboes reflexively vied for which culture would dominate the festivities in song and performance, Zeke spotted Phineas and Abigail threading through the crowd trying to reach the viewing stands where Lord Cumberland, Gerard, and Livinia were seated. He watched them from his distance now as if nothing else was happening at Redmond's Landing on the Bockboxen Forest Isthmus, all of it dimmed, the children's shouts, the music, the roil of the horde, the smells of roasting comestibles, only the scene from afar registered in his focus. He knew what was being said or, if left unsaid, foremost in their thoughts. Lord Cumberland was their savior, the one they counted on to bail out the farm. He saw them embrace, exchange words with easy smiles, and then Lord Cumberland called for someone from his retinue and a little man with muttonchops and a bedraggled suit of tails emerged buried in a mound of unwieldy photographic equipment, a deployment for daguerreotypes that swiftly descended into an opera buffa of the fellow frantically trying to set up the picture only to be forestalled by the utter collapse of the tottering tower upon him, a cave-in that occurred again and again until finally a vexed Lord Cumberland called the poor man over to have him remove his beat-up homburg to cuff him a single shot upon his dome. At this juncture, thwarted in his attempt at a photo with the Von Klobberts, the magisterial superintendent of the region now ordered the band of farmers, who were in the midst of a rollicking paean to cornfields and rutabaga patches, to strike up a ballad for the courtly couple to entrance the crowd with a waltz. They managed a shaky rendition of what Zeke thought to be "Blue Danube" and Gerard led with a mechanical rigidity devoid of all cheer, while Livinia seemed lost in a melancholic fog gamely adhering to duty. Zeke sank into a desolate ache of retreat, the terrible vignette foreshadowing the gloom of her formally entering Gerard's grasp. He glimpsed Ogden and Huxley and several farm scamps they'd befriended roving towards the far end of the viewing stand, and he could tell there was mischief in their movements. They were hiding behind the stand where no one seemed to notice them when they suddenly came barreling through an aisle towards the band and dance area and got close enough to Gerard to pelt him with a fusillade of crab apples. The son of Lord Cumberland took many such apple projectiles on the noggin, but carried on dancing, apparently unwilling to allow them the satisfaction of discontinuing. The boys bolted so fast that before anyone knew what happened they were already halfway to a copse for cover.

As the dance ended to scattered applause it became clear the hoboes were growing rowdier, louder, drunker, some of it a reaction to the Cumberland legion moving them with increasing aggression into a detached sector of the isthmus which the hoboes found insulting and unacceptable. The legion of constables who were Cumberland's personal guard began roughing up the more recalcitrant, hammered hoboes and these skirmishes escalated as combatants on both sides entered the fray in defense of their own. The children too intensified into a wild running pack of guttersnipes looking for maniacal hi jinks, mostly in the form of pelting the people with crab apples, swiping hats off heads, hurling epithets at easy targets, and ever looking to lure their victims, most often the legion of constables, into giving them chase.

Lord Cumberland sought to assert his power and stature by ordering the band of farmers to strike up a rip-roaring medley of John Phillip Sousa as he climbed the steps to the stage and boomed out to the crowd: "My good folk of our magnificent pastoral region, I beseech you to find calmness and cease this madness! We are here to have a good time, sing and dance and feast on roasted meat and your fine vegetables and celebrate our lives together—not clash like enemies in battle."

Some did pause in their fighting to listen to him, but most ignored him or reacted with rancor and outrage and threw vegetables at him.

"Why have you allowed the vile lowlife hoboes to come here and bother us?" a stout angry farmer shouted.

"It is your legions fault for attacking us hoboes who are here in the spirit of fellowship and solidarity!" an old hobo bellowed from the midst.

"Bumblelard the blowhard! You ain't from here and don't give a hoot about us!" another stentorian cry rose from the mob.

The picnic at Redmond's Landing was in a dire state of deepening chaos with the hoboes resisting the advance of the constabulary and making strategic gains of their own to reclaim the grounds nearest the meat-roasting tents. Their cause was somewhat undermined by the sizable number of hobo fighters, disarmed by the savory aromas of the flame-cooked meat, taking meal breaks to scarf down big thick cuts of beef and steak. Some of them and other picnickers not quite engaged in the donnybrook now heard Lord Cumberland on the stage orating: "Every farmer and burgher in this region I consider to be a child of mine, vibrant children bursting with exuberant capacities for commerce and plain hard work, but also headstrong, impetuous children who need guidance and control so they understand the limits of their station. That is why I am here, watching over you, protecting you,

FIFTEEN

reining you in against your own self-destructive tendencies. I am Lord of this fine land and care deeply that you all are healthy and happy." While some burghers and mostly his constabulary offered faint applause, a gathering crescendo of jeers and boos swelled up from the madcap violent welter engulfing the grounds, and Lord Cumberland visibly bristled and turned to his inner circle, including Gerard, and commanded: "It is time for us to leave these ungrateful buzzards! Peasants are more incorrigible than ever and they deserve the unpleasantness that is coming to them!" Turning to a uniformed officer on horseback: "Major Ethelbert! Lower the boom!"

The legion of constabulary soon responded to the major's subsequent screaming and sprung into a formation scheme of zigzags offset by "swinging fence" squadrons with seven or eight legions equipped with battering rams and oversize netting to immobilize their adversaries. While initially the hoboes sustained losses and several were restrained and taken into custody, the great majority adjusted to the onslaught with ingenuity and resourcefulness, and even some capricious tomfoolery. After all, they were liquored up and as such always hankering for some hilarious foray into lunacy. The constabulary increased in numbers until they stretched their configuration into a checkerboard pattern that continuously spun clockwise, while the "swinging fence," now grown into a surging "giant's whip," was comprised of more than thirty breast-plated constables clad in gray uniforms with coverlets. The hoboes found the regimented attack quite a formidable display of disciplined forces, yet equally recognized the overblown comicality of such an advance on them. They simply indulged their guffaws in evincing a nimble and agile retreat in convoluted whirligigs and spins and tumbling, a stunning show of sheer hobo exuberance fueled by alcohol, anarchy, and breakneck abandon. Zeke had by now taken the stage and wheedled some of the farmer musicians to stay put, despite some of their sodbuster brethren starting to leave because of all the fighting. Most of the farmers, Zeke was gratified to see, had remained to enter the fray fiercely in support of the hoboes and it was their reinforcements that truly made the difference holding the line for the nutty rail birds. The brawl slowed into a more strategic battle and without the farmers throwing in with them, the hoboes would have sustained heavy losses and been soundly routed.

Lord Cumberland and his retinue had already departed and it appeared Gerard left with them. Zeke saw no sign of Livinia and assumed she had left with the Cumberlands. He lost track of where Ogden and Huxley were but figured they were at the forefront of the scrambling antics of the children's brigade. Horst, Booth, and Mathias had simply disappeared into the welter of clashing. On stage with the ragtag farmer musicians that heeded his plea to stay, Zeke knew the critical moment for action had arrived. Someone had to step up and provide leadership, if not brinksmanship, to steer the day back towards sanity and a measure of amity before it became totally engulfed in devastation and violence. He thought if he broke through with a strong presentation of some kind that instantly captured everyone's attention and held them riveted long enough to truly hear his message of unity and fellowship and altruism he could bring a halt to the intensifying madness. He pointed at the band and bade them to strike up "martial marching band music with an ethereal fugue," which they seemed perplexed by. "Sousa rent through with a strain of baroque harpsichord ," he tried to further clarify. Finally, with a hint of chagrin in his voice he told them to "play anything as long as it is fast, loud, and moving and as though it is the last song you will ever goddamn play so you *have* to get it right."

Sure enough, the tubby wheat farmer with the van dyke and crescent moon stocking cap so long it fell onto the stage, Hop Quinine, began to blow a strong intro to "Our Milk Cow Named McTavish and the Carved Baker Figurine," the forgotten cantata of pastoral majesty and rustic strength. Yance Brollo, the wily faro shark who grew fine rhubarb and cereal grass, now blasted his trombone with such primal force it seemed to swell his entire countenance to make him look like a rotting pumpkinhead. The drummer, Ott Eschledy, a wayward cook who collected agricultural chapbooks with tall tales of spooky farmers, simply banged his one tom-tom with a visceral gusto. And then there was the skinny red-headed hooligan son of old Farmer Schmidt, Nathaniel, a bumptious rotter few could tolerate being around unless he played his guitar, on which he was quite proficient. They tore into a riveting rendition of "McTavish and the Carved Baker Figurine," a wild raucous careening roar that exploded onto the agitated crowd and made them pay some heed. Zeke recognized their raw power and decided to delay the speech he intended to give by interjecting himself over Eschledy as the lead vocalist. The drummer reacted with violent indignation and began smiting Zeke across his head and torso with his drumsticks, which only fueled the new singer's zeal to belt out the "McTavish . . . Baker Figurine" number with all the more sonority and spirit, a tussle many in the crowd found amusing. Zeke could only remember the first stanza of the traditional harvest/Walpurgis celebratory number and he ripped into it with every fiber of his being. "Our milk cow was named McTavish / And remember the carved baker figurine / While praise for McTavish was never lavish / On that dumb figurine I always vented my spleen / He was an erratic, sickly bovine, McTavish / But we all liked him just the same / How sad to see his form diseased and milk turned sour / And then the carved baker figurine forever appeared dour—and in the darkness a thousand such carved baker figurines began a torchlight march in the name of that milk cow named McTavish."

Zeke sang with the raw power of a man with little left to lose, as if his furious melodic shouting were a last ditch effort to seize control of the picnic, the brawling, the movement itself of providing a voice of leverage and hope to the disaffected, dispossessed, marginalized, and forsaken before it was too late to muster the confidence and fortitude in himself to rally folks for the struggle ahead, before all were lost for good. His performance was so utterly beyond the scope of description or classification by anyone noticing the farmers' band jamming on that stage that some simply stopped engaging in the great battle to watch the demented spectacle of that hobo Zeke and his band. He found a strange rhythm of lightning quick herky-jerky moves coupled with a slow dance with an invisible partner he twirled and laughed with, and intermittently screamed about "mobilizing and marshalling and uniting to conquer the world as we know it! Farmer and hobo believe in the same ideals and values and principals of humanity! Now we have to come together and fight!" Zeke was gathering more spectators all the time, not so much because of his oratory, rather the self-destructive singular show of mesmerizing lunacy drew them around the stage. Some of the Grange members thought it had gone too far and feared the hobo ploughboy from the Von Klobbert farm would hurt himself, despite the adrenaline kick Zeke seemed to infuse in everybody with his stage work. Deep within, inchoate and instinctual, Zeke understood he had seized upon a mysterious and preternatural power to command the crowd's burgeoning attention. While his oratory soared in stentorian rhetoric, it was more his strange and singular performance that appeared to captivate them, the question of whether he was going to implode right on the stage or soar into unimaginable heights of wonder. He spoke with vision and passion of the ardor of agriculture and the tribulations of rail-hopping and his voice boomed with a peculiar tone and he began to shake, slowly back and forth at first but ever faster and more violent. His entire frame soon began to spin in accelerating revolutions until he tumbled hard to the stage, and the crowd yelled for him to rise and continue when it seemed hopeless, and he was motionless. But Zeke sprang to his feet and gathering his cognizance began shadowboxing around the stage. As he bounced around with very nimble footwork and threw all manner of combination blows, he suddenly was seized by the notion to sing. He belted out an operatic interpretation of "The Cockamamie Cauliflower Clocked Farmer Palowski," a children's sing-along number he recalled from boyhood days with his mother in the tavern where she worked. The deep lugubrious version of the lilting melody he fashioned here was barely recognizable, but the plangent elegy of the crop turning the tables on the farmer resonated with the Grange members in the crowd as an inexorable metaphor apropos their current quandary. The finale crescendos with Palowski succumbing on his death bed with the last inexplicable utterance: *plapesto futerinzing.*

FIFTEEN

A foreign sounding phrase that appears fraught with meaning and augury, yet the more astute farmers in attendance, after some futile cogitation on the words came to recognize the randomness of the syllables escaping his last breaths and knew it to be Borshellac riffing on the pointless inanity of loveless lives disconnected from one another without working together on the common good for all. Similarly, the visionary performance encompassed a paean to movement, kinetic sweep of time, onward ever on the open paths through passing places, and this began with Zeke blowing a train whistle blast through his lips from his innermost depths, and it was a severe sound that kept resounding in deafening discomfort, frighteningly as a real train whistle but with much more warmth and solemnity and awe even, as you might hear such a train whistle in a maddening dream, and this of course engendered a jolting electricity of identification among the hoboes, and they stared at this odd figure on the stage who now broke into a riveting type of tap dancing that was so ineptly executed it was poignantly cathartic to them, and he was crooning now the old hobo classic for good measure, "Rumblin' o'er Wheat Fields in a Boxcar When Mornin' Light Comes," and the hoboes instinctually saw in Zeke one of their own.

But he wasn't done up there before concocting an improvised skit that harkened back to his time at sea when he perforce put on shows for the crew as the Fish Fellow. In this one he began playing Farmer Meade Critchley, a gangling, God-fearing sodbuster with a penchant for skipping instead of walking, until he only skipped and earned the moniker "Skippy." But Critchley had a thriving lettuce, tomato, and pig farm (he presaged the advent of the BLT) and to his detractors he skipped all the way to the bank. Until while taking inventory in a silo one day he takes a hard fall and upon regaining consciousness becomes inconsolable over his decision not to pursue astronomy, and suddenly concludes he is a failure and wants to do more for starving indigent people. But he cannot not figure out what that is, so he sails to the Continent to study painting for several years before nearly expiring from eating bad clams and having the epiphany that the answer was as plain as the nose on his face all along. In fact, he recalled his nose had been broken three times in his life, twice by pugnacious boozehound Arlen Daugherty back in his farm days, but that still leaves him in the dark about his way forward. Then one of his artist cronies suggests since he only draws farm scenes, dull "impressionist" ones at that, why doesn't he just go back and create the authentic article? That was the breakthrough Farmer Meade Critchley needed and so begins his journey home to grow crops for the poor and skipping again for the first time in years. Again, upon finishing his skit about the Farmer Critchley, Zeke stood tall on the stage without word or pose, simply remaining erect and still as the crowd hesitated to react for a good minute while not sure the performance was over, but then all at once bursting into a zealous ovation. As the clapping and huzzahs finally faded Zeke looked over the vast crowd still watching his every move, waiting, he thought, for him to do something more than speak and perform. He wanted desperately to provide that next level of direction, show them the plan to move forward beyond the status quo in which they had been snared for so long, and all he could do was simply jump off the stage and run into the crowd as fast as he could.

The clashes with the Cumberland constabulary had never really ceased altogether, as the rowdier hoboes coupled with the militant farmers continued in certain peripheral pockets of the isthmus, and only on the main grounds near the stage they collectively paused to take in Zeke's show. Zeke had hoped the temporary truce would spread to the outskirts but now that he found himself among the throng, he exhorted them to hold onto their anger, to maintain their will to see the struggle through, but to stand down and disperse as such fighting never solved anything. But it was no use, the blood was too hot in them, the tempest too far gone to unwind, and the constabulary was receiving a fresh boost of new forces to lace into the incipient coalition combatants. Far outnumbered and without any of the truncheons and blackjacks and other weaponry the constabulary had in surplus, the hoboes proved ingenious in readily adapting to the regimental advance of the legions by employing a complicated "reverse minuet in staccato," which hoboes traditionally trot out in evading bulls attempting to shoo them from trains. Loosely based on the Japanese art of hiding in plain sight while tripping aggressors, *Bisudo Tient Dak*, a.k.a, *Bitida*, the hoboes could not be contained by the vaunted "Swinging Gate" or "Giant's Whip" operational tactics continuously thrown at them by the legions, and they often punctuated their splendid evasions with gleeful teasing and exaggerated guffaws. The farmers were much more belligerent than their migrant allies, many quite liquored up and simply looking to "break some Cumberland heads open," and they managed to inflict major damage in several skirmishes when they isolated some constables, most notably when Big Uriah Wakefield and his Corn Whiskey Shuckers from the Shady Hills region worked a whole regiment over with their pitchforks and trussed them up like a big reddened bale of hay. Still, many farmers felt the brunt of the constabulary's armed advance as they were outmatched, and they too needed to retrench and adjust by adapting unorthodox strategies as had the hoboes. They enjoyed great success in thwarting the "Swinging Gate" by implementing drills from early farm manuals for new settlers, such as the "Moo Cow Cacophony," in which a phalanx of farmers disguise themselves as livestock (muddied faces, feathering and sheepskins) dart about in seemingly random patterns that are actually intricately drawn, all the while making a din of animal noise so the three "sun devil roosters" can screamingly sneak through swinging whips and scythes.

    Zeke found himself amid all the dust-swirling hostilities and ever-shifting configurations of conflict, shouting at first for his ranks to retreat and fight another day but soon his calls grew frantic with rage at the madness around him. Finally, it swept him up in its ferocious strife, and Zeke swung like a crazed beast at constables and connected with several haymakers before he started getting whacked with their cudgels, and he was in dire straits when he saw from afar a carriage driven by an apparent madman rampaging at full pelt through the fields. The horses blazed a sinuous path amid the raging battlefield, appearing in stark blinding barreling velocity intermittently as the smoke from fires suddenly burning everywhere engulfed the carriage now and again. The self-destructive breakneck pace of the vehicle held Zeke's gaze before it occurred to him the driver was Horst Schtuckgloo and he seemed quite berserk with booze and the two howling lads hanging off the back on some bales of hay were none other than Ogden and Huxley. How the guttersnipes laughed with maniacal exultance at the violent scene they sped through!

Zeke yelled: "Horst! Horst! You're going to crash!" and bolted towards the carriage and nearly got himself run over, narrowly dodging it and continuing to chase it, losing all visibility several times in the smoke and getting jolted and slammed by forms no longer recognizable in the fray. Knocked down he floundered before rising from a muddy stretch, a whipping fire precariously nearby, and here came Horst dead straight at him unawares and Zeke scrambled out of the way to simultaneously launch himself on the side of the seat, and here he clung tenuously while Horst roared incoherently and the boys screamed with desperate exhilaration, and then Og spotted Zeke hanging on the carriage side and the boys pulled him into the front seat beside Horst. And Horst shouted scripture to the skies as he sped harum-scarum right at the "Swinging Gate" which improvised a "Butterfly Net" of several constables breaking away to allow their carriage through their perimeter and quickly encircling them. But Horst evaded the snare by guiding the horses into a fancy caracole curvet maneuver that stunned everyone momentarily until he hit the reins again for a full gallop and they were now storming straight at a squad of scurrying and flitting hoboes who, at first glance, appeared to have succumbed to the stress of the conflict but were actually combining elements of traditional *Bitida* with *Boundstifling*, an old hobo high-hopping zag technique of evasion and confusion, and they were so nimble and unnervingly committed to the byzantine movements it left the boys in stitches with laughter and Zeke in wondrous admiration, while Horst was now madder and drunker than ever, standing with arms stretched to the heavens as he fulminated scripture in sonorous tones: "The Lord spoketh: I have come to cast

FIFTEEN

fire upon the earth . . . do you think I came to give peace upon earth? No, I tell you but division . . . Unless the grain of wheat falls into the ground and dies, it remains alone. But if it dies, it brings forth much fruit." He let out a thunderous holler that veered into a guffaw and he swigged his bottle of whiskey before falling backwards and losing consciousness, the horses now racing amuck towards the woodlands and stream as Zeke struggled to gather the reins and gain control of the spooked equines. The boys tended to Horst as Zeke desperately sought to slow the mad charge at the dense trees and certain crash. The horses charged inexorably, and he was only capable of threading through narrow trails and somehow steering them to the high grass and mire of the banks of the stream, their hooves ebbing and halting in the muddy terrain. The wheels of the carriage also became embedded in the muck and Zeke and the boys applied themselves to digging out, rocking the stuck wheels with the horses' pull, albeit it to no immediate avail when Ogden spotted her first across the stream traversing a meadow of wildflowers with the flickering scintillation of fireflies multiplying in the woodland twilight.

"Why, I think there goes Miss Livinia, yonder all alone!" he said.

Zeke perked up from being bent over a wheel buried in the muck, rising quickly to peer over towards the woman. "That's our dairymaid, I'd know her anywhere!" he averred before bolting in her direction and unhesitatingly fording across the stream that was up to his chest in places. "Livinia! Livinia! Are you all right?" he called once reaching the other side. When she became aware of Zeke's presence she turned and waited for him and embraced the hobo farmer once he reached her. "I am surprised to find you out here by yourself," he said, "is something wrong, Livinia?"

She regarded him warmly, almost smiling. "I am fine, Zeke," she assured. "I just wanted to get away from all the fighting and I wound up walking in the woods. I love it here where it is so peaceful and enchanting."

He looked around in agreement, as the crickets chirped and little birds warbled in low trees and the fireflies glowed as the stream burbled along. "Nothing like the woods," he said, "but how were you going to get home to the farm? I thought you left with the Cumberland retinue."

She looked away before answering. "They had more official visits to make, or something, and I was supposed to ride back with Phineas and Abigail. But with all the turmoil we got separated . . ." She grew pensive before suddenly brightening. "Zeke, your speech . . . performance . . . whatever it was, really was impressive. I've never seen anything quite like it."

Zeke felt good but inhibited over the compliment. "I believe in the movement, Livinia. Farmers and hoboes need one another and an ardent spirit comes over me when I must act to further that end. We're building an alliance to form the cornerstone of making things right."

Livinia chuckled to herself, quickly apologizing as Zeke was quite serious. "I was just thinking about the story in which you played all the characters." He wasn't sure if she really enjoyed his performance or found it too arcane, broad, or inane. "Well, somebody has to play them and it might as well be me," he reasoned coyly. "Some personas are in us and they have their own voices. I believe we ought to hear 'em out too."

The dairymaid let out a warm laugh and said: "Makes perfect sense to me."

They walked toward the stream and Zeke stated he would carry her across and she laughed and pushed him playfully, saying she would carry him. Zeke called over to the boys asking about Horst and Ogden hollered back: "He's out cold snoring up a storm!" Livinia asked about Horst and Zeke assured her he was just overindulging, and now he approached her looking to carry her across and she shoved him and darted away, running into the stream and wading across herself, and Zeke was right behind her.

Some rest and water from the stream seemed to have rejuvenated the horses as now they rather quickly were able to pull the stuck wheels from the mire—with Zeke and the boys' help—and the ride home was begun. Horst lay upon the bales of hay in the back with Hux and Og flanking him, while Zeke took the reins up front with the dairymaid at his side. The narrow paths through the forest in the fleeting twilight wove a mystical spell over Zeke as the insects stridulated and the darkening surroundings enveloped them. Horst snored vociferously and grunted at the nameless sphinxes tormenting his slumbers. Og pulled his slingshot out and was firing small rocks at the moving shadows of phantom critters, and Hux commenced whistling some familiar melodies, "Blue Moon" among them. Now the dairymaid was not really herself, Zeke knew, as who would be after such a tumultuous night of clashes and discord, but he perceived it was more than that. She was burdened, or even distressed, by the grossly untenable predicament she inhabited for too long and the cataclysmic events of the evening at Redmond's Landing on the Bockboxen Forest Isthmus appeared to be a breaking point. Zeke knew her dilemma well without words spoken, as she sat beside him leaning against his side, exuding a melancholy detachment. She did not want to disappoint her aunt and uncle but could not continue a courtship that her heart never countenanced. At least this is what Zeke believed and wanted to believe and thought he could liberate her from the quandary by becoming her beau. If Livinia felt even a small fraction for him of what he felt for her, he just knew all the untoward tensions she wrestled with now would disappear and everything would simply fall into place for both of them. And if there ever was a night for him to once and for all pitch his best woo and move it along between them, well, he knew this was that night. He felt the weight of her lovely form slumped against his and saw her eyes closed though she was not sleeping, more weary and frustrated. The timbre of Hux's whistling turned plaintive and fraught with mysterious meaning, Zeke imagined, as he tried to think of the right way he could begin a conversation now that a span of silence had supervened. He wanted to say something loaded with panache and sincerity and delight and wit, but not much along those lines were coming to Zeke. The gravity of the evening's events cast a portentous shadow over any manner in which he sought to look ahead, inasmuch as he saw no way forward without more tumult and unrest, until the inequities and oppression quelling the hopes of hoboes and farmers alike were rectified. And he now was an emerging leader of this new vibrant coalition and had to seize his moment and forge his new identity far and wide, for this time, he knew, he had found it, the true role where he could help folks improve their circumstances in life. But a hesitation, a pause, a reluctance held him back in both aspirations and he now realized they were inextricably linked, he could not pursue one without the other. If he failed to measure up in winning the dairymaid's heart his despondency would preclude his ability to lead his coalition. And if he proved unable to rise to the challenge his promising emergence as the leader of the movement now presented, well, his sense of defeat would undermine the core of his self-respect and sabotage his chances with Livinia in the bargain. Zeke simply saw the individual he could become, the exciting potential was laid out for him, being with the woman he loved and becoming the bellwether for folks he cared deeply about. They rode in silence, Zeke maintaining a slower pace to curb the jostling of her slumberous state, the words worthy of wakening her were not coming to him and he was quite content to quietly steer them through wooded paths of the still evening, his mind afire with propitious notions of love and the movement. He knew he was in a splendid moment in time wrought with tremendous potential for transformational change and he breathed in the air fully and listened to Hux whistling and the noises of the night creatures with close attention. When the wheels of the carriage finally rolled to a halt outside the horse stables Zeke hesitated before rousing the dairymaid to dismount. He thought how beautiful she looked with her eyes closed and appearing so peaceful when suddenly she opened her eyes and sat up with a start, gazing solemnly at Zeke for a good long space that transfixed him before she burst into a grin with soft chuckles and then truly stupefied him by planting a solid kiss on his lips, lingering there just long enough to let him know there was more behind it than simply good night. He was so delightfully dumbfounded and dazed with wondrous surprise he could not respond in any way but smile. The boys were busy rousing Horst out of his wheezing snooze and he came to in a foul irascible mood in which he thought the lads were up to their usual hi-jinks and he clambered up and began to give them chase, which, of course, they relished with much hilarity. Zeke hardly noticed their antics, so mesmerized onto the dairymaid he was, and it was she who spoke first: "Zeke Borshellac, you are a singular fellow! I never met anyone like you before, and you represent the only hobo I ever became acquainted with, as well as a good farmer—but there is much more to you. It got scary back there, people are so angry and desperate, but you stood up as a trusted leader. I can tell a destiny all its own is sweeping you up . . ."

"Whatever destiny has a grip on me I hope it's the same one that's got you!" he proclaimed.

She let out an amused laugh and kissed him again, faster and harder, and then hopped off the carriage and scampered off to the farmhouse.

Those moments that night with Livinia, and afterwards when he returned to his bunk in the hayloft and found himself recounting everything to Balthazar, were probably the happiest of Zeke's so-far peripatetic rather demanding life. "I am in love with that girl, Balty, yes indeed I am, always have been and always will be," he offered in conclusion right before turning in, "and she's real sweet on you, always has been." He smiled as he stroked the sheepdog's back. "I feel dizzy, Balt, nauseous or something." He laughed. "I guess I'm lovesick. So it is real." And soon enough he thought of the violence and the struggle, the clashes only deepening, the fires to come, and he swore he would summon all the strength within him to rise to the momentous times.

SIXTEEN

IN THE MORNING Zeke wakened to find Cy Undersnettle outside his hayloft preparing a mound of wooden slats and a great spool of wire on a horse-drawn cart. "Mornin' Zeke," he greeted his colleague, "some rough night out there, eh? At least nobody got killed."

"Yeah, it got out of hand," Zeke replied, remaining pensive in face despite the sanguine surge inside reflecting on his night.

Cy had a pot of coffee in the front of the cart and poured his pal a cup. "Phineas said we're all done planting, Zeke. He's pulling you from the plough."

Zeke seemed puzzled. "I still had the back acres past the rocky hillocks to do. Eggplant, scallions, and tomatoes."

"You're coming with me on the fence mending mission," Cy said plainly. There were thousands and thousands of feet of three-feet high fencing circumscribing the farmland, or at least was supposed to, and it was a perpetual chore to repair the fence and not a welcome task at that.

"Well, who's going to plant past the rocky hillocks?" Zeke stubbornly asked.

Undersnettle snapped that nobody was planting there, adding "Why does that matter so much?"

And Zeke knew by the question somebody was tilling earth over there. Zeke sipped his coffee and studied Cy's features, recognizing the uneasiness in his farm pal.

"Archibald Clupper," Cy soon murmured, "I think they may have given it to him."

SIXTEEN

Zeke pondered the name and remembered the butter-and-egg man who sold their eggs to some country stores, a lanky fellow who wore colorful overalls and a milkman officer's cap with a short brim. "Clupper had been looking for work on the farm," Zeke recalled. He found the eager butter-and-egg man quite engaging, albeit on the frenetic side, altogether a fine fellow with a penchant for holding a multitude of posts that left him too exhausted to function well in any of them. Having himself worked in many capacities, Zeke empathized with Archibald to some extent but also felt gratitude for moving past his itinerant past as he hoped to ensconce himself as a farmer and leader of the Grange movement. Working the soil had become part and parcel to his existence and he deeply wanted to maintain that gratification he derived daily from the sweat and blood he poured into the planting fields. So of course he was troubled by Undersnettle's appearance that morning announcing the reassignment of his duties to the wearisome task of fence repairs. They rode slowly along the narrow dirt path that circumscribed the farmland and talked about the violent clashes of the previous day, Undersnettle commending his colleague on his oratorical skills and courage for advocating tolerance and understanding among the groups of combatants. "Yessiree, Zeke, you are becoming the bellwether for us farmers. You sure have come a long way since our fights those times you tried to resist medical attention when you needed it."

Zeke bristled here: "I required no medical attention, Cy. I told you I was shouting loudly for Livinia across the field and she mistook my vociferation for physical distress of some sort. Now her mistake was understandable, the distance being a factor, but when you came charging at me to help it remains a mystery why you would not hear my assurances of being fine."

Now it was Undersnettle who entered a snit. "You are still denying the collapse that overtook you? You were in bad condition and I had to act."

The farmers went on like this for several more exchanges with each holding their ground, and the intensity only escalated to the point of nearly coming to blows once more over who was right about their series of brawls. But this argument faded once Cy introduced a new question of strategy about the movement: who had invited the mob of hoboes to the picnic? "That was a bad idea as they only provoked the legions," he stated.

Zeke riposted: "I invited them because it had to be done. The hoboes have a voice that must be heard. Farmers should recognize it and support their plight. Unified we are a formidable force, an important movement, Cy!"

They went silent for nearly a mile until Undersnettle halted his horse beneath a large fragrant linden tree that shed a berth of shade in a remote section of meadow abutting the forest. Cy jumped off and began unloading the wire and slats from the cart and Zeke was quick to help. "This *alliance* of yours Zeke seems responsible for breaking a lot of folks' heads. And it could have been worse. I'm not so sure the time is right for us to throw in with the hoboes," Cy said with a sober frankness.

Zeke tossed a few spools a wire onto the grassy earth and looked his crony in the eye: "The hoboes need us Cy, and we need to help them. They are destitute and hungry, and we grow crops. We have a moral duty to feed them. The administration owes them meals if there is no work, and they ought to compensate us. But we will have to make it happen. Sometimes that means shaking it up."

Zeke spent the next few weeks with Cy on fence mending duty, which turned out to be arduous work often in the outlying harsh purlieus of crag and hill. But he soon adapted to the physical demands and enjoyed the company of Cy as they continued their dialogues of Grange politics and agricultural strategies. He saw very few others during this period. Balthazar certainly in the hayloft evenings, Horst would ride out to the relegated twosome on occasion to share a few swigs and catch up, and Og and Hux would somehow still find Zeke to pull a prank and have some laughs. And he managed too to see Livinia at a few junctures, so of course Zeke felt just fine during this otherwise tough period. There was the day he knew they would be working by the

SIXTEEN

wild boysenberry and blackberry patches off the southern embankment spit, which was only a mile from the pastures where the dairymaid often tended to her flocks. He packed a loaf of bread, a hunk of cheese, and a bottle of applejack, and picking a fresh basket of berries he left Cy midday to jog over field and wilderness to reach her pasture and invite her to an impromptu picnic. After the initial shock, she appeared genuinely happy to see Zeke out there among her heifers and they set up their repast under a fine sycamore nearby. They exchanged comic notions of how the farm animals were acting haughty, and they expressed a new easy warmth with one another which began the night of the Redmond's Landing clash. "I'm always thinking of you, Livinia. Whether I'm hammering a new fence post into the ground or lying in the hayloft with Balthazar evenings, you are always there," Zeke confessed.

"Well, that is very interesting Mr. Zeke Borshellac. I'm afraid I can't say the same."

Zeke's face drooped. "You can't?" She was grinning now, chuckling, when she suddenly stole a kiss on his lips and cried that of course she can. "How could I ever stop thinking about a singular nutcase like you? Such a sweet nut at that!"

Oh yes, Zeke savored the few picnics he managed with the beautiful dairymaid, where each time he felt closer to her, seemed to laugh more, and there were always the kisses. He felt they were each other's destiny, and at times it scared him, but there were those moments too when he saw in her the anguish of her predicament with Gerard and Phineas and the Von Klobbert Farm's fate, and the pernicious tensions she still faced every day as a result of the Cumberland's son stubborn desire to have her, the consequences otherwise darkly adumbrated. Most days Zeke and Cy returned from their remote sites of fence repair too late to make the suppers at the Von Klobbert farm table, other days Zeke was simply too exhausted for anything but the hayloft with Balt. But he did show up for a few suppers with the dairymaid present, and the disquiet and anxiety in her and general unease now constraining everyone seemed palpable. Phineas had apparently achieved his goal as the banks backed off now and while he felt he had breathing room for the farm to bounce back, he also knew the Cumberlands were responsible for the good turn. And Zeke would listen to them talk about Gerard and his father in the way one discusses constables who keep watch on the land but can seem overbearing and invasive at times, the price of safety perhaps. Zeke could not refrain from watching Livinia at these suppers, her pinched face and glazed eyes and bloodless acquiescence, and feel a rage and gloom within that could barely be concealed. He occasionally saw her from afar while isolated somewhere with the fence mending, and she would be sauntering along a glade or across a verdant tract with Gerard at her side, and he knew she could not be happy. But could she decide such a sacrifice of joy and love was the right thing to do for the greater good? Such thoughts racing amuck would make him shiver with a nameless dread, and he would sip whiskey evenings and talk to Balthazar about it, who always seemed to buck him up and dismiss any such dark notions. Balt was always there to get him through the tough nights following days he spotted them on the horizon like darkening clouds and felt the stinging sudden sense of being lost.

The summer thus poked along and waned past the dog days until the nascent crisp cool of fall began to arrive, and Zeke felt that peculiar vim of regeneration September briskness can bring. He knew in some indefinable way that he stood on the edge of great shifts to be determined by the break of circumstances, and the vicissitudes would then blow all one way or another. He discerned the inevitability of the transformational sweep of events awaiting him and the others on the farm, only he never could have foreseen the earthshaking developments that summarily rolled in and overtook him. One windy drizzly late morning as Cy and Zeke labored in their fence duties amid the puddles and mire, they noticed a distant horse-drawn carriage approaching their way, a vehicle they failed to recognize, albeit unmistakably a conveyance of the well-heeled. It proceeded towards them at a steady, speedy pace, pulled by an enormous black horse with equine alacrity, the three figures on the seat coming into focus. Mathius Edgecomb, in the middle and wearing a solemn expression, was the only one they knew. He remained silent as the carriage drew close. The driver and the other man flanking Mathius' right wore the black and scarlet uniforms of the Cumberland legions, their kepis firmly upon their heads, jackboots to their ankles, great pistols holstered at their sides. The legionaries dismounted the carriage with a brisk authority and with taut strides approached the farmers standing by the fence surrounded by mud and wire and wooden slats. The larger legionary, tall and broad-shouldered, proceeded closer as his associate held back, and his jackboots let off a squeaking and grinding noise into the misty swirling air. He eyed the two farmers who stood erect awaiting his pronouncement, and the legionary whom he passed now looked back at Mathius, for direction apparently, and the veteran sodbuster uneasily pointed towards Zeke. The lead legionary strode with a dour gravity to the man he wished to address and, halting a few feet in front of him asked: "Are you Zeke Borshellac?"

Zeke did not betray the anxious worry roiling his insides and replied that he was. Now the other legionary had come to stand beside his cohort. The lead soldier now proceeded: "You are to come with us without delay to answer charges to be presented by prosecutorial authorities invested in the ministerial powers of Lord Cumberland, jurisdictional sovereign over these territories."

It was Cy who responded first with sharp incredulity. "What are you fellows' trying to pull here?! What could Zeke have done?"

The secondary legionary had moved towards Zeke and ordered him to clasp his hands behind his back. Zeke stared hard at the men, deciding whether to cooperate. "I demand to know the charge," he asserted.

The larger legionary shot back in a pique of impatience: "You'll know soon enough! At the farmhouse our squadron awaits your surrender."

The other legionary now sought to force a thick iron chain upon Zeke, threatening him if he continued to resist. Mathius was there now and spoke in a calm clarion manner, first explaining to Zeke that

Phineas asked him to assist the men in finding him. "I didn't want to, as piloting such constabularies to you seemed an ignoble business—until I realized better me than another. That's because I'm with you Zeke and will do my utmost to protect your rights in this travesty of justice they are perpetrating."

Again the legionary moved forward with his chain, the larger one now drawing his pistol ostentatiously and pointing it towards Zeke. "Are you going to cooperate with us, Mr. Borshellac? Or are you going to make this hard?"

Mathius stepped between them and declared: "I will not brook such thuggery upon this fine soil. There will be no need for firearms, you put that away and those chains and my friend Zeke will accompany you peaceably to the farmhouse to hear the charges against him." He gave Zeke a long look in the eye before Zeke nodded slightly, muttering "I have nothing to run from," and the legionaries obeyed Mathius' behest, and they drove in eerie silence the entire few miles, the larger legionary at the reins with Mathius in front, the other legionary with Zeke in the back.

The horse carriage pulled up at the farmhouse and they promptly strode inside, Zeke flanked on each side by the legionaries and Mathius in the rear. In the dining room sat two legionaries, the taller, thinner one decked out in a resplendent uniform, that, in addition to their primary colors of red and black, had a riot of ancillary hues such as violet, yellow, green and cerulean, as well as golden, embroidered ropes displayed vertically, tan-orange plaited epaulets, a garnet-and-silver striped sash swathed from shoulder to opposite hip, and a plumed, spiked helmet of shiny black-and-gray iron perched upon his dome. He was a striking figure, both fey and formidable, and the one who would be conducting the criminal procedure. Also seated at the long wooden table were Phineas on one end, appearing dour and worn, and Gerard, beside the chief legionary, wearing a stark slightly squinty glower, remaining silent and motionless while seeming to savor the proceedings. Zeke was seated opposite the chief legionary, the ones who brought him to each of his sides, while Mathius was bade to stand

SIXTEEN

back. The chief legionary asked Zeke in a sonorous preface if he was Zeke Borshellac, and he said he was in a steady voice. The garishly uniformed magistrate now, after surveying the accused from pit to dome with a scowl, presented the charge: "In the name of Lord Cumberland, presiding noble prefect over the regional lands upon which we stand, I am here to *inform you*, Zeke Borshellac, that you are hereby being arrested for organizing, assembling, and conspiring to engage in violent acts of sedition and insurrection against the power of authority invested in Lord Cumberland and his governance of these territories."

A heavy silence prevailed until Zeke answered in a straightforward manner of disbelief. "Sir, I cannot fathom whence such an indictment of my character comes. I assure you of my innocence and the inevitability of my exoneration. I demand to know the specific nature of these allegations!"

The chief legionary bristled, rankled at the impudence displayed by the apostate farmer, and scolded him accordingly. "Mr. Borshellac, you will make no such demands of this tribunal. The grand panel of criminal prosecutors have concluded a thorough investigation into your activities and associations and are prepared to prove to the superior regional court that you are a subversive agitator who has conspired and organized an uprising against the authoritative rule of Lord Cumberland. You would be wise to receive these charges without further outbursts, as this tribunal will not abide insubordination."

Now Mathius could no longer hold back his own outrage over the gross injustice suddenly befalling his colleague. "Sir, if I may speak, I know this man well and he is an honorable and admirable man who has shown nothing but decency and probity since he began work here at the Von Klobbert farm. This is a miscarriage of proper law being perpetrated and it cannot stand!" Mathius was animated with his outrage, gesticulating wildly, and legionaries from the periphery quickly emerged to quell him through close positioning. "Oh, so you will take me away for speaking the truth!" He turned to Phineas: "Phineas, surely you cannot allow this to happen without voicing yourself! Tell them what a fine fellow Zeke has shown himself to be on the farm, a harder worker we have never seen, his innate kindness, and devotion to his estimable sheepdog."

Phineas shifted uncomfortably in his chair as eyes fell on him. "You have grown fond of Zeke, Mathius, as many of us have. But these are serious crimes he is being accused of and none of us can prevent the inexorable grind of the law. Zeke must answer to these charges and will pay a harsh price for—"

Now Gerard stood with his patience apparently expired, as he erupted in fulmination. "Enough soft-pedalling the insurrectionist actions of the culprit! Enough ludicrous citations of *the truth* and the agitator's capacity for *hard work* and his dedication to his *mangy cur*! And the conspirator is so *kind to boot!* We know what this man has done, the uprising he led and instigated with his army of drunken lunatic derelicts, the so-called hoboes who shirk all responsibilities as citizens by refusing to work and looting and freeloading at will at the danger and expense of us all, this traitor summoned his hoboes to my father's annual Pig Roaster Summer Picnic at Redmond's Landing on Bockboxen Isthmus where they followed his plan to attack and upend and overthrow the Cumberland Legions present. Enough . . . move this forward!"

Zeke could not stifle a retort: "These men are out of work, good men who are hungry. They came peaceably in the hope of finding a good meal and enjoying the company of fellow picnickers. It was your legionaries who attacked them without cause and tore into the farmers who stood with them. You and your father should be doing all you can to help the hoboes through their hardship, but no matter, make no mistake, *our time is* coming!"

Gerard was standing now, exclaiming and pointing at Zeke: "The only *time* coming to you is going to be *inside a jail cell!*" He moved towards the chief legionary and furiously addressed him: "Now shackle him and move him out of here!!"

The chief legionary, impelled by his superior's command, nodded his head once to his left, and then to his right, and immediately legionaries surrounded Zeke and placed his wrists and ankles in chains,

SIXTEEN

and the chief legionary declared he would be remanded indefinitely to the Cumberland Eastern Territorial Jail at Frodtznjepple Peninsula.

Zeke now utterly sunk into a distressed despair that could only think of the dairymaid and whether he would see her again and his suspicions that his predicament here was precipitated by Gerard's jealousy of his relations with Livinia, and of course he thought of Balthazar and how his beloved dog would fare in his absence. After they began for the door, his gait encumbered by the two-foot chain connecting his ankles, he suddenly paused and called for forbearance in allowing him to see Balthazar. "All I ask of the tribunal is to say good-bye to my dog before we go." He looked for Phineas amid the figures around the room now and met his eyes: "Phineas, I implore you to grant me this one request, that I see my dog."

Phineas appeared to absorb the plea with compassion, reflected in his hesitant face, and he directed his response to Gerard and the chief legionary: "I would have no objection to granting Mr. Borshellac the modest wish to bid a proper farewell to his fine sheepdog Balthazar, that is, if you see fit to allow him such a moment. We have just heard conflicting accounts of the accused's character, but I will assure everyone that his sheepdog ranks among the finest working dogs ever to herd flocks on a farm anywhere, and such a superb, sterling canine deserves to see his master part for a dark and unknown future."

Gerard snickered snidely at the sentimental expression of Phineas and moved past everyone with his own attendants following. Finally, he replied: "Well, Phineas, you are magnanimous it seems to a farmer whom you provided an opportunity and who not only betrayed your trust but the very soil of your homestead. But since you petition me on behalf of this glorious canine, I will enable it." He chuckled in a derisive manner. "We certainly must consider the dog's part." With his stern countenance he made his way outside and strode hurriedly without meeting anyone's eyes, soon taking the reins of his own carriage and speeding away with the chief legionary riding beside him.

Farm hands were beginning to recognize the gravity of the situation and some already had gathered outside by the time Zeke and the legionaries emerged, and they turned to Mathius for answers to the horrid spectacle of their fellow farmer shuffling along in clattering shackles, despite the distilled stoicism engraved on the rookie farmer's face. Cy Undersnettle was there and others he came across on his way in to check on his fence-mending partner's fate. Horst Schtuckgloo stood erect, doleful and shaken, removing his hat and holding it against his chest. *"Who shall make accusation against the elect of God?"* he maundered lowly now with Scripture. *"It is God who justifies! Who shall condemn? It is Jesus Christ who died; yes, and rose again, he who is at the right hand of God, who also intercedes for us!"* And now Booth Booley was there to witness the sepulchral scene and was overwhelmed, as he asked Mathius simply, *what is this? What have they done to Zeke?* And Mathius had no answers for him or the others who quietly called out dumbstruck by it all. It was before Booth they halted for the tall legionary, the same who drove out to collect Zeke from Cy, to ask him: "Where is his dog, the sheepdog?"

Booth knew when he saw Mathius nod to him that it was a farewell, and he felt himself recognizing an inchoate sob. "He is working at the low pastureland by the bend in the river. His name is Balthazar."

They hastened Zeke to the same carriage in which he was brought in, bidding Booth to get in and guide them, and abruptly the horse was set in motion apace. Zeke sat in the rear seat beside a sizable legionary, and his chains rattled and he jounced with every dip and bump in the irregular path, but he was not all there. He was thinking about the dairymaid and whether she heard yet what had befallen him. He hoped not because he did not want her to see him shackled and ruined, while at the same time everyone present knew of her being Gerard's object of desire and as such the predicament was just too fraught. And he worried about Balthazar and how he would handle the news and who would watch over his beloved dog?

Zeke wasn't aware of it but his farmhand pals had piled onto Horst's wagon and were tailing his legionary carriage from a distance, as they could not allow him to disappear in such a dire state without being there for support, even if there was little they could do. Horst

SIXTEEN

stayed far back from the legion's carriage, as he knew where they were headed in the low pastures. He drove his horse slowly and no one spoke, Mathius, Cy beside him, and then the boys Ogden and Huxley saw them from where they were slopping the pigs a good two hundred feet beyond the cornfields, and they knew something was amiss the way Zeke looked in the legionary carriage and Horst then following, so they ran as fast as they could hollering for Horst and he eventually heard them and stopped to let them jump on the raised boards in the rear of the wagon. The boys murmured to one another as the somber silence of the men and the jostling advance of the wagon in pursuit of Zeke's vehicle had them apprehensive with lurid worries.

"Where are they taking Zeke?" Huxley asked them, then speculated aloud their dark hunch. "I'll bet Gerard is behind it. He always had it in for Zeke. Are they firing him from the farm?"

It was Ogden, the younger one, in his usual frayed overalls, blond mop tousled in the wind, who asked as he gazed fretfully at the passing landscape: "Are they gonna to hang Zeke?"

Only after a long wait did someone answer. Mathius partially turned to the boys and said: "Zeke is being charged with a crime he didn't commit. He needs us to be there for him now as he says goodbye to Balthazar. He'll be glad to see you boys there."

As they processed this the boys looked at one another and could not find words, their gazes then turning downward. When they pulled up behind the legionary's carriage, now stopped beneath a fine old elm, Zeke was already out and shambling out on the rolling swards of pasture, lengthy green blades blowing in the soft breezes, moving towards Balthazar somewhere out there lost in the functions of herding. Everyone from both vehicles now followed behind him, the two groups maintaining enough distance to watch the moment while affording Zeke some privacy with his dog. The legionaries may have glowered towards the farmhands gathered, but they left them alone, and did nothing as Booth made his way over to stand with his friends.

Suddenly coming over a rise to a declension they saw a great many sheep moving in an orderly manner under the careful control of Balthazar, trotting about in a series of zigzags to keep it just so. Zeke called to him, and the dog turned and seemed to snap from a trance as he ran towards his master. He came scudding and bounding over the undulant sward with his usual excited velocity at seeing Zeke, a joyous blur of kinetic sheepdog, until abruptly halting and sliding with forward motion, as if spooked by something he picked up about the scenario ahead. He appeared anxious, confused, as he sat up on his hind legs with his head cocked and then paced side to side, studying the odd assembly of individuals awaiting him further up the grassy slope. And there was something different about Zeke, wearing iron manacles and fetters on his wrists and ankles, shackles representing the most primal of fears in the canine psyche accustomed to freedom of movement. Zeke called out to him, sensing his consternation: "It's okay, Balt. Come on, everything is going to be fine." The dog, reassured by the sound of Zeke's voice, proceeded again but walked the remainder to his master. The two groups remained stock-still and utterly silent in watching the farewell unfold, respectful of their intimacy. They now approached each other, and Zeke crouched to receive Balthazar and hugged him with his manacles encircling him, while the sheepdog lowly whimpered and unrestrainedly licked his master. "It's okay, Balt, it's okay. I will be all right," Zeke kept assuring him and petting him as he liked it, somehow despite his restricted hands. He addressed the shackles, rattling them and declaring their transitoriness, that "the truth will come out and they will recognize their mistake and I will be freed." Balthazar appeared to become calmer as Zeke spoke. "You have to be strong, Balty, until this passes, and just as you always were there to buck me up through that great confidence you always have in yourself, I want to do the same for you now. I will not be away long and I will be fine."

With that he turned towards the gathering of his farm pals and called for Horst and the boys to come over and they did so without any interference from the legionaries. Horst strode with his upright sense of earthy probity, and deeply moved quoted scripture upon greeting Zeke, while Huxley and Ogden were struggling to hold themselves together by Horst's example but could not help the tears trickling down their cheeks. "Don't you worry about me, boys," Zeke began. "You fellas keep up the hi-jinks, and don't spare old Horst here none," he ordered about one of their favorite targets.

"It ain't right, Zeke! The bastards won't get away with this!" Huxley exclaimed as he cried.

"We'll get you out, Zeke. We'll spring you somehow!" Ogden added through his tears.

"I want to ask the three of you to look after Balthazar while I'm away. You know him well, what he likes, his routines. I'd really appreciate it."

They answered with effusive affirmatives and renewed tears, even Horst's eyes grew watery, as the separation of Zeke hit harder. "We'll take good care of Balt," Horst averred reverently, "he's like part of our family."

And as the boys now pet the restive canine, Huxley said astutely: "There ain't nobody on this farm more valuable than Balt so it will be easy to make sure he gets whatever we feel he needs. Without Balt in the pastures, Phineas knows he'll be in trouble."

A coercive call now came from the tall legionary in charge: "C'mon now, Zeke. You've had enough time with your dog. Let's move this along."

Zeke turned briefly with a slight nod, then noticed the boys suddenly jabbering in muted tones and asked them what they were so hopped up over and the youngsters looked at one another before it fell upon Huxley to pose the question: "We were wondering about . . . Miss Livinia, and if you will be saying good-bye to her? . . . because she's tending to the newborn calves this morning out in the pens by the creek . . . and sure as shooting she's in the dark on all this—"

"Let's go, Zeke!! Don't make this hard for us now!" came the sonorous cry of the tall legionary.

"You can wait one more damn minute!" Zeke shot back impetuously, then not entirely becalmed addressed the boys: "Listen fellas, I'd rather not put our dairymaid through the wringer with my departure. Just tell her I will be fine. My innocence will vindicate me and I will be back." He paused and reflected a moment and added. "Tell her I will miss her very much while away."

Booth Booley and Mathius had come over and stood nearby and they hugged Zeke too, promising they'd find him a good lawyer, and Booth counseled, "Keep a fierce spirit and do not be bowed, Zeke. Hold strong until we get you exonerated."

Before he turned towards the legionaries who were now coming his way, he said his final good-byes and the boys hugged him with tears flowing and Horst did so quoting scripture sotto voce and there was a last hug with Balthazar, who licked him through his whimpers and would not let him go until Zeke forcibly broke away after soothing him for a moment. But the wrought-up sheepdog bolted with a vicious growl for the legionaries, who drew their firearms and Ogden and Huxley darted for Balt while beseeching the men to withdraw their weapons because they had the distraught dog under control. And only after a bit of chasing and cajoling did they finally contain him in a frenetic scene out on the pasture that could have been a whole other catastrophe had they not succeeded.

They rode for hours through farmlands and forest and over narrow lanes twisting around hills and Zeke sat motionless in his shackles beside the burly legionary, ruminating on his infernal fate and the empirical reflections that revealed to him the incentives and motivations actuating it all, and he kept coming back to one impetus, one individual, and that was Gerard. Sure, he broke out as the true leader of the farmers' Grange movement at Redmond's Landing on the Bockboxen Isthmus, the promoter of hoboes descending on the picnic, the bellwether of consolidating the common interests of the two groups. But Zeke comported himself with high-minded integrity, never inciting violence as a measure but dazzled the throngs with his singular sense of showmanship and gave a performance the likes of which no one had ever seen. No, Gerard did not have him arrested for agitating the melee, or "insurrection" as the charge states, Zeke knew this much. Rather, the son of Lord Cumberland came with his father's soldiers to

SIXTEEN

take him away because he became aware of his burgeoning relationship with Livinia and his jealousy impelled it. As he sat in shackles being driven to the Frodtznjepple Peninsula jailhouse he lost himself in thoughts amidst the passing sylvan scenery, and he arrived at one perspective that hinted at the sanguine. Gerard's sudden fixation to remove Zeke and destroy him suggested that he was indeed making a resonating impression upon the dairymaid, those secret picnics together and scant exquisite kisses were real, she was starting to truly enjoy his company, and that was all Zeke needed during that long ride to the jailhouse to sustain him. But when they finally reached the Frodtznjepple Peninsula, a barren bleak rocky mass of land surrounded by sea save a slim thread connecting to the mainland, the waning afternoon already showing hints of dusk, the ominous looming sight of the disturbingly medieval jailhouse sent shivers down Zeke's back.

The legionaries ushered him inside straightway and through dim, draughty, rank corridors of echoing stone the prisoner rattled along, struggling to keep to their pace, arriving at a dingy imposing rotunda where a contingent of jailers in black-and-gray uniforms awaited the transfer. They stood like soldiers at attention, and once the legionaries stopped moving the head jailer declared they were prepared to receive the prisoner. And with that the burly legionary pushed Zeke from behind towards the jailers, causing him to stumble with his fetters and fall to the rock and clay floor on his chest and face. No one helped him get up, slow as it was, they all only watched him labor back to his feet. He was now directed by jailers towards the far corridor and they surrounded him as he shambled along, the incomprehensible exchange between the tall legionary and the head jailer over the confinement documents echoing behind him. The corridor grew increasingly dark and narrow as they proceeded, ever descending in a deep subterranean hell closer to catacombs, except for graves there were cells with solid iron doors having only slits to peer within. In the deepest dank bowels they finally halted and with a giant key a jailer opened one such heavy door and they shoved Zeke in so hard he again fell prone against the crud-coated stone floor, and long after they slammed the door shut upon him he lay there in pain and anguish. Here in this godforsaken pen Zeke would spend hard tortured days among the colonies of rats and cockroaches, without a vestige of sunshine, slop worse than what the pigs on the farm got to eat, and the unspeakable torment of never knowing when his case may be heard while the harrowing grip of utter loneliness proved most cruel.

SEVENTEEN

HE WORRIED after several days how much longer he could maintain his mind before it began to crack and break into irrevocable illness, and he believed if only he could spend his days writing, committing his thoughts to paper, then he could preserve his mental health while waiting for a way out of his ordeal. The turnkey who slid his bowl of mush under the door and looked in upon him seemed young with kind eyes, or at least Zeke imagined him as such as he exchanged the briefest of words with him every day. "Here you go. Chow time, mister," the even, low voice would come from the slit, and the young eyes, before the hot container of gruel was slid under the door. Zeke could barely swallow the fetid mystery mush at first but came to appreciate it more over time as his hunger compounded. Upon hearing movement at the door his mouth would water and he would hurry to the door and thank the turnkey for his meal. And after a while he would attempt to engage his only human contact in conversation, mainly to no avail but there were moments. Zeke elicited that his name was Jarvis and he was only working in the jail until he completed his studies at the Humanities and Fine Arts Academy in Kucklekroppsville, where he was pursuing coursework in glassblowing sculpture. Jarvis' father was a lieutenant inspector in Tanube and wanted his son to follow him in police work, so the jailer stint was a compromise. Zeke encouraged the young man to persevere in his glassblowing art, noting the long journey he'd been on himself in finding his own career path. Eventually, Zeke felt comfortable enough to outright ask Jarvis to provide him with paper and a pencil so he could keep a journal of his time in jail, a record of his observations and thoughts, mainly to preserve his mind and sanity. Jarvis chuckled at the request, citing the simplicity of it and that he wished he'd asked him earlier. The next day the turnkey arrived with not only the foul gruel but several notebooks and pencils, with encouragement to keep his spirits up. Writing became Zeke's salvation in prison, as he lost himself in committing his long simmering ideas to paper, recording his philosophies and plans to put in motion as the leader of the farmers' Grange movement and the looser, but no less potent, aggregating rise of hoboes. *The bountiful earth provides sustenance for all the lost and hungry, the weather-beaten hoboes should not be harried by want but nourished by the fruit of the soil.* An explicit strategy he could not yet envisage for the amalgamation of farmers and hoboes (whom he felt he was still destined to lead), only raw images, concepts, notions, even chimerical musings. He completely lived in his mind, suspending for long stretches of time the horror and execration of his cell surroundings. He wrote in a transported fever as glimpses of regeneration and the inextinguishable light guiding him to a faraway point of well-being, a fair and salutary place for all, would not dim. He descried a splendor of an existence where people were utterly free and full of love for one another and through the soil grew the sustenance they needed and together founded societies where folks could find the vocations and pastimes that exhilarated and enthralled them each individually. The central theme of his contemplations, the ne plus ultra, the desideratum and constant refrain, remained the plentiful crop burgeoning out of the soil and the lost nomad hoboes connecting to these benefactions of nature. When Zeke could catch some fleeting intervals of slumber on his rusted iron slab he dreamed of the corn in its husks on sun-dappled stalks up from the fine soil, good rows of corn soldiers ready to march in his battalion, the turnips round and dense born of the rich earth perched like volunteers waiting their assignments, the endless fields of cauliflowers resting in their leaves of coverings after their journey from underground to a sweet spot under the sun, the dark wondrous eggplants bent against their vines and knowing the glory of their patches was beyond human comprehension, the farmer leader-cum-prisoner dreamed of the soil and its fruits on a magnificent farm of the future where he envisaged an incipient better world.

But losing himself in his writing had its limitations and there was always the longing for those he left back on the farm. Balthazar was always in his thoughts as he would see him scampering across the pasture, masterfully herding his flocks, and in their nightly company and conversations up in the hayloft, he felt as if a piece of him had been excised, part of his very soul removed, and he simply could not abide it. While he was confident Horst and the boys would provide good care for his sheepdog, he worried how Balt would cope without him there. And his smoldering rage at his incarceration and urgent desire to exact justice for his persecution consumed him as well, making him shout at Jarvis more and more for his being allowed to see a lawyer, and where were his visitors? Zeke was certain Booth and Mathius and Horst would have attempted to visit him by now, and they were going to find him a lawyer. And then there was the constant deep ache he felt for Livinia, like a wretched sickness that would not relent as he thought of her beauty and laughter and singular spirit, the recent picnics, the kisses, and what might have been as he sat brooding in misery in his cell.

Then one day the eyes of Jarvis appeared in the slit and Zeke was curious as the feeding time had long passed. He heard the outsized metal key clanking in the lock and the massive iron door slowly opened towards him, and three uniformed men wearing dour expressions entered. Two of them had the black-and-gray uniforms of the guards he had already seen, though these men also had on silver kepis with fancy golden tassels, and polychromatic epaulets the size of cabbages. The other, clearly in charge, was in a yellow-and-gray flannel uniform with brass buttons, a black steel helmet of Prussian variety, and a long flowing cape of black silk with red felt piping. He was announced by Jarvis as Commandant Droochler, who approached Zeke in stiff strides with his high black boots and stood over him with a glare.

"Mr. Borshellac, the evidence is overwhelming that you are an enemy of the state who was leading an underground seditionist group that manifested in the uprising at the Pig-roaster Summer Picnic at Redmond's Landing on Bockboxen Isthmus, sponsored by Lord Cumberland. I've come here personally to hear your confession to directing the insurrection and failed attempt to overthrow the authority of Lord Cumberland!"

Zeke did not flinch as he responded in staunch outrage. "That, sir, is a patently false charge that I will refute and be vindicated as a victim of an oppressive despot and his son." Zeke studied the faces of all three men and asserted firmly: "I demand to have access to my lawyer. I have been denied visitors and this must be rectified immediately!"

Commandant Droochler fixed Zeke with a squinty glower and reached into his uniform pocket for a small tin container from which he drew a pinch of snuff and inhaled it in his nostrils. He continued sniffing as he joined his hands behind his back and paced around the cell, encircling Zeke three times in stark silence save the sharp clack of his boot heels on the stone floor, and again stood in front of the prisoner. "Mr. Borshellac, you must have misheard my requisition of your plea. You see, you have proven yourself to be traitor to the people, their ideals and values, the very soil upon which they live and raise their crops. You betrayed those who tried to help you and provide you work and shelter. You sought the violent removal of Lord Cumberland from the regional superintendence of his rightfully appointed duties, and therefore, you are unequivocally guilty of the crime of treason and you must confess it forthwith if your life is to stand any chance of being spared."

Zeke could hardly process the severity of such a pernicious charge, notwithstanding its spuriousness, and felt a dreadful nausea course through him before the shock turned to fury. "I will never confess to such a false indictment, an allegation so depraved it could only be hatched by a vile treacherous worm."

Commandant Droochler again reached for his snuff box and sniffled as he paced around, this time encircling Zeke four times in a manner of intimidation, at the conclusion of which he stretched out his right arm and one of his subordinates produced a very large cudgel and placed it in the commandant's hand. "Now Mr. Borshellac, about that confession," he stated in a cool expectant tone while padding again, cudgel pounding his palm, "please proceed and be done with it."

Zeke reiterated with more resolve that there would be no confession and to show Droochler that he would not be buffaloed he clasped his hands behind his back and began his own slow fraught gait in circling the commandant, who seemed stunned by the temerity and before Zeke made one complete revolution the caped officer exploded in rage and lunged at Zeke with the cudgel, but the younger man dodged its swing. The two subordinate officers instinctually started for Zeke but Droochler called them off, as he moved towards him again with the cudgel. "I will subdue him myself," he snarled. Zeke employed an unpredictable series of staccato angles in his defensive footwork and the commandant continued hacking away to no avail at the elusive target, growing increasingly frustrated and desperate with wild charges. Once Zeke caught a muffled chuckle escaping Jarvis as he watched by the door. When totally tuckered out and chagrined in front of his men, the commandant finally picked up his helmet, which had fallen off, and put it back on before adjusting his cape and pronouncing the prisoner "has the kind of recalcitrance I will relish removing." And he signaled his men now to go to work on Zeke and they rather swiftly had him down administering a stomping which became especially harsh once they newly fettered and manacled the prisoner, who gamely absorbed the beating with a stoic defiance until losing consciousness altogether.

He wakened strapped to a cold steel slab under the harsh lights of the prison infirmary, several stern bearded physicians in lab coats crowded over him. At first Zeke feared they were going to operate on him, but they were interested rather in performing a series of tests on him as their garbled exchanges seemed to indicate. His relief at not facing the knife turned to fright as the nature of the tests became apparent. "You are working with an underground organization of plotters, is that right, yes, Mr. Borshellac?!" the most rotund of the physicians began the interrogation. Zeke answered that he was not, and the most rotund physician rejoined: "Then you confess to acting alone in orchestrating the attempted insurrection?"

Zeke returned: "No, no, there was no such thing, with others or alone!"

The glowers and beards and white lab coats dissolved into blinding intense light. He shut his eyes and heard them murmuring incoherently, only a fragment of speech being intelligible to Zeke: "From his pain the truth will emerge." And Zeke opened his eyes to the blinding and now flashing light and the pain came in every unholy form, blood producing pokes, flame on flesh, deafening noise blasted into his ears, mallets crashing into bone, and they continuously asked him to confess to treason in the territory presided over by Lord Cumberland. Zeke screamed often in agony, cried out for mercy in the name of God and beseeched the wicked physicians with beards to find their humanity as men of medicine. But the latter only seemed to make them more desirous to crack him and they would chuckle with amusement at Zeke's naivety, often offering mock words of solace, such as, "surely your discomfort will subside once you stretch out a bit." Of course, Zeke got to know with terror that this did not mean he would be freed from the slab to exercise his limbs with movement, but that they were strapping him into the rack where the incremental tightening of the chains around the great spools stretched his arms and legs into unspeakable points of agony.

And while Zeke was taken from his cell for these daily horrors and dug deeper than ever for the fortitude to survive them, it was the regulated breaks taken by the physicians, announced by rather festive bells, that most sustained him. The breaks came every two hours unfailingly, a prison work rule for the physicians that lasted ten minutes, while the meal period announced after six hours via resounding celestial chimes was thirty minutes long. Not only would Zeke maximize these respites for his own rest and renewal of inner strength to continue enduring the torture, he calibrated his mindset to anticipate them in a way to withstand the nameless miseries inflicted on him by the demented, sadistic physicians. Knowing the intervals of repose were certainly ahead, no matter how brief they may be, made his tolerance of the daily barbarities committed against him possible, if tenuously so. And he observed the change in deportment and attitude of the six bearded physicians during these breaks, at first with astounded dismay but over time a broader understanding of the uncommon ethos and rule system entrenched in the Frodtzenjepple Peninsula jailhouse. When working on Zeke, pulling out all stops to extract his confession, the physicians were the most savage, relentless, and wickedly inventive torturers one could imagine, and they performed their duties with a tireless dedication. But once the bells rang they instantly fell into their interludes with a light-hearted affability which often involved easy badinage and the sort of comfortable small talk enjoyed between close colleagues. Such bonhomie was also transmitted to Zeke during these breaks, and as they got to know him better he became part of their downtime relaxed interactions, often forgetting along with them, as best as possible, the grim grind of their brutal work and his bearing the brunt of it. They told stories, jokes, shared snacks and drank coffee, and Zeke truly found the six physicians who were otherwise such demons of pain and suffering to be congenial, interesting, and funny associates to spend time with. And they likewise grew to enjoy Zeke's company and value him as a good egg with a humorous bent both subtle and odd. Their meal periods often were savory feasts of fine meats, cheeses, breads, and the most delicious pies, topped off with excellent Bordeaux on most Fridays, and Zeke very early on was invariably included to join his gracious tormentors in the partaking. Here he further honed his oratory skills with experimental postprandial speeches, or performances really, in which he delivered poetic imagery of the hobo riding trains under moonlit prairies and the noble indefatigable farmer working his wonders upon the soil and the magnificent horizon from which we must not flinch, where the Great Harvest for *all*, hobo and farmer alike, is one day due to yield its vast cornucopia throughout the glorious sun-drenched hills with the promise, the *redemptions,* of a new life of freedom and bounty and happiness. At times Zeke was carried away in such exalted visions of the poor nobodies who toil in the fields and ride the rails triumphing through the movement, founding a better life, a more just and humane existence, and during those fleet highs he could glimpse its coming like a castaway eying a distant ship on the seascape.

Occasionally he allowed himself to be swept up in these prose poem rhapsodies as a segue to the kind of singular performance skits of mad inspired arcana, the sort of strange sketches he had once improvised on the fishing vessels as a means of survival, the sudden peculiar shows forced upon folks along the dark highways as a Grackler. And when Zeke let himself go wholly into the realm of his skits, such as the entire baseball game, a grudge match he enacted as players who were all over ninety years old and spoke a grunting, guttural incomprehensible dialect, and were always fighting with one another and drinking bourbon and singing songs about the moon, which they feared like death itself, he felt some irreducible elemental truth excavated from his deepest recesses was finding expression. In his baseball drama of old-timers, he came to recognize a connection between the very young and very old and the shared uninhibited desire they often act upon to simply *play* and accept that as enough. He brought both nonagenarian teams to life with their slowpoke, crotchety geezer personalities and improbable winsome ways to keep the fans interested throughout the extra inning cliffhanger. In his whimsical, sometimes macabrely aberrant skits, sketches, and prose poems he gladly shook off his consciousness to fully inhabit and explore the outlying subconscious perimeters of his rough-hewn performance art. He reveled in the illimitable mysteries and inconceivably rare prodigies that rear up from nowhere, occasionally fraught with a heavy twist of danger, lures that stalk and lurk only in the raw and intemperate realms *beneath* consciousness. His broadsides composed in his cell inveighed against the societal structures that empower the aristocratic ruling class to subjugate peasants and laborers in such an ironclad system, while concomitantly he called for resistance and survival through the condition of oppression, outlast its awful yoke of despair, even extolling the many means of escape through small pleasures such as whiskey and nine pins and playing ducks and drakes on the breezy river banks under blue skies and having summer reveries stretched upon the grass. In short, the bearded team of torturers grew increasingly fond of Zeke over the weeks, found a common ground of fellowship and understanding and humor with the prisoner of their ruthless applications, and rather unconsciously, and so gradually as to be imperceptible day to day, the torture abated and the physicians at length fell into a pro forma routine consisting of an elaborate skein of pokes, probes, and "hotfoots" in which lit strings would burn until his toes were technically "burned," triggering a wiggly shimmy shake by the prisoner and leg-kicking in unison response by the physicians, and the rituals of abstruse movements as such would carry on. The pain and suffering had by this juncture all but faded from the program to coerce a confession from Zeke and was replaced by an undeviating daily protocol of increasingly curious patterns of motion that only seemed like torture, but was more about observance of the work's repetition and the budding comity between the physicians and their subject. While Zeke could not ignore the cogs they were in the greater iniquitous penal system, he also came to recognize their own needs for subsistence in steady employment and despite their fears of defying damnable orders he held out hope for their adopting scruples of reform. And for their part, the physicians could not deny their admiration and amusement in Zeke's idealism (extremely quixotic from their perspective) and unwavering, inexhaustible commitment and zeal to propagate and pursue his visions as leader of the gathering Grange movement uniting hoboes and farmers to rise up and force change.

Then one afternoon during Zeke's session with the physicians, who were standing in a circle and sending him while strapped supine on his slab (now tricked out with coasters) sliding across to one another in a new nascent ritual, three jailors appeared in the room. They were expressionless strapping men bursting in their black and gray uniforms, and the apparent elder, his frame bolt erect as he clicked his boots to ensure he had their attention, commanded: "Mr. Borshellac, you have visitors who will see you in your cell. Come with us now." Stunned, it took a full minute for Zeke to comprehend the meaning of the jailor's statement, as his inquiries about visitations and representation by counsel had been so thoroughly disregarded and dismissed that he had abandoned all such hope. They led him to his cell and told him to wait, imparting nothing else despite his excited questions. It seemed like hours passed before he heard footfalls in the echoing corridor, the jailors now exchanging words with Jarvis and the heavy key clanging in the ponderous metal door's lock, and then the figures entered and he saw the familiar faces of Booth Booley and Horst Schtuckgloo. Zeke was so overcome with sudden emotion he could not move but simply stared at his old friends, themselves likewise so affected they stared stock-still back at him until they rushed towards him and embraced in bear hugs. The jailors and Jarvis now left them alone, locking them in as the elder jailor called out they had a half hour.

"How are you holding up in here, Zeke?" Booth finally asked after so much unspoken feeling was already conveyed between the men.

"I have to go to the well of fortitude every day, Booth, but I'm just grateful reserves are still there to draw on." He thought a moment of them seeing him now after struggling with incarceration for so long and closed his eyes, as the old Zeke suddenly was someone he missed now too.

Booth asked him about his leaner appearance and the bruises on his face. Growing vexed, he said: "There are penal codes that must be upheld goddamnit! Are they providing sustenance?"

"I bear the brunt of my bad break, Booth. I'm fed some infernal mushmeal and they seek a confession by any means it takes, but I will never cooperate."

Booth looked at Horst and they shook their heads in disgust.

"What ever happened to the lawyer who you were going to get?"

Booth looked down and hesitated and muttered: "We are now talking to Worthington Asprauller, one of the finest legal minds in the region, and it looked all set that he'd help us almost pro bono. But he suddenly disappeared on us. He probably heard about the others we engaged. Gerard . . . we know he's behind the coercion. The Cumberlands are sly when leaning on folks."

Zeke began to ask if they had anyone else in mind but held off as he knew how hard it was to buck the Cumberlands and did not want to make his pals feel bad. "It is so good to see you fellows. I thought I might never see anyone from Von Klobbert farm again."

Horst stepped closer and clapped his hands on Zeke's shoulders. "You will survive this infernal dungeon, Zeke Borshellac! You are inexorable in your odyssey to a new enlightenment. All those back on the farm mourn the dark vacuity of your absence and see you more for who you are now. You will endure this harsh burden, Zeke. We will never relent until you are freed." He clapped his shoulders again and held his eyes as he backed away, murmuring Scripture, "We exult in tribulations also, they work out endurance, virtue, hope, because the charity of God is poured forth in our hearts by the Holy Spirit."

Booth related how he, Mathius, Horst, Cy, and everybody steadily pressured Phineas to demand they be allowed to visit him and make sure he was coping with prison and a lawyer is granted access. They threatened to not work until he confronted Lord Cumberland and Gerard about the welfare of Zeke. "We are going to get you out of here, Zeke, we will end this nightmare somehow I promise." Booth then told him what he most wanted to hear, shifting his large burly frame and scratching his close-cropped head before stroking his long black beard. "Balthazar looks for you every day, he is forlorn, Zeke, but he also seems to have faith you will one day walk into that hayloft and it will be just like old times. I can see it in his expectant eyes sometimes when I go over there and he doesn't see it's me right away. And the boys have been magnificent with him. They have been terribly distressed over your imprisonment, Zeke, and I'll tell you it has been hard for us to see them so glum without their old spirit for hi-jinks."

Horst piped up now with a sigh: "Even I miss the old piss and vinegar of the young fellers' monkeyshines, and I am forever on the business end of them."

Booth went on: "They're not the same lads you left behind, but Balthazar has done so much to bolster their outlooks. He seems to know how much they depend on him to lift their spirits, and damn if he don't act like a puppy playing with them now and again. Caring for your dog is so important to the boys."

Zeke breathed deeply and felt all the warmth of these tidings and the grievous losses his unconscionable jailing caused him.

There was a silence among them now, as if the anguish of the circumstances was suddenly too overbearing to address anymore, it simply hurt, the painful reminders they were to one another. And the one question that remained that Zeke had to know about, despite his trepidations, hung now over them defying any easy way to bring it up. "It's been rough on all of us on the farm Zeke, seeing you suffering so unjustly and missing you," Booth finally said. "Livinia nearly fell apart when she learned what happened." He shook his head, collecting his thoughts. "The day they came to arrest you she was secluded in the far meadows beyond the daisy hill wooded tract, leading her heifers into that less trodden grassland they relish, and she did not march them back to the farm proper until well past your departure. It was myself and Mathias who first saw her appear on the horizon with her heifers as she emerged from the distant hills, as we knew she had gone there and went to tell her what had happened. As she came closer I remember how blithe and sprightly she seemed in her element with her animals traversing the pastures, and how her disposition grew curious and concerned as she saw our sober expressions awaiting to greet her. We didn't bandy about our words because, well, bad tidings cannot be equivocated." His face turned to a grimace. "It was harrowing for us to behold the woe, the smite of unmitigated anguish that befell our beautiful dairymaid that afternoon. At first she would not believe us, and beseeched us to impart the full story that extenuated the news, that we could not possibly be telling her that you were taken to the jailhouse like some criminal. When she realized we could not palliate what happened, she slid into a frantic agitation, a pique of wretchedness that asked why we could not stop them and cried that it was an abominable disgrace perpetrated by the Cumberland authorities and wept and ran across the fields shouting that Gerard was an evil monster as she fell several times and picked herself up from the moist earth. Of course, we did our best to console her and offer solace, but it was no use. Livinia ran to rage in her delirium at Phineas and Abigail and everyone at the farm that we all should be ashamed as we could have done more to prevent such a brutal measure, that you were more vulnerable as your stature at the Grange had grown, but as she collapsed again and again into disconsolate tears that only blamed herself for not unqualifiedly terminating any relations with Gerard while reproving herself for not being more circumspect in her budding affections towards you, which only left you susceptible to the Cumberland wrath. We feared she may hurt herself in her overwrought condition, but she eventually found Balthazar—who greeted her with loving licks—and kneeling in the pasture petting him and telling him that we would fight back at the scoundrels and get you out allowed her some small respite from her dolor before she crumpled altogether into unconsciousness."

Zeke interjected an insistent question on Livinia's well-being and Booth assured him she came through fine. "Doc Hockers was rushed to minister to her and she wakened shortly thereafter and Cy, Mathius, and Doc Hockers rode her out to Blackmoor Bluffs where they have an infirmary. She spent a couple of days there." Zeke let out a deep breath and sighed with great concern. Booth said it was rest more than anything she needed, and they took good care of her. He reminded them that her father left the family to join the French Foreign Legion when she was a girl and her mother soon after was committed to a sanitarium. There were reports the father was killed in Tanzania, and that the mother's condition only deteriorated. Livinia only ever believed she would see them again. Zeke and Horst nodded solemnly.

"Livinia has had some bad breaks, much misfortune," Zeke said.

"The Livinia who finally did come back was not the same after that," Booth continued. "She was a broken young woman, Zeke, no longer the buoyant dairymaid who laughed easily. This Livinia has become withdrawn into a somber stupor who only seems still alive for her bovine creatures and Ogden and Huxley, whom she spends time with—who told us she only came back for the salary— and of course, Balthazar whom she takes for long walks over the fields. But she is broken by what they've done to you, Zeke, and bears guilt herself for letting her relations with you incite the vengeance of the Cumberlands. Gerard knew enough to leave her alone for a while, but lately he has been seen with her on the pastures and even with her riding again in his carriage. We are all apalled by it. She moves about in a trance of melancholia. Huxley confided to me she has lost all sense of hope and feels abandoned to her own prior mistakes of judgment and now has no will left to fight the Cumberlands' constant domineering control. She seems adrift in a torpor of defeat."

Zeke listened with a heavy heart and grave ire, as well as a bittersweet fleeting reflection that the dairy maid indeed really cared about him, all of which infused him with a new unyielding urgency to win his release from jail. Now he had to press his old friends again on their status in procuring him a lawyer. Horst frowned disgustedly at the thought while Booth began to recount more intimidation tactics from the Cumberlands, as odd provocations occurring in the town barbershop proved to be enough to dissuade no less than three prominent attorneys from continuing their engagements in representing Zeke. The first was Mylor Sandford Bleffrey, the six-foot-five esteemed scholar pettifogger known for suing shops with too low awnings that caused tall folks to clock their heads. Bleffrey, or MSB as some called him, was preparing Zeke's defense when he went to Nunzio's barbershop for a haircut and a light trim of his long luxurious beard. He was greeted by a dapper unctuous fellow wearing a porkpie and told that his barber Nunzio was "out of sorts" and his apprentice, Nino Foglio, would be honored to service the esteemed counselor. MSB was irked, not one inclined to subject the fate of his pride and joy whiskers to a novice, but the unctuous fellow spoke eloquently of Foglio's artistry with the scissors and soon they had MSB strapped into the chair, emerging later semiconscious, clean-shaven, and sporting a risible curlicue middle-part haircut with a permanent pomade. While the derisive whispers and overt displays of mockery over his drastic new appearance were for the most part light-hearted and benign, Bleffrey was shaken to the core by his suddenly hairless chin and odd oiled coils upon his head. His profound mortification damaged his self-confidence, left him traumatized with doubts and self-consciousness that so undermined his legal powers he self-medicated with booze, ran afoul of societal parameters, and in short order was committed to a sanitarium.

MSB's fall was precipitous, and Booth and Mathius were able to quickly pivot to another formidable esteemed attorney to represent Zeke, Flence Frick Frahlinger, aka FFF, whose incisive booming courtroom oratory had been lauded in picking apart the "Cruller Cover-up," effectively defending a modest baker from charges of poisoning a group on a church outing and proving the bad crullers were linked to curdled whey seepage dumped in the well water by the industrialist Endicott G. Emballows. Frahlinger eagerly agreed to advocating on Zeke's behalf, as he had a partiality to aiding plain folks in extremis, and while the compensation would be negligible to an attorney of his caliber he saw in it a chance to further emboss his reputation as a champion of the peasant class. A man of solid husky stature who believed in the benefits of physical exercise and was fanatical about his routines with medicine balls and Indian clubs, he naturally cared deeply about his appearance. He wore finely tailored three-piece suits, dangled a gold pocket watch, and often had a meerschaum appended to his mouth. But most of all, his well-tended dark beard, of such length he could tuck it in his lapels if he so chose, was his pride and joy and to his mind his signature feature. As it happened, after a meeting with Booth, Mathius, and Horst in a local tavern to discuss the case, he decided he could use a trim and on his own accord wandered into Nunzio's. Certainly the farmers would have cautioned him otherwise, but they later surmised that the Cumberlands must have calculated the well-groomed counselor would act alone. In the barber shop he was greeted, as MSB had been, by the very same natty, oleaginous fellow sporting a porkpie who explained that Nunzio "was on an African safari" but his apprentice Nino Foglio would consider it a privilege to provide his tonsorial talents to such a prominent gentleman. An out-of-towner, Frahlinger never heard of Nunzio and was nettled by the natty one, only wanting a quick trim and no nonsense, yet somehow they wheedled him into removing his Indian clubs from his satchel for an impromptu demonstration. Their knowledge of his devotion to the clubs, in retrospect, corroborated to Booth and the farmers that the Cumberlands were unmistakably behind what came next. As Nino attempted to execute a swinging movement with clubs in each hand, he clocked FFF twice, in the forward twist and then again on the backward maneuver, leaving the famed lawyer quite groggy. In a jiffy they had him in the chair propped up and strapped in, and Nino went to town in a madcap flurry of flying scissors and ruthless razor until Frahlinger found himself awakening in a nearby alley with a smooth clean-shaven face and a shiny completely bald head (except for three square patches inexplicably left in the occipital region of the skull). The horror of his transmogrification naturally overwhelmed him and his first instinct was to cover up and he purchased a trapper's fur cap in a dry goods store as well as a dust protector cloth to tie around his mouth and neck like a cowboy. Then he bellied up to the counter of the nearest saloon and proceeded to swig hard liquor and plot his vengeance on the rogue barber shop. When the dapper fellow and Nino Foglio finally issued from the shop at closing, Frahlinger shadowed them for a mile until they were on the outskirts near a deserted old mill and a wooded area, where he pounced and delivered such a severe beating to the apprentice barber he lingered for days on death's door in hospital, while the dapper fellow escaped the attorney's wrath and fled, ultimately fingering FFF in court and sending him to prison for a long sentence.

    At this point in recounting their travails in engaging legal representation, Booth paused with a reflective grimace, muttering over the frustration and emphasizing how they had to reinvent their search paradigm. "In a nutshell, Zeke, we had to find not only a capable attorney but one who was clean-shaven to avoid any further chicanery from Nunzio's Barbershop." And they thought they had their man in the form of Sandford Gray Larderot, an attorney from the panhandle with a sterling reputation largely centered upon his stout-hearted defense of the lothario cobbler Gilberto Pizza, who was charged with the heinous butchering of the woodwind section of the Topeka marching band with sharpened shoemaking instruments. Pizza walked and returned to his career in shoe repair, while the real killer was proven years later to be an apprentice butcher, Al Shepsi, of a Wichita meat shop who sought to frame Pizza because he was having an affair with the cobbler's long-suffering wife who tolerated his years of philandering. Booth and Mathius frankly did not think a lawyer of Larderot's celebrity stature would consider taking on Zeke's case, which was so fraught with political ramifications, but Horst pressed them that SGL, as he was also known, alone stood as their last best chance to spring the hobo farmer. And what clinched it for them was very reliable reports that Larderot had not only been clean-shaven throughout his career but his dome was as smooth and bare as a vine-ripened honeydew melon. Still, after their excitement of engaging the eminent counsel had abated, insofar as no one had actually met the man in person nor seen a photograph of him, there was anxiety as they awaited his coach to arrive at the town's station depot. Slowly the enormous attorney emerged from the rear seat, not without significant difficulty being so grossly corpulent, and upon setting foot on the earthen boulevard he stumbled and evinced surprising footwork in maintaining his reeling form to avoid falling. Finally, there before the desperate farmers stood none other than the great SGL, his radiantly grizzled beard the most thickly abundant and wildly voluminous of all others they had ever seen. While his head was as bald as advertised, at least the wide horseshoe span of top and crown were sleek as a newborn's labonza, the extreme hirsute state of his chin caused them serious trepidation. They decided someone would remain with the great attorney at all times as he prepared Zeke's defense, particularly steering him clear of Nunzio's Barber Shop where the dapper fellow endured in his managerial capacity.

It was Mathius on duty escorting SGL wherever he needed go one afternoon when the famed counselor indicated a desire to purchase laudanum in the downtown apothecary, as the big man had been complaining about his neuralgia and rheumatic pains and had been battling with severe diarrhea to boot. Mathius opted to wait outside and smoke a cheroot, sensing nothing potentially untoward within the apothecary shop. Yet inside monkey business was quickly under way once Larderot ordered his laudanum, as a jauntily tricked-out fellow manifested from the hidden rooms behind the counter, a charismatic sort eerily akin to the barber shop charmer (in fact, they were thought to be first-cousins it later emerged), and began a compelling line of jawbone that sold SGL on a vial of camphorated tincture of opium for his unruly bowels, as well as a fancy new witch hazel to apply to his pate. The jaunty fellow, dressed in a pastel seersucker suit and panama hat, insisted his customer sample the purchases and in a wink Larderot had swallowed several ounces of the opium preparations. An agreeable palaver between the men developed and the jaunty one soon offered a free trim of the hair on the back of his neck, and just like that the scene shifted and the massive counsel was maneuvered into a barber chair in an isolated back chamber, nodding a fair amount from the narcotic effect. He became increasingly languorous and somnolent and altogether unaware that a barber named Dino Carbone had now appeared in the back chamber makeshift shop, and the sizable barber pole lit up like a Christmas tree. Carbone wasted no time in attacking SGL's beard with the clippers and forthwith moved onto the straight razor to shave him tight. But the mysterious barber was not through yet, there was an element within him that would not leave it be. He wielded the clippers with a relentless mastery, an involuntary effervescence that seemed driven to mischief and havoc. His skilled scissor work rendered the sides of the bald pate an abstract "congeries of competing sheaves," as the jaunty one cryptically observed. Carbone was a sprightly barber who liked to wriggle and shimmy rhythmically while he worked, snipping noisily with specially made scissors and thrusting jabs of the clippers to shear and crop while humming familiar arias, all subject to the sweep and scrape of the straight razor. All that remained around the perimeter sides of SGL's head ended up being three parallel strips of hair at the temporal base above the left ear, approximately ¼ inch wide, 3/8 inch high, and 3.35 inches long, with a sizable crescent moon shape located just behind the right ear, and an approximately 2.75 inch patch up near the very rear of the crown that described an oblique triangle that also resembled a circus clown pushing a wheelbarrow. And Dino Carbone left one more signature imprint on his groggy customer's mug, eyebrows carved into bat wings with the pointy-toothed scowling bat face etched with indigo dye in the middle. When it was all over, they roused the big fellow enough to send him on his way, and so doped up he was his drastic new appearance never occurred to him as he tottered outside and slipped past Mathius, who was talking to a passing stranger who asked if he knew where he could find a good fishmonger who was reasonable. By some small miracle Sandford Gray Larderot, after traipsing through back streets and brush found his way to a fleabag hotel in the tenderloin sector and flopped on the torn-up old bed. One could only imagine the utter shock he received the next day upon gazing at his reflection, but we do know he straightway returned to the apothecary, not to seek retribution for the tonsorial malpractice but to stock up on his opiated medicines and decamp once and for all into a drifting life of hophead stupefaction.

 Once Booth concluded recounting the regrettable tale of SGL Zeke was dumbfounded and saddened by the futility of their efforts in retaining counsel for his defense, albeit he empathized with their frustration in challenging the Cumberlands. The three men went silent until Booth explained the jaunty fellow and Dino Carbone were clearly expecting Larderot to patronize the apothecary, and that had to be predicated on knowledge of SGL treating his chronic ailments with a variety of opiated preparations. "We have another attorney we are working on for you, Zeke, only this time we will keep him far away from the Von Klobbert farmlands while he prepares the case. And we'll put him in a disguise come the trial. Maybe a theologian or gypsy costume," Booth suddenly exclaimed with a strained sanguinity.

But to Zeke it seemed desperate and pathetic. He simply nodded. Another silence ensued until Horst piped up with news of the great harvest hootenanny they were planning through the Grange to have at the Von Klobbert farm, a momentous gathering of the growing Grange Movement uniting the forces of farmers and hoboes in one prodigious hootenanny commemorating the fall harvest. "We have been sending out circulars everywhere sodbusters and hoboes congregate, Zeke! Grange meetings, jungles, railroad junctions, taverns, farm socials, and the fervor for this hootenanny has been an extraordinary wonder to behold." Horst's eyes now had a faraway look as he recited Scripture: " 'If you have faith even like a mustard seed, you will say to the mulberry tree, be uprooted and be planted in the sea, and it will obey you." He paused a moment in reflection before continuing. "Out of the soil and through the rails comes a new conviction and fortitude, a transcendent sense of idealism and righteousness that joins together the strength of our burgeoning numbers, and we are beginning to believe *we can prevail*."

Booth and Horst searched Zeke's gaze now, allowing Horst's words to resonate, and finally it was Booth who declared: "And Zeke, but one individual inspires our movement like no other. The one they call the hobo farmer galvanizes them with a courage and passion for the struggles ahead like no one has ever seen before. They speak his name now with a reverence and hope, an unbowed sense of fighting back."

Booth looked at Horst who said: "That would be you Zeke, we're talking about you."

"So I'm a martyr for the Movement, eh?!" Zeke replied. "I hardly feel like the leader, or a martyr, but I will marshal all the power available to me to turn the tide in our struggle!" He asked Horst if he had a circular on him and he did, and Zeke kept staring at the urgent black print on the green paper, the remarkable drawings of farmers in their fields along with hoboes and their boxcars, the call to come together for the Hootenanny Harvest and celebrate the new solidarity. The message moved Zeke and he said he would like to hold onto the piece of paper, "to have it here in the darkness where it will remind me of its promise."

Booth nodded understandingly.

"Like a promissory note of better times ahead," Horst averred with a glint in his eye.

The farmers now embraced their old pal in turns before moving towards the cell door, where Jarvis appeared to escort them out. And then Zeke heard the harsh clangor of the thick metal cell door close on him and the lonely stifling quiet that followed. The empty ache of forlornness spread throughout his person and a miasma of despair settled over him as he fought to reconcile himself to the dim prospects he faced. He padded about and paused in a corner to squat with his head down, part of him wanting to lie prostrate in subjugation, but he just remained on his haunches gazing upon the crud-hardened topography of the cell floor. And now he saw what he thought he glimpsed from his slab bunk half-asleep overnight, strange ungodly insect creatures with the long springy legs of grasshoppers, translucent fluttery wings, bulbous eyes and antenna like alien membranes, these were grotesque little beings with whom he became fascinated, watching a band of them crawling around in some recondite martial drill he imagined, and they appeared to be multiplying. He conjured up their world down there in the corner of his cell floor and appreciated their pertinacity, their will to exist for who they were and admired them as survivalists. He thought of Livinia and Balthazar on the farm and missing them so much the ache burned his every breath, the life he left behind there and the Movement that began taking root before he was arrested, the leadership they said was invested in his imprisoned figure. And he knew he had to get out of that jail one way or another even if it meant dying in the attempt.

Eighteen

Commandant Droochler began showing up at his daily torture sessions with the bearded physicians, insofar as their transition to a soft-pedalled approach to instilling pain did not sit well with him. He always trusted them implicitly to be merciless in their maximizing of prisoners' suffering, so his sudden appearance signaled someone had informed him of the more relaxed routine into which they had fallen. They recognized the bind they were in, the Commandant expecting to see good old torture savage and barbaric while they were long removed from such tactics and in fact so rusty they could hardly muster a plausible feigned brutality upon their prisoner. But the specter of the Commandant seated at the head of the long table with his familiar cudgel in hand, pounding it now and again into his palm with a snap, was ample motivation for them to try to recapture their old fury for continuous torture. Now their routine of ostentatious but essentially ineffectual torture was out the window, the spirit of fellowship and conviviality that had grown among prisoner and torturers during breaks and meal periods could no longer exist, the oratorical poetic flights by Zeke of homage to hoboes riding rails under moonlit prairies and indefatigable farmers of unwavering backbones, his unique performance skits, all were henceforth proscribed. The bearded physicians had failed in all this time to extract a confession from the hobo farmer and leaks reached the Commandant of their capacity for unadulterated brutality weakening, so it was hardly a secret to them and Zeke that his appearance signaled their positions were on the line, and possibly greater consequences. As such they were under intense pressure to deliver serious pain to Zeke, and despite his being the recipient

EIGHTEEN

Zeke empathized with their plight and found himself partly rooting for their return to barbarity. And they mustered the flames that scorched him, the deafening blasts of noise, the strapping of his frame into the cursed elongations of the rack, the pounding of his form with large cudgels, all while Commandant Droochler monitored with his glower and ornately carved extra-large cudgel resting in his lap. But it was becoming apparent to Zeke that the physicians were not going as far as they might, the natural killer instinct necessary in torturers was lacking, whether consciously or not, and such faltering could only be ascribed to their fondness for the prisoner. The flames were a tad more fleeting, the rack not fully stretched, and the pummeling most of all seemed too tentative, fraught with a slight hesitancy.

For days Droochler sat with his team of black-and-gray uniformed adjutants at his side, his stern squinty glare scrutinizing the physicians' increasingly desperate exertions to prove they indeed remained consummate professionals who can be counted on to deliver the kind of pain that produces confessions. Their straining overcompensation for the evident loss of nerve in their administration of physical punishment was not going unnoticed, and Zeke felt Droochler's confidence in the physicians slipping away. The prisoner screamed louder and longer and with lachrymose histrionics that lent credibility, and a few of the physicians found the wherewithal to jab him with red-hot pokers and another thrashed the soles of his bare feet with the bastinado for an hour and a half one day. But it was not enough to convince Commandant Droochler that they truly meant business and were not still a tad palsy-walsy with the hobo farmer. He even wished there was a way he could confess to the charges of insurrection without condemning himself to the gallows or life in prison, insofar as a few words to that effect would surely vindicate their methods and preserve their positions at the prison. But such self-sacrifice served no lasting purpose in the march towards a just and free and auspicious world, and Zeke could not allow himself to perish since he was needed in the groundswell of the Movement. Moreover, the physicians at this juncture would not want him to confess to any of the crimes because they had to know he was innocent of all charges, and they performed their duties with a sense of ethical decorum. They not only had come to know Zeke as a friend and liked him very much, but they admired him as a fledgling leader with an unwavering idealistic vision. Then discord began to manifest among this erstwhile tightknit team of torturers, the pressure proving to be too much, as some argued for more fire and rack, others for bigger bastinados and water torture, while still others pushed for psychological torment such as endless macabre chanting by ghoulish figures in dim candlelight. Each day their focus and efficacy seemed to ebb more and Commandant Droochler continued his critical evaluation in his staunch silent disapprobation, punctuated by an occasional clucking of the tongue, angry grunting, whispers with his adjutants who often grew agitated with their disgust. Eventually rumblings of terrible consequences for both prisoner and his ineffectual torturers began to reverberate in certain sectors of the jailhouse. The physicians, the scuttlebutt went, would be summarily arrested for dereliction of duty and locked away indefinitely in the very prison of their employment at Frodtznjepple Peninsula while awaiting their trials in the Cumberland courts, which most considered of the kangaroo variety. Turnkeys in the mess hall were even talking about officials secretly preparing particularly inhuman cells for them in which low ceilings precluded their ability to stand up and punk sticks treated with raw sewage would burn constantly. Zeke, the skinny repeated over and over, would be accused of attempting an escape and executed through the hangman's noose or by a succession of hard blows to the skull with one of the large heavy-duty cudgel models brandished by Commandant Droochler and other senior prison officials. All of this of course raised the stakes and compounded the pressure the physicians and Zeke were under, as Zeke felt an urgency to act and break from the inevitable destruction towards which they all were headed.

  In harrowing moments of anguish he lamented the cruel loneliness of his incarcerated existence, now the loss of his companions, the physicians whose fraternity and palaver he relished during their breaks and meals. And it was shortly after the visit by Booth and Horst

EIGHTEEN

when Commandant Droochler took Jarvis to task for allowing Zeke's farm pals to stay too long, and the young jailor, whose company Zeke so counted on, was barred from all communication with the hobo farmer. Now Jarvis became a mysterious figure who guarded Zeke's cell and corridor in stone stark silence, a stolid form ever hovering in the near shadows of the prisoner's whereabouts, a young turnkey estranged and detached and coldly spooky to the forsaken Zeke. Jarvis had shared some tribulations he was going through with Zeke, his frustration in his work as a jailer, largely a position to appease his father the police lieutenant, and his aspiration to master the art of glassblowing. Zeke had counseled the young man and looked forward to their conversations, and Jarvis, of course, snuck him paper and pencils so the hobo farmer could keep a journal of his thoughts and ideas. But now that friendship, so important to Zeke to hold onto a right mind, the grace of sincere colloquy and a sliver of sanguinity, was gone. When he first became aware of Jarvis' diminished presence and silence he was perplexed, then dismayed as he heard of Droochler's edict. And there was disappointment in Jarvis for obeying it so readily and completely, even ire over the young turnkey's acceptance. But after spending that night in his cell he empathized with the fear the Commandant carried, especially with a young diffident fellow like Jarvis, and decided *he* would be the one to disregard such an edict. Zeke determined that he would simply continue talking to Jarvis as if nothing had changed and pay no mind to the silence coming from his interlocutor. He knew Jarvis was out in the corridor well within earshot, so he could provide unilateral conversation to the fellow whose company he so very much missed. He knew he was out there and hoped he was listening to his monologues about the importance of remaining true to one's struggle for meaningful identity and calling in the world, and not to succumb to pressure and convenience to conform to someone else's wishes and perception of one. And that might mean a policeman father who browbeat his son into accepting jailor work, he said without outright stating it. He spoke of perseverance and fortitude in not compromising one's beliefs and convictions, the commitment to the altruism necessary in the greater good of a free and just world. He stressed the importance of having the will and strength to recognize and pursue the aspirations and work that one truly wants and can derive the most happiness doing. Zeke recounted stories from his own divers fields of vocation, examining how random or disparate periods may have seemed at the time but when seen in retrospect, considering the goals and ideals carried in a clear course from his days at sea to the Von Klobbert farm and the voice that would resonate in the Grange Movement—a cogent progression emerges. He talked about the Gracklers and the Hobo Fund with which they deceived him, the Fish Fellow who became his survival muse, the great highwayman Dieter Schrampenkrieg and his philosophies of income redistribution, being roused from the hayloft as a boy in the wee hours by his drunken father upon his powerful steed and their mad moonlit rides through the woods, the hobo father who haunted him, the wave of new fairness coming across the land in the grassroots organizing of farmers and hoboes uniting for a better life and opportunities for everybody. And he never knew for sure if Jarvis was listening as the young turnkey held his utter silence throughout Zeke's lengthy discourses every evening, which went on for weeks, all the while the physicians continued to flounder in their strained but ineffectual, bootless sessions of torture, and each day they grew more flailing and desperate in their efforts to convince Commandant Droochler that they retained the capacity to actually extract his confession. It had become a pathetic sideshow of a kind for the Commandant and his team of adjutants and they appeared to savor the panicky scrambling physicians trying ludicrous, ill-conceived methods, such as spinning Zeke on a six-foot wood-carved top while serenading him with ominous Gregorian chants. The Commandant and his men would sit back and chuckle with derision, smoke large black cigars, and enjoy the squirming fear before them insofar as the rumors of the pending hobo farmer's execution and their imprisonment only escalated. It was repeated in every corridor of the jailhouse that Zeke would be apprehended for attempting a breakout, albeit whether they would provide him with an opening with which to cap-

EIGHTEEN

ture him, or simply declare him caught in the act before hanging him, was unclear.

All through these weeks of tormented fear Zeke kept talking to Jarvis at night, and watching the strange insects gather at intervals on his cell floor, amassing in their secret formations, and he found them fascinatingly diverting. Squatting in the corner and bent low he studied the busy maneuvers of the creatures, the marching in arcane phalanxes at changeable speeds, the seemingly capricious flourishes that always adjusted to a larger configuration which would soon become apparent. Each evening after talking for so long to Jarvis he would visit with the insects before retiring to slumber on his slab, and he began to believe they had forged a connection, man and insects, an intuitive communication through which the only living occupants of that prison cell at Frodtznjepple Peninsula understood one another. He sensed their yearning for proficiency and control and their deep commitment to one another as the source of their strength, insofar as alone they were negligible nuisances but when assembled as an army they commanded a respect and created an aura of dread among any arthropod enemies who would challenge their autonomy. And he could discern in his tiny cronies an abiding empathy with his plight as a prisoner, his sadness, anguish, even moments of despair in his wrongful confinement alongside them. They were there before his arrival and this was their home and Zeke stayed respectful of that fact, and he felt they knew he wanted to break out because he did not belong there, was unjustly sentenced there. And so he examined them with intense intuition every night, recognizing the mysterious contact he was having with them. Until one such night he was riveted upon the strange insects, watching them marching in many directions, compressing and contracting in flanks and all manner of geometric shapes, and he sleepily smiled down on their diligent ingenuity before turning towards his slab. But he caught something in his peripheral vision that he could not dismiss: the final flank of hundreds forming a spearlike thrust which resembled a quintessential door key, at least that's what Zeke saw, as they began marching away from their shadowy sector and towards the opposite corner. He followed them and watched them swarm upon a particularly darkened area of the stone penal wall, and he could not pull away from their sudden mission of boring in here. There were cracks and missing chunks and an intimation of looseness, a suspicion of untenable solidity, and he placed his palm against it as the long-legged bulbous eyed insects parted for him and he lightly tapped it with the tips of his other fingers. He knocked and listened with his ear against it as insects buzzed faintly in excitement that he was uncovering what they showed him, or so he imagined. The cracks evinced a penchant to crumble and Zeke sedulously worked on exploiting the decided frangibility and desired to know what lay inside, though he had a good hunch. With only his hands did he pick and pull at the splintered lines, the fractured segments, the chipped wavy pieces, and the time-worn wall proved increasingly vulnerable. He worked intensely in a trance, his strong farmer's hands instinctually finding the faintly moistened spots of pasty decay where he dug and burrowed with ploughing fingers like blades into hard earth. Once he looked down and was surprised his insect companions were in rows around him, watching him in an odd still silence, and he bent down low and met some of their unfaltering bulbous-eyed stares and could not decipher their intentions except he thought they wanted him to go. Not exactly because they rooted for his freedom, but perhaps so they would have their home again without the uninvited guest. Zeke couldn't say which, but either way he understood. As he continued to penetrate deeper and widen the indenture the notion of breaking through the wall altogether seemed possible and a buried cry of exultant catharsis reverberated dimly inside him. He worked faster and more skillfully than he ever would have thought himself capable, and he did so in a noiseless rhythm cautious of turnkey ears. He deliberated in a spell of antipodes, a haze of loggerheads that remembered well the rumors resonating throughout the prison that he would be hanged for attempting to escape, and naturally a suspicion rose in him that his discovery here was not all by chance. Part of him even considered the wisdom of going through

EIGHTEEN

any such hole in the wall, as it could have been Droochler's snare in which his capture would precipitate his execution. Of course, Zeke deliberated over this apprehension but he continued to dig into the wall every night and was making so much progress he had to find places in his cell to conceal the removed detritus, such as refilling the hole itself with the loose rock fragments, so it would not be noticed during the day. He never really doubted whether he would climb through the hole when the time came, for the mysterious connection he forged with the insects did not jibe with the notion of a set-up. It felt right to him, that he had to take his chances now or he could be confined to that cell for a very long time, and he was prepared for the worst although his cogitations would come back to the insects and a sense of sanguinity about their part in it.

And the night came sooner than he thought, the first glint of space past the wall, an apercu the size of a marble, made his heart jump. He paused to admire the milestone and thought of the farm and Livinia and Balthazar, the Harvest Hootenanny Horst and the Grange were putting together. A reverie of his sweet return floated through his mind, and he allowed himself its fleeting pleasure. He felt he earned it with his wall labors, and he squatted and smiled upon the insects assembled around him as was their wont now. He worked with a new intensity that night in breaking open the hole until it appeared a pumpkin would fit through. The next night he feverishly poked and pulled and punched his way to widening the width until he thought he could climb through, and except for one last nod of confidence to his tiny troops of support, he did not hesitate one moment in making his move. He went into the darkness head first and found his frame barely fit through the opening, and he could feel the tightness of a square rusted metal duct pressing against him. All he could do to move forward was push and slither himself along, each movement disturbing the long-accumulating rust from the surfaces enclosing him. Through the thick dust and darkness he wriggled and pushed his way ahead, coughing, knowing there was no turning back now, only the unknown of his hard path in this choking tight tunnel. It kept getting harder and more harrowing as he inched forward, the winding duct ever appearing to constrict him more, its inconsistent dimensions compressing him now and again to a near dead halt. The blackness and debris and rust-laden close air ever denser, ever more an impenetrable daunting barrier that induced constant coughing and gasping for breath. His progress only slowed as the duct squeezed him so he could hardly move, as he struggled to breath, and the disturbed flecks of rust floated into his mouth, nose, and eyes, and the coughing was uncontrollable. It seemed hours since he began his escape into the hidden duct, and though his movement had been painstakingly slow it felt like he had pushed himself into the deep and forgotten bowels of the primeval prison. And then he could not continue forward even a fraction of an inch, he felt the gripping encasement of the rusted duct pressing him like it swallowed him whole, and he could not breath. As his dire condition grew more ineluctable with every passing minute, a nameless terror pullulated up from his chest and overwhelmed his entire being, as time creaked ahead as if taunting his suffering immobilized immolation with the inevitable sepulchral upshot. To lose his life buried so abysmally in the entrails of the monstrous prison was a cruel fate and Zeke could not help but feel sorry for himself in his pain and shortening breaths.

And while it seemed impossible, his predicament took another turn into an even ghastlier torment. He heard them scurrying about in front of him, the patter of their footfalls suggesting several at the least, their low-pitched squeaking sounds of eerie communication, their eyes and teeth faintly visible to Zeke in the utter blackness. They made him shudder and swoon in dismay, wishing they would leave him expire in peace swaddled in his metal tomb. Then the rats, very large ones he sensed, moved onto his body in frenetic strides, sniffing and squeaking to one another, before he felt their sharp snouts poking into his face. His panic was modifying into a semiconscious dread as his breath grew ever more labored, the dizzying horror of his predicament too much to comprehend, the rats scrambling over him until they seemed to settle in their places of dealing with their prize. And now on his legs and back and hands and neck and chest and head and face he felt them nibbling at his skin, the ones on his back were already biting and gnawing and Zeke was groaning in the pain and fright. He thought in these moments of misery that this is how it ends for him, in the rusted old ducts buried in the prison gnawed by rats, and he wished so much he could have seen Livinia one more time among the blue skies and trees in her yellow dress she had on the first time he ever saw her, and he wished he could have had one more picnic with her and Balthazar, and that he could have danced a slow number with her one more time culminating in a kiss. He knew that he had always loved her from the moment he and Balthazar beheld her from a distance across the great rolling meadows, and knew it more with every stride he took to reach her, and converse with her, and to receive her beneficence in considering his plea to work on the farm. He knew he knew it in some primordial, profound, not always very cognizant way, and he even imagined he knew it before he and Balt appeared on that meadow that morning, like one just feels that heady urge to create something original and magnificent and understands it is in him to do it while not exactly sure the nature of such a marvel, only that it will be. Livinia was all the longing and desire and inchoate exhilaration he ever dreamed of the love he would one day find, she was the living embodiment of his romantic reveries, the beautiful laughter and smile just past all the loneliness. He struggled mightily to wrench and jerk his clamped form free, to no avail, and he began to succumb to his macabre fate as the rats continued to sink their knifelike incisors into his flesh. Now his blood was dribbling on him and it felt warm and caustic, deathly, as he heard them eagerly savor their easy prey. He thought of his father's drunken midnight equestrian rides and his coming into the hayloft for his sleeping son who was so frightened of being swept onto the saddle and galloping breakneck through the woods. He saw his mother in the tavern playing the wench to keep the collectors at bay, among the ruffians and rumdums and the gunsels and hooligans who knew her only that way, but he knew her differently. As a mother who would die for him, who loved him and did her best to protect him. The physical pain of his pierced flesh to the ravenous rodents was superseded by the anguish of knowing his premature demise would leave him nothing more than a work in progress, a raw unfinished struggling individual who never knew what it was like to really be in love and who was still discovering the potential that lay inside of him to become the leader of a movement he was truly born to lead. He felt trickles of his warm blood running into his eyes and mouth and continued his desperate efforts to extricate himself from his rusted metal tomb, to no avail. His misery and despair engulfed him with regret and anger, some self-loathing, at his horrible fate. He second-guessed his decision to climb into the tight duct, but also remembered he had to make a break from Frodtznjepple. He lamented his dream of helping the downtrodden being cut short just as he was finding his voice and hitting his stride with the Grange Movement. It had taken many years of multifarious pursuits through a long journey for him to find the right calling and now that he had, he mourned his grisly expiration at the teeth of such outsized rats. He felt them biting with a voracious glee and his blood streamed down his face and made him choke and gag. He knew the demonic little bastards had him, the darkness of Frodtznjepple enveloped him, the malignant authority of the Cumberlands now had him in their depraved vise grip, and he turned to God above in the firmament or deep within one's very own soul, wherever He may exist, and asked how could He let these lousy forces of malevolence and iniquity prevail against somebody like him who was only trying to make the most of himself in helping others?

Everything began to fade in a dizzy haze of choking grief and throbs and he thought of the good in each of his parents, his father's mighty horsemanship and fierce courage to envisage something more in life, despite his drunken mad dead ends, and his mother's unconditional love and devotion by any means necessary to provide for her son. He thought of his faithful sheepdog and the deep abiding trust and dedication to one another he and Balthazar always kept. And there was this irreducible and indelible image of his beloved Livinia that

EIGHTEEN

pervaded all his sensations, the glory of her beauty and the radiance of her whole personage, and he longed for seeing her one more time. He promised if he ever somehow was granted one more chance at life he would make the most of it, as now in his fleeting moments of existence he called out such a pledge to the Almighty without, within, wherever. "I will lead the hoboes and farmers into a better life of fairness, equality, and opportunity! I will give my heart and soul and blood to improve the fates of these people! Of all people cast aside and denied a fair shake in life!" He could not catch his breath and coughed in pain, then faintly whispering: "Balthazar! Livinia! Will I see you again?"

He was semiconscious as grating sounds began to reach him, distant noises that seemed to be growing louder caught his ear. He knew not where they came from or what they might be, only a rustling, occasionally clanging reverberation of something moving towards him, and the movement appeared to be inside the duct. They were coming for him, he now knew, the Droochler guards were onto his escape attempt and would capture him soon and hang him accordingly. In his dying suffering throes, down to last breaths and riddled with rats, Zeke felt a dim hope of rescue that was sorely tempered by the fact that the rescuers burrowing towards him were indeed those who would only kill him all over again in the bargain. Just as he had suspected they would, they set a trap and he fell right into it, and he rued his credulity for affording them the satisfaction to see him swing. He wished the rats would finish him off before they reached him. And his mind succumbed to the daze of a dying stupor which spun sickly with the bleakest of gray spidery shadows, as he faintly recognized they had his legs and were pulling him back, dragging him incrementally the way he'd come with each successive hard yank. He lost consciousness altogether until their arms with one powerful tug tore him out and tumbling onto the hard crud-laden floor. He sprung to his feet in a violent reflex of desperate defense, his head spinning in a blur of pain, his fear and delirium propelling his wounded shredded form towards those who pulled him from the strangle of the casing. His immediate charge seemed to catch them unawares, unprepared for one so hurt to have such fight left in him, and they went tumbling down, grappling and brawling in a tangle of punches and kicks until Zeke in his vicious maniacal cyclone of attack began to realize the upper hand. At least he felt he would destroy the one he was beating up, the others he could not account for, but they were yelling and crying out to him in unintelligible fragments and he just kept swinging with big roundhouses and slams of the body, clocking his foe with solid shots as he worked him over in the dim windowless room that looked just the place for someone to be beaten up. And he connected with a hard blow to the side of the head and felt his foe wobble, smelled the groggy recoil and loaded up another big haymaker that would have put him to sleep when a shaft of shifting light fell across his opponent's face and Zeke saw something familiar there. It startled him for the moment and he held fire on his fist and gazed with all the focus he could muster into that groggy mug before him, and exclaimed, "Jarvis!" And he crumpled in a strewn prone mess where cognizance could no longer hold sway, and only following considerable efforts of revival by the turnkey—who first needed recovery time himself—did Zeke begin to stir. Again his eyes adjusted to the shock of recognizing his rescuer (or captor) as Jarvis and feeling the sore stings of his wounds as he tried to get up.

It was dingy where they were in the prison, a close dead space they passed through where their exit from the duct somehow deposited them. Jarvis was crouched beside him gazing intently in his eyes: "How are you doing, Zeke? Are you hurt bad?"

Zeke looked around for the others. "Where'd they go?"

"Who?"

"Your cronies."

"Nobody's here but me."

Zeke tried to pick himself up but groaned in pain and sat back to wait. "So you *can* still talk?! Where's that cat who had your tongue cause I could have used him back there with those rats?"

Jarvis smiled slightly. "I may have been silent, but I listened to every word you said, Zeke."

EIGHTEEN

Zeke was grateful for his freedom from the casing and expressed so to Jarvis, but he was puzzled by him. He wasn't sure where he stood with him exactly. "I guess you'll get some citation for nabbing me escaping, eh?"

Jarvis digested this question with a look of skeptical reflection across his features, sighing through a deep breath before replying that he supposed there would be some recognition of service in his foiling the escape.

"They'll probably give you a promotion. Droochler himself will have to commend you and eat all his criticism of you." Zeke rose to his feet with a hand from Jarvis and tottered a few steps before righting himself. "Yeah, you'll be quite the rising star in this godforsaken hellhole. But frankly, Jarvis, I would not have expected this from you."

Jarvis was watching him pensively and now asked why is that. "Well, I thought you understood the cause I was fighting for—"

"But I do! I know it better than ever now."

Zeke had noticed the flintlock rod appended to his uniform belt in a leather case, as all Frodtznjepple guards were accoutered, and pondered whether Jarvis would draw it on him if it came to that.

"I've been listening to your discourses with keen interest for weeks now. Your ideas on organizing a grassroots coalition of farmers and hoboes challenged the orthodox social and economic theories of my education and experience. You've caused me to wrestle with my own conscience on what I believe to be the best route to a system of fairness and liberty and granting those with nothing a chance to work hard and make a good living for themselves."

Zeke carefully parsed Jarvis' statements, evaluating the young turnkey's true position at that moment. "And here you are having ferreted me out of the buried rusted tubes—where I would have met my end. You saved me and captured me at the same time."

Jarvis gazed at the prisoner he came to think of as a friend, one he then came to fear as the prison powers were watching his exposure to Zeke's radical ideas. Bold concepts expatiated evenings at length that caused him dismaying ruminations. "I saved you, Zeke, and I feel it was my duty to do so."

Zeke hesitated several seconds before replying: "You mean as a guard of the prison?"

"As a guardian of the principles of freedom and equality and the ability of all people to have a fair shake in life!" He moved closer to Zeke and placed his hand on his shoulder. "Zeke, I want to join you in your escape and work with you on your mission."

Jarvis' pledge produced a momentary surge of affirmation in Zeke, and the words lingered in his mind now with a sudden sense of accomplishment and promise. Here was a young jailor he came to know, a diffident, ambivalent fellow he encouraged to follow his heart and think for himself, one who was barred from speaking to him, yet Zeke continued his disquisitions every night not knowing if his pupil was listening. Now he knew he was, and wanted to join his cause, which meant if he could inspire and galvanize one individual such as Jarvis then why not a hundred, or thousand? Zeke felt moved by Jarvis' words and met his gaze with a mien of optimism as well as prudence. "Your spirit affords me auspicious notions," he said. "I am truly bestowed with real hope. But let's think through a judicious plan, Jarvis. I don't know the chances of my making it out of here, even with you on my side, but the smart bet would be that I don't. You could be shot dead with me. And even if we bust out clean you would become a fugitive at large along with me. I can't let you take on that kind of life."

Jarvis frowned: "That is my decision, Zeke. I am choosing to show you the way out of here and accompany you in your noble endeavor. Rejecting that help is an insult!"

Zeke regarded him with a searching gaze and shook his head: "Your help is beyond measurement to me, Jarvis. It will never be forgotten. I accept your help just not you coming. You can leave the job after a week or so and join my cause then. The Harvest Hootenanny will be a watershed gathering of the movement and I will need you there. You are far more valuable to me in such a manner than as a fugitive who abetted my escape."

EIGHTEEN

Jarvis pressed his case to join him, Zeke parried his pleas with great sensitivity, until Jarvis became quiet with contemplation. Finally, he met Zeke's gaze and declared with confident assurance: "Zeke, I will provide you the instructions on the best way you can break out of here. I know it can be done and you can do it. If it must be, I will hang back and join you later at the Hootenanny."

Zeke nodded with a warm smile. "Show me the way, Jarvis, and the movement will be at the Von Klobbert farm waiting for your presence."

And the turnkey led him through narrow dark passageways that wended sinuous paths through the bowels of the medieval monstrous structure that only one curious about its architecture would come to know. There were ancient rooms of torture they traversed long in desuetude with foreboding archaic apparatus, subterranean corridors littered with mysterious bones they crept among, secret surgical quarters they moved through rent with rats and skeletal remains of humans and the foulest stench. They maintained a quiet steady advance without communication until they came upon a door to a still lower level which old broken stone stairs brought them, and they climbed through piles of cryptic machines and equipment and saws before attaining the far wall where through a hole was a hidden square tunnel that seemed tight to Zeke when Jarvis said: "This will take you four-hundred feet to a terrace that overlooks the grounds to the forest. You will have to climb down four stories, make it across the grounds to the ten-foot wall and scale that." The tunnel sent a chill through Zeke, his horrific episode with savage rats very fresh. As if sensing his dread Jarvis said he believed the tunnel here was more accommodating. When Zeke asked how he knew that he replied: "I heard rumors of a tunnel built over a hundred years ago by three prisoners who labored stealthily for years before attempting to escape and were captured and sealed in their tunnel with hundreds of rats. I searched for it and found this, the one and same I believe."

Zeke chuckled slightly: "So my body will fit but will I emerge with my mind?" He embraced the turnkey one last time. "Whatever is in there I will go through it, and I will expect you at the Harvest Hootenanny."

Jarvis rejoined: "Whatever it takes, Zeke, I will be there. Godspeed to your journey." He told him to hang from the cornice on the terrace and use the hippogriff heads below to grip and lower himself. The wall to the southern sector was not far from the castle cylindrical building, he added, consisted of mortar and rock and was punctuated with jagged projections that should enable him to scale the barrier. The tunnel was daunting as Zeke crawled through the twisting confines of utter darkness, passing through several areas of obstacles clogging his advance that he concluded were the skeletal remains of the caught prisoners and the rats. He had to stop and collect his breath and will and stamina to continue many times, but he managed to reach the terrace and dash across to the edge and carefully begin his descent down the building using the hippogriff heads for his footing as Jarvis advised. Then the race across the rocky grounds—keeping to the darkest shadows until he attained the last and toughest hurdle before the forest and freedom, the imposing massive wall that seemed beyond his capabilities to mount.

Frodtznjepple was a chilling edifice from which few ever attempted to escape, none successfully, and the enclosing redoubtable wall provided the deterrence to anyone crazy enough to think about it. The first attempt to climb the wall ended with Zeke tumbling to the hard earth from more than halfway up, landing on his behind and causing him great dismay, expecting guards to open fire on him any moment. He could not see them but believed they were watching him, sure they were making sport of his tangle with the wall and would shoot him down once he made it to the top. He fell again, this time from a higher point and was badly shaken up but got so mad he came back with raging abandon and thinking of them gleefully observing him only made him bolder and more reckless in his ascent, which found a rhythmic fluidity as all tension left him, and then as he was finally able to swing one foot over the top, deafening shots rang out. He pulled the rest of himself over in a flash as a fusil-

EIGHTEEN

lade of bullets were fired at him and he jumped nearly the entire ten feet to the ground and, at least for the moment, his freedom. He ran like his legs were cyclones carrying him as they pleased and despite the chilling cacophony of firearms blasting nonstop behind him and now the barking frenzy of bloodhounds turned loose to chase him down, Zeke ran his fastest and surest in threading a path through the dense woods. It felt familiar all of a sudden to him, once again being pursued by hostile foes through thick brush and too many trees, but there was never more at stake for him. The reports of the guns cracked and boomed over him with ever intensifying volume and scope and the bloodhounds feral cries of hunting him down grew louder and broader with a swelling rumbling squall that would stalk him to the very depths of darkest consciousness. He thought a shot would wing him any moment, his blood would flow, and the hounds of hell would rip apart and gnaw his fallen form. But he kept running at his mad pace and neither his flesh was torn open by a bullet nor was he overrun by a pack of hounds biting him to death. He ran with such speed as he never deemed possible, even with the trees to weave amongst, the fear of the hounds and the exhilarating triumph of escape propelled him like a leopard at full pelt. For a moment he wondered what other powers lay dormant in a man until pushed to the brink. It was a chilly November night and he wore gray and white striped cotton prison garb, but he was not cold at all. It felt good, the fall air and the earth beneath his stride and running like a wild animal in the woods. As he neared the coastline he knew he had to remain in the wilderness until he found the connecting strip of isthmus to the mainland and beyond. And as he came upon it and raced through its hilly hardscrabble terrain, a new consternation seized him that now they would overtake him, the sparser cover of woodland left him exposed. And at some point the violent din of the hounds died and the last echoes of gunfire faded in his mind, sounds of menace that actually had quieted a good ways behind him. Yet he continued at the same clip apace and penetrated the deepest recesses of the forest by running for miles and miles throughout the night, resting only as day broke raggedly through the thick cover of trees and bush. He drank from a rushing stream and sat on a boulder enshrouded in overgrowth, reclining upon a dense bramble and closing his eyes. His brief respite provided some rejuvenation before he continued still early that morning, and he pushed onward into the remote wilderness that entire day, running most of the time and covering many more miles until crossing the craggy highlands and coming upon nearly impassable crowded forest which he navigated in the fading light of dusk.

Nineteen

It was after night had fallen when Zeke heard the singing, distant, obscure, and unrecognizable but strangely inviting and not fearsome. He found himself moving towards the voices singing to better hear them and the utter darkness of the forest eventually opened to a glade that he crossed to a trail as moonlight propitiously reflected the way now. The singing grew louder and more resonant, men harmonizing in deep solemn strains that sounded warm and strong to Zeke, at times vaguely familiar. Then he could make out across the clearing and a declension in the land a surface of water shimmering in the pale moonshine, and the singing began to stir him inside with a sudden cognizance of melody and lyric. He thought they were singing "The Grub Klepto of Yuma," and he smiled and chuckled to himself and accelerated his advance despite his exhaustion, then laughing in hearty peals as they broke into what he identified as "The Moon Looks Mean When I Pass Through Moline." And he just had to run when he heard them belting out a medley of "Del Schmaug Turned Rat Fink," "Lefty Malzone Was Right," and "29 Shots of Popskull Ain't Enough, Hey Mr. Bull We're Calling Your Bluff!" As he came to the edge of the descent towards the river Zeke was filled with a joy and ebullience that deeply moved him as he realized with certainty he had somehow stumbled upon a hobo jungle way out in the isolated forest, and the notion of whether it was providence that saw him here fleetingly passed through his mind. As he began to move among them, somewhere between a dozen and two dozen hobos sitting around fires with bottles of hooch and roasted mickies on sticks, others in a makeshift tent having a meeting, and of course the several standing around the main bonfire singing the old traditional hobo songs that led him to their far-flung jungle, he felt a profound gratitude to be there with his people. He wanted to help them more than anything and his vision to unite them with farmers and lead the coalition forward into a triumphant reckoning of opportunity and justice never seemed more urgent and auspicious to him. Aside from the illumination of the fires in spots the atmosphere was dim with shifting shadows and possessed a more serious and purposeful tone than other jungles Zeke had visited. He walked around with his head down, content for the moment to simply absorb their mood and environment albeit this anonymity was short-lived. Two hoboes, one older and in a battered derby and the other rangy and sallow-faced with a long mustache, were studying Zeke from the bonfire where they stood sipping their bottles. They soon approached him with the most disconcerted expressions, squinty gazes of consternation or plain awe.

"Mister, this camp welcomes all but who is it that comes in prison duds and is the spit and image of none other than the nonpareil Zeke Borshellac?" the rangy one put to him.

Zeke met their eyes, surprised at their recognition of him, and replied: "Gentlemen, I am Zeke Borshellac, fresh from an unfortunate stint at Frodtznjepple Peninsula."

They let out gasps of disbelief mingled with snarls of disdain. The older one looked him over pit to dome and called with shock and doubt: "Hey, Floop, Geets, Quigley, youse guys! Feller here claims he's Zeke Borshellac."

Those men came over from the bonfire, hobos with whiskers and loose long coats and one was smoking a corncob. They were muttering to one another, one chortled after garbling something about the "ghost coming back from the box." Others followed them, curious with their bottles, grungy figures who stood around Zeke, mumbling that "the poor bastard hopped the twig."

The two hobos who first discovered their visitor acted like hosts of some freak show. "So it's like this, feller," the older one began, "you may look like Zeke Borshellac according to the broadsheets, but you can't be our Zeke."

"Is that right? I think I know who I am," Zeke asked with bemusement.

The men murmured with uneasy laughter. One called out: "He does resemble the picture on broadsheets. I'll give him that."

The older one straightened Zeke out with a peremptory pronouncement. "You can't be him, chief, cuz they snuffed him out in the cooler, the bastards did. A great man, he was, Zeke, and they got him." He paused in silence a beat, then declared: "But he's in all of us!" A roar rose from the group seconding that sentiment, and Zeke was now truly stunned that they knew his name and were staunchly in his corner, albeit posthumously.

He looked around at their faces, unshaven, ruddy, coarse, but alive with a new vigor and spirit he had not seen in jungles. More had gathered around him now, swigging, murmuring in curiosity, gazing at the man they thought an imposter, yet some were unsure. He now saw just past them pasted on the side of the tent one of the broadsheets they referenced, and several such posters clung to trees in the encampment. He moved towards the tent to better see it and they eagerly got out of his way and stood around him. "HEAR THE CLARION CALL, HOBOES! FARMERS COME CELEBRATE THE GREAT HARVEST WITH YOUR BROTHERS! DESTINY, FAITH, AND CONVICTION UNITE US IN SOLIDARITY TOWARDS A BETTER WORLD COME IN THE SPIRIT OF THAT INSPIRING PALADIN WHO ROSE FROM SEA AND SOIL TO LEAD OUR MOVEMENT: THE IMMORTAL ZEKE BORSHELLAC COME TO THE HOOTENANNY HARVEST AT THE VON KLOBBERT FARM" There was a large drawing of Zeke looking upon idyllic farmland with a thoughtful mien, a train passing on the horizon. He could hardly believe what he was reading and became pensive a moment, considering the new notoriety greeting him with these hoboes and the mistaken credence they seemed to put in his demise. When he again looked up at them there were several more that came over to check out the mysterious newcomer who claimed to be Zeke, and he studied their gazes that were lambently lit by the flames casting a pale hue. Those who remembered him identified with his struggle and vision, he thought, and his reputation must have burgeoned by his wrongful imprisonment and then the news of his death elevated him to the role of martyr. He met their eyes as he surveyed the assembly and saw the righteous smoldering therein, the indignation harnessed for its stamina, understanding they were incredulous but intrigued by his strange presence and claim, perhaps even entertaining a jot of suspicion he could be who he says he is.

Then he felt an urge, a stimulus from deep within to consummate their noble struggle for improving their lives, to be not only who he said he was but the Zeke Borshellac they wanted him to be. The nomadic adventurer who rose from their own ranks with a personal connection and commitment to their cause and the ability and will to lead them onward to a better, more sanguine future. The long silence seemed to strain their patience, they wanted some singular evidence of validation from the man before them who turned up from the woods, that he indeed was the cataclysmic visionary come back from the grave or whatever darkness had enveloped him to lead them onward. Finally, Zeke simply let his instinct go by reciting the lyrics of the old hobo traditional number, "Coal Car Carl Cracking Wise Near Cleveland," as if it were a prose poem, sonorously enunciating the rousing but occasionally lugubrious account of the rangy hobo who had a cannon for an arm and could strike out anyone on a bet, could outrun any railroad bull and often taunted them to come give chase, and most memorably, always kept the other hoboes laughing and in good spirits with his jokes and sharp-tongued raillery. His disappearance jumping from the coal car into the mist of crepuscular canebrakes had inspired much lore and maudlin boozing over the years among hoboes, and some very real speculation that Carl was a revenant from the ghost world where baseball was played continuously amid intermittent sojourns to earth. "Here came Coal Car Carl cracking wise / The hobo camp full-throated with cries / Laughter soon swelled like a whirling calliope / As the flame-throwing hobo hurled brickbats at one particular dope." After a few stanzas a rowdy, liquored-up voice called from the rear of the gathering: "Hey, Zeke! If

NINETEEN

you're Zeke show us some of that old showmanship you were known for!" A broken-nosed grinning hobo in an oilcloth coat and flattened stovepipe yelled it. Zeke knew he had to convince them and he instantly launched himself into a spinning, squat-thrusting, hopping, diving maniac who belted a brilliant song of mad poetic incoherence that epitomized the poignance of a lonely night on a barreling boxcar. He only performed for a few fleeting moments there by the tent in the scant illumination of the flames far fluttering, but it was more than enough. There was stark silence followed by a kind of murmuring astonishment mingled with the burbling of laughter, they now knew Zeke was their man miraculously materializing in their twilight camp. One half-crocked hobo in a weathered tartan coat now called out what most had to be thinking: "Zeke, nobody comes out of Froddy once they go in! Unless they swung from a necktie! You beat the bastards!"

Zeke thought of Jarvis and answered: "I was lucky to bust out. I'm on borrowed time now. They'll be coming for me forever."

Another rugged loopy one responded: "Then they're gonna have to come for all of us, ain't that right, fellers?!"

And a sudden raucous roar rose like a clap of thunder among the surrounding crowd of hoboes, the entire jungle now yelling with intensity for Zeke. He was moved by their wild cries of heartfelt faith and unwavering ardent belief in him and the noble path he has been forging.

"Let's all move close to the fire and share our stories of struggle and survival and the singular esprit de corps that remains so ineradicable among us," the revered leader of burgeoning legend suggested, and they quietly followed him as he simply strode towards the effulgence of the flames and sat upon a large stone. As they all found places to recline Zeke noticed how the gathering had grown as hoboes were ever arriving, apparently aware of the campsite, and he also spotted a smattering represented in a contingent that did not seem to be hoboes. Upon closer scrutiny he pegged this group as farmers, which buoyed his spirit a good deal. He raised the bottle of whiskey the hoboes had provided him and spoke calmly and assuredly: "Our brothers of the soil are among us this evening, the finest of sodbusters who understand the true way forward is to partner with the lost peripatetic souls who carry on the good fight across the heartland under moonlit skies. In solidarity we press ahead for our existential rights, the crops we grow to feed the impoverished, the hungry ones up against it, the justice for farmers who cannot make a living anymore. Let's drink to our common cause of ensuring our voices are heard and collective power is felt in working for a better way of life for all of us." He felt the strength and conviction rooted in struggle and hard times in his voice. He was profoundly affected by the new sense of veneration with which they regarded him, the unanimous esteem, if not awe, they now invested in him as their bellwether and champion almost mythically risen from the road, the sea, the soil, and now miraculously resurrected through his astonishing manifestation. He saw the hope and belief in their upward gazes at him and would rather die than let them down. His jailbreak exponentially potentiated his advocacy stature to that of larger than life proportions, a legend in the making. And as Zeke came to fully comprehend this in the remote jungle, where he spent the night on a bed of straw in a tent they rigged up for him, he understood the grave responsibility as the leader of the movement he assumed going forward. Nonetheless, exhausted as he was from the most consequential, daring and exhilarating night of his life, Zeke slept soundly and straight through until dawn.

When he stirred from his tent, a cadre of hoboes and one of the farmers were there waiting to guide him to a fine breakfast of mickies and peppered rutabagas roasting over a new fire. They handed him a steaming cup of joe and he sat on his same rock from the evening, and all eyes were upon him, silent, adulatory, agog, almost as if reacquainting themselves with the shock of his arrival not being a product of bad liquor or illusory sensibilities of some phenomena or another. They appeared to be waiting on his addressing them, their numbers swelling by the hour and nearly double the hoboes he first encountered at the jungle the night before. He was pleased to observe most of the newcomers were farmers, hardy men of the soil who could no longer make it and heeded the movement's call to join forces with the droves of hoboes. He raised his bottle of whiskey and declared: "Let us as one swig a staunch eye-opener and gird our loins for the hard work that must be done. Together we will prevail and achieve a new and equitable way of life for generations to come."

They drank and let out shouts of approbation. Zeke paused until the clamor faded and remained silent for a minute before picking up three nearby potatoes and began to juggle them. It was a skill he acquired in his Grackler days and he was a proficient juggler, and quickly he had the mickies flying a good hundred feet into the air. Then he threw one to a farmer seated furthest away, immediately whipping one to a hobo also in the rear, and both men caught their projectiles. The third one Zeke held aloft and fulminated: "What we grow is ours to feed our friends in need! We will take care of all those who are hungry! The good soil offers sustenance and is everyone's earth of deliverance!" He surprised himself with the gravity of his statement, yet it came from someplace in him, an almost instinctual message that they seemed to want to hear.

He noticed from the corner of his eye a bespectacled hobo wearing a grungy raincoat and loose, tattered necktie, who was writing in a journal, the same fellow who was doing the same the evening before, and he realized he was some kind of unofficial recording secretary responsible for keeping a record of these momentous events. Now four hobo elders approached him from the side and the one with brindled long whiskers began lowly: "We think you will want to change from your prison garb, Zeke, and we have a suggestion of the sort of garb a leader of your caliber ought to consider."

Impressed with their solicitude and aware he would need civilian clothes, Zeke heard them out as they called upon a former chandler of rugged gear for farm, ranch and other hands who brave the elements in their work. Pud Stupilis was a slim, unassuming fellow who himself had fallen into the ranks of hoboes lately but had some surplus broadcloth and woolen material with which to fashion an apropos suit for the coronated front man. The hobo elders explained that they held a parley through the evening to determine the design for Stupilis to make his outfit and now Pud presented him the sketchpad with their raiment ideas. Zeke could not recognize what the squiggly scribbly drawings represented even on the most elemental level, the garment outlines and such, but he allowed them to steer him over to a jerry-rigged tent where the freshly-sewn togs awaited him. The crowd quietly followed them and before Zeke could enter the tent to try on the clothes, the hobo elders formally acknowledged the contribution of the chandler Stupilis to their great movement by his tireless effort to produce the suit they would shortly all see. While Zeke dressed inside, the chandler was tongue-tied and irked the elders failed to notify him he would be expected to give a speech. Overcome by nerves he began to shake, but managed to talk about his grandfather who taught him the value of appearance and fine clothing, despite himself being something of a homunculus who favored an old balmacaan with garish frogging and a cape so long tripping on it became his calling card. Stupilis grew tearful as he recalled his grandfather's irrational taste and stern detachment from his family, yet would find himself chuckling at recalling the man's lapses into adopting other personae for periods, such as the headless lion tamer's ghost, Flank, who wanted his head back but was reluctant to admit it for fear of implicating his lion.

    During one such rib-tickling anecdote of Pud's patter, Zeke emerged fully attired in the new suit Stupilis handcrafted for him. The trousers were a rich brown heavy, thick cut of worsted broadcloth with orange side stripes and trim to symbolize the earth and its fruits, the shirt a deep red with yellow to symbolize the sun as raiser of crops and provider of warmth, and the coat of sturdy oilskin charcoal with green trim as a tribute to those who ride the rails all night. Down one sleeve of his coat in amber threads was sewn an image of a pitchfork, and along the other was an orange bindlestick. A round patch depicting a locomotive crossing a moonlit prairie was sewn into the front right side, a similar patch showing a plough out past the cornfields in the fading light was on the left side. How Pud Stupilis ever made such a coat with such embellishments was an utter mystery to Zeke.

NINETEEN

Shod in a sturdy pair of black boots left for him as well, Zeke felt good in his new outfit, well prepared for the great challenges he knew lay ahead for the movement. A few hoboes now greeted him with claps and it began to catch on until they all stood around him applauding with loud fervor.

A visage of a short grinning hobo out among the aggregation seemed familiar, that cheeky glint in his eye and the beat-up derby cocked on a slant struck him as one he knew, and he moved towards him and now noticed the hobo beside him, lanky, long-haired, and laughing and the name fell from his lips, "Joke," and then he remembered the short one, "The Captain." Hoboes he met with Gunther one night in the back alleys of Bluddenville amid the ship propellers, only now more weathered by time.

"We played some horseshoes a long time ago," Zeke said.

The men chuckled and The Captain replied: "Yep, that's right Zeke. And you could pitch 'em. We knew you were with us back then!"

And Joke added: "And *one of us* all right. Yep, we knew it was you when we seen ya on the broadsheets back in Bluddenville."

They assured him a good number of hoboes were coming up from Bluddenville for the Hootenanny Harvest, and a smattering of shouts from the gathering vouched for his statement. Zeke smiled thinking of his Bluddenville days, albeit with an underpinning of darkness ever inescapable. Joke swigged a bottle thirstily and with great merriment called to him: "C'mon, Zeke! Let's pitch some horseshoes out by the pit we got set up!"

And that is where they all went. It was decided that the first shoe in the morning's tournament would be pitched by Zeke, and The Captain delivered a robust introduction of his "old pal" from yesteryear who one unforgettable evening around the "peculiar enchantment of wee hour bent pitched 'em like any of us who'd been at it for years!" Impromptu ceremony now guided the events of the makeshift horseshoe pit as Zeke felt compelled to offer a few remarks before launching his shoe, and he held the iron U-shaped plate aloft while projecting his bottle of whiskey outward with his left hand to pronounce symbolically the "triumph for hoboes, farmers, and all the disaffected disregarded folks who have nothing and come from nothing, we will persevere in pitching 'em until the lay of the land is made right and fair and free! The ringers may not come immediately, but they will come, and freedom will ring out across our land!"

A great roar of approval went up from the crowd and now they all began clinking bottles, and of course *everybody* had to touch bottles with Zeke with the "Cheers, brother!" refrain, so by the time Zeke was ready to actually pitch his shoe he sensed some of the air went out of the ceremony's momentousness and he sought to restore it with a classic hobo number, "Boozing and Rumbling O'er Prairies," which by the second verse the entire body was belting out one of the beloved anthems all hoboes knew by heart. The rousing sing-along soon segued into a stark silence as Zeke prepared to finally toss his shoe, and recognizing the significance scoring a ringer would provide he allowed himself a rather elaborate series of warm-up rituals which he thought would help his concentration. Prone to such rituals in the past, he usually limited them to deep-knee bends, a mélange of backwards sashaying whirligigs and heel-clicking, on this occasion he also included a manic running broad jump followed by a pantomime routine about a panhandler and a harried caballero. Most of the crowd found his dilatory maneuvers amusing, but halfway into the pantomime bit he could sense a low grumble of impatience beginning to manifest. It was time to throw the horseshoe and Zeke opted for a high spinning arc that came down a good four feet from the stake, greeted by a quiet murmur of sighs and groans. The Captain, an unsinkable master of ceremonies, strode grinning towards the stake with his hands out enjoining their patience, retrieved the shoe and returned it to Zeke. After another round of warm-up rituals, streamlined however by scrapping the pantomime except for the caballero's comically inept horsemanship piece, again Zeke pitched it, even higher but with less rotation and equally poor accuracy as it fell several feet off from the stake. The Captain quickly recovered the shoe for another throw, his grin and sense of control slightly reduced, the importance of Zeke, as the leader of the movement, scoring a ringer here to kick off their tournament not lost to either of them or the hobo elders or most of the hoboes and sodbusters assembled. Several more pitches fast followed, each one different in the nature of the warm-up ritual albeit it the caballero's schtick slued increasingly frantic with song, while the throws themselves were consistently errant, a couple even landing among the crowd and one especially pie-eyed hobo getting clocked topside. All told, it took Zeke upwards of forty pitches to finally score a ringer—a couple of leaners along the way proved controversial as some hoboes deemed that sufficient for ceremonial purposes but were shouted down by the throng—and the tournament, almost anticlimactic by then, was able to proceed.

Later, the sodbusters had sought Zeke's presence to commence a tournament of their own that invoked the old-time pastoral game of Sack 'n Slip So Long, aka, Sanslipso, a traditional contest best described as a combination of potato sack races, Johnny on a Pony, ducks and drakes, bocce, and running bases. The ranks of farmers at the jungle continued to grow apace, many arriving out of desperation having lost their farms to foreclosures by banks. The hands they employed were likewise cut loose and showing up broke, lost, and indignant. Among these furious forlorn farmers was one that caught Zeke's attention, a familiar face he recalled from one of his visits to the Grange meetings, the raw-boned sodbuster who wanted farmers to build their own stores to sell their crops, Wyatt Plantwater. He still smoked a large pipe, generating clouds of smoke, which Zeke waded through to greet the man. Plantwater lost his farm and was a study in despair and appeared stupefied by Zeke's presence. "The word around the rails I been hoppin' is that you perished at Froddy," he began, "like all the poor bastards who end up there." He puffed on his pipe and gazed at the movement's last best hope with marvel. "I lost my farm and everything I owned. My family went to my mother-in-law's. But I'm with you all the way, Zeke."

Moved by the man's misfortune and utter sincerity of trust in his leadership, Zeke could not refrain from plumbing his memory for any tidbit of information, any morsel of news regarding the Von Klobbert farm, noting his erstwhile connection to the Grange and Horst Schtuckgloo and Booth Booley, particularly in the most inviolable beatings of his heart, Balthazar and the dairymaid, but the once vocal Grange member had nothing to offer. He hadn't been to a Grange meeting in many months, hadn't seen Horst or Booth or any of those fellows since he saw Zeke at one way back. "I'm no longer a farmer trying to survive, Zeke," he expounded, "I'm a human being trying to survive. That means I'm a hobo now truth told, like a lot of farmers who've lost everything. We're all hoboes."

Plantwater assumed master of ceremonies duty as the farmers gathered on the sloping grassy field adjacent the campfire that was designated for the Sanslipso game, thought to be a morale booster in the vein of the hoboes' horseshoe competition. Of course, ceremony was necessary as prelude to the start of the contest and that naturally revolved around Zeke. A roly-poly farm hand with a long beard and bulbous red nose known as Corn Cavendish, who worked on Plantwater's farm for years, assembled all the farmers around the field in an oblong potato-shaped circle before assiduously folding one of the potato sacks and marching high-step style across the middle to present it to Zeke. "Thank you, farmer," Zeke said, clueless as to what they expected him to do. He hesitated, and for a long span of uneasy stillness nobody moved until Corn Cavendish pivoted caddy-corner in a confused shuffle which collapsed into a hard fall. The man was obviously embarrassed but his attempt to mask his discomfort by guffawing in a histrionic conniption only made it worse for himself as his farmer brothers mocked him and playfully hurled clumps of weeds at him. Pelted on his forehead with a sizable dirt bomb, Cavendish launched into a series of backward somersaults and highland yodeling he picked up in the Black Mountains as a boy, and it occurred to Zeke that the farmers themselves knew no ceremonial maneuvers to kick off a game of Sanslipso. Plantwater appeared baffled and chagrined, only shrugging as Zeke gazed at him. Therefore, Zeke decided he would invent one himself simply to move things along.

NINETEEN

Opening the sack with a flourish he jumped into it, pulled it up to his chin, and began jumping around the field curiously proclaiming improvised poetry. Meanwhile, spinning on his back in circles was Corn Cavendish. The farmers approved and the vocal wild one with a blade of tall grass jutting from his mouth and candy cane striped suspenders and a shock of blond hair, Dirk Freckler, whipped the baseball at Zeke, who caught it barehanded, which prompted everyone to cheer before Zeke spotted a young farmer suddenly bolting for a base and pegged him out with a powerful throw to Hunter Boogle, the aging chicken meister, who easily put the tag on Jeffrey Plystrock, who got a late jump and was a poor runner. Still, the audience whooped with delight and before settling down broke into the traditional farmers' anthem, "Sodbusters Sockeroo." They sang standing tall and proud, belting out the beloved classic lauding the agricultural way of life that for them carried a poignant wistfulness invoking the threat of modern times and so-called "progress" on their work of the soil. Perhaps that is precisely the reason they sang with such vociferous defiance mingled with traces of tears falling from some of their eyeballs, it was hard and painful to be reminded of the cruel downturns many had been through since their boyhoods on farms singing that same blithe number. But it was *their* song and damn the world itself if they could not sing it loud as hell with heads high and a sense of hope, however faint and fleet, in their hearts. And they were drinking their whisky with gusto as a result which soon lent the game of Sanslipso a rougher, more harum-scarum dimension not usually associated with it. The farmers played with reckless abandon and a gratuitous violence they seemed to relish and laugh off, and Zeke couldn't tell if they really didn't know the rules of Sanslipso or were simply feeling their oats and having fun. It looked to him that they were just beating the hell out of one another while hopping around in the sacks and skipping rocks in the streamlet by the wooded area, while intermittently chucking baseballs at one another amidst roughhousing in a mindless free-for-all. Yet there was a score being painstakingly maintained by a grave geezer in suspenders and a broad-brimmed hat, who the players all deferred to in his rulings and general control of the game. Every so often this geezer marched onto the field and with fingers in his mouth whistled like a crazed bird before executing a series of complicated arm signals. Some even appeared to comprehend his apparent rulings. Zeke could not decide if the Sanslipso match was a random tumultuous free-for-all with inexperienced players or a game of such byzantine facets and nuances that to the novice it simply appeared violent chaos. In the end it did not matter to him, as the farmers unequivocally appeared to revel in the fierce competitive challenge of the madcap sport and continued playing, punctuated only by periodic tobacco and whiskey breaks over by the stream (which many soaked their heads in to refresh themselves), well towards the waning of afternoon with dusk pending. And over on the adjacent fields the hobos too went well into the afternoon with their horseshoes tournament, as many new arrivals joined the action and a festive spirit of solidarity swelled among the spectators in belting out the old hobo numbers of yore, such as "Hey Mr. Brakeman, Your Choo Choo is A-Chug-Chugging While We Chug-A-Lug It," and "Roamin' on the Lost Locomotive with Duke and Chet," and they were roasting mickies and boozing with a boisterous fellowship of swaying and roistering, mostly singing the hobo songs with an undeniable ebullience.

    As the shanks of the coming evening settled over the air both groups began to wind down their games and gradually made their ways over to the great bonfire, already stoked up and roaring now, to begin the supper of mickies and root vegetables contributed by some of the arriving farmers for roasting on sticks. It was a jovial supper of farmers and hoboes, fresh off the playing fields and exhilarated by the momentousness they all seemed to sense, as they stood around the great fire with their sticks of flame-cooked yield from the good earth and ubiquitous bottles and hard-won stories of struggle told with gusto and even humor, they seemed to feel the change that was coming, they wanted that great cataclysm of progress to break open to be able to ride it home for all those to follow their path, and they were ever so ready to fight for such a new life of opportunity and dignity, a fair shake goddammit, and the man of the times, one of their very own, the mythic phoenix who would lead them, now stood among them and addressed them with his bottle in hand in a postprandial speech which the slight farmer, already seen around as the recording secretary of sorts, was close by with pencil in hand and head down transcribing his words. And they were plain words the men understood, words that delivered episodes of his own journey that connected with such men, words that knew not just the pain of hardship and defeat and calamity and lostness, but resilience and perseverance and faith, and he told them that at morning's first light they would be moving out on a march to the Von Klobbert farm for the Hootenanny Harvest. "There we will join with our brothers both hobo and farmer, the lines are blurring fast my friends, and together we will make our movement known, let them see who we are and what we demand, and our cause will advance towards the destiny of history." He stepped away from the crowd and the fire and moved toward a tent with hobo and farmer elders at his side, where they had a large map spread across a makeshift table and with a long stick in hand Zeke began planning the best route their march can take through mostly woodland and hills to the Von Klobbert farm. The Hootenanny Harvest was on Saturday afternoon, they would set out Friday at dawn and would just make it, at least so they thought according to the calculations of logistics. It was an old worn map wanting for topographical detail and the territories were limited in pinpointing the locus of many villages and even the general propinquity of burgs seemed fatuously arbitrary. The hobo and farmer elders in the tent recognized the formidable obstacles that lay ahead of their march as none seemed to recollect how they even made it to the present jungle constituted in remote uncharted primordial woodland. Not a single arrival, farmer or hobo, had any familiarity with the far-flung region and could hardly be relied upon as a guide. Zeke himself penetrated far deeper into the forest reaches in his escape than he thought imaginable and was utterly lost in the isolated surroundings. Yet all eyes looked to him as he bent over the map on the table and brandished his long stick in the manner of a general strategizing a plan of attack, then pacing around the table with the stick now carried horizontally behind his back. He padded deliberately, slowly, reflectively. He knew there were serious challenges and not just making it to the Hootenanny on time, but to their making it there at all, so deeply remote was their point of origin. But it was his duty to project confidence in their course insofar as he could tell everyone had concerns over the harsh terrain and doubts about their capability to find their way to the farm. Zeke remained steadfastly sanguine in his command of the march and set a southeasterly route for them to commence at dawn, and every one of them believed they would slog forward on the right path that would transport them there. Everyone, that is, except Zeke himself who harbored a residue of misgivings despite convincing himself for the most part that their march *had to make it to the Von Klobbert farm* and nothing could prevent the momentum of their movement from meeting with its destiny, certainly his own fate with the woman he loved and the dog he missed so terribly, that those marchers would join countless others converging at this Hootenanny and his contingent *would show up out of nowhere if it meant providence itself guided them there.*

Outside the tent they heard the deep raw notes of a lone trombone, mysterious but also jaunty in a strange way, and the elders waited for Zeke to emerge first from the tent and he saw the assemblage had swelled around them, extending deep towards the bonfire beyond. A rangy hobo in a long plaid coat and banged-up trilby stood up front and blew his old slipstick with intensity and proficiency, handling the slide with the panache of a crowd-pleaser. And then an old farmer with a long mustache, a red scarf with a corn design, and a floppy hat began playing a harmonica, ripping a solemn yet stirring melody that blended with the horn to create a true sound of their moment in time, for it struck robust notes of the earth and the rumbling speed of a train at night. A soft, steady tattoo of a drum now could be heard and then a young fellow, a skinny tatterdemalion with shaggy brown hair, appeared from the throng with a single drum harnessed to his chest that he beat with a rousing current of the mission and adventure ahead of them. The newfound combo infused a tone and texture of sweeping auspicious gravity, punctuated by pixilated riffs, to the present solemn moments and the hoboes and farmers watched Zeke with a transfixed sense of hope and yearning as he moved before them with the elders. They wanted him to assure them again that their time had come and he would lead them into the yawning breakthrough of progress, into the landscape of history, the faces remained riveted upon him and he tried to really meet their gazes, many now with wonder, awe, and new faith seeing him in the flesh for the first time, the weathered, the dog-tired, the angry, the drunken, the pale wind-burnt, the black enraged, the black beaten-down, the black resolved, the brown inspirited, the brown boisterously eager, the red wild and daring, all the beleaguered farmers stripped of soil but not will to fight back, all the broken, alienated, unwavering undaunted hoboes, all of them he looked into their eyes and saw himself and he opened his talk with the words: "It is always those born well, those on the other side of power that want to clobber us with it, exclude us like wild animals at bay, and that, my friends, is a lousy dirty trick. Well, they can't get away with it any more. I say to you, 'What about us?! What about our lives in this world?! Aren't we here too?!' Our day is coming and theirs is waning. Tomorrow we begin our journey to a new beginning. We march to the Von Klobbert farm and there the meaning of our sacred alliance of hoboes and farmers will be delivered." Zeke thrust his whiskey bottle aloft and shouted, "Godspeed to every sodbuster and tramp who walks with us!"

And they all took lusty hits and the band struck up a heartening melody, low at first, a warm poignant tune they all seemed to know which they began by humming the rhythms and then singing in unison in strong throaty fullness. After the first verse the band struck up accompaniment that really swung the harmony into a full bustling grand number that transformed the sound into something sublime and deeply moving. They all knew the song so well too, Zeke reflected in marvel, and the musicians were so deft and fervently lost in their instruments, and it was a song he had never heard before. How can all these hoboes and farmers and the little combo know it so well, so passionately and masterfully, and it be utterly foreign to Zeke? The mystery soon cleared as Zeke listened to the lyrics they sang with such heartfelt gusto. "Out of the sea and up from the soil / Zeke Borshellac came and to him we remain loyal / He traveled the land and struggled through much / took a lot on the chin as hobo and farmer and such / Zeke we trust cause he's one of us, by goddy / like a phoenix he busted out of cursed old Froddy / Out of the sea and up from the soil / Zeke Borshellac came and to him we remain loyal." The new anthem of the movement was written that day by, fittingly, a hobo and a farmer, who woodshedded with the harp player in a copse by the bend in the stream while the others were playing Sanslipso and horseshoes, and later they introduced their work to the trombonist and the drummer and a core group of hobo and farmer singers to learn it.

"Out of the Sea and Up from the Soil" was an instant hit with everyone from the moment it was penned and first sung by that small cadre, and by the time Zeke issued from the map tent the entire throng knew it and loved it very much. He was deeply moved as he stood before them, surveying with wonder the chorus of committed faces, so deeply touched by the beautiful song about him that he felt goosebumps and a surge of profound duty and honor at their investing so much in him as their leader. And the depth and weight of such responsibility suddenly unleashed a terrible fear within him as he thought about those yearning faces out there and how they were counting on him. But the fear was part and parcel to his being the one out front for them and he understood that. He knew it was indispensable because it represented the irreducible doubt in them, and him, of their prevailing one day and rising above the pain and suffering of their oppression and exploitation. Facing that fear would propel him forward to find the fortitude, the path ahead. But right now, the magnificence of the stirring tribute tune left him greatly moved, exhilarated, yet ineluctably there was that fear lacing though it too. As the number wound down it was apparent the throng expected their leader to address them with a few remarks, and when Zeke demurred they filled the awkward quiet by spontaneously continuing the song with the humming Zeke heard before, a great embracing sea of the glorious melody of their new song, and Zeke felt the warmth and bolstering elicitation to oration in their rhythmic buzz. He began to speak, noticed the meager farmer who was chronicling it all peering up at him like a longing little boy with his pencil and notepad cocked and ready, offered him a smile of confidence before proceeding. "I look out at all of you and know the hardships, troubles and travails, that every one of you has been through, and the perseverance and strength it took for you to make it here to form our great coalition. I may be the one out front in the leadership role, but you are inside me—*I am you, we are one*— and together that is what drives our movement forward. I don't have any specifics, you know that, there is no time for all that. We're going to rectify the lopsided imbalance of power and privilege that precludes us from the better lives we deserve. We are going to assert that right cause it is the natural right of everyone in existence." He paused a few moments before deciding he had said enough and then stepped away, the elders steering him towards his tent for the evening, as the crowd broke into uproarious applause and raucous cheers before serenading Zeke as he moved through them with another round of "Out of the Sea and Up from the Soil."

Twenty

HE WAS UP before any of them and lit a fire under a small pot of coffee, which he drank with whiskey while walking in the darkness. He strode down by the stream, listening to its gentle purl and the susurrous stirrings of animals and faint chirp of birds heralding the imminent dawn. Once the earliest light appeared he told himself he would have to waken everyone for the journey, as getting a good jump was not only necessary to cover the miles but important for morale. Some ruffling snorts of snoring men reached him now and he mused upon the dreams they may be having, especially after such a spirited evening of sanguine sentiments. He nibbled on some pemmican still in his pocket and moved towards the jerry-rigged stick tent where he thought the musicians were sleeping and, spotting the trombonist curled under a blanket, he shook him awake and bid him to play his slide. "I need you to wake 'em up, Tommy," he said with a half-smile. Tommy Dunkirk, an affable popular fellow in the jungle, appreciated being tapped to rouse them for assembly. He blew a roaring rhythmic blast from the old hobo number, "The Grub Klepto of Yuma," and could hardly refrain from chuckling in amusement as incrementally hoboes and farmers began coming to consciousness in not always the most accepting manner, some even hollering in dismay. But it worked quite well and all in all they rose rather quickly from their impromptu bunks and without any direction from Zeke or anyone else, instinctually mustered in rows on the grassy field and stood somewhat at attention as Zeke now came to address them. He moved past their half-asleep, barely upright postures, gazing at them, sizing them up and tilting his cogitations towards preparing them for the long march. He

TWENTY

said they would be moving out after they had some breakfast (roasted mickies again) and knocked back some coffee and whiskey. He hoisted his own bottle and led them in the ceremonial eye-opener, all whooping as he did to accentuate his swig. Then he stressed the importance of being loose and resilient, open to the vagaries of the path forward, and began shaking and twirling and convulsing higgledy-piggledy in a paroxysm of sudden madness, and so they all did the same until Zeke flopped onto the earth in a final flourish. Then he sprung up as if agitated pell-mell and again exploded in a fit of jerky spasms before suddenly flopping once more, and they all mimicked his lead, and he continued again and again until everybody had enough and was in stitches and yapping like monkeys over nothing except Zeke drilling them in such cryptic up-and-down calisthenics without uttering a word throughout. By the time he was through and ordered everyone up, many were out of breath and needed a break. So Zeke led them in a solemn but passionate rendition of the old hobo classic heard in jungles everywhere, "Paducah Rain Tastes Salty, Mr. Entwhistle," which worked its cathartic medicine into their resuscitation and soon they were assembling near the great black bonfire cinders, two abreast, farmers and hoboes paired up just as Zeke called for them to do, the formation for the march he felt was right despite their falling short of farmers and eighteen hoboes would have to march with themselves.

Zeke was about to declare the moment had arrived for them to break camp and move out when he noticed a contingent of farmers, the sort still new to the migrant existence and fresh from their farm calamities, kicking up a half-crocked incoherent rhubarb with some hoboes. They were sore over waking up to a hobo melody and then Zeke going and singing the old hobo chestnut, or so Zeke thought. When he launched into "Don't Eat Pegler's Goo Goo Crop," the old farm ditty, he thought the bracing good-time rendition he offered would suffice in balancing the musical selections of the pre-march, but he never got through half of the number before they drowned him out with guttural incomprehensible chants.

"We don't want it that way!" the one in heavy oilskin overalls and a long-brimmed wheat-colored cap, known as Averill Overbalker, stated very clearly in stentorian deep tone.

"We ought'n have to ask for such a thing, Zeke!" a lugubrious lanky farmhand rigged out in some odd preacher get-up, Seward Snover, clarified the point.

But when Zeke acknowledged these lubricated testy farmers and again started to call for their breaking camp to begin the march, they once more began squawking about the dearth of farmers' songs throughout the morning so far. While seemingly a minor flap that could have been ignored with a bracing reminder of the larger collective goal at hand, Zeke recognized the importance of his finding the right resolution without appearing to take sides. He paused in pensive reflection as a quiet fell over everyone, all eyes on their leader as he began to pace with his gaze down and stroking his chin. As a flock of geese flew over them in stark contrast to their protracted silence, Zeke looked skyward while maintaining his forward movement and the glare of morning sun disoriented him just as his step caught a slick patch of grass and cottontail poo, and he found himself falling backwards onto his rear end. Before such an image of buffoonery could plant itself in their minds and undermine their confidence in him, Zeke instantaneously sprung to his feet with such theatrical verve he left no doubt that surely his tumble was performed on purpose. "The songs we sing inspire, strengthen, and propel us forward in our movement. We revel in both farmer and hobo songs. We are each other, powerfully together . . ." he proclaimed before breaking into an improvised amalgam of the farm and hobo classics, "When the Bastards Bury Me I'm Growing Back as a Cornstalk" and "The Corncakes Skunk Loomis Cooked Us in Muscogee." As Zeke belted out the hybrid number he transformed himself into a stage version of a burgeoning cornstalk as well as playing Skunk Loomis preparing his corncakes with the very same freshly risen corn. And he somehow melded the two melodies and lyrics into a fine tuneful number all its own, thereafter known as "Cornstalks to Corncakes" among the marchers and the movement. A bravura brilliant stroke of showmanship put across by Zeke which no one who was there could ever forget. And, after a lengthy pause in which everyone appeared to bask in the glow of the extraordinary song that for a few moments transported them, they quietly fell back into the two lines, hoboes and farmers partnered, and began walking behind Zeke.

There was no cognitive awareness that a momentous march had indeed officially commenced, rather it simply advanced in a natural way as they proceeded across open fields of grass and hills canopied with tall trees. Even the slight fellow who had been busily recording his observations in his notebook did not reach for his pen. He seemed reflective, pensive, moving forward with the others as an act of inevitability not unlike a vessel sailing from its dock out to sea. It was time to go and off they went, but soon after they traveled a couple of miles they began to sing and that seemed to summon their sensibilities to the challenges ahead. They sang softly and in fine warm harmony that struck Zeke as evidential underpinning to their unity and esprit de corps. They alternated hobo and farmer numbers until they sang "Out of the Sea and Up from the Soil," the trombonist now adding notes soon to be joined by the melancholy rhythms of the harmonica player, the drummer finally providing backbeat. The marchers sang their new anthem and paean to Zeke many times and in a variety of forms that morning, Zeke the only one who withheld his voice. He felt self-conscious singing about himself, but the powerful tune moved him deeply and he swore once more he would rather die than not lead them to a place where they can find a fair shake and better lives.

They maintained a brisk pace and hopeful spirits through the morning and much of the afternoon, penetrating deep into the forest and surmounting rocky hills, wading across many streams, and coming upon a barren wasteland of rubble and earth spotted with abandoned crumbling buildings. They could feel the lives once lived amid the endless deterioration and desolation, the people who left the ruins behind as a reminder to those chancing upon them, and the marchers were quieted by the utter bleakness. As if to counter the enveloping darkness they began to hum "Out of the Sea and Up From the Soil" in solemn restrained tones. After a while as the despair grew more ominous and oppressive around them, Zeke joined the hummers and he too once again felt sustained by the singular song that was written about him. He fended off a jolt of doubt about their course and called out for the marchers to halt and take a break, as he hopped upon a mound of broken bricks and stone, a cairn he imagined, and led them in a toast. "To the souls who once walked these ruins we pass through, and the hopes and dreams that once carried them through their days!" he bellowed to the swarm around the dirt and rubble. "Who were they, Zeke? Were they good folk?" Zeke paused and thought about that. "What does it matter who they were? They were people, and people are intrinsically good. Sometimes we have to fight for the good in ourselves, sometimes against the bad in others." He paused in reflection. "But I believe people are mostly good." Shouts of approval went up and they all drank, some crying out about "fighting the good fight!"

They pressed on as night fell and after climbing a weedy foggy rise came upon a meadow of scrub and high grass and an occasional enormous tree, threading their advance through the overgrown but vast fields. It was Clyde Quigley, belying his aging haggard form with a crazy-legged jig of excitement, who first sighted the tracks glinting in the moonlight projecting from the great forest that reappeared on the horizon. "Hey! Yonder the rails are shimmery! Whereupon tracks show up a train to somewhere ought to come around!"

Much ferment and clamor ensued as the march soon came to a halt. An incipient row began to grow among the men, one side headed by hoboes Floop, The Captain, and Quigley pressing for following the tracks, the other, consisting of sodbusters Rye Boogle, Dirk Freckler and Averill Overbacker arguing to stay the course. The dispute broke down according to affiliation, all hoboes for the tracks and all farmers for bypassing them. Zeke saw promise in the tracks simply because he knew they were utterly lost in the deep recesses of uncharted forest and a railroad line had to lead somewhere, he reasoned. The old map he consulted again with the elders proved useless, except it seemed to confirm they were indeed standing on land, not afloat at sea. But the farmers were not having it and mainly, he concluded, because all things railroad were associated with hoboes, and they would not cede such a matter of importance to their itinerant brothers.

"We must not attach untoward identifications to what we come across, as they may speed our journey," he declared to the assembly of men. "Would I reject a tendered ear of corn to stem my hunger because it is the product of the farmer?" He surveyed their faces, swigged some whiskey, and answered his own question. "No, I would not." He padded about as that sank in with them, then added, "Would I reject a slug of whiskey to ease my pain because it was tendered by a hobo?" He waited a moment, padding. "No, I would not."

Floop darted from a tree towards Zeke and histrionically took a pull on his bottle, echoing as if in song, "No, I would not," and he elicited a smattering of laughs. When the hard-nosed whilom wheat farmer Dirk Freckler let fly a "No, I would not!" of his own, a much more defiant declaration also with a twist of lyricism followed by a pull on his whiskey, the crazy-eyed sportive Rye Boogle added a sentiment shared by many: "I wouldn't turn down a slug of hooch from nobody."

A long heavy silence ensued before the band instinctually struck up a splendid melody of "Our Milk Cow Named McTavish and the Carved Baker Figurine" and its beguiling but moving stark notes seemed to effectuate an almost metaphysical contemplation among everyone for several minutes afterwards until they all simply began marching along the railroad tracks into the forest.

After a few miles they were enveloped in complete darkness, surrounded by dense trees and bush far removed from the kind of woodland people can traverse. The tracks alone cut through the vegetation, though increasingly the marchers had to push through it as it had grown over the rails onto the crossties. Quietly and with an increasing anxiousness among them they pressed onward, Zeke out front maintaining a staunch confidence via singing an oddly syncopated dazzling version of "Our Milk Cow Named McTavish . . ." which left the men more confused and distracted from their deep forest oblivion. And it wasn't long before the tracks were completely overgrown with unrestrained plant life, skeins of dominant weeds filling every void, albeit this hardly mattered as the railroad tracks simply terminated in the dark tangled bowels of the woods. Consternation and chagrin coursed through the throng of blocked hoboes and farmers who massed among the unruly vegetation and looked to Zeke for direction and leadership in finding a path forward. Zeke felt a nameless sense of guilt in their lostness and a lonely sickness of despair in contemplating a next move, as he sought some reassuring pronouncement he might make to the marchers. They were chastened now from their earlier buoyancy, shadowy figures hitting whiskey bottles without much to say to one another, at least nothing of confidence or hope. They could only turn to Zeke, one of almost mythic proportions to them now, the hobo farmer who busted out of Froddy and seemed sent by providence to aid them. He called for the band members to come forward into a tiny clearing amid the trees where he stood on a rocky little mound of red earth, and slowly the musicians emerged, heeding the call of duty despite their drunken frustration, and Zeke welcomed at his side his trombonist, harp player, and drummer, three fellows he had grown quite fond of since they had shown up at the jungle. But another came out of the crowd, a shaky tow-headed man in baggy striped trousers and an old double-breasted olive coat, a madcap sort of fellow who seemed very determined, and he toted a banjo. Zeke had never seen the fellow before and studied him a moment, wondering if he could actually play his instrument but quickly sensed the uninhibited performer in the stranger and could but chuckle when he let rip a sonorous roar from the bottom of his lungs, a cry of cryptic meaning or perhaps peculiar tongue. He jumped up and down and howled and strummed his banjo with a rare energy and mastery, and the lanky Tommy Dunkirk spun around and squatted and sprung up with his slide thrusting while blowing big notes, and wiry shaggy young hobo Rupert Yuckens began tapping his snare, while the harp player started up with his great mustache hanging over his harp.

But this was introduction music, all build-up for the one they wanted to dig inside deeply as they knew he could, every one of them looked to Zeke to make it right with his nonpareil showmanship. He began with simple shrugs of the shoulders, lightning fast jerks while he slowly executed clownish deep knee bends, his arms describing circles and elliptical shapes. He pointed at the harp player, whose name was Stublinski, and he blew a pensive melody while Zeke launched into a number he improvised about dark forest at night in the rain. "In the forest nobody becomes lost / because it doesn't matter out here / we gather our strength in the bush / the road to the Hootenanny Harvest beckons us / and we *will make it there* /because rain, mud, tree, hills, or slipping far astray in the nowhere *can ever stop the united will of hoboes and farmers!*" And now he really began whirling and shaking like he was having a seizure, but these were controlled convulsions the crowd knew, and he motioned to the young Rupert Yuckens to crescendo a rising backbeat and Tommy Dunkirk introduced his tumultuous squall of slide that sent the song soaring as a full-blooded juggernaut of intensity. Zeke sang a series of traditional hobo and farmer songs with an unimaginable gusto, mixing and slicing and concocting odd medleys of powerful lyrics and rhythms that left the marchers speechless and inspired. He threw himself with reckless abandon and full-throated ebullience into mud and rock and tree, and too often crashed and slammed and stunned his game frame into a pause for re-gathering his wind. The rain came in sheets through the forest and the mud swelled under them, the gales strengthened and violently shook and swayed the trees, but the band continued to play because Zeke would not quit his performance, because he would not take cover and give up their ghost. It was plain that only when his heart ceased beating would he relinquish his duty and mission as leader of the Grange, his good folks in their desperate dire ordeals, hobo and farmer alike. He knew they were irretrievably, impossibly, gravely *lost* and had no practical or realistic plan with which to find their way back to charted known territory, let alone the Hootenanny. That every one of his marchers felt this dark void of buried lostness but for one glimmering beacon of hope, one individual who completely captured their belief, inspiration, and undying loyalty, the one and only Zeke Borshellac, only exacerbated Zeke's anguish at coming to grips with such a dark and stark realization of their *utter and calamitous lostness*. He knew he could never show them his doubt, his looming sense of confusion and pending doom, his stymied perplexity at charting a course out of the punishing wilderness, as that transparency could quash their last remnants of faith and only hasten their demise. Zeke chose to ride his mythic rise as a folk hero with the marchers as a source of faith and conviction, for their belief in him sustained his last irreducible sense of belief that persevering onward would be rewarded. That's all they had, one another to feed from and build upon this irrational belief of deliverance. And so his performance would only end this night in the tempestuous forgotten woodlands when he was wrung out and exhausted into total collapse. Nothing stated his commitment, intrepidity, and preternatural bona fides as the one who will lead them to the enchanted Hootenanny than such a passionate, maniacally puzzling and self-destructive performance.

Always in his thoughts was his beloved dairymaid, who now occupied a sacrosanct place of apotheosis in his mind, of the *truest of sublime ineffable romantic love,* and his beloved sheepdog, who held his own position of *immortal unconditional love and devoted friendship.* The hoboes and farmers administered to their crumpled leader, reviving him in the rain that would not relent, and regaining consciousness Zeke felt good and confident and led them in a thunderous, rousing rendition of "Cornfield Confidential: Fourteen Ears, Fifteen Hoboes, and No Damn Butter," as they began in hearty spirits once more marching through the thick black night forest. The more lost they became in slogging forth in the soaking woods the more spirited and ebullient Zeke became, eliciting an almost equally defiant ardor from the marchers. They took his cue and evinced a crazed embrasure of the severe conditions and lost backwoods oblivion trapping them. The symbiotic crescendo escalating between them rumbled and fulminated into strange and wondrous moments, but when it began to ebb ever so slightly from its iconoclastic energy Zeke felt the brunt of his doubts again. It was when he saw the recording secretary beside him, scribbling in his journal with a frantic excitement, all agog describing the events of their march, particularly limning the mythic figure leading them, or so Zeke thought, that suddenly this image of the earnest scribe was enough to shore up Zeke's sagging spirit. The marchers struggled mightily through the thick black forest in the hard rain, the squalls, the deepening mud, until their progress stalled in a marshy hollow and they were even more lost. But Zeke would not let them surcease. They pushed forward with a furious zest and nihilist appreciation of their absurd path to utter oblivion. The wet foggy dawn broke with a dim gray luminosity that slightly improved their visibility and allowed more progress. By the time they reached an opening to a clear stretch of grassland the morning had fully arrived and the little sparkle of the low sun broke through clouds and suffused them with a measure of warmth. Soon they came upon a river winding gently through an expansive meadow of curious vegetation and wildflowers and they drank the cool water and rested.

It was Saturday morning and the Hootenanny was that afternoon and Zeke knew there was no gainsaying the fact that they were so far gone in the wilderness their making it there did not seem auspicious. Averill Overbalker, removing his long-billed cap as if entering a church, began offering the morning toast, but their bottles were hardly raised when Geets joined him by garbling a notion of extending a joint toast, farmer and hobo, and that was the way it happened. Such careful attention to the appearances of their alliance would allow them to strengthen in solidarity, Zeke thought approvingly. Though all could be for naught if they remained bound to the woods, he also considered. Not reaching the Von Klobbert farm in time was the darkening specter worrying him, for that was his duty as leader and meant so much to the Grange movement and himself personally. Even if, he increasingly came to recognize, he would very likely find himself captured and hauled back to prison once they marched onto the farm and his presence was known. They followed the banks of the river for a while and came upon a town that seemed faintly familiar to Zeke, and he hollered some such notion, which was taken by many that he knew the area and way to the Hootenanny. The marchers perked up with eager anticipation and new optimism. It was a barren burg of only a few rocky streets and wood-frame attached houses with worn wooden sidewalks. There were a few people moseying around, mostly older folks with dour expressions. One lanky old-timer in a buckskin jacket with fringes sized up Zeke and made a contemptuous grunting noise. Zeke thought he knew this man and was grateful when he gathered he was not the fisherman Haggerman from his days at sea, but an utter stranger. He asked the man the name of the town, where they were, the proximity to the farm, and he was only returned an icy glower. All the older folks here only offered cold stares, and Zeke felt they were foreigners or xenophobes who wanted no company. Zeke called out now that this was not the place he initially thought it was, that they could not waste more time there and must continue moving forward.

"Now hold on there, Zeke," Dirk Freckler called out from the crowd and moved towards him with his head down and thumbs hooked under his candy-cane suspenders. He stopped in front of Zeke and said: "A lot of us feel you know exactly where we are but are testing our resolve by making the journey seem ground to a halt cause we're too lost."

Zeke stared at Freckler and cast his eyes around the crowd. "No, Dirk. That is not the case. I do not *test* hoboes or farmers. I am going to lead you to Von Klobbert farm and there our movement will be heard."

A murmur rippled through the men, one of bright energy and nodding heads, and the hobo Quigley called out with a robust cheer: "We know you know the way, Zeke! You just want to make us *earn our way* in to the thing! That's all right by me."

They proceeded through the bleak streets and plastered on the wall of the last wooden structure was a jarring poster Zeke happened to gaze upon: WANTED DEAD OR ALIVE, and there was a picture of Zeke staring back at himself. Everyone swarmed around the wall of the old building to get a look at the poster, which announced the escape of

TWENTY

a dangerous convict, Zeke Borshellac, from Frodtznjepple Prison and much buzzing and muttering ensued until Steward Snover, standing on a bench with his long frame bedecked in a somber black coat redolent of a preacher, shouted: "We knew they'd be coming for you, Zeke. But you must know that before they take you down they're going to have to take all of us down . . . ain't that right, fellers?!"

A furious roar of approval rose from the crowd and Zeke nodded his appreciation with a smile, gesturing with his hands for them to wind it down, and when silence finally came he declared that their journey was in the hands of providence now, and he had faith they were on the right path and would reach the farm soon. "Our mission is too important to the history of working people and I am confident our movement will have a transformational impact on their ability to attain a fair shake and live better lives. They are depending on us and we will be there." He gave the poster one more glance and quipped, "Not a bad portrait of me, and done so quickly to boot!" And the throng let a good collective laugh as they began marching once again.

Hours it seemed went by as they traversed meadows and streams and dense, lush hills rank with the traces and trails and of hidden woodland creatures. The marchers were tired and aching with the miles covered over the long night, the dearth of grub, but no one complained as they marched onward with an increasingly desperate fortitude because time was simply running out. Only the anxious carping sodbuster in his long chestnut duster and farm cap, Jeffery Plystock, openly questioned whether it was a mistake that they delayed leaving the bonfire jungle until the morning. He levied his reproof indirectly, singing way off-key an old scythe swinging song that aggrandized and mythologized the poignant lonely farmer Slome, a solemn wheat grower who had a penchant for playing the provocateur with agricultural politics. Only silence followed Plystock's criticism, and they hummed again as they trod through great stretches of pristine woodland. Then Zeke glimpsed a wooden structure from a distance, a place with smoke emanating from its chimney and as they neared the old place Zeke began to believe he had been in the building before. He grew more convinced of his memory of the tavern, which he now identified it to be an inn for wayfarers passing through the forest. As they descended a sloping stretch of mud and weeds into the valley where the inviting tavern sat, Zeke in his eager excitement bellowed: "I know that tavern! I drank fine brew in that tavern! My horse waited outside while I drank brew inside that tavern!" He burst into joyful laughter knowing now he would know the way to the Von Klobbert farm, as he thought the tavern was the one he chanced upon the night he galloped far afield with Catapaltus and secretly espied Gerard carrying on drunkenly with several strumpets. Zeke soon was running towards the tavern, whooping and exclaiming about the Hootenanny being in their propinquity now and that he could almost hear the musicians playing and smell the roasting meat, the longing for Livinia simmering for so long now pervading his thoughts. The marchers were right behind him, hopeful too but not quite as elated as Zeke, perhaps sensing the distinct possibility of him remembering erroneously. But when Zeke drew near the stone and wood structure with opaque sectioned windows he became quiet, slowing his stride to a walk while peering intently at the place. He furrowed his brow as he circled the building and the marchers remained massed at about twenty feet back watching with some concern as he proceeded with his curious examination. Finally, he turned to the men and chose his words carefully in acknowledging his misapprehension once again: "A long time ago I could not sleep and took an all-night ride on my fine steed Catapaltus, culminating in a woodland tavern with my witnessing the wanton deceit of my nemesis as a farmer. While what I saw was very real, I did not see it in this particular tavern." While the perturbed murmurs and sighs were less pronounced as before, Zeke was troubled to hear them but buoyed by their abiding supposition that he was only testing the limits of their will and endurance in the build-up to their grand arrival at the Hootenanny. While Zeke did not openly endorse this inference of theirs, he also did little to discredit it after his earlier denial, deciding the marchers believing him a character-building stickler better than a hopelessly lost pudding-head.

TWENTY

They moved onward more quickly than before and set out again through the valley and into the thickest forest section of all, where the dense trees were larger than anyone had ever seen and the air amidst them was darkly hazy. A trepidation of passing time and fading light informed Zeke's every step in the immense forest enclosing them, his lonely secret of their utter lostness aching in his every fiber. He could do nothing but continue to lead them through the nearly impenetrable woodland and maintain their spirits by not disavowing their steadfast belief in his navigation abilities. His overland route was merely his desire to instill a lesson in perseverance in them. He wished it were as they believed; he simply could not let them down. It would kill him, he knew. He pushed himself forward, leading them without knowing where, their unbreakable, unwavering belief in his knowing the way gave him stamina and faith beyond all reason that he would find the farm. Providence would deliver them there somehow. He heard them behind him humming again with real vigor "Out of the Sea and Up From the Soil" and the band softly accompanied the melody with instrumentation, and after a while Zeke could not handle the absolute conviction they invested in him, as he thought about being so lost, and he began singing "The Old Bag Hangin' Wash Gave Us Soup," the old hobo number. The marchers fell in line and immediately joined him in chorus, and after that Corn Cavendish broke into "Sodbusters Sockeroo," and then a hopped-up Geets launched into the hobo elegiac ballad "Stu Bleavins Dropped Dead." They came upon a clearing and climbed a hill covered in weeds and beyond was a stream that struck Zeke as familiar. He began to run towards it trying to ascertain how he knew it, soon connecting it to the time he fled Bluddenville with Balthazar and they chanced upon a doe and her fawns lingering for a drink. Now an exultant relief rose in his chest as he neared the stream and knelt beside its glimmering easy burble and drank its cool freshness. He yelled with jubilance to the marchers as they arrived behind him, "I know this stream, I came upon it on my way to the Von Klobbert farm so long ago! Balthazar drank from this stream! Now I know that we are on the right path!" The men all drank from the stream that now gave them hope and a sense of making progress, but as they slaked their thirsts Zeke was already racing up and down the banks in further investigation of the source of his recognition. He took a slug of whisky in studying the burbling flow of the stream, then waded in and stood for a moment with the water up to his waist and his gaze upwards at the sky. At length he turned to the men gathered at the bank, riveted on his every move, and offered his by now usual recantation: "While my fine sheepdog and I indeed encountered a doe and her fawns enjoying the fresh water of a stream, I now can avouch that that stream was not this stream." There was a protracted silence afterwards, as Zeke stood in the stream looking around in all directions trying to determine the way to continue.

Hunter Bogle, the old chicken farmer, was the first to call out. "That's all right, Zeke. If I didn't know you were playing some game with all this, preparing us for the trials ahead, I'd say it's time we got to the Hootenanny! It's getting late!" Others followed with similar sentiments, stating they trusted Zeke knew what he was doing, but questioning at the same time the obvious, the day was slipping away from them.

The Captain stepped forward and led them in a toast: "We will follow you until we pass your test, Zeke, but the Hootenanny beckons in the light of this day and we know you'll deliver us there, even if our education must wait!" They threw back their whiskies and yowled in robust concurrence, the band struck up "Out of the Sea and Up From the Soil," and Zeke climbed from the stream, moved by their devotion while also crestfallen insofar as he had no idea where they were or which way to go.

It now was extremely hard for him to maintain the veneer that he knew the way forward but had to first teach them an important lesson in persistence and grit, yet the alternative of disclosing his utter lostness remained unacceptable. He led them onward at a brisker pace, racing against the waning day and going by pure instinct. There were several more sightings of familiar parts of the forest, a copse, a beaver dam, a small clearing of verdure fluttering in the breezes, a

TWENTY

field of wild berries, that all duped him into believing he recognized them from his wee hours rides on Catapaltus, and therefore could find the farm from there. But his celebratory cries invariably led to reassessments of his memory of the places and the admission to the men that he had once come across a beaver dam, for example, just not *this beaver dam*. He struggled to conceal the desperation that was becoming too insistent and intense to not address any longer. The fellow scribbling in his journal while observing Zeke's every move, evaluating his every word, grew more and more brazen with his subject, posing questions now after sidling up to him while marching, queries that caught Zeke off guard and made him bristle, but think as well. Zeke was out front marching at such a speedy clip the bespectacled unofficial recording secretary could not keep pace alongside him without scurrying intermittently, his old raincoat flapping behind him, as he frequently adjusted his wire-framed spectacles and had his head in his notebook scribbling much of the time. "We all know you know the way, Zeke, but what would you be thinking now if you really were lost in the forest? Hypothetically speaking, what would you do?" the zealous scribe asked. Zeke had no answer for such speculation, and wondered if Crokus, as such was the journalist's name, suspected the terrible truth. Zeke accelerated ahead of him and Crokus scurried then to catch up. "One day a great many people would be interested to know your thoughts at this critical juncture in the Grange's march to the Hootenanny Harvest. The hoboes and farmers have great faith in you and the impact the movement can make. Can you speak through the constraints of the time and space, and address history as to what you are feeling and the cataclysmic upheaval you seek?"

Zeke heard the question ring out behind him and could not help thinking of an answer as he paced forward, sensing the marchers at the front of the lines picked up what Crokus asked him. The question seemed to hang in the air until at length Zeke paused to turn around and hazard a reply, and as he did so the marchers were disconcerted enough to halt in anticipation of Zeke's words. "I don't know what the upshot of our movement's struggle and dissent will be, but I have a good notion it will carry forward the great ideals of freedom and justice and opportunity for folks who have nothing and are willing to work hard. All I know is that the status quo cannot hold and we have all had enough. Maybe years from now they will say it began right here with us, because it will take time to forge lasting change. All we can do is reject the choices we have now and set in motion a vision and plan to improve the lives of the forgotten and destitute."

The scribe wrote it down in his notebook as the hoboes and farmers, after a brief pause once Zeke stopped speaking, began to shout and cheer in raucous and hearty approval. And a mighty epiphany swept over Zeke just then, culminating in a thunderbolt of dizzying recognition of the power that had been present in him and the marchers all along. The belief the men had in Zeke and faith in his leadership was so intense and strong and undying that all he had to remember when his own doubts arose and sewed hesitancy and trepidation was the *reality of their belief and to continue believing in their belief*. Here he was in the deepest stretches of unknown forest, wrung out and beaten down in utter frustration as the specter of leading his marchers to nowhere instead of the Hootenanny, where the call of momentousness awaited them, the shadowy prospect of that awful specter stared at him with a taunting ignominy. He understood that he was not truly rising to the role he found himself in, the figure of inspirational leadership in a great struggle that would result in historical consequences. He had to embrace and become the leader they believe him to be and harness all the enormous impassioned inextinguishable belief they had in him. And alchemize their symbiotic strength for the great clashes ahead, as the one out front expanding in renown, out of the sea and up from the soil, the one who represents his folks as only one can when he is one of them, and uniquely capable to spearhead a revolution for the times at hand. He marched with a springier, surer step and could not stop thinking about the absolute belief the men behind him invested and entrusted in him and he simply allowed all that belief to become the foundation of his consciousness, he let it come in and fortify as an unshakable bedrock of his reality, his true persona, foibles

TWENTY

and all the peculiarities of this figure they believed in *was Zeke Borshellac and nobody else was leading them onward to a better life*. So he had to do it and he had to enable *that Zeke Borshellac*, the one who would get them there, to come to the fore and take the reins. He had to give them who they wanted and needed by giving all of himself and more of himself, and that of course meant wise decision-making, strong direction, and brilliant, singular showmanship. He still had to first lead them out of the deepest, most isolated primordial forest, and he could only veer against the grain of linear, rational, practical thinking. He remained utterly lost and hopelessly circumscribed to the uncharted woods and sadly he wished he was the self-assured figure whose men believed he knew the way and was only playing with them. Zeke forced himself to think like the men and therefore think like the Zeke who could march them to the Von Klobbert farm any time he chose. And he kept thinking this way, powerfully locking into that unwavering mindset. And the marchers picked up on that new confident stride and moved faster with sanguine expectations as they sang "Out of the Sea and Up from the Soil" to the band's deft accompaniment.

The afternoon sunshine yet spread its glorious rays over the meadows and valleys they crossed between forest stretches lined with streams and the wild hills of dark earth. Zeke strove to stay focused on every passing moment as he intuitively picked his path through the magnificent wilderness, summoning and holding close like a living prayer the profound expectation of coming across the farm very soon. He could feel the farm just ahead, *knew it was there* waiting for their arrival in time, the marchers behind him sore and aching and exhausted, many with bleeding feet and hobbled gait now, but none complaining one iota. Rather they were eager with optimism, persevering onward with that unshakable faith in Zeke Borshellac, back from the grave of Frodtznjepple Peninsula, feeling somewhere beneath all their pain and fatigue the stirrings of the exultance to come through the Hootenanny awaiting them on that farm, once they located it. The symbiosis of belief and confidence only strengthened and intensified between them, Zeke and his marchers, evident in the speedy certain stride of Zeke and the commensurate acceleration by the men in line behind him, by the heart and will in Zeke's face and the complete absence of doubt in his mind that he would find that farm, and the soulful conviction with which the marchers sang "Out of the Sea and Up from the Soil" with the otherworldly musicianship of the band in accompanying them. Zeke saw everything in every passing moment, birds, trees, beetles, plants, and he was sure he would recognize signs of the farm as it came in focus. But this did not happen. Instead he heard distant sounds, faint and mysterious, that piqued his interest. Over the undulating grassland scattered with black oak and larch and birch and beech he charged forward towards the faint tones resonating, his audibility seemingly increasing with his movement, even if in barely appreciable increments, as he splashed across another rushing stream and climbed a rocky steep slope the faraway cadences of life and people and quite possibly musical instruments playing into the winds led him with the lure of discovery. The marchers slogged right behind him with an intense recognition of the transitory urgency of this last best tangent of Zeke's and, while not doubting his will to take them there they instinctually refrained now from singing the farmer or hobo numbers and the band remained quiet to allow him to hear the obscure sounds. Zeke obliged his mind to stay connected to the marchers' belief in him and this he felt found him the sounds to follow, that in some deep unutterable way this faith between them was somehow lifting them from the buried wilderness.

    The sounds seemed rhythmic and melodious the more he chased after their source, and he could only keep thinking this was a Grange band of farmers playing at the Von Klobbert farm. There were moments the tenuous noise seemed like songs he recalled from the Pig Roaster at Redmond's Landing by the great farmer combos that performed, such as "Our Milk Cow Named McTavish and The Carved Baker Figurine," but it was so faint he wondered if his mind molded the melody as he desired to hear it. He rushed towards it trying only to find the musicians, if it was a band he was hearing, and Hop Quinine, the chubby wheat farmer who played trumpet with gusto, kept popping into his head. Yance Brollo, the trombonist as well. And then he could not avoid thoughts of his mission being ultimately suicidal, at least to objective observers, for his appearance at the Hootenanny could see him arrested immediately and remanded back to prison, or worse, being shot in broad daylight. But nothing could deter his efforts to make it to the farm once he had that chance again, he simply had to go there, his life as he wanted it to be depended on it. The awakening resolve and lifeblood of the Grange movement was gathering there to start a new beginning, the hoboes and farmers who admired and followed Zeke were there mourning their martyr, the woman he loved more than anything was there, as was his beloved sheepdog. A fleeting reflection passed through him on whether he would seek out the farm with such vigor if he knew that he'd be shot dead or imprisoned again in Frodtznjepple, and he decided he would make the quest no matter what with so much there waiting for him. Not going would equally destroy him, he knew. The glorious afternoon appeared to be on the wane now to Zeke, the sunshine a shade tinted to the shadows and the gentle breezes becoming windier, and Zeke charged at a pace that included running intermittent with walking. The land seemed to have fewer trees and stretches of wilderness and as they ascended each lengthy rise it became another inclining slope towards a top of sky, which once attained a new upward rise of grassland, pastureland, now with hardly any trees greeted them. The music continued to grow louder and Zeke felt a surge of excitement and even a sense of gratitude that he was on the right trail, that this was the Grange band playing, it had to be. And finally they ascended the last long rise of earth and came upon a vast open land of grass that yawned outward to a distant horizon. Zeke now began to run, a steady jog at first increasing in speed as his urgency to know it was the Hootenanny just yonder towards the horizon impelled him run faster and faster, until he perceived far away across the vast range of pastureland the obscure remote stirrings of people gathered around the sounds of figures on a platform who had to be the band. The white structure set behind them had to be the Von Klobbert farmhouse. He slowed to a stop and let out a short laugh of jubilance at his recognition, then turned to wait for the marchers who had fallen a good ways behind him. "We made it, fellows!" he called to them as they came into earshot. "The Hootenanny Harvest is there on the range ahead of us."

TWENTY-ONE

BRIEF MERRIMENT ensued among them as they caught up and absorbed the news, constrained then by the enormous challenge ahead of them now in confronting the spectacle of the Hootenanny. Zeke peered out at the tiny faraway aggregation and realized everything that meant anything to him in the world was out there on the pastureland horizon. He wiped off the dirt and brush that accumulated on the fine new suit the chandler Pud Stupilis made at the jungle for him, felt the craftmanship of the thick brown trousers with orange stripes, the deep red shirt with yellow, the oilskin charcoal coat with green trim and the sleeves decorated with images of a pitchfork and a bindlestick on respective arms, the patches of a locomotive and plough sewn into the jacket. He led them on the last long leg of the march across the grassland, striding in a good strong pace but not running now, the endless mass of farmers and hoboes gathered out there becoming apparent to the marchers as they approached them from behind with most of the crowd facing the band on the stage. There were welters of roiling turbulence out among the still distant figures, agitation between groups around the fringes. The legions were likely overzealously maintaining order, which has the opposite effect of provoking unrest, Zeke remembered. The music carried across the pasture well enough for Zeke to make out the song the band was playing, "Sodbusters Sockeroo," and he thought the stocky animated horn player was Hop Quinine. The pasture was on a slight incline as they marched towards the crowd and band and at about five hundred feet some of the hoboes who were standing farthest from the stage began noticing the large contingent of men coming their way in long rows of two. The magnitude of the crowd continued to leave the marchers in awe as they drew nearer, and now word was spreading among the hoboes in the rear that a regimented band of their own was approaching out of nowhere. Zeke saw the great flames rising from roasting pits dug into the earth, and an abundance of meats and fowl strewn on steel grills and hung from immense racks spanning the fires. The multifarious plenitude of the harvest bounty was ubiquitously evident in the good earth's yield, the corn, onions, broccoli, potatoes, beets, cabbage, tomatoes, cauliflower, green beans, and all the others, some he himself had worked the soil to bring forth. And the wooden kegs of ale lined in numerous stations around the grounds, vast profusions of brew signifying the festive spirit of the gathering, more beer than Zeke had ever laid his eyes upon. Swirls of excitement and pockets of general hubbub rippled through this periphery of the crowd and the band finished their spirited rendition of the farmers' anthem and a man on stage made an announcement over one of those raw new jerry-rigged amplifiers known as loudspeakers that was incoherent from the marchers' distance.

The band started playing another number well-known to the marchers, "Turnips and Wheat Folks Must Eat, Pete," and then it became plain some of the hoboes and farmers were recognizing Zeke and registering utter shock and amazement in watching him lead his march towards them. They stopped whatever they were doing upon perceiving the man out front to be Zeke and remained riveted in wonder of his return from the grave, as they believed he perished in Frodtznjepple. "Zeke! Zeke!" a few here and there began to shout, "It's Zeke Borshellac back from dead to lead us forward! A miracle!" For most turning to make this discovery words were inadequate and stifled by their sheer astonishment that stole their breath and the groundswell of powerful emotion overcoming them. Here was the heart and soul bellwether of their movement, one of their own from the ranks of hoboes and farmers alike who rose to inspire and galvanize them and ultimately sacrificed his very life in carrying out his commitments to the cause, now reappearing like a phoenix on the pasturelands of the Hootenanny Harvest to once again rally them for-

TWENTY-ONE

ward. One by one the isolated scuffling with the legions on the periphery simply ceased as the participants recognized the man leading the march out on the fields. The legionaries also were astounded and confused and suspicious of this sudden arrival of the famed hobo farmer who had become a martyr since his banishment and presumed death on the cursed peninsula. The light across the farmland was just starting to ebb and cast a time-toasted hue of otherworldly mystery upon everything, the autumn crisp air and occasional wind lending a deep sense of time and gravity sweeping through it all. Wave upon wave of hoboes and farmers, engaged in the passions and tensions of the great event, many skirmishing with the heavy presence of legions in altercations of acrimony and physical strife, now upon beholding their flesh-and-blood chief stunningly there on the field went suddenly silent and still with eyes wide and mouths agape, awed by the incontrovertible return of the extraordinary man many knew personally and heard all the lore about.

Once the marchers reached the main mass of the enormous crowd that numbered well in the thousands, beyond anything Zeke or the marchers had ever seen, the Hootenanny attendees in their stunned fevered quietude parted the middle for their new arrivals. It felt to Zeke as if they were moving down a river as folks receded around them and fell into whirls and eddies, appearing profoundly moved in shock first, then joy. The strange silence and roiling that now met the forward marchers continued until the band on the stage, the fine Grange band of Hop Quinine and Yance Brollo and the skinny red-mopped young hooligan on banjo, Nathaniel Schmidt, and the mercurial cook Ott Eschledy on drums, broke off the number "Candied Parsnips and the Clapboard Shed of Big Chet," and the only noise now was the scrambling sounds of the legions in positioning their regiments to best contain and confront the manifest threat of Zeke Borshellac. Zeke now could plainly see those on the reviewing stand off to the side of the stage, still a good distance away but he could make out the middle of the top row, between Phineas and Abigail, who appeared older and more dour than he remembered them, and Gerard and Lord Cumberland, both men wearing frowns of disgust at the marchers' disruption, was the dairymaid he loved so much and now through a lens of apotheosis after his extended absence in a living hell. The glimpse he got of her made his heart race and a strong surge of warmth and rapture shot through him, though it was tempered by the odious presence of the imperiously repellent Gerard at her side, no doubt dominating and controlling her every move, he thought, by having broken her will. She seemed pale and languid, withdrawn and somber in her reclined form sunken in resignation, not a smile or laugh possible in her. Zeke wasn't sure whether word reached them on the stand that the hurly-burly throwing things for a loop out amongst the swarms was indeed caused by Gerard's old nemesis, but Zeke suspected Gerard was directing the clampdown containment effort. The legions near him certainly knew who he was and they were maneuvering and flanking their forces in some byzantine strategy to contain and trap Zeke, they were forming a great circle around the dangerous insurrectionist as the band went silent and the hoboes and farmers in stupefied awe watched him, waiting for him to lead them or show them what was next. Zeke sized it all up and took measure of the legions vast numbers moving every which way to surround him, their firearms at their sides, and he thought about the potential powder keg for bloodshed. Just then he heard barking familiar and magnificent, a balm to his heart as he felt the exuberant canine pounce of his beloved sheepdog leaping against his side, up from the swarms of people around him, suddenly he was hugging and petting and receiving effusive licks from Balthazar. He called out his sheepdog's name and kissed his happy kinetic snout and stroked his fine thick coat and for the moment the tension eased. They shared a profoundly happy and grateful moment together, their singular bond inviolable and everlasting, and the folks around them all seemed to know how much Zeke's dog meant to him, and they deferred to his brief rejoicing in their reunion.

  Word was still spreading through the vast throngs that Zeke Borshellac indeed arrived, he came out of nowhere from the dark deep tunnels of death, from the ghastly grip of Froddy itself, and great excitement and inspiration among the hoboes and farmers continued to grow. But now the identity of the new arrival's leader reached the stage and viewing stand and Phineas was bounding up where the band had been playing and he spoke into the microphone hooked up to loudspeakers. "We have to continue with the program," he began, "our newcomers are welcome, but you have to settle down now. We need you to proceed in a calm, amiable, and orderly manner if you wish to participate in the Hootenanny Harvest festivities." Phineas headed towards the viewing stand, where Gerard was already making his way to the stage and in the corner shadows of the platform they conferred, Gerard animatedly giving the farm owner an earful.

It was plain to Zeke and anyone around him and his marchers that they were not the ones responsible for the agitation and antipathy escalating, but the legionaries who were moving against them as unwelcome intruders. The legionaries were fully engaged in a strategy of confrontation and intimidation, cutting off the marchers and attendees around them by running a crazy eight formation through their ranks and splitting them into two separate masses and surrounding both. In accomplishing this tactical maneuver the legionaries rode roughshod through the hoboes and farmers in their way, deliberately clearing them aside in bruising fashion. Corn Cavendish was clipped from behind and knocked down, only to be kneed in the dome while struggling to his feet. The Captain was tripped and then kicked while prone on the ground.

Again Phineas strode to the stage and microphone, calling for a "peaceful enjoyment together of our great Hootenanny," and "this is no place for disruptive belligerence and confrontational discord. We will not stand for it, and if you newcomers are prudent, you will stand down. Don't push it or you will pay a very dear price." But all the hostility of the legions and their encircling nooses of physical menace only seemed to intensify and it seemed to Zeke they were just itching to unleash an all-out attack. The hoboes and farmers who marched with Zeke now began singing "Out of the Sea and Up from the Soil," lowly at first but soon swelling in passion and volume as an answer to the baleful warning from Phineas.

When Seward Snover, the staunch farmer who dressed like a preacher, took a blackjack bash across his back and went down a scuffle ensued but Zeke waved the marchers back, and Tommy Dunkirk began blowing his trombone to support the singers and quickly their band was in full swing as their anthem blared in full-throated ardor. It stirred the conviction and deeply felt yearnings of hoboes and farmers throughout the massive crowd that seemed to have grown exponentially as word spread of Zeke's incredible arrival, and they took turns singing with roaring fervor the great traditional hobo and farmer numbers that have been such vibrant elements of sustenance over their years of hardship and the incipient Movement. Here rose from the hearty unyielding throats of men, lyrics borne deep from their chests, men who have had enough inexorable oppression under which they were fated to fall far short of the full and rich lives they knew they deserved, magnificent rousing songs such as "One Swiped Mickie Equals One Split-Open Head," "The Corncakes Skunk Loomis Cooked Us in Muscogee," "The Old Bag Hangin' Wash Gave Us Soup," and "The Grub Klepto of Yuma." And the farmers were just as uproariously thunderous in belting out their agricultural favorites, such as "Cornstalk Hideaway with Wanda Purvey," "Scythe Swaths, Width Eighteen Feet," and of course "Sodbusters Sockeroo." The vast crowd continued to swell in numbers as it became more widely known that Zeke Borshellac had returned from the clutches of death in the stygian nightmare of Froddy, the intensity and volume of the singing only rose accordingly, the farmer and hobo bands all accompanying the old melodies with heartfelt musicianship, and eventually realizing their spirit would not abate any time soon Gerard bounded across the stage and grabbed the microphone to snarl over the loudspeaker words of intimidation: "A sick enthusiasm out among you boils over by demented drunken delusion and misguided tragic belief in the escaped convict agitator who comes here only to cause harm and destruction, a maniacal nihilist who sews hatred, violence, and annihilation of everything good people hold dear to life." The great throngs that now stretched for what seemed miles into the undulating pasturelands clear to the horizon became more raucously loud as the son of Lord Cumberland spoke, a motley mass swaying and moving in rhythm with a collective force of unbending strength, skirmishes with the legionaries in fringes multiplying.

Zeke saw that the situation was perilously close to blowing up into full-scale fighting, but it seemed irreversible now, and then they once again broke into "Out of the Sea and Up from the Soil," the entire endless sea of hoboes and farmers all knew the tribute number to Zeke by heart now, and the bands were jamming with such delirious intensity it seemed to convey *we are not acquiescing anymore, not to threats of violence or arrest, we are prepared to fight for a better future!* Gerard continued to spew his insults and intimidation, though he visibly grew more furious with the ever increasing volume and endurance of the singers and musicians, until his father Lord Cumberland stood in vexed chagrin and slowly ambled his sizable form onto the stage and over to Gerard, where Phineas and a Legionary Major gathered to discuss the impasse raging now with the huge and growing throng defying their demand to stand down and submit to their control. The hoboes and farmers sang Zeke's song with such deafening rhythmic spirit that it seemed to come from another source of mysterious power, sprung loose from the soil beneath the vast stretching masses of vocalists, caught soaring above the historical moment in time and reverberating with such undying belief in the meaning of their movement that Zeke felt moved nearly to tears with a palpable core of courage lifting him to press forward.

He stroked his beloved sheepdog, his truest ally and confidant through his own struggles, once again at his side, reunited for the battles ahead. He glimpsed the frenetic Crocus to his left near Averill Overbalker, the wild bearded farmer singing with fevered abandon, and the bespectacled scribe in his torn raincoat was scribbling madly in his notebook. Now Zeke felt a brawny arm around his shoulders and quickly saw it was Booth Booley, his black beard flowing and his head held high as he sang Zeke's song at the top of this lungs, squeezing

Zeke with his powerful grip as he met his eyes and cried: "I have goosebumps, Zeke!" Adding after a few moments, that he never doubted he would make it back. "They love you Zeke. You were born to find our farm and lead the movement."

Cy Undersnettle followed, singing zealously, wringing Zeke's hand to say he was with him all the way, and referencing their old scraps over his mistaken medical condition, said, "You don't need a doctor Zeke, but we all have your back."

Balthazar barked and barked in great excitement and it occurred to Zeke that perhaps the sheepdog was singing along in his own way. The legionaries seemed to tighten their enclosures and many now were brandishing their firearms, only awaiting the word from the Cumberlands to put down the burgeoning rebellion for good. Gerard was the most animated among the group on the stage discussing the disturbance, his arms flailing and his raging voice arguing to unleash the brunt of the legionaries, albeit his father, ever magisterial in an annoyed petulance about it all, appeared to voice concern about the sheer numbers of Zeke's supporters out there. Gerard approached the microphone again and the melodic din of the masses overwhelmed him. "If you don't stop singing we will have to *see* that you stop, our patience is wearing very thin and the legion is close to taking matters into hand—" The melees around the edges and in other sectors now were escalating and Zeke saw hand-to-hand brawling starting and then gunfire erupted, only shots fired into the air to disperse such engagements, though no one scattered.

Now Lord Cumberland himself ambled across the stage and he received an uproar of attention as he took the microphone. There was a great rumble of boos and catcalls and raspberries, and a piercing chorus from a contingent of wild farm boys, rowdy rascals with plenty of moxie, several up in trees near the side of the stage, belting out "Lord Bumble-lard slid his jib, Baby Bumble-lard choked on his bib! Lord Bumble-lard does nothin' but make life hard! Baby Bumble-lard, look he's hoisted by his own petard!"

TWENTY-ONE

And Zeke spotted Ogden highest on an oak branch, Huxley adjacent him on a sycamore, and Zeke just had to smile, and as he thought they were looking his way he waved his arm and they both waved back, laughing their heads off while singing their old epithets. Lord Cumberland attempted a more conciliatory tone, saying if the singing does not end the Hootenanny would have to come to a premature close, adding they had several more musical performances scheduled and all he was asking was a return to calm order and silence. "Shove it, Bumble-lard!" a half-crocked, irate farmer yelled. "Bumble-lard the blowhard!" another cried.

And a chant that began far away in the furthest reaches of the crowd now was spreading towards the middle and soon it became audible to Zeke, stark and simple in its staunch demand. "We want Zeke! We want Zeke!" Lord Cumberland stood at the microphone now, his stout form motionless beneath his jutting chin, surveying the vast fired-up crowd, his expression one of impatience, concern, and cunning as he stalled after several tries to begin his address, the impassioned singers of "Out of the Sea . . ." only amplifying their rally number but now coupled with a swelling counterpoise of the insistent thunderous chant of "We Want Zeke! We Want Zeke!" He finally began: "The individual you are so enamored with and believe to be the one you have been waiting for to lead you forward, the one who escaped prison for crimes he must pay for, is not who you believe him to be. He will disappoint you and lead you into ruin . . ." Just when it seemed impossible the volume and fervor of the crowd could increase, it went to an altogether volcanic boom of rage that stopped Cumberland from continuing. He crossed his arms and stepped to his son and Phineas and the Major of the Legion, and they had another discussion. Lord Cumberland always prided himself as a prudent magnate, as a judicious practical evaluator of difficult, volatile predicaments or controversies, a man of reason and artfulness, and at this juncture he came to the decision that allowing Zeke Borshellac to address his followers was the wise feint to disarm their crazed belligerence that teetered on a riot. Despite his son's strenuous arguments to the contrary, calling for a restoration of order by the legions right then, Lord Cumberland's mind was made up.

Zeke had grown increasingly concerned that had not a momentary compromise been reached, a calamitous bloody clash would result, and he considered calling on the singers and chanters to take a break before the out-and-out violence could begin. The perilous deadlock could not hold at such immense levels of unchecked combustion and emotion, but then Lord Cumberland was at the microphone now stating that Zeke Borshellac would be permitted to come up to the stage and speak to everyone.

"The Von Klobbert Farm was good to Zeke Borshellac," he began, "and by all accounts Zeke was a hard-working farmer with a natural affinity for tilling the soil. Phineas and Abigail Von Klobbert have fond memories of Zeke's early months on the farm when he learned how to plough and work the land. *Before* he became a rabble-rousing demagogue. In the spirit of that good will and opportunity the Von Klobbert's showed Zeke, we will welcome him to this stage to address this venerable Hootenanny Harvest that has eclipsed all previous attendances of all such events in these territories." Lord Cumberland knew what he was doing, let them have their glorious moment in which they can exult and holler and cheer for their fair-haired boy, allow them that brief thrill of catharsis in seeing Zeke take the stage and deliver the platitudes and pie-in-the-sky fantasies they wanted to hear, and afterwards, as the Hootenanny finished with a whimper and the snockered and sated throngs dispersed, Borshellac would be quietly arrested and remanded back to the Frodtznjepple Peninsula. The raw exalted tumult that rose in crescendo was so loud now that to Zeke it seemed like the mass of noise was riding over them, a deep echo of the firmament, as if the singing and chanting and cheering melded into a single sound so big and noisy and awe-inspiring that it hovered over the masses like the disembodied yowls of a million ghosts who were watching from somewhere. And he heard the bands playing together as one great band, all farmer and hobo bands blowing and riffing and wailing Zeke's song with a rollicking looseness and improvisational brilliance that made it wondrous and singular and uniquely powerful to experience.

    As he made his way through the sprawling crowd, the reverential crowd, *his* crowd of loyal and desperate stalwarts of farms and railroad jungles far and wide, men who saw in his rise their hopes and visions of a better world where agriculture is prized and the boxcar nomads of the night can always count on the bountiful crops of farmers for nourishment and survival, he beheld them truly, up close, fleetingly but intensely. They were jubilant faces he moved past in his path now, hundreds of beaming, admiring, awe-struck visages that met his glancing eyes, scrambling in mad jostle to clear the way for him, trying to shake his hand, many calling out words of encouragement, "We're with you Zeke, all the way!" "Zeke, this is our time, you're the one, we believe in you!" "Zeke! Nothing is going to stop us! We all got your back!" They were singing "Out of the Sea . . .," their anthem, in a warmer, slower, more touching manner now, infused with an underpinning both holy and inextinguishable, while the "We Want Zeke" chants still sprung up in merry raucous waves as now the profound excitement and eager anticipation throughout the vast pastureland continued to build. Yes, it was happening, their standard bearer, Zeke Borshellac, the fabled Hobo Farmer, was threading his way, faithful sheepdog at his side, through the throngs to the stage. And Zeke saw in their faces and heard in their voices a cry for better fates and was again humbled by their true belief in him to lead them there. He knew those faces and voices out there, disgusted, disappointed, frustrated, but not yet beaten, not defeated quite yet, plenty of reserves somewhere inside prepared to fight and ride second winds as far as possible. He knew them because he was one of them, and boy did he ever have a fire burning in him fanning into a conflagration by a sure second wind poised to push the Grange movement forward. Zeke knew it was in him and had to come out, as he sensed all along while not cognizant of its source and content, and now he felt all his struggles and undying desire to help people, all the pain and persevering, all of it culminating in his emergence as leader of the Grange Movement. Many hoboes and farmers he encountered along his path to the stage were men he knew, such as the amiable tramp Quigley who sprung upon him with worshipful eyes and slapped his back, Dirk Freckler, the vociferous wheat farmer shouting incoherent words of encouragement in his ear, the indefatigable hobo Floop performed a brief jig and tipped his battered porkpie, the skinny harp-playing Vigalor and his pal Spodio, hoboes he once encountered on a ride deep in the woods now beamed and wrung his hand, and then came out of the crowd his old pal Mathias Edgecomb, who Zeke embraced and told his former farming mentor that he could always depend on him when the tide turned against the newcomer they all pegged as a hobo.

Mathius spoke with solemn emotion. "You always had the heart and the will, Zeke, I knew you were destined for something beyond our farm. No one could work the plough like you. I know you will be great up there addressing everyone."

A little farther in his momentous approach to the stage he came across his beloved old mentor and warhorse sage of the agricultural struggles, Horst Schtuckgloo, the veteran farmhand who had taken a shine to the hobo who was willing to sweat blood over the soil and introduced him to the Grange meetings. The rangy whiskered old-timer, surrounded by Grange leaders, placed his hands on Zeke's shoulders and smiled with stark surety at the protégé who had returned heroically and dramatically. "Zeke, we could never but believe that somehow you would emanate from that Gehenna and reappear here for our unfinished business. Remember the Corinthians. 'And one night the Lord said to Paul in a vision, 'Do not fear, but speak and do not keep silence; because I am with thee, and no one shall attack thee or injure thee, for I have many people in this city.' " Horst gripped Zeke's shoulders tight and held his eyes with his fiery gaze for a few moments before releasing him.

"Out of the Sea and Up from the Soil" continued to roar with the might of thousands of voices singing with the passion of their lives, and the formidable waves that broke over the vast stretches with "We Want Zeke," and the several bands of hoboes and farmers blared their instruments in improvisational brilliance that few could ever have imagined.

Zeke pushed onward towards the stage and Balthazar let out an excited bark and the enormity of the moment, weighing on Zeke now, suddenly occurred to him with a jolt. And he saw her now on the viewing stand seated where she had been all along, still seeming withdrawn and bleary and listlessly broken, yet stunningly beautiful, tragically so he thought all the same. He felt all the indignity, the outrage, the subjugation of the once naturally cheerful and blithe dairymaid and he swore he would rescue her from the thrall of the Cumberlands. Then for a moment, a sweet luminous instant, he met her glance and thought he sensed the old connection there, the spark in the glimpse that said so much, and he was heartened and buoyed with exultant sensations. Then it passed when hovering over her were Gerard and his father in animated intense discussions, Phineas and the Major of the Legion now walking with them to the edge of the stage from the viewing stand. His reverie darkened, he wondered if he had experienced a tender moment with Livinia or if he had imagined it.

Doc Hockers emerged from the crowd to pump Zeke's hand, smiling with tired eyes, the physician of Von Klobbert farm who administered first aid to Zeke a few memorable occasions, said in a hoarse voice: "Zeke, remember they used to call me when anybody became ill or got injured on the farm? It seems we're all calling on you now to lead the way forward." Zeke took his words to heart, told him he'd do his best up there.

And no sooner did he move past Hockers when he came upon a familiar figure, a young fellow with soulful eyes gazing at him. They both were speechless for a few moments as they peered at one another. "Jarvis, you made it," Zeke said. He was gratified and moved to see the brave turnkey who befriended him in prison and helped him escape. They embraced.

"Nothing was going to keep me away, Zeke. I had to be here for the Movement, for you. You're making some kind of history."

Zeke nodded with a half smile. "If it wasn't for you, I'd be rotting in that hellhole still. I am forever grateful."

"No, I am the grateful one, Zeke. I listened to your lectures from your cell. Without you inspiring me I too would be rotting in that hellhole. Now I want to join your cause."

Zeke smiled. "We need people like you, Jarvis. We need you."

He neared the stage and the swarm of folks surrounding his progress seemed to intensify with their great anticipation of his performance, their wanting to see him up close, and so many forms and faces jutted towards him to shake his hand and offer statements of support, these followers who had so much faith in Zeke Borshellac. Balthazar began to bark and wag his tail with excitement as a small commotion occurred just ahead, and then the two boys who took Zeke's confinement to prison very hard sprang out of the crowd from below, from a hidden place they found beside the stage, and the sheepdog was greeting them happily albeit allowed them to rush Zeke and simultaneously hug the hobo farmer whose return they never gave up on.

"I knew you didn't croak in that joint, Zeke!" cried Ogden, his feistiness, mop of blond hair and frayed overalls just as Zeke recalled. "I never bought that bunk that was going around!"

The taller Huxley grinned showing his crooked teeth and echoed his younger pal's words. "Same by me, Zeke! I knew there was no damn slammer that can hold you! Not even Froddy. I told 'em all you'd be bustin' out there. I knew it. We missed you, Zeke."

Zeke laughed with all the affection and appreciation he always felt towards the two wild urchins who reveled in harum-scarum hi-jinx. "How did you boys make it over here from the tree so fast?" he asked, not expecting a response. "We had some fun on this farm, did we not? Let's play some Shrike on the Fruitwood . . . again, eh?"

Ogden replied keenly: "You got it Zeke! We got your number in Splatterbrain Suggsy *Whoa! Whoa! Whoa!*"

The multitudes sang Zeke's song and the musician's played the melody with mad virtuosity, a constant thunderous roaring, resound-

TWENTY-ONE

ing, and Zeke surveyed the crowd surging all around him wanting to touch him or just catch a glimpse of him, and he was continuously humbled by their trust and unadulterated faith, swearing to himself that he would never let them down. He took his last few paces to the stairs at the side of the stage and began to climb them, now moving on the raised platform he was able to truly take in the endless sea of folks stretching in every direction, no one had ever seen such a mass gathering, he thought. He felt all of the deafening reverberations of their singing his song, marveled at the aggregation of musicians playing as if they had been one band for years, gazed out at the faraway silos of worn white paint he knew so well, the barn to his side he slept in for so long with Balthazar, the farmhouse he esteemed so much and ate suppers with the Van Klobberts and hands, the direction his first field lay where he learned the trade of ploughing so thoroughly.

The chants of "We Want Zeke!" were louder now than anything he ever heard and he absorbed it all for a few moments as he looked for Balthazar, who had climbed to the stage with him, and waited for his splendid sheepdog to find a suitable place beside him to sit and watch him deliver his speech. He glanced the dairymaid's way several times and felt he saw enough connection in her eyes to convince himself their time, like the Movement's, had come now and he knew in his bones somehow they would come together. He fought off any doubts that he was engaging in wishful thinking of some kind and imagined his performance would waken the lost dairymaid from the grip of her tormentors. He turned to Balthazar one last time and their eyes met before he moved closer to the front of the stage where the microphone on a stand awaited him. He had never seen a genuine microphone before and marveled at the dynamic steel design of the instrument. He glanced at the loudspeakers projecting from tall poles on each side of the stage and blew into the mic, creating a sonorous sloughing that carried for miles it seemed, as loudspeakers were strung up on trees and poles throughout the grounds. The singing gradually began to fade and the chants seemed to cease rather quickly, as they all anticipated Zeke's address was about to begin. As the din diminished and a stark silence suddenly fell over everyone Zeke was shaken by the pressure as he began to form his first words. But nothing formed in his mind and nothing came out of his mouth. He cleared his throat uneasily, worriedly, with nothing to clear but his head that was devoid of a worthy thought to articulate. He adjusted the fit of his custom-made coat that Pud Stupilis fashioned out of broadcloth for him at the jungle, wiped off some traces of dirt on his sleeves, glanced again over to his sheepdog who seemed concerned to him. He peered upon the viewing stand to his immediate left where Livinia sat in abstracted introspection, a melancholy haze it seemed to Zeke, Phineas and Abigail to her right appearing shaken and indignant, and Lord Cumberland standing with his arms folded over his ample midsection, talking to the Major of the Legions, a husky fellow himself with a brindled mustache and high boots, and Gerard stood closest to the stage, looking daggers at Zeke with a smirking malice that sensed a stumble by his old foe who returned from the dead to steal his thunder with such gusto. Raw anger flared in the hobo farmer, an instinctual fury that wanted to beat the Cumberland son up, a wrath he had to control and channel into his address to the masses stretched as far as one could see. But it only threw him further into a tongue-tied tizzy that writhed in a hole of consternation deepening with every tick of a silent clock. He became conscious of his breathing as it grew irregular and labored, his onset of panic leaving him frozen and free falling deeper into an abyss of speechlessness. The inexorable silence continued choking him as his vision shrank into a fuzzy portal of still forms gawking at him groping up there, thousands of figures riveted on him waiting for words but witnessing an impossible implosion of unprecedented proportions. The painful seconds piled up and Zeke remained immobilized like a clay sculpture, and he felt woozy now, light-headed and dizzy, about ready to faint when he thought maybe if he could start his speech they would think his long-delayed silence had been purposeful for dramatic effect. He struggled mightily for opening words as vertigo and nausea took their toll and rendered him teetering on unsteady legs. The stark silence carried on disturbingly over the massive crowd, only a rustle of leaves here and there stirring in the wind was audible.

Finally he forced out an utterance in an act of pure will, a vocal release hoarse and low that seemed a declaration of sorts: "Hoboes, farmers, all of you out there . . . I was lost at sea . . . consumed by the soil . . . left for dead . . . but here I am with you at this Hootenanny Harvest . . . to begin our journey to a better world and better lives!" After several seconds as Zeke hesitated to continue a tremendous volcanic roar rose from the great throng and it went on and on, breaking into the chants of "We want Zeke!" and the heartfelt singing of "Out of the Sea and Up from the Soil" all over again. Zeke waited for his exuberant supporters to quiet down, smiling occasionally and eventually waving his arms in a manner asking them for silence. When they finally gave it to him he once more found himself bereft of words that seemed right to say, nothing to his alarm came to his head that his tongue might utter. Again a long uncomfortable silence ensued before the crowd showed signs of impatience, distant catcalls few could make out, whisperings of exasperation, restless movement of the once stockstill audience. Zeke searched his mind and sweat blood to push past his stage fears to find his next line, but he knew his address had to be beyond anything they had seen or might expect. While he had nothing, felt empty and dizzy, during the transitory moments ticking away up there on the stage he instinctually recognized the intensifying stakes for him to perform extraordinarily for his folks, this was the supreme do-or-die juncture. In that regard, the long silence worked in his favor, dramatizing the hobo farmer's presence on the stage as his imminent ignominious flopsweat failure vied with his elemental hardiness of spirit to come back with something to thrill his followers. He called a few musicians to the stage, the red hot trumpeter Hop Quinine of course, the young harum-scarum hellraiser Nathaniel Schmidt on guitar, Ott Eschledy on drums, the tandem of trombonists, Yance Brollo and the ever affable Tommy Dunkirk, the hobo harp maestro Stublinski, the drummer Rupert Yuckens, and he told them in a soft but assured voice that he wanted to open with the beloved hobo classic "Coal

Car Carl Ain't Dead Yet." The musicians seemed uneasy as they waited for his cue to begin, Zeke called out to for some hooch to wet his whistle and several hoboes and farmers responded with alacrity, the first bottle reaching his hand he took a good hit as the crowd grew more restless and it did appear Zeke was stalling. Then he turned his back to the crowd and raised his left arm, grasping the microphone stand in his right hand, his right foot tapping to a beat only he was hearing. When his arm came down they struck up the rousing chords that kick the number off, and Zeke transformed himself into a performer who transfixed everyone with his moves and voice and hypnotic aura, a feat of astonishing will and unbridled surrender to instinct. While he crooned the bittersweet lyrics attesting to the everlasting Carl's durability and inexorable hobo spirit, the crowd understood that Zeke was really singing about himself and the Movement. It was in the utter raw sincerity he summoned, the dual evocations of bravado and vulnerability that came across in his voice, and the improvisational footwork of his dance flourishes that saw him swing the microphone stand overhead in blinding circles, culminating in a series of launches into the air which he caught in stride with assured panache each time. The ovation he received after this number was so loud and long it alone corroborated that Zeke had something up there truly singular and unprecedented. He waited for the applause to finally quiet and now began to describe the next numbers he was going to perform, "Corn on the Cob and a Cup of Joe, Brother Farmer!" and "Wheat Fields Swayin' While I Watch 'Em With My Whiskey," and "Boxcar Slim and the Turnip Patch Fluke," fine old classics whose central themes underscored the symbiotic connection that had thrived naturally throughout hard times, the hoboes' reliance on beneficent farmers and their bountiful crops for sustenance and likewise the brotherhood of hoboes always looked out for the foreclosed farmer and hands to befriend and welcome into the jungles and train hopping milieu.

"Hoboes and farmers have always taken care of one another in the most natural and necessary ways, through nourishment both physical and spiritual, food grown from the soil and friendship straight from the heart," Zeke explained, calling then for several more musicians to join him and his band on stage in the performance of these beloved songs. "The agricultural life will forever live on, we must grow our crops and raise our livestock, it is who we are. And the hobo spirit of adventure and new horizons must forever remain a key part of us. Together we will maintain our farmlands of abundant harvest, together our hobo rambling spirit, camaraderie and solidarity will carry us forward!" And he began to sing the aforesaid songs with a genuine belief in every lyric, a staunch serving of truth in every vocal inflection and harmonic swing. His movements were equally honest in their simple dexterous display, crisp footwork pivoting sideways integrated with sharp kicks at 3 o'clock and 9 o'clock outward angles, while his torso undulated spasmodically and arms performed complex circular motions punctuated by right hand chops against an unsteady left arm to suggest some arcane sign language. His voice was in perfect form and the crowd bathed in the inspired yearning notes of desperate striving, while his movements simply perplexed and stunned them before they caught on with revelatory gratification the complicated emotional terrain he was traversing over. At some point while exploring the subtleties of the turnip patch serendipity of the Boxcar Slim number, Zeke radically veered from the framework of the song and broke into what appeared to be a prose poem. He waxed poetic about the land and the importance of protecting its purity and productivity, its beauty and fertility and, most of all, their control of it, ownership. "The good earth provides subsistence for us all. The farmer makes a living, the hobo comes across some grub, more crops will become necessary in the jerkwaters and boondocks as more hoboes start appearing on the byways by way of the railroad jungles. We must harness the mutual strength and potential of both." As he delivered his lines in a rhapsodic soaring bellow that interpolated deep lugubrious moans, the hobo farmer allowed his feet to improvise a blinding tap dance, brilliantly bungling, that segued into a series of bends and twists that wiped out in several hard crashes, each time his bouncing back more manically determined to perform better with an expanding array of musicians on stage for his experimenting with new songs and increasingly daring dance moves.

At this juncture in his performance with the crowd completely charged, Zeke decided to unleash his discovery about the Cumberlands' secret plan to sell off the region's farmlands to industrialists who would erect smokestack factories throughout and forever obliterate the pastoral splendor and agricultural world that existed for centuries. He dropped this bombshell through a series of extempore skits that told the story of the wild overnight rides he took with Catapultus, the exhilarating release they provided him, the philosophical flow of thought they afforded him, and he presented these scenes by scampering about the stage in a clippety-cloppety manner that ingeniously suggested he was horseback. He broke into a spontaneous "Ode to Catapultus," an entrancing swerve into verse, before embarking on the Forest Tavern skits that recounted the story of Zeke stumbling upon the drunken Gerard, off in a corner ensconced with a bevy of harlots, rambling on about his and his father's stealthy plot to sell off all the farmlands. The skits inside the tavern initially were character studies of the tradesmen he observed, such as the wainwright who smoked a pipe and met his old pal, a stocky silversmith, and they spoke of fond memories as boys. Eventually, Zeke concocted a woodland ghostly figure who wore a tweed cape and deerstalker and haunted the forest as well as the tavern, a chimerical character whose perspective was critical to communicating the revelation about Gerard with the apposite tone and details. Zeke's woodland ghost sang and danced to comic effect, strutted about the stage regaling the crowd with reminiscences of his experiences as a ghost circumscribed to such a remote area, all as a prelude to the stunning scene in the tavern he bore witness to that evening. The ghost, who called himself Sturgiss, went on to describe in a straightforward manner the spectacle of himself Gerard Cumberland made, not protracting the salacious tawdry elements of his carrying on with his harlots, albeit not omitting that part either, but underscoring the high-handed statements he had made when his sloshed tongue divulged the scheme of his father and him to sell the farmlands.

As a device of the skit, Sturgiss referred to a strange horseman who tippled alone, obviously Zeke observing as well, and the denouement of the skit shows Sturgiss and Zeke in dialogue about the evidence of a plot they eavesdropped upon. The conversation crackles with scattergun non sequiturs about irrigation techniques and hobo terminology, and the crowd, already mesmerized, simply ate it up. There were accented allusions to the plot that Sturgiss and Zeke molded into melodies, such as "Cumberland Wants a Garrison with a Regiment on my Cornfields," " More Mills and Factories Mean More Taxes For Their Coffers," "Farms Go Away We Are Industrializing!" and "The Old Remittance Man Sneaks Back into London, While the Son Shall Rule!" And they sang a duet about the magnificence and faith and honesty inherent in the agricultural life and the importance of defeating any threat to its existence. It was a wonderful exultant number that deeply moved every farmer and hobo present while rousing their fighting spirit even beyond the courageous will they already had shown. The ovation shook the earth of the pastures for what seemed miles, the folks would not stop the crazy exhilarated applause as it went on and on, and Zeke brought Balthazar to the mic and the beloved sheepdog barked a message that sounded very sanguine, and with a twenty-two piece motley mix of musicians standing to his sides Zeke led them through a few closing numbers, old classics in creative interpretive versions, among them "Don't Eat Pegler's Goo Goo Crop," "Lefty Malzone Was Right," "Stu Bleavins Dropped Dead," "The Moon Looks Mean When Passing Through Moline," "Hoboes at the Hootenanny Laughing it Up," and finally a slow, solemn, viscerally uplifting finale combining "Sodbusters Sockeroo" and "Woke Up in Wichita on the Cannonball When a Bull Clubbed Me Over the Head" and, of course, "Out of the Sea and Up from the Soil." When he had finished his eyes were on Livinia, where they had frequently wandered, and they locked their gazes with a fervency that told him she was once again herself. She was standing on the reviewing stand and now began hurriedly towards him, as the crowd continued their sustained ovation that managed to once more top their previous thunderous volumes. Gerard had been conferring with his father and appeared quite agitated for some time, they were talking to the Major of the Legion as the dairymaid darted across the reviewing stand and leapt to the stage and soon was joined with Zeke in a passionate embrace, tears running down her cheeks, before they kissed in the way only long lost lovers know how. Balthazar jumped in the air and wagged his tail, Ogden and Huxley, now on the stage happily hugged the exuberant sheepdog as the three stood beside the smooching couple they'd always rooted for.

TWENTY-TWO

L̲ORD CUMBERLAND and Gerard were surrounded by Phineas and other farm owners who were jawing their rancor in no uncertain terms, the gist of Zeke's disclosure about the pending industrialization hitting home with them and explaining all the tours of the properties Gerard had been conducting with men of commerce in big city suits. It suddenly became clear to the farm owners the monumental betrayal the Cumberlands were surreptitiously seeking to perpetrate. The dispute escalated and became increasingly furious as the Cumberlands tried to tamp down the bitter distrust and shaken confidence in their governance duties, and the acrimony approached violence as Gerard became aware of Livinia's departure into Zeke's arms and began shouting for the Legion to arrest him. He shouted this order several times to no avail and the crowd was rumbling in a disarray, seemingly waiting to see what was coming, nothing of harm to their beloved leader Zeke Borshellac or there would be hell to pay. Finally, amid all the chaos of confusion and imminent utter madness and melee, Gerard rushed to confront the Major of the Legion himself, thrusting his bellowing mug into his face and commanding he instruct his troops over the loudspeaker to arrest Zeke Borshellac immediately. When the Major still hesitated after much badgering, himself questioning Lord Cumberland's commitment to rural life, Gerard flew into a rage of condemnation, swearing he would have his badge taken as a Legion officer. Gerard bolted for the nearest microphone by the reviewing stand and again boomed the order to those in uniform closest the stage, albeit his menacing voice carried over the loudspeakers to the legions spread throughout the grounds: "Arrest that man immediately! Arrest

Zeke Borshellac now!" He eyed Zeke with malice and pointed at him as the hobo farmer stood on the stage with Livinia at his side. "Arrest that agitator for subversion, he is an insidious insurrectionist that is responsible for this damnable uprising!" He went on and on accusing Zeke of plotting a violent overthrow, of perfidious schemes of a dangerous incendiary bent on destruction of decent society, but it became apparent well before he ceased screaming commands that the legions were not listening to him. The many uniformed legions amassed near the stage and viewing stand, the others spread throughout the grounds, remained stock-still with their firearms undrawn and their sympathies undergoing a tectonic shift. Gerard in vicious frustration once more confronted the Major of the Legions, who was listening to Lord Cumberland attempting to explain the industry magnates seen strolling the pastures with himself and Gerard so frequently, and he demanded he obey his order to arrest the insurrectionist Borshellac or suffer the consequences of his own arrest and imprisonment.

"And just who is going to arrest me, Mr. Cumberland? I'm afraid in the court of public opinion of which my legions are part and parcel, your credibility as the administrators of the region has been irrevocably damaged, if not criminally implicated."

Lord Cumberland, ever the sly equivocator, the temporizing finagler, sought to obfuscate the narrative now becoming obvious about the probity of his superintendence. "Major, emotions are overwrought at the moment, let's not resort to hyperbolic reckless speculation. The man escaped from the Frodtznjepple Peninsula where he was imprisoned for crimes against the state. He will be arrested soon enough with or without your legions. Regiments of the greater jurisdictional constabulary will be by soon enough. Perhaps you hesitate in the moment to exercise prudence, considering the performance of Borshellac hypnotizing his followers?"

The Major of the Legion looked at Lord Cumberland like one would regard a confidence man who folks were now wise to, and simply said, "The situation is far beyond prudence, wouldn't you say? I think Zeke happens to be one of those extraordinary brave souls who tell us the truth and the whole shoddy infrastructure of the establishment comes tumbling down. You sir, appear to be on the wrong side of the tumbling."

Meanwhile, Gerard had already given up on assistance from the legions, who were all celebrating with beer and esprit de corps joy with their farmer and hobo brothers for as far and wide as the eye could see, and the raging humiliated son now made his way to the stage where Zeke held court with Livinia, Balthazar, Ogden and Huxley, Horst, Booth, Mathias, several elders from the Grange, and there were old hobo pals around him too. Phineas and Abigail were congratulating him on his unforgettable performance and thanking him for his commitment to the agricultural life and inviting him back to the farm in an elevated role of farm management. "We had such a fine harvest, Zeke," Phineas related, "a real bumper crop, and to think they were still talking about foreclosure—"

Zeke smiled. "The Von Klobbert Farm can never go under. It will always be a thriving farm, Phineas, because the land is fertile and the people work so hard and are so kind. It made me who I am today, and I'll never forget it."

Just then Gerard made it to them and he yelled for Livinia to come to him. "Don't throw away your future, Livvy! Come here and forget about this foul rabble-rouser who cares only about himself! When the smoke clears from his day out here with the legions losing their minds, he will be back in Froddy and my father and I will remember very well who seized this opportunity to betray us!"

The dairymaid held onto Zeke's arm and addressed her nemesis in a clear-eyed, peremptory manner: "Your privilege and coercion no longer have power over me, Gerard, nor any of us around these parts. I love Zeke and hope to never see you again."

Everyone on the stage now stared at the Cumberland son in his rejection, hoping he would withdraw, but he was not through with the woman he manipulated for so long. "You have lost your mind, Livinia! There is no other explanation for you to fall for this vile radical, this grungy miscreant! You *will come with me for your own good!*" He lunged towards the dairymaid and tried to grab her, but Zeke stepped in to block him. The others on the stage called for Gerard to leave it alone, pleaded with him to back off.

"Come on, Gerard, Livinia could not have been more direct. You should just go away now. Please," Phineas implored.

But Zeke was not asking him anything, he was *telling* him, "Scram or you and me will have to scrap it out."

Gerard smirked and snickered with the words: "So the living piece of crud who blighted our land with his odious presence all these months thinks his time has come, eh?" He laughed derisively. "The legion will come to their senses and all this madness will go away, and you will be sent back to Froddy for a date with the hangman's noose, my poor dead tramp!" The great crowd was again singing "Out of the Sea and Up From the Soil" in their jubilance and triumph in winning over the legions to their cause, and surging swarms were now surrounding the stage watching the encounter with the newly unfrocked Cumberland son and the man of the hour Zeke.

"I don't think so. Now as I said, beat it or you're going to get yours," Zeke told him plainly.

Gerard promptly threw a punch that Zeke ducked and the fight was on with everyone on the stage scrambling amid much yelling and Livinia pleading with Zeke not to engage with him. Great agitation rose from the viewing platform where Lord Cumberland was shouting now for his son to leave it be, "the greater jurisdictional constabulary will be around soon enough to settle the score!" The bulky regional administrator began charging towards the stage to expostulate with his son but was restrained by several legions, compelling him to watch the bout as a mere spectator like everyone else riveted around the combatants.

It was well past the point of intercession now as the two men squared off right there on the raised platform where all could see, and there were thousands of spectators in rows amassed around the bout, their partisanship for the hobo farmer as ardent and full-throated as the utter unanimity of their numbers would allow. Never had such deafening roars of support for a fighter been heard anywhere by anyone present, his number "Out of the Sea and Up from the Soil" entering the din in intermittent waves of a mass chorus. It began with Gerard the aggressor boring in wildly and throwing big roundhouses that Zeke dodged and bobbed around on his nimble bouncing feet. Gerard screamed and swore at his kinetic opponent, charging in swinging and desperately looking to tackle him or land a barrage of blows. But Zeke was too quick for him, invariably keeping two moves ahead and evading the Cumberland son's every punch with crowd-pleasing verve. Zeke never felt so fast and agile and supremely confident in his boxing brilliance, not that he had much experience in the sweet science but his triumphant return to the Hootenanny and his dreamlike reunion with the dairymaid afforded him such a boost he invented his own style of boxing replete with crazy footwork, frenetic dancing feints, jerky evasive maneuvers . . . the kind of dazzling display of wizardry which was largely about the performance. One truth that Zeke came to understand and embrace in his long journey from sea to soil was the importance of performance in so many of life's pursuits and challenges. Whether fair and just or not, the showmanship of one's approach to achieving a goal can be the key element to realizing success, he recognized. Zeke's singular boxing exhibition he put on with the rampaging Gerard rushing him to no avail from every angle was a show no one would soon forget. His arrhythmic, unpredictable, unorthodox freeform manner all at lightning speed was confusing and impenetrable to Gerard's advances as Zeke repeatedly faked and dodged his pursuer to such an extent Cumberland found himself so off balance he'd fallen to the floor more than once. The crowd was delighted by Zeke's offbeat defensive approach that again and again made Gerard appear like a raving rabid oaf, and Zeke obliged by providing the evasive razzle-dazzle while holding off on clocking the Cumberland son despite many opportunities. It went on with Zeke playing the fleet-footed matador to Gerard's mad bull, over and over Zeke would cleverly elude the wild charges and blows while expending minimal energy as Gerard became increasingly fatigued and spent.

Until the Cumberland son tried a zigzagging approach that ostensibly cornered Zeke to the rear of the stage, but when he bore in with a last maniacal advance—ponderous, unsteady, lurching from utter exhaustion—Zeke was ready and sidestepped him with a nimble flourish and Gerard found himself airborne going off the stage. His inanimate form crashed into the well-trod, hardened dirt below with an ugly thud, landing on his side and remaining as such in a motionless heap for several lengthy moments before slightly stirring with arms and legs until he was able to sit up and simply totter in a half-conscious haze with a bell rung sufficiently to keep him on his rumpus for a good while past that. The crowd erupted in uproarious cheers and jubilant cries and thunderous joyous noise at the magnificent knockout scored by their hero, the hobo farmer himself, in his own inimitable amazing thrilling way which rendered his malevolent adversary unconscious without ever laying a fist on him. They clapped and cried words of congratulations, and they too began again singing Zeke's song in a new slower solemn tone, affording him space on the stage as he embraced Livinia in his moment of triumph, received Balthazar's giddy excited leap for a hug, and Og and Hux, Horst, Booth, Mathius, all offered their heartfelt wishes for such a courageous and stunningly singular manner of victory.

So many made their way to the victor, tendering hearty congratulations and words of abiding support, dozens of farmers and hoboes demonstratively extending their elation over his knockout win, wringing his hand or slapping his back or simply embracing him. The musicians struck up an enchanting medley of hobo and farmer songs with a rough spontaneous quality that somehow sounded rousing and poignant at the same time. It was a true harvest homecoming for Zeke, for he knew all the struggle and perseverance of being on the road, his simple objective to help folks while remaining righteous throughout, was truly worth it. He had made his mark but was just getting started and felt a surge of gathering momentum carrying him forward, a second wind driven by a vision of idealism. The Grange elders now came by to shake his hand with broad smiles and plainspoken kudos, a sincere dignity ever at the core of their roughhewn rusticity, and these seasoned sodbusters in the autumn of their years saw in Zeke the very future of agriculture life and its abiding prevalence. Partnering with the hoboes was his transformational idea that paradoxically seemed limiting and even foolhardy but was indeed a revelation of bold-spirited thinking that would be hailed as an obvious, necessary alliance to future generations. The veteran hoboes who were considered the brain trust also approached Zeke as a contingent and were quite animated with their whooping and hollering and laughing with their beloved bellwether who came through for them so much, and soon Zeke was huddling with a joint committee of the two groups.

The Grange elders apprised him of the Riverbank Jamboree that was planned in one week to take place in the city of Porsnaugen. It was another mass gathering of farmers and hoboes to further their unified momentum as a force of change and fellowship while concomitantly preserving the farming life and freedom to roam and seek new horizons. Angus Fletly, the octogenarian potato farmer active in the Grange for most of his life, saw a true follow-up opportunity in the Jamboree in Porsnaugen. "Zeke, whatever happened here at the Hootenanny we knew we needed another rally to keep the Movement going." He patted his shoulder twice and looked away. "Your memory frankly is responsible for drawing the massive crowd today . . . a posthumous tribute was the thinking I'm afraid . . . but now that you are with us flesh and blood, think of what your presence will mean to those attending the Jamboree in Porsnaugen."

Zeke nodded at Fletly's earnest plea and knew at once his place to be next was Porsnaugen, which had a rough-and-tumble seedy image as a river city and would certainly attract a great many hoboes regardless of the convocation of the Movement. "Well, I hope the news of my continued existence will be a boost to our folks showing up!" he chuckled. He turned to Livinia and met her beautiful eyes with his gaze, while asking the committee for a few moments alone with the dairymaid. "It feels like a dream, Livinia, making it to this Hootenanny and finding you in my arms. A dream I never want to wake up from and I could not bear being separated from your presence ever again—"

The dairymaid laughed her lovely laugh and he seemed bemusedly nonplussed. "Of course I'd be very pleased to join you, Zeke, in your trip to Porsnaugen. If that's what your beating around the bush to ask me!"

He smiled broadly and she exclaimed: "Porsnaugen or bust!" And they embraced and kissed and when they stopped he said: "It's you and me and this great Movement that will protect farmers and provide succor to hoboes."

"I'm so excited to be part of it, Zeke," she declared buoyantly, "it truly feels like the beginning of revolutionary change coming from the people. They needed someone to be out front, the right leader. I'm so proud of you." She paused, then: "We all thought the worst."

Her face for a second reflected the anguish she felt during his imprisonment and Zeke embraced her, telling her that he thought of her every day in the godforsaken Frodtznjepple. "The faith I had in one day achieving my freedom and seeing you again Livinia is what really sustained me and kept me alive in there." They held one another and declared their love for each other in such a deep earnest manner Zeke felt it resonate to his very core and knew it was a moment he would forever remember. He knew she felt the same by her slight trembling, her tight embrace, her eyes. Zeke broke the silence as they separated: "Porsnaugen may not be Paris, but with you at my side it will feel like a trip to a paradise."

The crowd, continuing to sing and celebrate and revel in the splendid events of the day, the legions continuing to partake of the festivities with a hearty gusto, the Cumberlands now contained somewhere as the Major of the legionary troops had taken charge of matters. When Gerard finally had shaken the cobwebs from his brain after his tumble he became quite volatile and truculent towards the Major, demanding Zeke's arrest, until he had to be subdued by legions and taken into custody himself. Zeke was already preparing for the journey to Porsnaugen as it would require at least three full days and nights from the farm, the joint committee recommending he leave that very night to ensure his arrival on time. Many hoboes and farmers wanted to join Zeke on the challenging trip, to be part of history and to ensure protection for Zeke now that he was such a controversial figure whose fame held varying meanings to people, some certain to stamp him a demagogue or dangerous agitator. Not because he felt vulnerable did Zeke decide on appointing an entourage to travel with him, but rather because he was so elated to see his old pals once again and thought they'd be valuable connecting with farmers and hoboes and deserved to be included in the long journey to such an important rally in the Movement's beginnings. They would have to ride horses and horse-drawn wagons to make it to Porsnaugen on time for the Jamboree and Zeke asked with great sentiment and trepidation about the status and availability of his old cherished horse, the powerful Catapaltus, and when Livinia assured him the black steed was indeed still in fine fettle, well-cared for by his friends in his absence, the hobo farmer choked up a little in his throat with relief and immense gratitude. Immediately a contingent of farmers were dispatched to deliver Catapaltus to his true owner, and a fine sorrel by the name of Macklemore, the horse the dairymaid most often rode from the farm's stable, was sent for as well. Those he chose to accompany him to Porsnaugen were honored and thrilled to go, most of the riders he assembled were selections one would expect. Horst Schtuckgloo of course was tapped first, Zeke sidled up beside him wrapping his arm around his shoulders, telling him simply in a low voice that he needed him to come, and the old farmer nodded with a slight but beatific smile. Booth Booley breathed deeply and almost teared up when Zeke quietly asked him over a few hits of beer together. Mathias Edgecomb was engaged in singing and beery dancing with a bunch of legions and young farm hands when Zeke spotted him and called him over to broach the trip. "Wouldn't miss it for the world, Zeke. We've come this far, and we're going all the way!" he exclaimed. Cy Undersnettle was visibly moved to get the nod, and Wyatt Plantwater inquired if Zeke was traveling with a group and volunteered his presence for the journey, citing his status as a

Grange officer, and Zeke felt obliged to invite him. Doc Hockers was chosen so the caravan would have a medic on hand who can perform first aid if necessary. Corn Cavendish did an impromptu jig, his rolypoly form and long beard whirling about in delight over Zeke requesting his presence on the Porsnaugen ride. Joke, his excited gangling figure so happy to be included he hugged Zeke and The Captain, his derby-topped squat pal also invited. Floop and Geets, well along in the wassails could not refrain from pie-eyed hobo horseplay to show their pleasure at being picked. And Quigley, well, the loopy capricious but ever unwavering hobo committed to the cause, dropped to his knees uncharacteristically in solemn gratitude to make the cut. Crokus was added as the chronicler, Zeke considered him a capable scribe sympathetic to the movement and, moreover, the only such reporter around. It took Zeke and others a while to locate Jarvis, who had gravitated towards the maple tree near the potato fields where he quietly celebrated with a tall beer and a group of admiring farmers asking him about Zeke in Frodtznjepple, but when he did, as several people were watching, Zeke asked in a more formal manner for the erstwhile turnkey to join their journey to Porsnaugen. "It would be my honor, Zeke," Jarvis said. "The honor is mine, old friend," Zeke answered.

 A welter of hurried hullaballoo followed as those travelling with Zeke now moved to gather their equine conveyances and whatever they deemed necessary to pack for the road. Here now came the magnificent black steed Catapaltus, so imposing and powerful, led by Cy Undersnettle and the boys Ogden and Huxley, the assiduous tenders of the horse in the hobo farmer's absence. Zeke was very moved to greet his old steed again and felt a surge of grateful stirrings as he stroked him, and the tremulous whinnying bespoke a reciprocal appreciation. And right on his heels was the splendid sorrel Macklemore, trotted out by Abigail Von Klobbert herself, who proudly presented the horse so cherished by Livinia for the Porsnaugen adventure. "I'm going to make this official, Livinia. Macklemore is *your horse going forward*. You can count on him to carry you to Porsnaugen!"

TWENTY-TWO

Phineas had come over to congratulate Zeke and express his undying gratitude for his courage and strength in prevailing over the Cumberlands and being such an exemplary farmer in leading the Grange in establishing a new incipient agricultural era. The fatherly farm owner robustly embraced him and his matronly wife followed with a smiling kiss on his cheek, before they led him to the stage again. There the Major of the Legions greeted him with a solid slap on the back and hearty handshake. "You taught us all something important today, Zeke," he said. "Never give up the ghost when you know you're right. We all owe you a great debt, my fellow."

The dairymaid was at Zeke's side and Balthazar at his foot as Phineas approached the microphone and addressed the crowd, which had become more boisterous and raucous in a mad boozier sort of revelry. "I always admired Zeke Borshellac's stamina and zest for farming, but an ethereal streak can detract from his being taken seriously, and I was guilty of seeing him that way at times myself." The farmer patriarch hesitated as he collected himself. "But I'm here to tell you all that this man saved this farm all on his own. And *he willed* the wonderful bumper crop the soil yielded for our fine harvest, no one could plough a field like this man." He smiled and glanced at Zeke. "All he needed was an old ox named Gomer." His face became somber. "They threw him in Froddy on false charges, sought to destroy him . . . but *here he is back among us* . . . and he may have single-handedly saved agricultural as a way of life for us farmers. And I see now why he brought in the hoboes. They are our brothers and it is our duty to nourish them and doing so will save all of our souls. Come farm our land with us, good hobo friends. The farmers will adopt your freedom of spirit and sense of fellowship." Phineas paused with his head down, perhaps deciding if he had anything further to add. After a long uncertain silence he finally said: "And now it is time for us to hear from Zeke one last time before he departs for another rally in Porsnaugen. He is a leader for our times and our causes, whether you are a farmer, hobo, legion, or anyone who cares about progress as a people, this is a remarkable individual one can truly believe in and get behind. One who truly emerged out of the sea, as the song says, and came up from the soil. I give you Mr. Zeke Borshellac!"

The ever-swelling crowd with new arrivals, mostly hoboes, still pouring in now erupted in a deafening rumble and roar of emphatic approval and they spontaneously broke into "Out of the Sea and Up From the Soil" as the disparate sections of musicians struck up the notes once again in accompanying the full-throated roisterous singing that amplified more and more with passion and exultance. Zeke moved towards the microphone as Phineas gently placed his hand on his back before withdrawing, the intensity of the singing and music continuing unflaggingly for several minutes as Zeke stood and smiled slightly, humbly, he knew he must wait for them to quiet down, couldn't rush them if he tried. It seemed an interminable space of time to Zeke before the choristers and revelers finally went silent, as Zeke felt the tug of modesty while allowing his supporters the full expression of their joyous gratitude. But when they settled into that inevitable quietude of a crowd that hangs replete with the expectation of profound oratory delivered with memorable eloquence, Zeke, as he had done earlier, felt his sense of articulation seizing up on him and fast disintegrating into a maelstrom of blankness. He tried to modulate his breathing and find the modicum of equanimity necessary for him to deliver the right words, but the specter of the consequences of an abject failure to produce a fine parting speech proved a formidable foe. He fiddled with the microphone, adjusting its height and tilt protractedly, and began clearing his throat in a variety of raspy harrumphs and other cacophonous emittances from the bowels of his flop sweat fears, until he precipitated a full-blown coughing fit that elicited the attention of Cy Undersnettle and Doc Hockers. They administered him a glass of water, Zeke managed to kid Cy about their duking it out once more, and soon he was alone on stage, frozen, with a rapt crowd waiting for his words. The seconds kept stretching into minutes as the massive crowd grew restless and riveted to the dramatic spectacle of their new vibrant leader, the famed hobo farmer, one of their own who rose to lead their Movement, who appeared to be

TWENTY-TWO

struck with a paralyzing fright but who they knew better and believed that he had something powerful up his sleeve still. It was the familiar bark of his sheepdog that communicated a capability to proceed, he glanced over to Balthazar sitting up behind him and understood the tone and message of his bark that had been his counsel, the wise canine confidant in the past. Just move onward and the words will come, let the words emanate from your core, and with that Zeke broke into a sudden paroxysm of shaking and twisting and daring acrobatic somersaults through the air that crashed hard to the stage.

While this untoward further delay did not detract from the crowd's confidence that Zeke fully intended the rocky start to his farewell address, had the hobo farmer failed to rise with alacrity from the deck and deliver the meaningful speech they fully expected, well, it may have done some damage to his aura. But he indeed jumped right up with a rejuvenated urgent sensibility that now recognized the moment in social and agricultural history to which they all found themselves—and the importance of the leadership entrusted in him. He moved to the microphone and stood straight with his arms at his side and began: "There was a time not very long ago when people generally believed the Von Klobbert Farm would inevitably be closed. Some of us had faith that it would not. Deceivers in positions of power conspired to sell the land to industry, but we preserved our good soil and protected our farming way of life." The crowd erupted here in spontaneous applause and wild cheers, even a few verses of Zeke's "Sea . . . and Soil" theme song. After patiently awaiting their silence again he continued. "In the deepest forest I was lost with my sheepdog without any prospects of opportunity, until we came upon this farm, and they bestowed a plough upon me and assigned me a harsh field to harrow . . . I am forever grateful to the Von Klobberts and I never wavered in believing, despite the setbacks, that one day we would have the bountiful harvest we had this fall." Again the throngs broke into thunderous cheers and more of the Zeke's "Sea . . . and Soil" theme, the musicians sounding their notes for a ripping short span as well. Once quiet again, Zeke went on. "We all have hoboes deep inside of us, the call of wanderlust, whether we ever rode the rails or not, and we all have the desire to raise fine crops that will sustain and nourish us. We must never lose faith in the abundant harvest the soil will yield. We must always persevere in the good and noble prevailing over the false and insidious, the just and trustworthy over the perfidious and malevolent. The hobo wakens in a boxcar to a sunrise spread across the swaying wheat fields and glimpses the exalted wonder of a new day. The farmer in the field spots his brother rumbling across the plains on an adventure towards the beckoning horizon and envies his freedom. They may even wave in a gesture that recognizes themselves in one another. The farmers will gladly support their peripatetic brothers with sustenance, and hoboes everywhere will always welcome a farmer hit by hard times into their singular fraternity of nomads. Remember when all seems hopeless, don't succumb but believe all the more that a better life is just a little further past that clearing and over the elevation in the woods. When you are irretrievably lost, never waver with doubt that you will one day find your way. Believe beyond all reason and you will also discover yourself in the bargain." He remained there at the microphone for a long space of reflection, his gaze inward and low, and utter stillness held as they waited to see if he would add more words. But he did not, turning to the dairymaid and she hugged him. The great crowd erupted in the most thunderous and fervent reception yet to Zeke's oratory, a speech they knew would be his last before his departure for Porsnaugen and the sweep of destiny propelling him forward.

 It would be known as his "Von Klobbert Farm Farewell Address," a venerated impromptu speech recorded verbatim by Crokus. Now he stroked his hand over Balthazar's head and coat and the sheepdog wagged his tail and nuzzled Zeke. Phineas came over smiling contentedly and wrung his hand vigorously, his eyes imparting his esteem for the hobo farmer he too often hedged on when the Cumberlands vilified him. Abigail grinned in captivation of Zeke's moment, holding his gaze a moment while grasping his arm with affection. The brilliant Indian summer afternoon had waned into the shanks of a

TWENTY-TWO

cool, breezy fall evening, the sun now low and diffracting a splintered dusk sky of pale, pink and purple. On the ground to the side of the stage, set back apart from the throngs, his cavalcade of old pals and trusted associates had gathered with their horses, some with horses and wagons such as Horst and Doc Hockers, readying for the long ride to Porsnaugen. And just as Zeke now glanced towards them, he saw Catapaltus being walked around, watered, and readied by the harum-scarum rascals Ogden and Huxley, as they and the others prepared their saddles and bags with provisions and supplies, larger articles of equipage were packed onto the horse-drawn wagons. Beyond the busy entourage preparing for their imminent departure, far off but visible near the old silo seldom used, Zeke perceived here was the detention quarter designated to hold Lord Cumberland and Gerard. There were several legions standing guard outside the opening to the silo, where the Cumberlands were no doubt contained, and Zeke made out the blue and white plumed shakoes of a cadre of officers presiding over their apprehension.

 He left the stage with Livinia at his side and Balthazar at his foot, the throngs surrounding their leader with admiring well wishes and parting a path for them while remaining close enough for a last close look at the larger-than-life hobo farmer. The majestic sorrel Macklemore was being groomed, hydrated, and fed cracked corn rolled oats by several Von Klobbert farm hands, dairymen and women who knew Livinia so well, and they were beaming for their dairymaid in her splendor, so proud they were to prepare such a fine handsome and robust horse for her to ride. She stroked his neck and uttered his name and kissed her beloved stallion on the forehead. Zeke made to assist her mounting the saddled horse, but the dairymaid was a superb equestrian and sprung herself up from the stirrup and atop Macklemore in an effortless motion of grace. Zeke moved towards Horst, already seated at the reins of his wagon with Wyatt Plantwater his passenger beside him, Corn Cavendish and Quigley on the bench behind them. He thought of the saddlebag he once carried the still growing Balthazar in during horseback rides of yore and proposed to his old mentor that his sheepdog find a place under the heavy-duty tarpaulin covering the supplies on the cart. Horst grinned eagerly and stated it would be "an honor to transport the greatest farm dog to ever herd livestock." And with a slight boost up from Zeke the sheepdog launched himself with nimble ease into the nearest corner, ensconcing himself there for the haul.

 Zeke saw now that everyone in his convoy was ready to begin their journey. Booth, Mathius, and Cy were in the saddles of their horses, as were Jarvis and Crokus, the latter a grateful recipient of a donated horse by kindred spirit farmers of the Grange. Doc Hockers was at the helm of his horse-drawn wagon and riding with him were The Captain, Joke, Floop, and Geets, the exalted and humbled hoboes sitting tall with earnest sparkle across their ruddy features. As Zeke moved towards Catapaltus he saw everyone was gazing his way now, just waiting on him to lead the way. The urchins Ogden and Huxley stood straight and dutiful without a trace of their smirks, quite proud in their role of presenting the magnificent Catapaltus. Zeke noted he never saw them so serious and intent in a process, and even allowed a fleet notion that perhaps they were going to pull some joke on him. But as they shook his hand with broad smiles before he drew himself astride his great black steed, he almost wished they were up to one last bit of hi-jinks. Never were there truer and more trusted pals to a fellow taken for a hobo, a stranger showing up out of nowhere on a farm. They had already beseeched him in their brazen sort of palaver to let them join him on his journey, but Zeke had to quash that. He felt bad about denying them the adventure, but it was for their own good. He got Catapaltus started with a great flourish of kicking his front legs high and circling in a trot around the convoy of riders who were watching and waiting, soon settling into an easy amble towards the front position. Livinia maneuvered her sorrel nearby as Zeke spun Catapaltus once more to face his team with a few last words. He realized the entire crowds of hoboes, farmers, and legions had gathered around them as their departure seemed imminent. The scattered singing and playing of instruments and general noise of the masses now became utterly silent.

"Farmers will always nourish hoboes, hoboes will always inspirit farmers. Inevitably it is *performance, perseverance*. It is in us and has to come out. If we are to realize who we are. Let it out, everybody. Let it out. And follow it all the way. Now it's onward to Porsnaugen!" He prodded Catapaltus sufficiently to rouse the great horse into an explosive gallop that began across the gaping panorama of farmland slowly rising in elevation towards the distant forest hills, and Livinia kept pace not much behind to his right and then the panoply of riders, Booth, Mathius, and Cy, the drawn wagons, and Jarvis and Crokus bringing up the rear. He heard the band of musicians strike up his song and the impassioned chorus of everyone singing it, and the music only faded as they rode away.

But before it dissolved completely from earshot, a disturbing crack reverberated across the firmament, followed by the shouts and clamorous uproar of the throngs as the song abruptly stopped. In a murderous rage Gerard had broken out of his detainment in the silo, snatched a shotgun from the back of a legion and running towards Zeke's receding company fired off a round. As Zeke slowed Catapaltus to a halt another report split over the sky and soon he and his riders had all pulled up and swung around to see the distant tumult unfold. The throngs of farmers, hoboes, and legions pounced upon the younger Cumberland right after the second shot, thin plumes of white smoke still evident, and the constabulary now manacled his hands behind his back and dispensed very rough treatment, partly from chagrin at his escape, in dispatching him back to confinement in the silo. Zeke and his riders watched in silence, the wind picking up as the twilight expanse over the pastures seemed to wax darkly iridescent, the violent scene behind them starkly underscoring the challenges ahead. After gazing fixedly on the faraway crowd and the capture of the would-be assassin, Zeke eventually noticed sitting on the cart with Balthazar, arisen from under the tarpaulin and looking back along with everyone else, the harum-scarum guttersnipes themselves, Ogden and Huxley. They turned to find Zeke shaking his head, his reproachful gaze upon them, and all they could do was shrug, betraying the slightest of smirks. Balthazar, it nonetheless appeared to Zeke, was delighted to have the company of the boys in his cart for the journey. And Zeke could but evince the barest of chuckles. He then addressed his riders. "There will be others taking shots at us. Best to get used to it. Hopefully they will continue to miss. It will not deter us from our cause one iota. Our work has just begun." And he swung around Catapaltus, checked in on Livinia with a smile, and cried, "Onward to Porsnaugen!"

THE END

Appendix: The Songs of Zeke Borshellac

The Songs of Zeke Borshellac

Chapter One

The Fishhead Fellow:

- "Floundering with Belly Full of Poor Papa" (play)
- "Fishsticks in the Crawlspace, Half-cooked" (poem)
- "Apace Molders a Moonpie" (ballad)
- "Catfish Confidential" (play)
- "Mud Flaps Mojo" (play)
- "Monkfish Lasso Pasquinade" (play)

Chapter Two

Zeke sporadically bursts into "Greensleeves" when his reflection appeared in a window or large puddle.

Zeke sings songs while demolishing the old house Ma Moody wants built into a gambling palace:

- "Tailor, Shorten My Trousers Please"
- 'In a Canoe with Mrs. Ledoux"
- "Pixie Dust and Spaetzle"
- "Skeleton Charlie at Dead Man's Jamboree" (pirate chantey)
- "Klondike Cappy Gets Shot by His Patootie" (old 49ner song)

And in his final assault on the house the following old songs he sings:

- "Pancakes on a Promontory in Toledo"
- "Fritz in the Pumphouse"
- "I Love Mr. Marshmallow But Not Today"
- "Marbles in My Head Make Me Who I Am"
- "The Rolling Pin Imp Came to the Party"
- "Hootenanny Hellcats in Polka Dot"

- "Fourteen Clams For Forty-Eight Fellers" (old miners' song)

Chapter Four

Hobo in hobo bar played songs on his harp:

- "Rock Island Line"
- "Orange Blossom Special"
- "Playing Thimblerig with Hoyt on the Night Train to Norfolk"

Zeke performing for hoboes with his horse Scunj, sings:

- "Sleepin' Off the Sneaky Pete in Coal Car #3"
- "Woke Up in Wichita on the Cannonball When a Bull Clubbed Me Over the Head"

Rollo, standing on his horse facing backwards sings:

- "There Ain't Enough Clumps of Coal to Make One Lousy Meatball"

In an improvised version of The Gracklers' Salzburg Circus Skit, "Oh Tannenbaum" is sung for the Kaiser (at Simon's behest.)

Chapter Five

The Gracklers ambush the cavalcade of a wealthy count and present The Salzburg Circus Skit.

In it the Kaiser sings:

- "The Rain That Falls on My Head Strengthens My Resolve and Trickles Off My Helmet"
- "We Move Forward Together With Carbines and the Will to Kill the Enemy"
- "My Kaiser Blood Lifts Me Up to Lead Us On to Conquest (And Eleven Thousand Kegs of Pilsner Beer!)

Zeke as Rube Doolittler sings:

- "Seven Frolicsome Tumbleweeds Scudding in the Gusts, Mocking My Lonesome Despair, Until I Set Them On Fire" (sorrowful cowboy ballad)

The Prussians sing German drinking songs:

- "Prost! Schnell! More Beer, Madchen, Before This Soldier Meets Herr Shrapnel!"
- "Beer Runs Through Me Like a River and I Run Through Mortar Shells Like Uncle Otto"

The grand finale song:

- "We Are All in This Together Unless We Decide Not To Be Anymore"

The Gracklers bushwhack two coaches of metaphysicians (among them Windsor Adair Frappe, author of *Snveling Mopes Languishing in the Root Beer Paradigm*) and launch The Milkmen Guild's Wildcat Strike skit.

Simon as John L. Lewis on horseback sings the old mining songs:

- "Desmond the Brave Parrot Hopped the Twig and Now It's Our Turn, Gents"
- "The Lung Turns Black and We Tip Our Hats and Burn the Company Store to the Ground"
- "Hexton's Hot Finger Romp" (sung by Rollo as dairy tycoon Hexton Torborg)

The Gracklers attack the coaches of the Flemish plutocrat, Anders Stupenier, and soon follow the songs from the Johnny Appleseed in a Pagoda skit:

- "Cold Cold Plantanos, No No Grow"
- "Yes, I'm Johnny Bananaseed"
- "Monk, Pagoda, Apple Anyone?"
- "Muck Dooka and Digging Deep in the Pagoda Dustup"

CHAPTER SEVEN

Outside the hobo bar performing with his horse Scunj for hoboes:

- "One Swiped Mickie Equals One Split-Open Head"

- "Hopped-up Hoboes at the Hootenanny Laughing it Up" (old elegy heard in jungles far and wide)

Numbers from the traditional hobo songbook:

- "The Farmer on a Tractor Waved as We Rolled By, Or Was That an Italian Salute?"
- "The Stumblebum and the Quaker"
- "Del Schmaug Turned Rat Fink"
- "The Corncakes Skunk Loomis Cooked Us in Muscogee"
- "Paducah Rain Tastes Salty, Mr. Entwhistle"
- "The Tiresome Preacher at the Jungle Outside Chi-town Wasn't So Bad"
- "Lost My Bindlestick, Found a Gladstone With a Suit Inside That Don't Fit"
- "Stu Bleavins Dropped Dead"
- "The Grub Klepto of Yuma"
- "Wheatfields Swayin' While I Watch 'Em With My Whiskey"
- "The Old Bag Hangin' Wash Gave Us Soup"
- "Lefty Malzone Was Right"
- "Living Off the Fat of the Land, Except Sheboygan"

Hoboes began chanting cryptic slogans:

- "Corn on the Cob and a Cup of Joe, Brother Farmer!"
- "Riptide Over the Side, Come and Get Me, Slowpoke!"
- "29 Shots of Popskull Ain't Enough, Hey Mr. Bull We're Calling Your Bluff!"
- "We're Getting the Hell Outa Here, Ain't Time For No Bum Steer, Regardless There Better Be Beer! Got That, Admiral Johnny? Do you read me, General Willie?"

After Zeke is defeated in his bout with the hobo father, the harp player and banjoist strike up:

- "The Melancholy Hobo Ate Franks and Beans All Alone in the Alley in Muncie"

Chapter Nine

While hoboes are playing horseshoes in the old shipyard, the hobo known as The Captain plays "St. James Infirmary" on the harp.

Chapter Ten

At the Oilcan Conclave following Cyril's triumphant poetry appearance, songs sung by the crowd in thunderous jollity:

- "Gut Ten Pikes and Call it a Day, Uncle Nobby"
- "Sea Legs and Scurvy, Ain't That a Pip!"
- "Sturgeon Smoking, Jonus Jumped In"
- "The Scrimshaw Swindle of Guy Schmutzie"
- "The Seines of Skeleton Isaiah Jammed With Stinkfish"
- "Shrovetide Dusk Skedaddle" (a rollicking paean to the lam)

As Ma Moody berates Zeke, the band strikes up:

- "Flotsam Trunks and Jetsam Shoetrees, Who Jettisoned My Chiffonier?"

Chapter Thirteen

During wee hours ride, Zeke comes across some hoboes (Vigalor, Spodio, and Hogan) in the woods at a campfire, and they jam for a few songs:

- "The Moon looks Mean When I Pass Through Moline"
- "Cornfield Confidential: Fourteen Ears, Fifteen Hoboes, and No Damn Butter"
- "Coal Car Carl Cracking Wise Near Cleveland"
- "Hey Mr. Brakeman, Your Choo-Choo is A-Chug-Chugging While We Chug-A-Lug It!"
- "Boozing in Boxcars On the Way to Hobo Heaven"

Chapter Fourteen

At the Grange meeting with Horst:

- "I Grew an Eight Pound Onion on a Banker's Grave"

After Zeke's speech at the Grange, the farmers belted out old farming numbers:

- "Sodbusters Sockeroo"

- "Don't Eat Pegler's Goo Goo Crop"
- "Farmer Stroud and the Eleven Glommed Beets"
- "How Many Harvest Pecks on a Pontoon?"
- "Scarecrow Artie Used to be a Yellowbelly"
- "When the Bastards Bury Me I'm Growing Back as a Cornstalk" (The Grange's traditional number)

Chapter Fifteen

At the Pig Roaster Summer Picnic at Redmond's Landing on the Bockboxen Forest Isthmus, farmer bands played:

- "Cornstalk Hideaway with Wanda Purvey"
- "Haystacks and the Dead Swede"
- "Scythe Swaths, Width Eighteen Feet"
- "Our Milk Cow Named McTavish and the Carved Baker Figurine" (the old forgotten cantata)

Zeke takes the stage and sings:

- "The Cockamamie Cauliflower Clocked Farmer Palowski"
- "Rumblin' O'er Wheat Fields in a Boxcar When Mornin' Light Comes"

Chapter Nineteen

After Zeke escapes from prison and runs miles into deep woodlands, he hears distant singing and comes upon a hobo jungle. The songs he knows, hobo songs, which we have seen in earlier chapters:

- "The Grub Klepto of Yuma"
- "The Moon Looks Mean When I Pass Through Moline"
- "Del Schmaug Turned Rat Fink"
- "Lefty Malzone Was Right"
- "29 Shots of Popskull Ain't Enough, Hey Mr. Bull We're Calling Your Bluff!"

While pitching horseshoes with hoboes at the woodland jungle:

- "Hey Mr. Brakeman, Your Choo Choo is A-Chug-Chugging While We Chug-A-Lug It"

- "Roamin' on the Lost Locomotive with Duke and Chet"

A hobo and a farmer at the woodland jungle collaborate on a song about Zeke:

- "Out of the Sea and Up from the Soil"

Chapter Twenty

Tommy Dunkirk, a hobo trombonist, wakens the hoboes and farmers at the woodland jungle playing "The Grub Klepto of Yuma"

Zeke leads them in a solemn but passionate version of "Paducah Rain Tastes Salty, Mr. Entwhistle"

Zeke, trying to appease some farmers with one of their songs, gets halfway through "Don't Eat Pegler's Goo Goo Crop"

To resolve the song controversy, Zeke melds a farmer song ("When the Bastards Bury Me I'm Growing Back as a Cornstalk) and a hobo song ("The Corncakes Skunk Loomis Cooked Us in Muscogee") into a number that became known as "Cornstalks and Corncakes"

When hoboes and farmers are at loggerheads about whether to follow the forested railroad tracks, the band strikes up "Our Milk Cow Named McTavish and the Carved Baker Figurine"

Zeke leads the hoboes and farmers through the woods in the rain and becomes increasingly lost. Leads them in singing "Cornfield Confidential: Fourteen Ears, Fifteen Hoboes, and No Damn Butter"

Terribly lost in the forest the hoboes and farmers hum "Out of the Sea and Up from the Soil"

Zeke sings "The Old Bag Hangin' Wash Gave Us Soup" and the marchers soon add their voices, "Sodbusters Sockeroo" and "Stu Bleavins Dropped Dead" soon follow.

The band plays "Out of the Sea and Up from the Soil" and later the marchers sing it again.

Chapter Twenty-One

The Grange band plays at the Hootenanny Harvest "Sodbusters Sockeroo," "Turnips and Wheat Folks Must Eat, Pete," and "Candied Parsnips and the Clapboard Shed of Big Chet"

During the clash with the legionaries at the Hootenanny Harvest the hoboes sing "One Swiped Mickie Equals One Split-Open Head," "The Corncakes Skunk Loomis Cooked Us in Muscogee," "The Old Bag Hangin' Wash Gave Us Soup," "The Grub Klepto of Yuma," and "Out of the Sea and Up from the Soil." The farmers sing: "Cornstalk Hideaway with Wanda Purvey," "Scythe Swath, Width Eighteen Feet," and "Sodbusters Sockeroo."

At the Harvest Hootenanny Zeke addresses the crowd and sings:

- "Coal Car Carl Ain't Dead Yet" (after crowd launches into another big rendition of "Out of the Sea and Up from the Soil")
- "Corn on the Cob and a Cup of Joe, Brother Farmer!"
- "Wheat Fields Swayin' While I Watch 'Em with My Whiskey"
- "Box Car Slim and the Turnip Patch Fluke"
- "Ode to Catapultus" (Verse in tribute to his great horse, after the series of skits in which he affects a duet with the ghostly woodland figure of his, "Sturgiss.")

Zeke closes with the twenty-two-piece band on stage:

- "Don't Eat Pegler's Goo Goo Crop"
- "Lefty Malzone was Right"
- "Stu Bleavins Dropped Dead"
- "The Moon Looks Mean When Passing Through Moline"
- "Hoboes at the Hootenanny Laughing It Up"
- "Sodbusters Sockeroo"
- "Woke Up in Wichita on the Cannonball When a Bull Clubbed Me Over the Head"
- "Out of the Sea and Up from the Soil" (sung by the crowd, played by the musicians)

✷

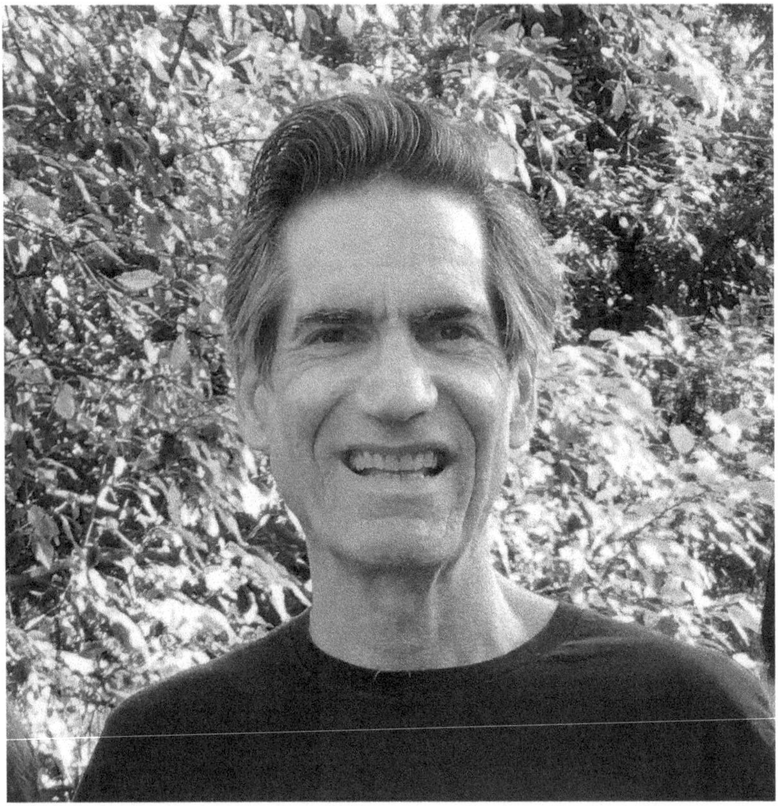

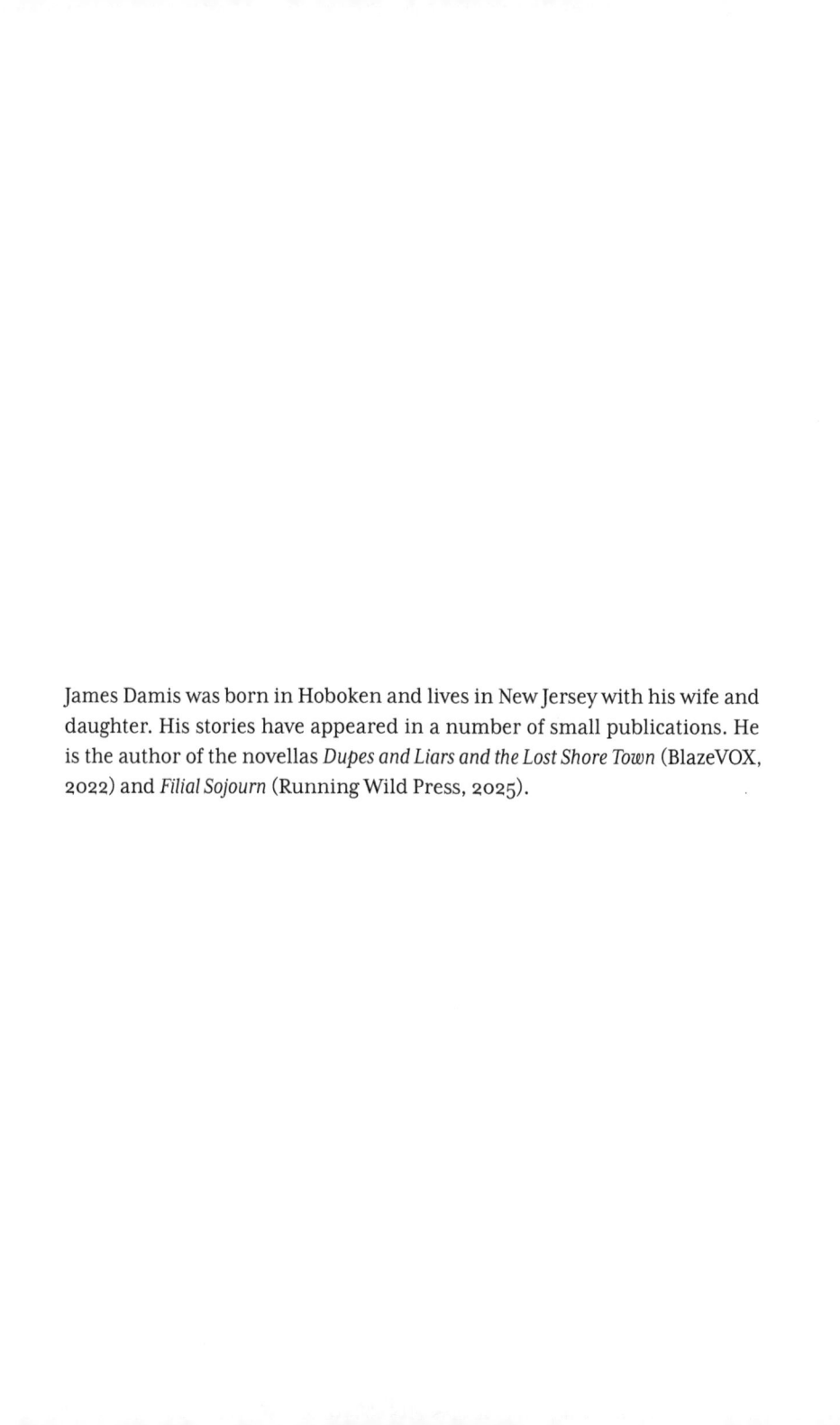

James Damis was born in Hoboken and lives in New Jersey with his wife and daughter. His stories have appeared in a number of small publications. He is the author of the novellas *Dupes and Liars and the Lost Shore Town* (BlazeVOX, 2022) and *Filial Sojourn* (Running Wild Press, 2025).

Milton Keynes UK
Ingram Content Group UK Ltd.
UKHW031206111124
451035UK00006B/642